Also by M. E. Morris

ALPHA BUG

THE ICEMEN

C-130: THE HERCULES

SWORD OF THE SHAHEEN

THE LAST KAMIKAZE

THE LAST KAMIKAZE

M.E. MORRIS

Random House · New York

Library of Congress Cataloging-in-Publication Data
Morris, M. E.
The last kamikaze/by M. E. Morris.
p. cm.
ISBN 0-394-57634-9
I. Title.
PS3563.087444L3 1990
813'.54—dc20 90-53132

Manufactured in the United States of America

24689753

First Edition

For the generations on both sides who gave up their best years to fight the great Pacific war and who are now passing into history. Despite their diverse cultures, they had one thing in common: they loved their respective countries without reservation. Because of that, they fought with their own personal sense of honor and dignity. Those who follow would do well to remember them.

"DO NOT STAY ALIVE IN DISHONOR."

—Excerpt from *Sanjin Kun* ("The Ethics of Battle"), promulgated by
General Hideki Tojo, Imperial Japanese Army

Author's Note

This is, among other things, a flying story.

The events and characters are fictional and the aerial scenes involving the accomplishments of the Zero are based on the author's own experience and the actual performance capabilities of one of the world's greatest fighter aircraft, the Mitsubishi A6M-2 Type Zero *Reisen* (abbreviated form of *Rei Sentoki*) or Zero Fighter. The Zero, along with the later-arriving Grumman F6F Hellcat and the Chance-Vought F4U Corsair, set the course of four years of intense naval aerial fighter warfare during the 1941–1945 time frame. When flown by well-trained, experienced pilots, the A6M-2 was in every case a formidable foe.

Mention must also be made of the valiant men who flew and fought against the Zero in less capable aircraft, such as the Curtiss P-40, the Bell-39, and the Grumman Wildcat, in many cases achieving kills by sheer determination and superiority in fighting technique. They deserve singular remembrance.

American aircraft and American pilots, along with their allies, all progressing to the point where they were so much more capable than their adversary, eventually defeated the Japanese fighter.

Finally, this story is written to, perhaps, temper the bitterness that still exists among those individuals who have such valid reasons to be bitter. There are a number, American and Japanese, and the war cost them so much.

Fifty years have passed. It is time.

Acknowledgments

The author is indebted to Mr. Hatsuko Naito, whose book, *Thunder Gods* (Kodansha International Ltd.: New York, 1989), provided a personal insight into the minds and hearts of those men who, a long time ago, were the *kamikaze*.

THE LAST KAMIKAZE

Prologue

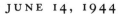

The low-soaring birds of the sea climbed and dove and banked and plunged through the salty spray to skim the whitecaps in their unceasing hunt, their prey the slim dark shapes performing their own graceful ballet just inches below the surface of the western Pacific Ocean. Darting fish meant that death was the pursuer, and the vicious kills of underwater predators scattered tasty tidbits of flesh and viscera along the surface. There, the bloody debris was immediately scooped up by the dipping claws and open beaks of the feathered scavengers, their sharp cries at once signals to one another and expressions of excitement.

Even in his intense pain, the pilot of the Mitsubishi A6M-2 Type Zero *Reisen* could not ignore the antics of the feeding birds far below him. They were too much the perfect flying machines, their instinctive understanding of the laws of aerodynamics far superior to his own. If only he could have been born a bird.

He would have easily bested the aggressive American who had finally managed to put a stream of steel pellets through the thin aluminum fuselage of the Zero—one round was in his right upper leg at the moment and the tightly tied scarf was doing little to stop the flow of blood. Fortunately, the American had most probably been as low on fuel as he, for the stubby blue Hellcat had turned away just when its kill had seemed certain.

There was another reason the Japanese pilot had looked for and found the birds. There would be land nearby. Too late in the battle he had realized that the American had worked him away from his base area. Now, confused by the pain, he was not sure just where he was, and too much fuel had been used in the desperate climbs and tenacious tailchases he had exchanged with his adversary. He would never make it back to the coral strip from whence he had risen over seven hours before—even if he knew where it was. But he had a flyable airplane, a precious asset to the dwindling forces of the Imperial Japanese Navy. He might die from the bleeding, but his airplane must live to fight again.

A masterpiece of engineering and design, the Zero had been a startling surprise at the outbreak of the war. In the hands of pilots seasoned by several years of aerial combat against the Chinese, the Zero had little to fear from the P-40s of the American Army Air Corps or the Wildcats of the U.S. Navy. Extremely light and thus highly maneuverable, the Mitsubishi fighter had early run up an impressive kill ratio against its heavier and less agile American counterparts. Too impressive, perhaps, for the overconfident Japanese had elected to stay with the *Reisen* design, modifying it only slightly to gain some measure of improved performance. The Americans, on the other hand, had taken the lessons learned and had come out with new designs, notably the rugged Hellcat and powerful Corsair, and the air war took on a new dimension. More heavily armed and more heavily armored, the U.S. fighters were faster and sturdier than the Zero, and the American pilots adopted combat tactics to exploit those advantages. And the lone, wounded Japanese pilot making his way eastward across the Pacific was just one of the latest victims of allied aerial superiority.

Carefully, he leaned his fuel-air mixture a tiny bit more. The engine would run a few degrees warmer but the decreased fuel flow would give him another few minutes in the air and that could mean several miles of distance. He checked his other instruments. Propeller revolutions were as low as he dared set them: seventeen hundred revolutions per minute. Any lower would be counterproductive as efficient propeller pitch was a function of the amount of manifold pressure he kept on his engine. The present combination was giving him a very economical fuel flow, eighteen gallons per hour, at one hundred thirty knots of airspeed. Of course, with the fuel gauge indicating almost empty, how many gallons actually remained was unknown to him.

His jaw hung slack from the fatigue generated by the intense throbbing in his leg and his breathing cycle reflected the toll the wound was taking on his body. His own intakes of life-sustaining air, like those of his aircraft's engine, were slow and measured for maximum efficiency, but his exhales, again like those of the Zero's Nakajima power plant, were sharp puffs of spent gases. He knew that he was close to incapacitating shock.

Pushing back the canopy, he let his head lean into the slipstream. The cool air brought back a small measure of his reasoning power and he knew that he was at least heading in the direction of several atolls. There were many in the Marshall and Caroline islands, a number of them still in his countrymen's hands.

If only he had some water. His mouth was almost void of saliva and his tongue stung where it touched the backs of his teeth. Swallowing was merely an exercise in procedure; nothing passed down his throat.

Ahead, down through the large gaps in the clouds, he thought he saw a thin white thread of surf. He lowered the nose of the Zero and let it descend through the clear wide valleys between the fluffy mountains. There! It *was* surf. Soon, he could see the entire arc of one side of a large circular reef. It enclosed a blue-green lagoon and in the middle was a large island completely overgrown with rain forest. Its peaks were nudging twenty-five hundred feet and a number of them were obscured in the thick gray mist of afternoon rainstorms. Several smaller islands dotted the open water between the large island and the reef, and just to his left was one with a ribbon of white sand on the near side.

Once more he glanced down in the cockpit at his instrument panel. The needle of his fuel gauge was no longer flickering at the empty symbol; it was rigid against the stop.

The pilot aimed his airplane for the thin strip of beach. As he passed one thousand feet, his engine noise died. Now, he was truly like the seabirds, riding the currents off the big island in one last effort to reach the smooth sand of the smaller one. He would not lower his landing gear. That would increase the drag of his airframe and cost him distance. It would be a bad decision, anyhow, as the impact of the tall landing gear on the soft sand would most surely flip him over on his back. No, he would belly his aircraft in.

At one hundred feet, he lowered his landing flaps and slowed to his minimum safe speed. With his canopy open and his engine silent, he could actually hear the waves building and breaking across the gentle slope of the beach. There was a noticeable offshore cross-wind and he dropped his upwind wing to keep a straight path down the shoreline. Just before touchdown, he lifted the wing and raised the nose.

The Zero settled onto the surface and slid smoothly across the packed sand, then unexpectedly encountered a depression and pitched forward on its nose. The tail rose high into the air, and for a moment, the pilot feared he was going over on his back. But his slow-speed approach paid off. The Zero balanced for a moment on its propeller spinner and then flopped back down in an upright position. The pilot reached across his lap to unfasten his seat belt, but the pain of his wound and the fatigue of his last desperate hour shut down his brain. He sat there, unconscious, with one hand in his lap, the other still grasping a useless throttle.

AUGUST 14, 1945

"Saburo Genda!"

The call of the one-legged Imperial Navy lieutenant, adding Flight Petty Officer Genda's name to the list of the dead, was joy beyond belief. Within the next two days, Genda would be climbing into a special, modified Mitsubishi Type Zero fighter and striking the American fleet in the waters off Japan. In the tradition of the samurai, he would go forth anointed by his peers and fly into the open arms of his ancestors. Saburo already knew what target he would select. It would be one of the big carriers and he would carry his five hundred-pound bomb straight down onto the center of its crowded flight deck.

Saburo stepped forward and joined the line of three men called before him. At the command of the lieutenant, they formed a small unit of two ranks, two men to a rank. An equal number of honor guards joined them, two sailors in front and two behind.

The lieutenant saluted the squadron commander and, keeping a strict cadence with the tap of his crutch, marched the eight-man formation into a small temporary building beside the main hangar. Inside, Saburo and his three companions were left alone. Before them were four bare tables and beyond the tables a small raised wooden platform. On it sat four wooden buckets full of steaming hot water, and beside each was a large bar of yellow soap. A much larger wooden tub stood beyond them, easily eight feet in diameter and four feet deep.

The chosen ones removed their uniforms and carefully folded them before placing them on the tables. Then, they wet their bodies with water from the buckets, soaped themselves, and rinsed off the lather. Finally, each walked over and lowered himself into the large tub.

Saburo involuntarily gasped at the extreme temperature of the water, but with discipline typical of his new station in life managed to sink deeper into the water until he was covered up to his chin. He had a strong urge to urinate and knew his companions were fighting the same feeling. After a while, he simply relaxed.

"Saburo," the companion across from him said, "I am glad your name was on the list." The other two nodded enthusiastically, one adding, "We have been together from the beginning. What a glorious day this is."

"And tomorrow," joined in the third, "will be even more glorious."

"Yes," Saburo agreed, looking in turn toward each of his comrades. The march to the bath building under the crisp cadence of the one-legged lieutenant was still fresh in his mind, as were the deep bows his assembled squadron mates had rendered as Saburo and the other three marched before the ranks. Now, clean and refreshed by the water and flush with the anticipation of his assignment, he felt as if he were a god, such a dramatic belief strengthened by the knowledge that to those still outside, he and his companions were legally dead and for the rest of their time among mortals they would enjoy the respect and reverence of their unique status as living ancestors. Tomorrow, their souls would become guardian spirits and would join those of the ancient samurai at Yasukuni Shrine on Kudan Hill in Tokyo. Saburo lay his head back on the rim of the tub and thought of the events preceding this moment of supreme honor.

He would never forget the sadness in the face of his mother as he told her that he had been selected for the elite naval flight training program that produced pilots for the *Tokkotai* (Special Attack Corps), nor would he ever forget the look of pride that bathed his father's face when he offered the last handshake and with some effort bent his arthritic back to bow respectfully to his son. Saburo had never seen his parents after that day of parting, his duties having kept him occupied day and night until just four days back when he was told of the bombing of Nagasaki. Just one airplane. One bomb. A repeat of the Hiroshima attack. And his father and mother were among the thousands of instantaneous casualties. There would not even be any remains for a loving son to attend to and pray over. All he could do was light prayer sticks in the base temple and swear vengeance.

His devastating sadness was at least tempered by the fact that he was a pilot in the Imperial Navy, a third-class flight petty officer who had graduated at the head of his flying class while just sixteen years old. And sitting around him in the tub were numbers two, three, and four, each only a year older than he.

As anticipated, they had been selected for the singular honor of joining those before them in setting the example of how the Japanese would fight the final battle of the great war. Now, at the Atsugi Air Base, southwest of Tokyo, their day had come. As if of one mind, the four rose, stepped from the tub, and began drying themselves. To an observer, had there been one, they would have appeared almost as oriental clones. Except for the slight individuality of their facial features, they were identical, each with cropped black hair and close to five-and-a-half feet in height. Broad shoulders capped sharply tapered torsos. Lean hips, an extension of tightly rippled stomachs, outlined identical triangles of dark hair from which hung genitals still limp from the relaxing effect of the hot water. Like most Japanese of their generation, their legs were short. Their thighs and calves bulged with youthful muscle, the result of the physically demanding exercise program they shared with their squadron mates. For a moment, they stood there looking at one another, each seeing himself in the forms of his companions.

Their uniforms were gone from the four tables and in their places were the white robes of the dead.

Saburo wrapped a cotton loincloth around his groin and waist and pulled on the flowing *yukata*, tying the sash of the summer kimono neatly and tucking the ends out of sight. Finally, he stepped into the wooden *geta* provided him.

Each of the four young pilots stood behind his individual table while a young woman entered. Keeping her eyes averted out of respect for the four "dead" young warriors, she lifted small white porcelain cups of warm sake from a black lacquered tray and placed one on each table, then backed out the door, her delicate dancelike movements emphasizing the extreme femininity that was the hall-mark of the Japanese female.

The men raised their cups to eye level.

"Banzai! Ten thousand years!" Saburo toasted.

"Banzai!" the others cried in unison. The warm sake went down the four throats at precisely the same moment.

"Fuck Babe Ruth!" Saburo added spontaneously, borrowing one of the provocative battle insults his brother had said was shouted by Japanese ground troops when engaging American marines. The four young men laughed out of control at Saburo's obscene depar-ture from tradition. It was a hilariously bittersweet moment as each of the four nervously tried to hide his own first fear of certain death from the others. After a few moments, they composed themselves.

The one-legged lieutenant was waiting outside and wordlessly escorted them to a sleeping hut beside a small shrine on the perime-ter of the airfield. Each was shown into a separate room.

Saburo removed his *geta* and slipped on white cotton slippers before entering and sliding the wood-and-rice-paper *fusuma* shut behind him. A low table, shiny and hard with its lacquered surface, sat in the middle of the room on one of a dozen tatami mats covering the floor. Nestled in the *tokonama*, a niche on the far wall, was a thin cloisonné vase. The scaly maroon of its primary color was a perfect compliment to the single white chrysanthemum rising from its slender throat. Beside an adjacent wall rested a rolled maroon *futon*. Saburo crossed his legs and lowered himself on the opposite side of the table.

The beauty of the room was its simplicity and purity, the maroon vase and *futon*, along with the black table, being the only color-accent objects. The walls, translucent natural rice paper stretched on unstained wooden frames, passed through a measure of the early evening sunlight but not enough to form strong shadows. A single paper lantern waited for its time.

This was the first moment he had had to himself since hearing the one-legged lieutenant call his name, and despite the lump of fear that had hung in his throat while he bathed, he found himself strangely at peace. There was no one in the room he had to impress. His countenance and demeanor could reflect his true feeling and he was pleased that the fear was fading and being replaced by a tremendous pride of being selected for the highest of combat honors. In the tradition of ancient Nippon, in the footsteps of the samurai of the shoguns, he would die in battle for his emperor and he would do so at the controls of a fiercely competitive aerial fighter.

The recall of his initial solo flight caused his lips to curve gently upward. For that first time, he had lifted his two-place A6M-2K Zero off the ground without the comforting presence of his instructor. Crouched in the open front cockpit, the wind whistling around his helmet and grabbing his scarf, Saburo had climbed steeply into the clear skies south of Tokyo and enjoyed an hour of the most glorious freedom he had ever experienced. He had wheeled and soared in great arcs. Gaining confidence, he had climbed steeply and dove sharply, each time pulling himself level with a steady grip on the joystick. He was a warrior unsheathing his sword—an airborne samurai who would go on to polish his killing skills and soon engage the Americans. When he returned to his base and touched down on the mother soil of Japan, he was forever changed.

By the time he completed the all-too-brief training course, there was no other concern in his life but the Zero. When he wasn't flying it or studying its systems, he was standing or resting beside it, letting its lean lines remind him that even after four years of world conflict, the Mitsubishi-bred fighting machine was still one of the premier military aircraft in the hands of a competent pilot. And Saburo was determined to be one of those few remaining competent pilots. His affection for the airplane went far beyond that normally attributed to an inanimate object. It was a love affair, and when Saburo was in the cockpit, his hands and feet positioned on the controls, he and his machine were as much lovers as man and woman coupled in the human act. They moved together, one an extension of the other. Their foreplay was his preflight inspection, which he meticulously carried out with a loving touch, feeling and probing and stroking all of the vital parts of the airframe and engine with an anticipation that bordered on the unbearable. Airborne, they eagerly entered the unique world of flight, masters of a limitless heaven where there were no constraints on their lovemaking. They could cavort about the sky in the throes of a passion that was as intense as any Saburo had known, and in the presence of their enemy they would carry each other through an exhilarating crescendo of turns and dives and rolls to finally reach a state of all-consuming effort. Only then, when one of the aerial adversaries bested the other, would a climax be reached. Saburo knew that death could be the orgasm, but even that would be a welcome outcome as long as he could share it while mated with his beloved Zero.

His lips straightened when his thoughts proceeded to his graduation and first operational flights under the tutelage of pilots only a few months senior to himself. The American task forces were just over the southern horizon, and every day the devilish blue Hellcats and Corsairs screamed in from seaward. Saburo had thrown his Zero at them with complete disregard for his safety, but he was no match for the seasoned carrier pilots who had fought clear across the Pacific. Within the first minute of his first engagement, he was trapped by a pair of weaving Hellcats. He would turn into one only to have the other attack from the opposite side. Reversing his turn was a futile tactic for then the first would turn and have an advantage. The pair of Hellcats methodically stitched his aircraft so full of holes it began to come apart in midair. Opening his canopy and rolling over, he released his seat belt and dropped free just as the Zero disintegrated within a bright orange ball of fire.

Floating down, he had a front-row seat for watching the rest of the lopsided aerial battle. Every one of his five companions was being destroyed and there was only one other parachute in the awesome blue sky around him. Warily, he watched one of the snarling Hellcats circle him much as a shark circled its victim before attacking. Then the snub-nosed Grumman turned in and sped toward him. Saburo unholstered his revolver and began firing at the American, convinced that every moment was his last. He could see the ugly black holes of the Hellcat's six wing guns before the American broke sharply away, passing so closely that Saburo could read the obscene epitaph thrown his way by the lips of the helmeted and goggled pilot. But the American had not fired.

Saburo knew that under the same circumstances but with reversed roles he would not have let the American live.

His thoughts passed, and for the first time he noticed a loosely rolled towel on the table before him. He unrolled it to find an envelope, a sheet of paper, a carbon pencil, and a small pair of scissors. He clipped off thin slivers of fingernails and a lock of his hair and placed both inside the envelope before writing his *haiku*, the obligatory farewell verse of the warrior. Saburo knew that he was not a poet so he simply wrote down his feelings:

> As the cherry blossom reaches its peak
> of beauty just before it falls, so shall
> I honor Nippon with my death.

He folded the paper, inserted it also inside the envelope, and ran his tongue across the bitter glue on the flap prior to pressing it shut.

The *fusuma* through which he had entered the room immediately slid open to reveal a young girl gathering her kimono as she dropped to her knees. She bowed deeply before rising, hobbled gracefully over to the table, and squatted to pick up the envelope, scissors, and towel. She looked at him only one time, with just the trace of a smile, before she bowed again and backed out the opening to kneel once more and pull the *fusuma* shut.

Saburo knew that the parts of his body would be passed to his brother, providing he returned from his war, and subsequently would be placed at his parents' memorial plaque on a field high above what used to be Nagasaki.

The *fusuma* slid open a second time and a different female repeated the ritual of kneeling and bowing before approaching Saburo. An older woman followed her into the room and placed a shiny wooden bowl of clear broth and vegetables before Saburo.

"*Ozori,*" she announced.

Saburo knew that the forthcoming meal would be special. *Ozori* was normally served only at the time of the New Year and was a festive soup. Perhaps the delicious treat was meant to signify his new role as a dedicated warrior who would not see the next New Year. As the older one backed from the room, the younger woman placed a thin, silk-covered, cotton pillow beside Saburo and sat next to him.

"I am Tomoko," she said, lowering her eyes.

"Saburo—Saburo Genda," Saburo responded, somewhat embarrassed. He had no experience with women, having finished his schooling during the demanding days of a faltering war and immediately entering the rigorous flight training when only a day away from his parents. The young woman beside him was wearing the white face and exaggerated makeup of a geisha. Her tightly wrapped kimono was the most beautiful Saburo had ever seen, a silk brocade of deep blue with large red-and-orange flowers. The matching obi was easily twice the size of any he had ever seen his mother wear.

"I know, Genda-san. It is my honor to attend you." Tomoko pulled back one of the large hanging sleeves of her kimono and with the forearm exposed lifted a small white ladle of the soup to Saburo's lips.

Saburo let the hot mixture linger in his mouth. It was exquisite, with a clear taste of the sea and subtle hints of ocean fish and crab. Small square pellets of glutinous rice provided substance. Tomoko delicately touched his lips with a white linen towel. She repeated the ritual at just the right pace and as Saburo savored the last of the soup the older woman returned, this time with hot tea and several covered dishes. She placed them on the table, retrieved the soup bowl and serving spoon, and left. Tomoko lifted the covers of the dishes and Saburo's saliva glands became very excited, stimulated by the sight and smell signals of broiled ocean bream garnished with pine needles; moist *nori*, seaweed; and the deliciously tart *wasabi*, green horseradish paste. The other dish held *sekihen*, a thick mixture of boiled rice and tiny red beans, itself a celebration food served on special occasions. Finally, there were light brown rice cakes dotted with bits of Hokkaido rock lobster meat. Saburo had never seen such a feast.

Tomoko offered a pair of smooth sandalwood *ohashi*. The Japanese chopsticks were rounded into thin, long conical shapes as opposed to their squared-off Chinese ancestors, and in the manner reserved for the dead, they were sticking upright in a bowl of white rice.

The bream was moist and full of flavor, the meat falling apart in Saburo's mouth before he could put his teeth to it, and he fell upon it with hardly a pause between mouthfuls. Tomoko kept his teacup full and giggled behind raised hands when a sliver of fish subbornly refused to leave one of the chopsticks. Then, as he nibbled on the rice cakes, she plucked the three strings of a samisen and softly sang of the mountains and shores and streams and lakes of Japan during the time of the samurai. Saburo leaned back and listened, his belly full and his mind at ease.

The last lilting note of an ode to Fuji-san faded and Tomoko raised her eyes to look directly at Saburo. "If my lord wishes, I will sing of the Thunder Gods, for my lord is truly one of those mighty warriors."

Saburo was extremely pleased to be so honored. Originally conceived as sacrificial pilots of the *Ohka* (Exploding Cherry Blossom) flying bomb, the Thunder Gods had been expanded to include those who would pilot conventional fighters and dive bombers on *Jibaku* (self-crashing) one-way missions. The *Ohka* craft had been the original vehicles of such missions. Carried to the outer perimeter of the attack area under the belly of modified Mitsubishi G4M2a "Betty" medium bombers, then released to execute their rocket-propelled attack dives, the *Ohka* units were now sorely depleted, over 438 of their kind having been lost during the Okinawa campaign with only a sunken American destroyer to testify to their bravery. But the premier *kamikaze* pilots of the *Ohka* squadron, who rode their wooden, twin-tailed monoplanes to their deaths, had inspired hundreds of their comrades, including Saburo, and their example was now sacred within the tradition of the Imperial Navy.

"I am not worthy to be so honored," Saburo protested.

"It is I who am not worthy to sit in the presence of so mighty a warrior." Tomoko bowed low and placed her samisen in position.

Her words sung of the beauty of sacrificial death and the honor and dignity of such ultimate service. She sang of the Buddhist precept that held the nature of life as a fragile, transitory thing and how death could be viewed as crossing into another plane of existence. She repeated the Confucianism concept of absolute loyalty to the lord emperor and finally allowed the refrain to stress the Shinto belief that warriors were descendants of divine beings, and upon dying, the Thunder Gods, too, would become deities.

The melody continued by describing how the purity of the heavens spawned perfect warriors who dove at their targets with short-winged craft symbolic of the *kantana*, the long sword of the samurai. Just as the *kantana* sliced through clean air to dismember the enemies of the samurai's shogun, so did the Thunder Gods slice downward at the enemies of their divine emperor, Hirohito.

Tomoko continued, her story concluding with the refrain that the Thunder Gods were the vanguard of a mighty wave of *kamikaze* pilots who would turn the tide of battle as decisively as had the great typhoons that destroyed the Mongols first in 1274 and again in 1281. The last note faded and Tomoko kept her eyes downcast in a final mark of respect.

Saburo was moved to silence but kept his eyes fixed on the geisha. He wanted to study the beauty of Tomoko, but the white mask of the geisha made it difficult for him to detect her actual features. He had no such trouble with the second woman who appeared in the doorway.

Tomoko rose, placed her hands on the front of her thighs, bowed deeply and bid Saburo good-night. "It has been my honor and pleasure to serve you, my lord. May this evening be the worst you shall ever have to endure."

It took Saburo a somewhat puzzled moment to unravel the true meaning of her parting wish.

The second woman was a bit older, perhaps by two or three years, but still barely into her second decade. She did not wear the makeup of a geisha, but her lips were red-tinted and her slightly downcast brown eyes were outlined with barely perceptible dark lines and sat atop delicate, high cheekbones. Her exquisite black hair, instead of being upswept and looped in the formal way, hung down her back, and Saburo felt his loins tighten as he let his gaze drop from her face to her throat and then to the open collar of her white kimono. It was very loose and she appeared to have on no undergarment, for when she kneeled and bowed, Saburo's eyes were drawn down into the deep shadowed valley between her breasts.

"I am Emiko."

"I am Saburo Genda,"

"I know," she said, repeating Tomoko's words. Standing, she unrolled the *futon* and waited beside it. Saburo rose. Emiko spoke again. "A determined warrior going into battle must reap his reward before he unsheathes his sword, for afterwards he will be with his ancestors." Reaching forward, she untied the sash of Saburo's kimono and pulled the garment back and over his shoulders. Saburo took an eager step forward.

"In a moment, my lord Genda-san." Delicately, she placed a restraining hand on his bare chest. "Lie down."

Saburo practically dropped onto the soft *futon*.

Emiko giggled. "On your stomach, lord."

Saburo obediently rolled over but kept his head turned back over his shoulder. Emiko folded one of his arms as a pillow and gently pushed his head back around.

Saburo could not see but heard the soft whisper of Emiko's kimono sliding down her body and onto the laced reeds of the tatamis.

Then he felt her hands unwrapping his loincloth. He eagerly raised his hips as Emiko pulled the garment away from him.

The scent of a thousand spring flowers filled the room as Emiko poured a clear thin liquid into her hands and leaned over Saburo. Starting with his shoulders and then the top of his spine she began to rub the liquid into his skin, working outside to his upper arms then back in and down to the small of his back. She glided them across his firm buttocks and to the backs of his thighs before beginning a kneading of the soft skin over his kidneys. Saburo felt that every muscle in his body had dissolved—all except one.

Emiko's hands indicated he should turn over and he did so, seeing for the first time her nakedness. Saburo had often jested and lied with his cronies about girls, and he had suspected that they were often doing the same with him. But he had never seen a nude adult female and certainly had never been in the erotic situation in which he now found himself. Emiko was without reservation the most beautiful creature he had ever seen, even in his imagination. His entire body strained with desire.

She knelt beside him and began massaging the liquid into his chest, then his stomach, and finally his groin and around the inside of his thighs, casting fleeting but admiring glances at the rigidity caused by his sexual excitement. Saburo could not lie still another second.

But Emiko continued to restrain him. "Wait. It will only be another moment."

Saburo was in a state of near ecstasy as Emiko straddled him and lowered herself onto his stomach. Leaning forward to flatten her breasts against his chest, she placed her open mouth over his. Saburo hungrily pulled her against him. As they kissed, he felt her slide down and lift slightly. Saburo could not suppress his involuntary gasp—the pleasure was almost unbearable as she took him inside her.

The long shadows of the rising sun slowly shortened as Saburo and his three companions finished dressing. Over the upper arms and legs of their flight suits they loosely tied strips of cloth, each inscribed with several signatures of their squadron mates. Should they suffer a wound in any of their extremities they could quickly tighten the bands and slow the loss of blood, perhaps enough to make the difference between success and failure of their mission. Finally, they placed the traditional *hachimakis* around their cloth helmets just under their raised goggles. Tracing their heritage back to the sweat-bands worn by the samurai, each symbolic headband carried the blood-red Kanji characters proclaiming the wearer's devotion to the emperor.

The one-legged lieutenant and the four-man honor guard returned and escorted them to a position at the head of their assembled squadron mates. A petty officer brought forward a tray upon which sat five cups of sake. Their commanding officer took one, Saburo and his comrades the others.

"Banzai!" the officer yelled.

"Banzai!" The four repeated the toast, but their words were almost lost in the roar of their squadron mates behind them.

"Banzai! Banzai! Banzai!" With each cry, the men removed and energetically waved their caps.

With his squadron ground crewmen lining the ramp, Saburo marched alongside his three companions, stepping aside when he reached his own aircraft. "I shall be waiting for you at the Yasukuni Shrine," he called after them.

Proudly, he returned the deep bow of his mechanic. A slight chill ran up his spine. Just as Tomoko had foretold in song, he was a Thunder God. In just a few moments he would be slowly guiding his fated craft between the ranks of cheering men, returning their continuous chant—"Banzai! Ten thousand years!"—with a stoic forward stare, symbolic of the samurai's single-purpose concentration and nonswerving intent to lay down his life for his emperor. In some ways, his last departure would be Kabuki theater at its ultimate, for Saburo was no longer a common man from a poor suburb of Nagasaki; he had taken on the role of the dedicated warrior, similar perhaps to the heroic character Ikyu in the classic play *Sukeroku.* For a brief period, Saburo would have the power of the samurai, the power to oppress the enemies of his emperor, and in the way of *mie*, the dramatic Kabuki acting ploy used at the climax of a play, his face would be frozen into picturesque immobility, showing only the one emotion his real-life drama demanded and not necessarily the more human emotions carried within his body.

Before climbing into the cockpit, Saburo presented his mechanic with a white chrysanthemum, a memento of his night with the woman, Emiko, who with a deceiving shyness had introduced him to the joys of unrestrained manhood.

Strapping himself in, Saburo sat motionless while his mechanic checked the tightness of his shoulder harness and seat belt.

"Genda-san," his mechanic whispered, holding out another white headband, "your ground crew would be honored if you wore this *hachimaki* as well as your own. In that way, we will be participating in your glorious mission."

Genda took the headband, signed by his squadron mates, and fastened it over the one he already wore. Looking in his mechanic's eyes, he pledged, "You and the others will share in my victory."

The older man nodded gratefully, placed a subtle hand on Saburo's shoulder, and gave a reassuring squeeze before stepping down and positioning himself to the left and in front of the Zero. Leaning forward, Saburo started the powerful Nakajima engine and a great cloud of dust raised behind the plane, the first breeze of the Divine Wind.

He was almost ready and the Zero strained forward, as eager as he to carry out its ultimate mission. Saburo could already envision his death dive, the great target of an American carrier growing ever larger through his windscreen, the rising red tracers threading the sky around him in a futile attempt to stop his attack. But the gods would be with him.

What would the final impact be like? For the first time, the reality of his act touched him. There would be no pain, certainly, his consciousness being instantly destroyed. Perhaps there would just be an unfeeling darkness, a lack of awareness, a complete void. No, there would have to be something else, for his journey could not end with the flaming crash of his Zero on the warship; he would still have the journey to the warriors' shrine on Kudan Hill. *What a joy that would be!*

He settled in his seat, forcing himself to follow the routine procedures despite his anxiety. A strange calm came over him—as if he were detached from the activity taking place around him. His body was a participant but his mind seemed to be only an observer.

As if controlled by some outside force, Saburo turned on his radio. The crackling words in his ears were the last he had ever expected to hear.

"All aircraft, shut down your engines. Pilots, in the obedience of your samurai tradition, return to your briefing room."

What?

The message was repeated.

No!

Unbelievable words followed. "The struggle is ended. Our beloved and sacred emperor will be speaking to us shortly."

No! No! No! This cannot be true! I will never give up this fight. To do so would be a violation of the code of Bushido. This cannot be.

Saburo added power and started to jump his chocks, but several of his squadron mates joined his mechanic in front of the aircraft and held up their hands in protest. Angry and confused at the sudden development, Saburo slammed his mixture control into the idle-cutoff position. As the engine died, he angrily ripped off his headbands and helmet and slung them onto the ground. Furious, he climbed out of his aircraft and stalked back to his ready area. There, he found his fellow *kamikaze* candidates milling about in a state of confusion. Some were as angry as he. Strangely, a few seemed relieved. Others were looking around aimlessly, unsure as to how they should react. A number were weeping. A few minutes before noon, their officers assembled them before the outdoor speakers.

Saburo instantly recognized the first voice, that of Chokugen Wada, Japan's most popular radio announcer:

> This will be a broadcast of the gravest importance. Will all listeners please rise. His Majesty, the Emperor, will now read his Imperial rescript to the people of Japan. We respectfully transmit his voice.

The inspirational strains of "Kimigayo," the national anthem, followed, and at the end there was only a brief moment of silence before the Emperor's high-pitched voice was heard for the first time by Saburo and others all over Japan. Even then, it was a recording, the reverence for Japan's man-god dictating that he not be heard directly. There was a slight distortion to the record, and the Emperor spoke too softly and in the Imperial tongue, which was difficult for the common Japanese to follow. But the message was all too clear.

With heads bowed, Saburo and his squadron mates stood at attention.

> To our good and loyal subjects: After pondering deeply the general trends of the world and the actual conditions obtaining in our Empire today, we have decided to affect a settlement of the present situation by resorting to an extraordinary measure. . . .

It is true. Saburo listened carefully to the awful pronouncement, his thoughts at first riveted to the Emperor's words. But as the declaration continued, his despair and rage interjected recent memories. The faces of his parents, caught in the firestorm at Nagasaki, wept with him.

> . . . Despite the best that has been done by everyone—the gallant fighting by military and naval forces . . . the war situation has not necessarily developed to Japan's advantage. . . . Moreover, the enemy has begun to develop and employ a new and most cruel bomb. . . .

Saburo felt his fingernails digging into his palms. If only he could break ranks and run to his Zero. There would be others who would join him. Together, they could— They could do nothing to change the moment. And such disobedience to the Emperor was not in the tradition of the samurai. Disgrace and death were the only acceptable reactions. But Saburo would not die; that, he was determined. Startled, he heard the Emperor almost reading his mind.

> . . . Beware most strictly of any outbursts of any emotions which may engender needless complications. . . .

Saburo tried very hard to take his Emperor's words at their value. They were still divine commands. The hurt was numbing but the fact that it was shared by the Soul of Japan would make it bearable.

> . . . Let the entire nation continue as one family. . . . Cultivate the ways of rectitude; foster nobility of spirit; and work with resolution so as ye may enhance the innate glory of the Imperial State and keep pace with the progress of the world.

The war was over. Tears continued to blur the visions of Saburo and his squadron mates. After citing them for their bravery and devotion, their commander dismissed them and they walked away, shamed, most still confused as to what they should do next. A gunshot split the air. A few moments later, another.

Saburo knew what he would do. He strode resolutely out onto the airfield and faced south, where the American fleet steamed just over the horizon. His body was rigid, his face red with rage and moist with the fluid draining from his eyes as his resolve burned itself into his soul.

I shall never forget this time of shame. Someday, somehow, somewhere, in the memory of my mother and father I shall strike back. I swear it.

THE END OF SUMMER, 1991

Chapter 1

Captain Saburo Genda, Japanese Maritime Self-Defense Forces (JMSDF), retired, stood spread-legged on the windswept rocky beach in front of his cottage on the southwest shore of Hokkaido, the northernmost island of Japan. The strong sea winds worked against his stance but he remained firmly planted on a large flat rock that was his favorite spot for meditation. The winds carried a premature autumn chill and would do so for the next weeks until they became quite frigid with the onslaught of the Japanese winter, but on this day the only concession Genda made to the early-evening cold was a slight movement of his forearms as he slid them further into the hanging sleeves of his wool outer kimono. Overhead, dusty white seagulls hovered and squealed their defiance at the sea, the forward thrust of their flapping wings exactly equaling the force of the sea wind.

During the last hours, the solid overcast of stratus clouds had been lowering until now there was less than one thousand feet between their ragged wet bases and the surging surface of the water. Genda knew that such a sequence of clouds and winds forecast a slow-moving warm front, but he doubted that the temperature after its passage would be significantly higher, perhaps only a degree or two at this time of the year.

He enjoyed the changes of the weather, particularly when one season was replacing another. The annual cycle of warming and cooling along with the sky changes as the weather fronts approached and passed were reassuring things to him, evidence that the nature of which he was a part was the very essence of his physical existence.

The cycle was predictable because it was infallibly repetitive and had been so since the first circuit the earth had made around its star. On the other hand, he, like the flowers and trees and grass and animals and the fishes of the sea, was but a temporary visitor to the house of the dragon that was formed by the islands of Nippon. Thus, his life, as that of all living things, had not been predictable. The events of his life-cycle had all come unforetold. Yet, in retrospect, there had been a certain purposeful order to them, whether they had been pleasant or tragic, for each had evolved out of the one before and each had led logically to the next. And now, as it became with every human, his cycle was almost complete.

As it was on every day he was at the cottage, this was Genda's time to try to remove all logical discursive thought and place himself in communion with the All, with nature. Like the world around him, for a short while he would simply be. His communion with the rocks and water and even the gulls above would be complete.

His outward appearance implied that sixty-three summers, two of which had been spent in the Imperial Japanese Navy and thirty-two in the maritime arm of the JSDF, had taken less than their anticipated toll on his stocky muscular physique, although his hair was touched with the dignity of gray and there was the beginning of a relaxation of the ramrod-straight back. The tone of his skin was that of one who lived not just with the elements but *within* them, and his face radiated an inner strength that reflected a lifetime of serious purpose although the weathered skin was a bit off-color.

As well it should be. Flowing through his arteries with every beat of a heart that had known all of the pleasures and agonies of a full life was a new adversary, a relentless one that would hasten certain decisions, but he would fight it as he had all the others. And bolstered by the strength of his Zen discipline, he could stand there and disregard his mortality for a precious few minutes. There would be time later to contemplate his ultimate destiny.

His private stretch of Hokkaido coast, eight kilometers southwest of the village of Urohoro, was the perfect home for the old warrior. The harsh climate that accounted, in part, for Hokkaido's being the least settled island of the Japanese archipelago challenged him daily. Here, in the past few years, he had found the solitude he had long sought. On this stretch of barren, rock-strewn coast, he was his own person. As a point in fact, there seemed to be no other place for him, or those of his kind, in modern Japan. The incomparable crowding of people in the major cities and the supersaturation of roads and farms and railways on the islands of Honshu and Skikoku as well as parts of his native Kyushu had no appeal for him, and the ever-burning memory of the fiery deaths of his parents would never allow him to resettle in the city of his birth, Nagasaki.

There was also the consideration of the overbearing attitude of the entrepreneurs of the new technological and financial Japan. The sight of his old cronies in their Western business suits and white shirts with striped ties hurrying about Marunouchi, the economic heart of Tokyo, brought sour phlegm to his throat.

"Saburo," they would say, "this is another time. The old ways cannot cope with the new destiny of Japan. We must adapt."

Adapt? No, that was the one thing he could never do. The years in the JMSDF had been hard enough with the emphasis on keeping Japan a subdued military power with no chance to regain her former armed strength. Japanese troops were not even referred to as military; they were "defense forces" only. "Puppets" would have been a more appropriate term; puppets of the great conqueror, America, who had drafted the postwar constitution that swept away Genda's world.

True, he had found some satisfaction with his career in the maritime arm, but there had been too many years of frustration as he tried to convince senior officers that along with her financial and technological emergence as a world leader, Japan should rebuild her military. Such traditionalist thinking had been considered as blasphemy, of course, and most probably the reason he retired with stripes and not the tiny cherry blossoms insignia of an admiral. As for any "second" career, he would never let the code of the warrior be replaced by the pursuit of the yen. Instead, he had planned to remain here on the windswept rocky coast, living out his days in meditation, writing of the great war, and placing his watercolor impressions of the beauty around him on small squares of raw silk.

Except for his old Imperial Navy flight petty officer uniform and his dress blues from the JMSDF, he had disposed of his Western clothes. And his only concession to the times was an eight-inch color Sony module that allowed him to watch—mostly with disapproval—the major events of Japan's passage into the world of the West. That he did with a passion and an ever-building feeling of regret that the land of his birth was paying for her new position as a technological and financial world leader with the sacrifice of her ancient culture.

A fresh wind caused him to place one foot behind the other as a brace, and he found it difficult to properly meditate. Too many thoughts of his past life and irritations with the modern world were overriding the need to clear his mind. With consideration for his aching joints, he carefully lowered himself into the more classical seated Zen position with legs crossed, arms still tucked well up into his kimono sleeves.

The dark swelling waters of the northern Pacific matched the mood of the relatively tiny human sitting so determinedly on the rocky south shore of Hokkaido. The rise and fall of the surface somehow seemed to reach out and synchronize the expansion and retraction of Genda's chest as he slowly breathed in the salt air and let his eyes search for a sea that was not there, a Japanese sea stretching all the way to Hawaii. That is what it should have been.

As so often they did on these occasions, Genda's thoughts drifted back over the years. Now that he was on the far end of them, he realized how quickly they had passed. The time with his precious Emiko had been but a moment; the career with the JMSDF a matter of years unbelievably swift in their passing, more like minutes than long cycles around the sun. Now, the days of retirement, so short that they seemed to be overlapping, one beginning before the previous had even ended, and each cycle shorter than the one before.

On the grand scale of eternity, Genda could not even put his life into perspective. Such a reconciliation was beyond him, but the realization that his life was passing more rapidly with every sunrise made him acutely aware that if he indeed had a destiny, it was yet unfulfilled. Of all his regrets, that was the most painful.

All men had a destiny; a few were singled out for greatness. Genda had long ago resigned himself to the fact that he was not one of the great. But he was a man of honor, a product of a people whose lives were governed to the smallest detail by heavy traditions: strong family bonding, loyalty to one's warlord, inoffensive consideration of all men except those who would deny one his path in life. Toward that person, a Japanese was a formidable, never-yielding foe. The very code of the warrior—Bushido—set forth the standards for such conduct, and above all else, Genda considered himself a warrior. A warrior with an unfulfilled destiny. And that greatly concerned him.

Only a few hours earlier he had returned from a summons to his physician's office in Sapporo. It had been only a brief consultation, one that centered on the findings of recent tests. The leukocytes— white corpuscles—in Genda's blood were multiplying too rapidly. His lymph nodes, spleen, and liver were all enlarging. The diagnosis had been devastating.

Sitting there on his great rock, he sought peace of mind. He must place himself in the plane of solitary existence. It took a while, but finally, with the deepest of concentration, he forced all thought out of his body except for the realization of the power and beauty of the coarse nature around him.

Here, in this remote place, all was in order, the balance of trees and foliage perfect in the traditional way of ancient Nippon. The large gray rocks at the foot of the bluff upon which he sat were rounded from centuries of pounding surf and had been forced into a symmetry of mutual support. They would move no more until they felt the force of the tsunami.

Winding back to his cottage was the curving pathway of small black rocks, each one personally selected by him and collectively arranged in a series of curved lots, each bend with a radius precisely 1.2 times the radius of the next closest to the cottage. The shore scrub had been thinned but not altered in its natural pattern, and its rough cover was in sharp contrast to the carefully arranged pathway. The cottage itself was of all-natural material and simple in the way of the warrior. Like Genda at the moment, it was in harmony with its surroundings.

But the harmony of nature did not extend into Genda's soul, and his concentration once more faltered. For all of his effort to embrace the pure principles of Zen Buddhism, he was a bitter man, one who had spent his life in suppressed vengeance against the enemy who, forty-six years earlier, had not even let him give his life in the service of the divine Son of Heaven, Hirohito. Genda's sense of disgrace was barely tempered by his recollection that over the subsequent years he had served his country with distinction. But even that service had a dark side. Had he always taken the wisest of courses?

Certainly, his tenure with the maritime air arm of the JSDF had given him purpose. First as a flight leader, then a squadron commander, and finally a wing commander, he had steadily climbed the promotional ladder, eventually serving on senior staffs.

For almost three decades, he had worked side by side with the Americans in his antisubmarine warfare specialty. As a senior pilot in the American-built Lockheed P2V ASW aircraft used by the JMSDF, he had participated in joint exercises and attended American ASW operational training courses, hungrily devouring every bit of tactical information, information that he sometimes used for a secondary purpose. That purpose had seen him serving two masters, but primarily for the greater glory of Nippon. Financially, considering the extra income, he had planned well, and there remained in his account at the Bank of Tokyo a substantial sum that would see him comfortably through his remaining years. Grimly, he realized that now there might even be too much money to spend in the little time left. Shaking his head as if to clear away the thoughts, Genda gave up on pure meditation. Too much was in his mind.

With effort, he rose and walked back along the precisely curved path into his cottage. A shallow brass container of hot water sat on the hibachi in the main room. Genda tapped a small portion of shredded tea leaves into an earthen teapot and covered them with the hot water. As the mixture steeped, his eyes were drawn to his pair of swords resting quietly in their cradle across the room. Both were housed in black lacquered wooden scabbards and each handle was wrapped with the skin of the shark to provide for the firmest of grips. Small gilded cherry blossom fasteners held the sharkskin in place, and from the grommeted end of each handle hung a tassel of orange, his chosen samurai color.

The swords were held horizontally, the shorter one over the longer, their gracefully curved forms symbolic of the *torii*, the entrance gate of a shrine.

Perhaps *seppuku*, beginning with the ritual slicing of his stomach, would be a more honorable way out of the awful days ahead. Even now, in the twilight of his years, his body weakened, he could salvage his honor by drawing the short blade across his belly, being careful not to cut more than three inches deep to avoid the extremely painful severing of his intestines. He would then raise the blade and place it against his carotid artery and pull it sharply forward.

But he would need an assistant for when he pitched forward, someone to use the long blade to deliver a final compassionate but swift blow to his neck. Perhaps his old friend in Urohoro.

However, the irony of such a consideration was that he was already near the end of his time. *Seppuku* would be sapped of its purpose.

He poured himself a cup of tea. For a moment, he thought that perhaps he should eat something. But he was too troubled. Instead, he would drink the tea and after a while try to sleep. He dreaded that moment, for he knew the nightmare would return.

"Saburo!" The terrified call of his wife, Emiko, caused Genda to lunge forward and sit upright on the *futon*. Reality quickly returned, but the dream lingered. Would it never leave him?

They had been so happy, he and Emiko. Surprised that she had wished to marry him even after the disgrace of his aborted last mission, he had eagerly undertaken the joys and duties of a husband. The Occupation years had been grim with life-threatening shortages of food and medicine, and for the first year Genda had only his uniforms to wear. Stripped of insignia, the drab and worn garb was a constant reminder of his failure to protect his Emperor.

After a series of menial jobs, he and Emiko had managed to put together a small business, and the hardships of those years had been more than compensated for by the love of his wife and her wise tempering of his hate. "My husband," she would say, "the war is over. You fought honorably. It was just not to be. We are young. We have our lives ahead of us. That is all that matters."

He had been starting to believe her. Their business had prospered and they had acquired a prime location in Tokyo, operating a sidewalk shop of pearls and china on the Ginza. The Americans would buy anything they placed on the tables, the 360-to-1 exchange rate of yen to dollar making the average occupational troop outrageously rich by Japanese postwar standards. Most of the Americans had been polite and considerate and not at all like Genda and Emiko had imagined they would be. Some had even befriended them, and on occasion one would take Emiko to the lavish American military base exchange at Yokasuka and in response to her shy requests would purchase some of the necessities that were unobtainable on the starved Japanese market. In turn, Saburo would grant their benefactor special prices on such prized items as Mikimoto pearls and Noritake china.

But there had been a few, mostly young replacement troops who had not seen combat, who belittled and mistreated the vanquished and subdued Japanese.

Two of such a kind, half-crazed by the strong Japanese beer and sake, had forced their way into Genda's hut behind his stalls on a hot August night and raped Emiko—on the very day she had learned she was carrying their first child.

Genda would never forget the horror and anguish he had experienced as the huge Americans held him powerless while each assaulted Emiko. Every vivid detail of the attack remained in his memory and returned so very often in his nightmare.

By the time the Americans had fled and Genda could gather his wife into his arms, she no longer sobbed or spoke. Her mind was gone. He had tried to comfort her, to talk to her and assure her that it was all over. She had only stared straight ahead.

Genda had laid her gently back on the *futon* and covered her. Perhaps if she drank. In retrospect, he knew that he should never have left her even for that short period of time. When he had returned, Emiko was standing in the center of the room, her tiny mouth set and her eyes wide with determination.

"No!" Genda had screamed as he saw her upraised hands and then the blade of a kitchen knife starting down. He had leapt across the room but had been still in midair as she plunged the knife into her abdomen.

"No, Emiko! No, no, no . . . !"

As on that awful night forty-five years back, Genda's body shook with the sobs of his great sadness. Emiko, with her gentle and forgiving nature, had almost healed his wartime hurt, and then the two drunken Americans had renewed it and added an even greater injustice.

The offenders had been quickly caught, and American military justice had been swift. They had been sent back to the States for a lifetime of hard labor and the trial council of the military court had even apologized to Genda for the acts of the soldiers and had given him a small sum of American occupational script. But to Genda, it would always be another tragedy that equaled the cruel and senseless bombing of his parents. He would never forget—or forgive—either atrocity.

Genda stood. He could sleep no more. The instant that was yesterday was past. Despite the low overcast that was just beginning to release its moisture, the horizon to the east was showing the first light gray signs of dawn.

Perhaps it was just as well that the nightmare had interrupted his sleep, for it once more reminded him of his vow made so long ago. A vow that had slipped farther back into the recesses of his mind as he enjoyed the comfort and serenity of his cottage. Now, his illness changed his priorities. He must bathe and dress and go into Urohoro. He had a most vital phone call to make.

Chapter 2

The angry sea the night before had forecast the steady light rain that
was falling onto Urohoro, and the narrow dirt side streets of the
small village had drunk their fill within the first few hours. Stub-
bornly, they refused to absorb any more of the sky-cleansed seawater. Genda's ancient Datsun made its way along the muddy paths
much as an embryo ice skater would take the first tentative strokes
across a freshly prepared rink. But he had driven the streets before
and despite the sliding and the occasional necessity to veer close to
the wooden houses lining his way to seek firmer ground, he made
sure progress toward the only public inn in Urohoro.

Stopping directly in front of it, Genda disregarded the rain while
walking the few steps to the entrance. With just five rooms available,
it was the only facility for travelers in the village. A small anteroom
adjacent to the owner's living space held a registration table and a
telephone that Genda often used.

"*Ohayo gozaimasu*—good morning!" Genda called toward the
room off the entrance. A faint echo responded, followed by a series
of hacking coughs.

Genda dialed a special number from his past and gave the access code to the female on the other end of the line. There was some delay and Genda's heart began to quicken. Suppose the code was no longer useful! The last evening's decision had been based on the possibility of acquiring outside help. But his concern was quickly erased as a familiar voice reached his ear.

"It has been a long time, old friend. I am surprised to hear from you."

Genda was pleased that the tone was friendly and the words arranged to conceal any aspect of either his identity or that of his control. He knew that on the end of the line there was a special Soviet embassy phone but precautions had always been taken. Politely, he responded, "It is good to hear your voice. I have a request."

"Business?"

"In a way. I must meet with you."

"Our business terminated several years ago. You have something for me, still?"

"No, my friend. And it is only in desperation that I need something from you. I only ask that we meet so that I may speak of it."

"I am not sure that would be proper."

"For thirty years of loyalty?"

There was a pause, then, "I will see you as a friend, nothing else."

"That is sufficient for the moment."

"Where shall we meet?"

"Do you remember our walk in the fog when we spoke of the days when we would no longer be in the business?" Genda asked.

"Yes. It was a rare time between us."

Genda smiled and nodded to himself as he also recalled the time. "Then, let us meet there again, at the same hour as before."

"And the day?"

"I can be there tomorrow. Is that too soon?"

"No . . . no, I think not. I will look forward to it, old friend. I must confess you have aroused my curiosity. I and my associates are in your debt for many things. If I can be of personal service, I shall be honored."

"You are kind to an old man. I will see you, then?"

"Of course."

The owner of the inn and the cough entered as Genda hung up. "Genda-san, you should not be out in this rain."

"It is but a mist. I had a call to make—and it is you who are threatening to tear the linings of your throat. You need to keep the hibachi working on nights such as these. The cost of the call will be on your bill. Please advise me."

"Nonsense. It is a small thing to do for one who has served his country as long as you. I am a man honored."

"And also a man of little funds if I judge the hollow silence of your rooms to be indicative of the lack of travelers."

"Ha! You are perceptive. But there is one room engaged. It will more than pay for your rare phone calls. Do you have time for some tea, or warm sake, perhaps, to counter the chill? Beer?"

Genda could appreciate the anxious look in his friend's face. It had been a while since they had visited. "It is early. Tea might be more appropriate."

The innkeeper held the two cloth panels aside as Genda entered the tiny living quarters. The man had tea water already hot on his small wood-burning stove. While Genda cupped his hands around the warm container and waited for the flavor of the leaves to saturate the water, the innkeeper took a bottle of Asahi Lager from a small refrigerator. Opening it, he held it up before his toothless grin. "To old times."

"To old times."

"We had a similar-tasting beer on Okinawa," the innkeeper mused, "a great supply, actually, and we drank it furiously just before the Americans landed."

"Those were hard days."

"No, those were the days of glory. We welcomed the assault and the chance to show our superiority—our officers told us we would march down the streets of Tokyo after the war with bags of American testicles hanging from our belts. And we fought well . . . we did indeed fight well." The innkeeper raised the Asahi and took a long swallow. Wiping his mouth with the back of one hand, he shrugged. "But they also fought well and there were too many! I don't remember anything after being hit until I woke up tied to a stretcher among wounded Americans. They were marines and very young." A faraway look came into the man's eyes. "One of the aid men gave me a cigarette."

"And you honor *me* as a warrior?"

"You fliers were special to us."

"I never got off Honshu."

"No, but your comrades did, and they dove their aircraft into the bowels of American ships with a great fury. You would have, also."

Genda was not anxious to discuss the battle of Okinawa. That was where the first Thunder Gods had made their debut and that is where they had failed miserably at the cost of too many precious lives. One of the lesser-known incidents had also been the *kamikaze* mission of the last great battleship, *Yamato*. With the same single-mindedness of purpose as their airborne brethren, the crew of the *Yamato* had sailed to certain death, their impossible mission to break through the American fleet and beach on the shores of Okinawa. There, the mighty eighteen-inch guns could continue their task as fixed shore guns and the crew in a last desperate act would join their army and marine comrades on the doomed island in a fight to the death against the American invasion forces. And like the *kamikazes* of the air, the mighty ship had died in her attempt.

For a while, the two men sat and sipped their drinks and enjoyed the soft sound of the drizzle on the hard clay roof of the inn. It was inevitable that they recalled the closing days of the war and the special relationships they had with their comrades. For the inn-keeper, such memories were precious, but for Genda, they brought back too much pain. The innkeeper reached for the tea. Genda held up a hand in polite protest.

"You are kind but I have much to do." Genda stood, took the offered arm, and squeezed it warmly. The man's other arm was still on Okinawa. Stepping away, Genda bowed. "Ten thousand years, my old friend."

The innkeeper's face brightened. *"Banzai!"* he whispered strongly. "Ten thousand years, Genda-san."

His contact arranged, Genda drove north across the western bulge of Hokkaido, yesterday's rainclouds still draping a gray moist veil over the tops of the lush mountain foliage. The weather front, originally spawned by a large low pressure cell over western Siberia, had lost most of its heavy moisture in the high mountains of the Republic of Mongolia, but enough remained to wet down Hokkaido for at least two more days. After its passage, a rapidly moving cold front would follow and bring temperatures that would emphasize the arrival of winter weather, and the next front of the series would most likely provide a white mantle of snow. Genda knew that the drive back to his beach house could be much more hazardous.

Turning south at Takikawa, he soon entered the freeway system that served Sapporo. The region, originally inhabited by the Ainu, the "proto Japanese people" who predated the arrival of the first settlers from Korea and China, lay in the fertile valley of the Toyohira River. It was one of Genda's special areas, with a beauty that defied capture by his paints. He had tried often but had yet to reproduce the right shades and composition of harsh greens, purples, and browns that nature wove into patterns much more subtle than the strokes of his brushes could manage. He could only imagine the awe that the first settlers had when they saw the valley. The new Japanese had reached Hokkaido in the middle of the nineteenth century and began an intensive agricultural development of the area. They had rapidly prospered, despite the hard long winters, and in slightly over one hundred years the city of Sapporo became a metropolis of one million people. Laid out in grid fashion similar to North American cities, Sapporo was easily navigable, however Genda would not have to contend with the central city on this trip.

His destination was the Sapporo airport, and despite the rain, he arrived in time to catch an early-afternoon flight to Tokyo. At Tokyo's Haneda Airport, which provided most of the domestic air service to the capital city, he made a timely connection and one and a half hours after lifting off was looking down at the city of his birth.

Nagasaki, the first port to be opened to the outside world and the only one from the sixteenth century to the end of the nineteenth, lay on the northwest side of Kyushu, nestled on the edge of a fjordlike inlet and protected by offshore islands. As the airliner passed over the city to position itself for its approach to the airport, Genda gazed down on the great shipyards that opened onto Nagasaki Bay. Several giant supertankers were in various stages of construction, propped upright in their huge dry docks like giant earthworms resting after a herculean meal of raw steel.

From the air, there was no remaining trace of the devastation that had been visited upon the city in the closing days of World War II, but Genda could clearly see the Peace Park in the Hamaguchi-machi section of the city. There would be the memorial that marked the epicenter of the burst of the second atomic bomb, and all around the area was the rebuilt section of the city of a half million. Genda wondered if the more than twenty-five thousand souls released on August 9, 1945, were still lingering in the same heavens through which his airliner was passing. If so, there were two whom he would like to hug and kiss. Of course, as an aspiring Zen Buddhist, he could not accept such a ridiculous concept, but as his parents' son, he wished it were so.

Departing the Nagasaki air terminal, he hailed a taxi and soon arrived at the Hotel Hakuunso, where he would spend the next two nights. He habitually stayed there on his many pilgrimages to the city and the staff welcomed him with their usual cordiality. Although the last years had seen him quite content to sleep alone, the manager always inquired as to his wishes. As expected, Genda declined the discreet offer. Now that his urges were milder, it was easier to remain faithful to the memory of Emiko. But there had been other nights in the Hakuunso. . . . The memories were sufficient to satisfy him now.

The next day, at the appointed time, Genda stood before the memorial in the Peace Park. Here, he once again reflected, was where the awful fireball began, spreading outward before the eyes of the old couple less than an eighth of a mile away could even blink. In that next awesome moment, his frail birdlike mother and erect, always protective father had been turned into ash. All during his clandestine career as a foreign operative he had chosen this place for the exchange of orders and information. Each visit renewed his hate and softened the pain of betraying his own service. His subterfuge had been a necessary thing, for it gave the chief adversary of the United States a few more pieces of the tactical puzzle that would give it the edge should an ultimate conflict occur. Such a conflict was an improbability, but Genda was determined that, if it did, the ideology of Marxist-Leninism would survive. That, Genda felt, his people could combat. They would never shake off the American influence. Just the opposite. To Genda, his fellow Japanese seemed determined to make themselves oriental clones of the Western world. But superior clones, with intellect and capabilities far outreaching their role models. Even so, such a thing would be the end of Japan as he knew and loved it.

A small group of touring visitors, apparently from nearby Sasebo, approached and stood with him in silence. Genda kept his head bowed and eyes closed. After a few minutes he heard them walking away and he allowed his eyes to open. One of the group remained beside him, a man about his age but with oriental features more Mongol than Japanese. He wore a brown cloth overcoat, the collar buttoned at the neck. A matching fedora with a brim a bit too large was pulled tightly over his head, causing bushy gray hair to erupt from around its sides.

Without looking aside at Genda, the man softly spoke. "You are aging."

"As are we all," Genda replied, also keeping his eyes on the memorial.

"Yes." There was a touch of resignation in the one-word reply.

"Thank you for coming."

"You are doing well?"

"I miss the activity."

"I should have left when you did."

"Why did you not?"

The Mongol shrugged. "I do not know. I suppose I was afraid."

"Of what?" Genda asked.

"Of growing old. Of being useless. Of going back to Kimchatka and spending my days watching the grass grow in the summer and the snow fall in the winter. I am sorry, I did not mean that to sound as it did."

Genda chuckled. "There is something to be said for watching the grass grow—and the snow fall. But it is a very legitimate fear, that of growing old. I am experiencing it."

The Mongol grunted in understanding. "Then tell me what service I can perform for you."

Genda looked over and caught his companion's eyes. "I am dying."

The Mongol's eyebrows rose and his look softened. "I did not know."

"I only found out two days ago."

"What is it?"

"My blood. The medical people define it as a too-rapid multiplication of white corpuscles. It is losing its ability to sustain me."

The Mongol looked genuinely shocked. "Leukemia."

"Yes."

"You should be in a hospital. There are treatments."

Genda pulled back, offended. "And lie in bed and shrivel up and groan with pain until someone puts enough substance into my blood that I just lie there as a turnip?" Realizing he had reacted too harshly, he calmed and continued, "Yes, there are treatments. The injection of powerful chemicals or the painful replacement of bone marrow are the two most common. But to what avail? Another three or four years? All spent in excruciating pain? That would rob me of my vitality faster than the disease."

The Mongol reached over with one hand and gave Genda's shoulder a gentle squeeze. "How long do you have?"

"Four, five months, perhaps a week or two longer. What do they know when it comes to precise timing of such things? If you help me, it will be long enough."

The hand remained on Genda's shoulder. "What can I do?"

"Forty-six years ago, I was poised to strike a blow against the enemy of Japan and I was denied. I made a vow that I would someday take up that mission again. I want to strike the Americans one time before I go."

The Mongol removed his hand. "Saburo, my old friend, the Americans are no longer the enemy of Japan."

"They are *my* enemy. They murdered my parents and raped my wife. Need I remind you, they are your enemy, too."

"Only in ideology. Remember *glasnost*?"

"Do not try to mislead an old hand at misleading. Nothing has changed behind the silver words of Gorbachev. The goals remain. Do not insult me with the mention of such a farce as *glasnost*, the Russian fad of the dying eighties. It was an exercise in semantics, nothing more. Another rabbit from the Soviet hat to generate American sympathy through the last winter of the decade. With the satellite countries abandoning political support and seeking their own identities, Gorbachev had to come up with something."

The Mongol's voice took on a harder edge. "*Glasnost* preceded that debacle."

"It preceded actuality only. The disintegration of the world party was already under way. The outside world did not know of it, but Moscow did. *Glasnost* was a poorly prepared attempt to forestall it. It didn't work. And overnight—isn't that amazing?—the political climate of Eastern Europe was changed. Despite *glasnost* and the release of Eastern bloc obligations, you barely made it through that crisis without a major in-country collapse. Last year was just as difficult. Ha! Where is Gorbachev now? What are his latest words on *glasnost*?"

"Officially, I must take exception to such remarks."

"Officially," Genda repeated with the slight trace of a smile, "I would expect you to do so. But, it is of no consequence to my problem."

"Saburo, the war is long over. Forgive me, but you are an old man, a dying old man. Why not put it all behind you?"

Genda's eyes narrowed. "Every night when I close my eyes I see the terror-stricken face of my Emiko. I see her body being ravished by two brutal American soldiers. I see the despair in those precious eyes turn to shame—completely unjustifiable, for she was an innocent in that horrible encounter—then I see her look of anguish fade into a blank stare and there is no life left in her eyes as her hand opens her stomach and destroys my seed in her womb along with her own life. As if that is not enough, whenever I look in the skies over Kyushu I see the tiny radioactive particles that are all that remain of my mother and father. I have lived with it for almost half a century—will you help me or not?"

The Mongol again touched Genda's arm and turned him aside. "Let us walk a bit. I should tell you—there may be little I can do."

The two men slowly strolled the peaceful pathways of the park. There was a biting chill in the air and only a few other visitors.

Genda persisted. "You have contacts, ones that can be of service to me in this."

"What do you plan to do?" The Mongol was at least interested.

"I have no definite plan yet. Perhaps a blow against American military installations. Maybe their embassy. Anything that will cause a rift with my country."

The Mongol remained silent while he considered Genda's request. Anything, however small, that would disrupt the bond between Japan and the United States would be to the advantage of the Soviet Union. However, he could not see how anything significantly consequential could arise from one old man's efforts. "It will take much more than what you may be able to accomplish, Genda. The bond is too strong to be weakened so easily. That has been our problem all along."

Genda sighed impatiently. "I will do it by myself, if I must. It will be easier if I have help."

The Mongol could only think of one rather weak reason for offering any assistance: the impending U.S.-Japan treaty. Word from Moscow was that it had some far-reaching provisions and initial intelligence indicated that the treaty could weaken the Soviet

Union's position in the western Pacific, although not all of the details were known. With the unprecedented decline of Soviet political influence during the past two years, the Soviet Union must rethink its expansionist goals. Indeed, self-preservation was more the goal at this point. Perhaps assisting Genda in his intent to strike the Americans would cause a slight but critical disagreement between the United States and Japan. Anything would help. But he would have to keep direct Soviet participation out of the picture. This was not the time for the U.S.S.R. to be suddenly connected with acts of terrorism, and that was just what Genda seemed to be considering. There was one possibility but the Mongol held little confidence in the group that came to mind, even though it would confine Genda's actions within the Japanese sphere. He stopped as if to admire the beauty of the neatly manicured grounds and without looking directly at Genda, said, "There are those who would help you do such a thing but they are small in number and would require financing."

"I have funds I will never use."

The Mongol cocked his head as if hesitant to continue. But he did. "They are fanatics. Irrational. Your own countrymen."

"So much the better." Genda stood motionless during a long pause.

The Mongol did not feel that he owed Genda anything, but the Japanese had served him well in past years. There was some slight feeling of gratitude—and sympathy. After all, a dying man should receive some consideration of his last wish. And there *was* another factor, perhaps of greater importance. Since the 1989 collapse of Party control in Eastern Europe and the subsequent political changes within the Soviet Union, his services within the KGB had been almost exclusively those of a paper pusher. It would be nice to go out with some type of recent positive action on his record. Whether Genda's operation would be successful remained to be seen—but if it was, the Mongol would retire with distinction and several more rubles per month to ease his old age. Quietly, he offered, "I can give you a name."

"And arrange a contact?"

"Yes, I believe so. And I can provide necessary papers—IDs, passports, whatever you require. Perhaps even some hand weapons and funding from my personal contingency fund."

"I said I have funds."

"Genda, if you truly intend to go through with this, the persons I put you in contact with will come up with some ideas, I assure you, but in all probability they will require more money than you have. I may be able to convince my superiors that there is benefit in this for us as well. There is one caution, however. The people I recommend to you are completely irresponsible and have no head for any kind of coherent planning. They will do anything, but they must have a leader to follow. The money will not only buy their services but also their allegiance as long as they are killing Americans. You should also know that they are not averse to killing their own countrymen if it suits their purpose."

"Have I heard of such persons?"

"They have been underground but largely dormant for years. Your sudden desires are just the cause célèbre that could awaken them again."

Genda's mind suddenly tightened with alarm. "I will have nothing to do with the *yakuza*."

The Mongol shook his head. "No, I am not speaking of those thugs. To begin with, their outrageous tattoos and idiotic missing fingers make them far too identifiable, and you know as well as I that the romanticized characters we see in films are far removed from the drug-dealing extortionists we know the *yakuza* to be. I am speaking of another group, equally as fanatical but with some semblance of a political purpose."

Genda felt relief as his mind opened wider. Of course. "The Red Army?"

"The same cell that sent Yu Kikamuru to the United States in 1988."

"They are unprofessional. Kikamuru panicked at the mere sight of a police vehicle and was caught needlessly."

"So, they need a leader. And you need followers."

"Give me the name."

"Toshio Goto. I will set up a first meeting. After that, it is up to you. I should tell you that he is not a strong leader; that is one reason we have heard little from him in recent months. But his followers are loyal and they may easily adapt to your goals."

Genda was not inwardly pleased that he must deal with the Japanese Red Army group. Mainly disgruntled former students, they were terrorists without a real purpose and had little effective organization. "An immature man will not understand the intensity of my purpose. I am not a terrorist."

"Goto is one of the originals. As for being immature, he is in his forties now and much more receptive to guidance by someone with wisdom and stature. He will listen to you and his people will listen to him."

"Where will I find him?"

"It will take me a day. You are staying where?"

"At the Hakuunso."

"Of course. I forgot you are a man of habit. Tomorrow afternoon, I will inform you."

"How will I recognize him?"

"I will see that he identifies himself to your satisfaction."

Genda's former control left as unobtrusively as he had arrived. Genda remained standing for a few more moments, deep in thought, before returning to his hotel.

The next afternoon, Genda received his message from the Mongol. He must travel north of Tokyo to Takaragawa Hot Springs. Goto would contact him there.

Chapter 3

The bus ride to Takaragawa Hot Springs was a welcome relief for Genda. His return Nagasaki-to-Tokyo flight had been typical of air travel in Japan during the end of the holiday season: busy, crowded terminals, hassle at the security gates, and a full fuselage of chattering, excited travelers overburdened with carry-on luggage, bright straining shopping sacks, and the ever-present camera bags. Everyone was exhausted and anxious to be home and prepared for the winter. There was still enough afternoon heat to cause thermals, however, and for most of the flight seat belts were required. Although Genda had spent a lifetime as a military aviator, he was a poor passenger and always preferred a forward aisle seat. He could board the airplane last and get off first.

By contrast, the bus was quiet and had a soothing sway as it passed rapidly away from the crowded city and through the suburbs and countryside on the short journey to the springs. The passengers, seated by large tinted windows, could enjoy the passing scenery in silence. On buses, Genda preferred a window seat.

After checking into his room at the inn, he proceeded to the men's area of the springs and disrobed, wrapping one of the large fluffy towels around his lower body and then tightly coiling a smaller towel around his head to form a dam against the perspiration that would surely come.

He was early for the appointed meeting with Goto and he used the time well, alternately soaking for long periods of time in the hot springs that bubbled up through the volcanic rocks and immersing himself in the frigid mountain streams that ran through the thermal springs area. In places, early autumn ice already lined the edges of the water and very few of those present matched Genda's determination to use both the hot and cold waters, but each cycle rejuvenated him and eased his joints, providing some freedom from the constant stiffness that they had suffered for the last years.

While he soaked, he studied the shapes of the huge black stones lining the streambed. How had they come to their present positions? Some ancient earthquake? An ancient landslide triggered by prehistoric flooding? More than likely, just the slow evolutionary process of constant pressure as the massive eight-thousand-mile-wide Pacific plate ground against the coast of northeastern Honshu. Those great round rocks counted their ages in millions of years.

The hot springs, themselves, were small pools of varying depths, fed by the mysterious furnace that forever burned deep beneath the surface of the earth. Most of the steaming waters were covered by open-sided sheds that gave protection from the winter snows. By contrast, the wide stream that rapidly flowed through the center of the area was a roaring torrent of frigid white water, cascading down a series of plateaued rock beds and swirling around and over the dark boulders that rose above the torrent as much as several feet. Upstream, hanging partially over it, was the inn, its three tiers of simple accommodations topped by a pagoda roof of weathered green slate, and all around the area were the great oaks, their autumn leaves almost gone. An abundance of perennial greenery and rock fern thrived along the humid banks of the stream. As Genda and the men walked and soaked they exchanged bows and pleasant small talk. The place was certainly not crowded. At the moment, Genda had one small pool to himself.

Eventually, a younger man joined him.

"*Aiie!*" the newcomer exclaimed as he lowered himself into the hot pool. "The fire in the center of the earth must be burning hotter today." He positioned himself opposite Genda.

"Yes, it must be very close to one hundred and ten degrees. Do you come here often?"

"On occasion. I usually prefer the hot mud down at Beppu."

In years past, Genda had also visited the town of more than four thousand thermal openings in the earth's crust. South of Tokyo, Beppu was a much larger hot springs area and noted for its red "Bloody Pond Hell" outcropping of water at almost two hundred and twelve degrees. No one bathed in that!

"I prefer it here," Genda said. "I like the quiet and the isolation."

"Yes. Beppu is much more crowded."

Genda judged the man to be in his mid-forties. His hairline was trying to creep back over his head and was already near the top but what remained was full and still dark. His upper body was lean but the wrapped towel failed to disguise a soft middle. There were some acne scars on his cheeks and his teeth were not well cared for. But his look was pleasant and he was not unhandsome. Probably had been good with the women in his youth. Genda had noticed that the man's legs had a slight bow in them when he had initially approached. "Are you staying at the inn?"

"No. I will be here just the day. You?"

"Overnight only. I live in Hokkaido."

"Are you on holiday?"

"In a way. I spent two days over at Nagasaki."

"That is a nice city."

The man was friendly enough but did not seem to want to volunteer any personal information. Yet, when Genda had his eyes averted he had a strong feeling that the man was studying him. He was not too surprised when his companion made a suggestion.

"I have had enough for the moment. Would you like to join me in a walk?"

"I may spend a few more minutes." Genda prefered to leave the door open should the man not be his contact.

"There is a beautiful bend downstream where we can dry ourselves and enjoy what there is of the sun. We may even see a white chrysanthemum."

White chrysanthemum! That had been Genda's code name during his contacts with the Soviets. The man knew the right words to identify himself. Obviously, the Mongol had given them to him knowing that Genda would immediately pick up on the phrase. It could not be a coincidence as at this time of the year there would be no blooming chrysanthemums, even around the hot springs. The man had to be Goto. Wrapped in their thick white towels, the two men picked their way over the rocks downstream and around the bend. A light breeze had risen and the number of men hardy enough to brave the increased cold had dwindled drastically. Most had left for the indoor pools. A small open shed, its supports anchored among the large rocks, sheltered an unoccupied thermal pool. Genda and his companion sat on a flat-topped boulder by the pool. They were the only ones in the immediate vicinity.

The man smiled briefly before speaking. "I am Toshio Goto."

"Captain Saburo Genda."

"I understand we may wish to do some business together."

"Perhaps. I am used to a disciplined organization, however."

"We are as disciplined as our purpose requires."

"Certainly. My one condition is that I guide the effort. I will select the targets. The method and time I will leave to you."

"That is satisfactory—as long as it is in keeping with our own goals."

Genda looked around before continuing. They were still alone. "I must confess I am unfamiliar with your goals."

Goto raised one leg and crossed it over the other before using the towel to dislodge some small rocks from between his foot and thong. "The furtherment of socialist progress by world revolution."

Genda tried very hard to keep his face from responding to the foolishness of the remark. Socialist progress in Japan? A country rapidly becoming more capitalist than even the United States?

Goto sensed Genda's amusement. "I know we have not been very effective the past few years. A matter of funding."

Certainly, the Soviets had withdrawn their support, thought Genda. There were other, quite more critical, demands for their diminishing supply of rubles. "I want a series of operations against the Americans. Does that fit in with your goals?"

Goto pursed his lips and switched his legs to clean his other foot. Was Genda suggesting the killing of Americans? He could see no immediate advantage in murder for murder's sake, even the murder of Americans. But continued inaction could be much worse. Already the preoccupied populace of Japan looked upon the Red Army as no more than a tragic nuisance. Working with the man, Genda, might restore some political clout. It certainly could generate headlines and even a waning movement could benefit from headlines. Cautiously, he answered Genda, "Indirectly. Ours is a slightly higher purpose but the means may well be the same. You can provide financial support?"

"Yes. Not without limits, of course."

"One million yen immediately?"

"That is no problem."

Goto bit his lower lip as if contemplating whether his next question was appropriate. "Why are you doing this?"

"It is personal. I would not think that my reasons would be of interest to you as long as your purpose would also be served."

"A matter of security. You could turn us in."

"I would be turning myself in as well."

"You were an officer in the JMSDF?"

"I still am, but I am retired."

"What did you do?"

"I was an aviator and later a member of various staffs."

"For how long?"

"Long enough. I do not believe that my past is of any concern to our relationship."

Goto was not satisfied. "I think it is. You were a career military officer. You worked with the Americans. And now you want to kill Americans. Something must have happened."

"Only American military. As for my motivation, it is something that happened a long time ago. I will speak no further of it. I have offered you a proposition."

Goto shrugged. He could see little political gain from an association such as Genda was suggesting, but there could very well be personal gain. A renewal of his reputation within the national party would be almost reason enough. And he was restless from inactivity. Why *not* take the old man on? It would surely beat the clandestine life of petty crime he and his associates had been forced to follow just to keep the cell together. And anything could develop. "Good enough. When do we start?"

"Now."

Two thousand miles southeast of the pool of hot spring water where Genda and Goto were sealing their pact, two sun-baked American aviation enthusiasts were looking at the results of a year's very hard labor. They stood on one corner of the international airport on Pohnpei, the capital island of the Federated States of Micronesia.

Behind them, the mountainous rain forest island rose over two thousand feet, its central peaks piercing the bottoms of rainclouds. This was a banner day, and around the makeshift hangar was a group of excited, chattering natives, women and children as well as men. A number were running back and forth, leaning over until they would almost fall in order to peer inside the hangar at the shadowy shape of what appeared to be a single-engined airplane. For the past year, few had been privileged to see exactly what the Americans had been up to, but over the months word had passed all around the island and now all had been invited to the unveiling.

Consequently, almost all of the island's population were there, and a number of the less shy were impatiently clapping for the activity to begin. The pair of Americans waved and nodded in appreciation.

Of the two, Patrick McMahon, Jr., was perhaps the most excited. His father had fought against such a plane from the straight decks of the old *Essex*-class carriers. Not only had the father willed his son his tall tapered body and his fighter pilot's unruly shock of blond hair, steel-blue eyes, hawk nose, and squared jaw, he had instilled in McMahon, the younger, his intense love of flying. When the son had been ten years old, his dad had purchased a basket-case P-51 and restored it, converting it into a two-seater in the process. Patrick had grown up in the rear seat of the Mustang and on his sixteenth birthday he had soloed it. Ten years later, in the fall of 1984, the senior McMahon had died and the twenty-six-year-old Patrick had inherited the P-51 along with his father's lucrative Buick dealership. His flight log now contained entries describing 2,267 flight hours, including time in restored Hellcats, Corsairs, B-17s, and the twin-boomed "Forked Devil" of the European air war, the Lockheed P-38.

By contrast, his partner, Terry Simpson, barely came up to McMahon's shoulder and weighed perhaps one hundred and twenty pounds soaking wet. Skinny, hyper, always cheerful, Simpson had grown up as a "ramp rat" on a dozen small airports, trading dawn-to-dusk menial tasks for flight time. A natural mechanic, he had rebuilt his first radial engine before he had been eligible to drive his first car. At the age of twenty-one he had met McMahon and the two had found a strong common bond in their shared love of aircraft restoration projects.

"Let's roll it out," McMahon said.

Together and with the help of a small group of native children they carefully pushed the low-winged aircraft out into the sun. For the two Americans, but even more for the older natives watching from a distance, it was a magic moment. The relic rolled back the calendar fifty years to the time when its presence on Pohnpei was a routine thing. The fresh dark-green paint on the upper fuselage and wings had been mixed to match perfectly the original wartime colors used by the Imperial Navy. The bulging cowling over the restored Nakajima NK-1C Sakai 12 radial engine was a bright black and the silver-spinnered propeller seemed anxious to feel the force of the surging 940-horsepower, 14-cylinder engine. Bathed in sunlight, the emerald airplane shone like a sparkling ghost of the past.

A hearty cheer erupted from the small band of native onlookers, punctuated by a smattering of applause.

The two Americans walked around the airplane examining their handiwork. It was as close to factory-fresh as they had been able to restore it. By the time they got it back to the States it would be an almost priceless possession.

Finding it had been the first miracle. Finding it in a restorable state had been the second, for the aircraft had crash-landed on a small island in the Pohnpei lagoon some forty-seven years ago.

Their good fortune had been accidental. In the summer of 1989, while on a scuba-diving expedition to the Caroline Islands, McMahon and Simpson had visited a local *sakau* bar in Kolonia, Pohnpei's largest village. A bare seven degrees north of the equator, Pohnpei was the largest of a collection of western Pacific islands that included the more historical Truk and Yap. The Americans had been the only Caucasians in the bar, and at first the natives treated them coolly although politely. Once they saw how willing the two outsiders were to sample their native drink, however, and how unpretentious the white visitors were in laughing at the mule-kick effect of the pounded root solution, the natives accepted the Americans as friends who could appreciate their island culture. The Pohnpeians had loosened up and began sharing their traditional tales. Toward the end of the evening, McMahon and Simpson had listened incredulously to the story of one old native, who told them that back in 1944, while fishing in the lagoon, he had witnessed the wheels-up landing of a Japanese warplane on the beach of a nearby tiny island. The native claimed the airplane was still there, hidden under thick foliage. At first, McMahon thought that it was the *sakau* talking, but as he listened and ran the details through his mind, he began to believe the native. Simpson was a bit more skeptical.

Pohnpei had been bypassed by the Americans during the fierce island-hopping of the Pacific war, although a sizable Japanese Army garrison had been present on the main island. The native claimed that the officer in charge had established a salvage party, but lacking the ability to safely disassemble the aircraft and get it across the lagoon, he had elected to preserve it where it landed. His men dug into the sand and under the direction of the wounded pilot were able to lower the landing gear, then drag the airplane away from the water. The officer had his men wash it down thoroughly with fresh water and spray it inside and out with the tropical preservative they used to protect and preserve their weapons. The work party then built a floored shelter, hauled the aircraft inside, and sealed the small building with an overall cover of thick tar except for a small round opening. The building was completely filled with smoke to drive out the humid island air and check for leaks. Finding none, the Japanese left the dry smoke filling the interior and sealed the hole. It was their intent to come back at some later date and recover the airplane, but the war ended before they could do that and in the excitement and confusion of American occupation and the repatriation of all Japanese troops back to their homeland, the incident was forgotten.

Over the years, tropical growth had completely covered the hut and it lay undisturbed until the day the two Americans were led to the site by the aged Pohnpeian. It took hours of backbreaking work to remove the interwoven island foliage, but they finally managed to break into the hut.

"Holy Jesus, Patrick, look at that!" Simpson had exclaimed, his skepticism completely gone.

In the dim light, a gray-and-green metal mummy from the past stood on its tall gear in all its glory, preserved with the same efficiency and care the ancient Egyptians had used to lay their royalty to rest. McMahon crawled up onto the wing and gingerly pulled back the canopy. "I don't believe this. It looks like we could just step in the cockpit and go flying."

But closer examination revealed that there were areas of major corrosion. Still, the airplane was basically undamaged and certainly restorable.

Returning to the States, the two overjoyed men had enlisted the financial and technical aid of a number of their companions and had formed a small nonprofit corporation to restore the airplane. The engine and propeller were removed and sent to Guam for a complete rebuilding. New tires and rubber fittings were obtained. Every square inch of the entire skeleton and skin was examined and replacement sections formed and substituted in the areas of corrosion. All fuel lines, hydraulic lines, and electrical wiring were replaced. New fabric was placed on the control surfaces. The canopy and windshield were fitted with new Plexiglas, and all of the flight and engine operating instruments were overhauled. The two 7.7-mm fuselage machine guns and the two wing-mounted 20-mm cannons were broken down, cleaned and oiled, and restored to firing condition. The only concession to the modern era was a set of state-of-the-art radio and navigational equipment. Now it was complete and sitting for the first time in the bright Pohnpeian sunlight.

"It is beautiful," Simpson muttered, prayerlike.

"Wait until we see how it flies!"

For the two Americans, it was almost a religious experience. The object of their admiration was not just an aerial classic, it was a very rare one. There were only two other flyable survivors in the whole world.

At one time, there had been over ten thousand.

Chapter 4

George Kohji Sakai, second-generation Japanese-American, entered the newly refurbished White House presidential briefing room and found a seat along the wall. A forty-three-year-old ex-marine—if there was such a thing as an ex-marine—Sakai was completing his third year on the Japanese desk in the State Department's special operations section—a synonym phrase for antiterrorist matters. It had been his assignment since returning from a six-year stint in the Tokyo embassy. The briefing really had little importance for him; there were no antiterrorist provisions in the new U.S.-Japanese mutual defense security arrangements. But his boss had said be there, so he was.

Sakai still carried his five-foot-five frame marine-erect, and his one hundred and forty-three pounds of muscled flesh was kept in the proper place by frequent trips to the basement gym. With a ready smile and a gregarious office personality, he was well known within the department.

The division heads and section chiefs already occupied a number of the tall-backed chairs arranged around the long, green-felt-draped conference table, and the most comfortable chair, a leather-cushioned swivel wing, was waiting for the president. A large projection screen was on the viewing wall, and off to one side of it was a highly polished cherrywood podium with the presidential seal emblazoned on its front.

Most of the underlings were already seated around the walnut-paneled walls of the room and Sakai made his way toward an empty seat on the far side.

"Wanna booster chair, George?"

Sakai sat down next to the teaser. "At least my knuckles don't drag on the rug when I walk by."

One of the men on the other side of the room caught Sakai's eye.

"Gotta bail out of our match today, George. Debbie's mother's coming over and we're doing the dinner-and-theater bit. Sorry."

"No problem."

"Match?" the older man on the other side of Sakai asked.

"Racquetball. You play?"

"God, no."

The majority and minority leaders of both the Senate and House walked in and seated themselves at the long conference table. The two senior division heads and their action officers who had worked on the treaty with Japanese counterparts followed and took chairs near the foot of the table. One of the action officers started nervously thumbing through a thick folder of assorted papers and graphs; the other poured coffee.

Christ, Sakai thought, *if you aren't ready for this briefing by now, it's too late to read your notes.* He had read his copy of the proposed treaty the night before even though he had not taken an active part in its drafting nor did he anticipate any direct responsibilities with respect to it. He did know that it was the result of eighteen intensive months of conferences and work sessions with the people from the foreign ministry of Japan and there were some rather radical provisions. The conversion of the Japanese Self-Defense Force to a full-fledged military service was certainly the most controversial provision. It would require a change in the Japanese constitution. Sakai had to wonder if old "Dugout" Doug MacArthur was turning in his grave over that one. The second most interesting proposal was the sharing of American nuclear ship-propulsion technology with the soon-to-be resurrected Japanese navy. That was directly contrary to Japan's long-held stand against any form of nuclear weaponry. However, the provision had been inserted by the Japanese, so they must have considered all the ramifications. Besides, they had over twenty nuclear power plants in the country and certainly had the basic expertise.

Sakai noted that the big table was almost full, and as the wall clock clicked to exactly five-thirty P.M., a hush fell over the room.

"Gentlemen and ladies, the president."

Everyone stood as President Dave Donaldson strode into the room followed by the secretary of state, Don Baldwin, and several of the president's White House staff. The president took a moment to nod to the assembly before lowering his lean lanky frame into his chair.

"You've got quite a tan, Mr. President," commented the Senate majority leader. "How do you get tanned in Washington in the winter?"

"Spent part of the Texas trip in Corpus, Senator. You should have gone along."

"Too many duties on the Hill, Mr. President."

"I'm sure there are. Are we ready, Don?"

With a precision worthy of a Broadway production, the secretary took his position behind the podium, the house lights dimmed, and a classification slide lit the screen.

"This briefing is classified secret, no foreign nationals," the secretary began. "Mr. President, at your direction we have completed the draft treaty with the sovereign nation of Japan for a new level of mutual defense in the western Pacific. Our Japanese counterparts have worked alongside our own action people every step of the way and have agreed in principle to each of the provisions contained in the treaty and all provisions have been informally reviewed by Prime Minister Hoikata. He will be receiving a similar briefing by his Japanese staff within the next twenty-four hours.

"Our briefing will address the file of talking papers we have prepared for you to be used in your meeting with Mr. Hoikata on Thursday.

"We do not anticipate any surprises with respect to your discussions with the prime minister, but there are several points which we believe will give you increased bargaining power should he have any second thoughts about the treaty.

"As you know, this draft has been prepared quietly and very few details have been leaked to the news media. We anticipate that the public release of the provisions concerning the restoration of Japanese army, navy, and air forces and the incorporation of nuclear power in their military ship-building program will generate considerable opposition on both sides of the Pacific and will be the most difficult provisions to run through Congress and the Diet. Be that as it may, I would like to begin by presenting the obvious."

A bright slide with a list of several statements appeared on the viewing screen and the secretary began reading them.

"Japan is now the number-one financial force in the world and the yen is on the verge of a one-hundred-to-one ratio with the American dollar. There is talk of a revaluation which would place it at one-to-one and it would become the world's premier currency. And the startling truth of the situation is that such a revaluation of the yen can be absorbed by Japan with hardly a pause in its day's activities.

"Since the mid-eighties, Japan has been the world's leading creditor nation. Every working day, the Japanese people and their corporations generate over a billion dollars worth of savings—a gigantic money pool.

"In deposit ranking, all ten of the world's leading banks are Japanese.

"Nomuro Securities Company is the largest securities company in the world and still growing. It dwarfs Merrill Lynch.

"There is so much investment money within the Japanese economy, they have been buying up art, land, and buildings on an international scale and at an increasing rate and at formidable prices that no one can match."

The secretary paused to allow his words to germinate. Looking directly at the president, he continued, "I realize you know all this, Mr. President—they have been rubbing our noses in it for the last two years. But what it says is that they can jolly well afford a military force. All it takes is a shift of the allocation of applicable percentages of the Japanese national budget to accommodate a modern, fully equipped army, navy, and air force. At worst, it may call for slightly increased capital gains taxes, but it is obvious from these statements alone—and I could have provided you with a dozen more applicable factors—the Japanese economy has plenty of money for any required tax increase. Under this treaty, we shift most of the burden of the defense of the Japanese islands and the western Pacific from the American taxpayer to the Japanese taxpayer, where it rightfully belongs. And I believe we all agree that it is about time. If Japan is to enjoy the prestige and power of an international force, she also must undertake the responsibilities of such an achievement. Those responsibilities must include a capability to provide a military response in the event their national interests are threatened. I would remind Mr. Hoikata that there has never been a dominant financial and political power without it having a corresponding military capability."

The next slide appeared on the screen, a series of budget figures for NATO and Japanese defense and proposed modifications.

"As you directed last June, we have come up with figures that we feel are realistic in terms of our revised commitment to NATO and the Japanese. The key to this paper is that despite our reductions as a result of the Soviet situation since late 1989, we are preparing to further scale down our financial and military support of NATO and we will have one hell of a job doing that if we do not take equally drastic steps with our commitment to Japan. Mr. Hoikata must understand that a half century of America carrying the burden of the free world's defense cannot continue any longer. To do so risks the economic stability of our country. We have pushed this argument with NATO and we must push the same argument with Japan.

"We cannot expect our European allies to react favorably to our new NATO posture if we continue to provide over ninety-five percent of the military defense of Japan."

The third slide appeared, a ranking by strength of currency, technological achievements and capabilities, international investment, balance of trade, and military strength of the ten leading world powers. In the first four, Japan was first; in the fifth, tenth.

"This, sir, is absurd. The message will be obvious to the prime minister. He just needs to see it laid out in front of him."

The president held up a hand to interrupt the secretary. "I fully agree with what you have presented so far. The handwriting is on the wall, even to the Japanese. And those are all good points to have at my fingertips. But I also want to emphasize to the prime minister that there is no compromise in our position on this. Thus, Hoikata is going to be one tough son of a bitch in arguing for some tit for tat."

The secretary clicked to the next slide. "At the action officer level, everyone is happy. Japan gains our nuclear ship-propulsion technology and license to manufacture our F-117 advanced stealth fighter and the B-2 for their own air forces, and we will lease the U.S.S.

Midway and *Coral Sea* with complete air wing hardware to their new navy until they complete their own first two carriers. As part of the package, we will retrain their carrier air wings—"

"Tora, tora, tora. . . ." The faint voice from the end of the conference table caused even the president to join in the laughter.

He turned around, able to relate very well with the comment. His own youth had been interrupted by those very words, and he had fought against the Japanese in the Pacific as the navy's youngest aviator, a twenty-year-old dive-bomber pilot. "I know that those of us who are old enough to remember have some gut feelings about the wisdom of all this, but I also know that all of you have my grasp of the inevitability of restoring the Japanese military. We just can't delay it any longer. We must have some relief from the terrific burden of policing the western Pacific and Japan has to grow up and shed her pampered position for one of Pacific Rim responsibility." The president seemed pleasantly surprised at the enthusiastic round of applause that greeted his statement.

As it died, a State Department aide nervously entered. "Excuse me, Mr. President." He hurried over to the secretary of state and handed him a note. With some initial irritation, the secretary scanned it, then looked up at the president, his irritation replaced by concern.

"Mr. President, an attempt has just been made to car-bomb our embassy in Tokyo."

"My god!" the president exclaimed. "Were any of our people injured?"

The secretary looked expectantly at the aide, who immediately answered the president. "Yes, sir, but not in the embassy itself. The bomb exploded short of the embassy and injured some of those reporting for work. We are awaiting a complete casualty count."

The president stood. "I suggest we continue this briefing later in the day. I believe our first priority at the moment is our people in Tokyo. I will be in the oval office, Don. I want to know the details the instant you have them."

"Yes, Mr. President," the secretary of state replied.

As the president turned to leave the room, his eyes sought out Sakai. "George, this is right in your old area—looks like you've got some work for a change."

Sakai stood. "Yes, sir, Mr. President, I'm afraid I do."

.   .   .

George Sakai stopped by his office only long enough to grab a couple of red-lined files before hurrying to the State Department's Situation Room. His boss, Bert Thompson, head of the Far East Division, Special Operations Section, was already there, as was the secretary of state. Jim Clarke, division FBI liaison, and Jesse Simmons, Clarke's CIA counterpart, were in a huddle as the secretary and Thompson watched an on-site report over the department's secure-circuit TV link to Tokyo.

Ambassador Tim Oroku was briefing. "Twenty minutes ago, at seven thirty-two A.M. Tokyo time, a car bomb exploded—prematurely, we think—within one hundred yards of the main entrance to our embassy. Twenty-three people were killed, including the driver, and fifteen are injured. Eleven of the dead, including one American, and three of the injured are embassy employees who were approaching the embassy for the day's work. Japanese authorities have the area secured and are investigating the incident. There have been no prior threats and no one has declared responsibility for the event."

"Do we have the driver's identity, Tim?" the secretary asked.

"Unknown at this time, Mr. Secretary. We don't even have a sex or nationality. Nothing much left."

"Are we sure the bomb was intended for our embassy?"

"The car was proceeding at high speed toward our main gate. We can only assume that we were the target."

"I agree, Tim. However, it's completely unanticipated at this end. How about you? Any signs or warnings?"

"No, sir. Motivation factor is unknown. I would speculate random terrorism."

"Can we get a shot of the scene?"

"Stand by. We'll patch in the local TV coverage."

The screen flickered black for only a second before the bombed-out car came into view. Firemen were still roaming the debris. Cloth-covered bodies were strewn about the sidewalk and ambulance attendants were beginning to load them into the waiting vehicles. Japanese police had the area cordoned off and were dispersing several small crowds of onlookers. The street was obviously closed to car and pedestrian traffic. The narrator was Japanese.

"What's he saying, George?" Bert Thompson asked.

"Just routine coverage," Sakai replied. "Time of event and what happened. A description of the scene and some witness comments.

Everything was apparently normal when the vehicle came speeding down the street and just blew up."

The secretary removed his glasses and began wiping them with a clean handkerchief. "You still there, Tim?"

"Yes, sir."

"We'll look forward to your follow-up. Anything else for now?"

"No. For the moment, we intend to let the Japanese authorities handle it. We have a liaison officer working with them. As soon as I have anything, I'll contact you."

Sakai interrupted. "Would you ask the ambassador who the U.S. fatality is?"

The secretary nodded in response and continued. "Am I correct in understanding that all of the dead and injured are Japanese nationals and employees of the embassy except for one? Who is it?"

"Patricia Bender, Mr. Secretary, one of our legal staff. We're trying to notify her next of kin now. Since she is the only American casualty, we're content to have the Japanese handling this."

Sakai shook his head. She must have been assigned after he had left the embassy.

The secretary turned to Sakai. "Any other questions, George?"

"Yes." Sakai took the offered handset. "Mr. Ambassador, this is George Sakai. Would you happen to know if there have been any foreign visitors to the embassy in the past weeks—other than Japanese, of course? Any recent employees who don't seem to be working out too well or whom you've let go recently?"

"I'd have to check with my people on that. I've seen no one, but I normally wouldn't be aware of such day-to-day details. Why?"

"Just trying to cover all the bases, sir. Thank you." Sakai returned the handset to the secretary.

"Keep us posted, Tim." The TV link faded to black. The secretary accepted a cup of coffee from the State Department duty officer and sat with the others around the table. "Any thoughts, anyone?"

Simmons, the CIA rep, was the first to speak, "The Red Army comes to mind, sir, but they've been out of the picture for a couple of years. And they've been primarily an internal group with internal goals. The Japanese police have been keeping them pretty well harassed into impotence. They have little source of funds."

"George, this is your area."

"Mr. Secretary, the Red Army would be my first thoughts, also. However, I would not discount a completely different source. As for any warning or even premonition, this attack is out of the blue as far as I am concerned."

The secretary thought for a moment before continuing. "There are some considerations that I feel we should remind ourselves of—and they all have a bearing on the upcoming treaty. While our relations over the past twenty years—the period of time Japan has emerged as a world power to be reckoned with—have been generally quite satisfactory and mutually beneficial, there have been conflicts in policies. Tariffs come to mind, of course. And there has been some strong dialogue over our wishy-washy system of instituting and then canceling import restrictions. There's also the radical right, who have been violent at times, but they have always directed their violence toward their fellow Japanese. Perhaps they are concerned about the treaty—what they know of it.

"The main provisions are still secure, by mutual agreement. The president and the prime minister want to make a simultaneous announcement at the signing. But it's the biggest political development between us and Japan since the end of the war. How in hell we've kept most of the provisions secret from the media is a miracle in itself. The reemergence of Japan as a military power and our agreement to furnish them with a large chunk of our most advanced weaponry will shock a lot of people on both sides of the ocean."

"There is another factor," Sakai suggested.

"What is that?"

"Maybe someone else has obtained knowledge of the key provisions of the treaty and is embarking on a campaign to disrupt U.S.-Japanese relations to make approval difficult if not impossible. The Japanese may not want the treaty if it means internal unrest, and we may not be so crazy about it if we think there is a possibility the radicals can take over and use a rearmed Japan to resume the physical expansion she started over fifty years ago. She certainly has the technical and economic knowhow, now. We've seen some signs of that type of thinking in the past few years. Small scale, but some of it the voices of influential people. And there is the obvious: the Soviet Union is not going to receive this treaty with any kind of enthusiasm at all."

The secretary raised an eyebrow. "Outside agitation? Soviet interference? Always a possibility, but we would have had some under-the-table discussions with them by now if that were the case. The whole world thinks that the treaty is primarily a trade agreement at this point. No, I think the Soviets are primarily in the dark about the still-classified provisions of the treaty—but certainly concerned that there may be some. I really would expect some indications from them before they would embark on such a course. They're a lot more sophisticated than that—and I never thought I would refer to the Soviet Union as sophisticated. But, they are. My vote goes to the Red Army. But why now? All of a sudden."

"There is a third possibility," Sakai said.

"Ah?"

"Palestinians. Iranians. They are completely unpredictable and would do such a thing just for the act itself."

"I don't know. Why in Japan?"

"Why not?" Sakai countered. "It's as reasonable as anything else they have done."

"True enough." The secretary sighed as if someone had stepped on his chest. "It's a shitty world, gentlemen. But I need to tell the president something."

The duty officer interrupted. "The Japanese have to tell us something first. It's really out of our hands for the moment."

The secretary nodded his agreement. "Let's go back to the Iranian-Palestinian connection—but only to rule it out. The Japanese environment around our embassy has always been considered one of the most stable in the world. We can't overlook a sudden Middle Eastern input, but it is so unlikely. For one thing, our counterparts in the Japanese Ministry of Foreign Affairs would alert us immediately if any suspicious persons passed through customs, and the Japanese have a most efficient internal security force. Add to that the fact that any non-Japanese sticks out like a redwood in a pine forest. If there are any Arabs or Iranians in Tokyo, you can bet your last yen the authorities know it and have already checked up on their whereabouts at the time of the bombing. Unless the remains of the driver have Muslim written all over them, I say we count the easterners out."

Simmons lifted his arms in frustration. "That leaves the Red Army."

"No, that leaves Japanese nationals who may be Red Army or Soviet agents or some unidentified radical. That will be my preliminary report to the president. But it tells us also that we have to intensify our security of the treaty provisions with respect to the two key agreements on reinstitution of the military and the sharing of advanced military hardware and know-how. If this attack is just coincidental, then we sure as hell don't want to throw gasoline on the fire."

Sakai's file on the Red Army had not received an entry for almost two years. "I'm having a hard time blaming it on the Red Army. They haven't even been making any noises lately—and they are good at making noises. Politically, they're isolated from all of Japan's major parties and they have never received any support from the Japanese people. They just don't fit into the Japanese psyche. And they would be the least likely group to have any information about the treaty."

"Well, someone had a bomb in that car," the secretary persisted.

"Yes, sir, that is true, but we need more to go on."

The secretary held his glasses up and seemed satisfied that they were clean. "Let's kick this around for a few minutes. Staying with the treaty as the cause of this attack, let's consider the possibility that the security of the working committees may have been compromised on the Japanese side. Not to the press, obviously, or it would be front-page news all over the globe. The inclusion of the articles creating a stronger military could very well have triggered somebody. But it is unlikely that the somebody would have popular support despite the fact that we are practically repealing article nine of their constitution. In my last conversation with the prime minister, we reviewed a number of factors that are critical considerations with respect to the acceptability of the treaty by the Japanese. For example, there has been a gradual shift to the right in the mental attitude of the Japanese since 1970. Before that time, the Self-Defense Force had not even been mentioned in the press despite its creation back in 1957. In 1978, eighty-three percent of the Japanese electorate were in favor of it. In 1988, that figure was in the nineties.

"Add to that aspect the fact that the Japanese have become very confident in their ability to do *anything*. So much so, they are no longer condescending, they are arrogant. And arrogance is a combination of ability, ambition, and extreme self-confidence plus one other critical ingredient: the feeling of superiority over everyone else.

"Ninety-nine-point-nine percent of the population of Japan are pure Japanese, all descended from the first five hundred people who originally settled Japan. Collectively, they have the highest IQ in the world. And they know it. And unless we make a habit of lying to

the face in the bathroom mirror, we know it. They feel a together-
ness we will never know.

"Now, consider one last factor. Oriental face, the overriding
necessity for the oriental to maintain his honor and dignity. The
most powerful financial and technical nation of the world loses a bit
of face when it has a so-called second-rate military. Sure, the JSDF
is a modern, high-tech, professional organization, but it is small,
almost a token force, and defense oriented. Yet, the jump from
where the JSDF is today to an official army, navy, and air force
capable of carrying out its national policies and protecting its national interests is not very far. So, as Prime Minister Hoikata has
indicated, there should be overwhelming popular support of the
treaty. I agree; Japan is ready to come out of the World War II
closet. Car-bombing the U.S. embassy just doesn't fit in with that
premise."

The secretary paused as if expecting a question. Hearing none, he
spoke to the duty officer. "Stay in touch with Ambassador Oroku
and let me know when Patricia Bender's next of kin have been
notified. I'll want to call them." Turning to Sakai, he added,
"George, you've had plenty of time over there. I want you to go
over and assist in any way you can and also see if you can work with
the Japanese authorities in finding out what's behind this. Any
objections, Bert?"

"None, Mr. Secretary. It's a good idea."

"God-damn yes men all around me," the secretary observed with
a tired grin. "Either I'm one hell of a decision maker or I'm surrounded by pansies. Have a good trip, George, and keep Bert right
up to date. I'll want a daily briefing on this until we find out what
the hell is going on. And let's continue the treaty briefing first thing
in the morning."

The evening rush hour traffic was at least past its usual impenetrable
peak, but Sakai was a bit edgy by the time he arrived at his town
house in Olde Towne. There was much to do before grabbing the
red-eye special out of National Airport for Seattle, where he would
have a two-hour layover before boarding the Northwest 747 flight
to Tokyo. He could hold some of his calls until the layover, but
there were some he must make before leaving Washington.

He left his car double-parked. It would take at least a half hour
before someone called it in and the tow truck could arrive. He

hurried upstairs and grabbed his ready bag off the closet pole. Everything he would need was inside with the exception of his toilet gear. While he slipped on a fresh shirt, he dialed Alicia's number.

"Hello." His ex sounded as if she had a cold, but even a stuffy nose failed to alter her ante-bellum Southern accent. It was as unchanging as her habit of never appearing for breakfast until her "face was done" and her "body prepared." The daughter of Emily Tate Tweedy—of the Jackson, Mississippi, Tweedys—and the Honorable John W. Richards, former ambassador to Australia, Alicia Jane dripped with Southern charm and diplomatic poise—except when she was angry. At that point, both characteristics disappeared.

"Alicia—George. Something's come up. I have to go to Tokyo for a few days."

"No, George, not again. You have the children this weekend. They haven't been with you for over three months."

"I can't help it. There's been a car-bombing."

"I saw the news, George. And you can *never* help it! You fight me to keep them here in the District but you can never take them when it's your turn."

"Alicia, I can't argue with you right now. I have to get out to National Airport. Please explain it to them."

"I've run out of explanations, George."

"Then tell them the truth. I have to leave town. It's that simple. It's my job."

"It's always been your job, George. You were a bigamist, married to two wives, your job and me, in that order. I couldn't take it then and I'm not sure the children can take it now."

"They can if you support me. Regardless of our disagreements, you owe me that."

"Then come back to me, George. There are other opportunities. We can still make it. Give them a home where their daddy will be at home in the evenings and weekends."

"I didn't leave you, Alicia; you left me. As for my time with the children, this is worse than our marriage ever was."

"Not for me. It is one hell of a lot better."

"I'm sorry, Alicia, I really have to run. It's important."

"So are your children."

Low blow, Alicia. "Of course they are. But there are things I simply have to do. I promise. As soon as I get back, I'll take them for a whole week."

"And that will be when?"

"I don't know."

"And I don't know what I saw in you, George. You're a workaholic of the worst kind."

"Alicia, we had seven great years . . ."

Their brief years together had been great, and despite their disagreement over Sakai's career, a serious conflict that had led to their divorce, they still retained a troubled affection for each other and on occasion their physical relationship survived the break. Alicia might be stubborn enough to divorce him as a matter of principle ("The children would be better off in Australia") but she seemed to share his desire for a continuation of their intimacy. Sakai considered it just compensation for the ungodly disproportionate check the court decreed he must present her with each month. However, he also retained enough respect for that remnant of their marriage to remain faithful. And he strongly suspected Alicia shared that loyalty. Still, she could be a real bitch when their relationship strayed from sex.

"Alicia, I *have* to go."

"Have a lousy trip, you bastard."

"Alicia . . ." There was no sense in continuing his plea to a dial tone.

The other calls would have to wait. The steady drizzle matched his mood as he ran to his car just as the tow truck arrived. Throwing his bag onto the backseat, he ripped the ticket from the windshield and shoved it into the glove compartment with the rest. When he arrived at National Airport, there was an empty State Department parking slot. At least not all of the gods were mad at him.

He was the last to board.

"I'm sorry, sir, we haven't any more hanging space," the male flight attendant chirped. "You'll have to stow your bag in the overhead."

Sakai looked down the long tunnel of the stretch DC-8. His seat was somewhere in Maryland and the few open overhead compartments were already full. He stuffed his bag under the center seat in front of his own. Groaning and creaking with the weight of a full load of passengers, the tired old Douglas lifted reluctantly off into the night sky over D.C.

From the level of service rendered, it became apparent to Sakai that the flight attendants were overpowered by the sheer number and demands of their passengers. They passed out the midnight snacks with all of the courtesy and consideration of overworked guards at a maximum-security prison. The boiling cold front over the Midwest not only woke Sakai from a cramped nap but terrorized the infant sitting behind him. Two scotches didn't help; he spilled both and was unable to request a third because the flight attendants were forced to belt themselves in along with the passengers. Someone on the other side of the aisle threw up.

By the time he felt the *solid* thump of contact with the Seattle runway, his personality had sunk to the level of the flight crew's.

His VIP card got him into the first-class lounge. Orange juice, coffee, and a Danish restored some of his faith in humanity. A cold water wash in the rest room also freshened his outlook on life, but it was a temporary respite. His book-at-the-last-minute seat on the 747 was in the middle of the coach pack. After takeoff, he leaned his seat back and pushed the plastic headset into his ears. The movie screen lowered and the words "Return of Lassie" appeared.

Figures, he thought, and placed the headset into the pocket of the seat ahead.

The embassy driver was waiting as Sakai glumly exited the deboarding tunnel at Tokyo's Nakita International Airport. His watch, set to Tokyo time, read 8:00 A.M. He had flown for seven hours and it was just an hour later than when he had departed— despite the fact that it was the next day.

"We have you booked at the Fairmont, sir," the Japanese driver said as they pulled away from the terminal. His English had only the slightest trace of a Japanese accent.

"I'd rather go straight to the embassy, please."

"Yes, sir."

Sakai relaxed and enjoyed the drive into the central city, his eyes smiling as he recognized most of the streets and buildings. They skirted the Akasaka section, the playground of the Japanese politicians and well-to-do and the home of one of the few remaining Geisha Exchange buildings. The traditional dinner companions mostly lived in their own apartments and traveled to and from their places of employment in man-drawn rickshaws, their white-painted faces staring straight ahead and their exquisite coiffures protected by small rice-paper-and-bamboo umbrellas. The streets were lined with discreet and very expensive restaurants and entertainment houses where more than a few of the taxpayers' yen wound up in the pockets of shrewd proprietors who catered to a very special clientele.

The United States Embassy, just to the east of the Akasaka section, was a veritable fortress, the huge red-brick-and-concrete structure set well back off of the access street that in turn provided access and exit to Sotoberi-Dori Avenue, one of the main east-west arteries across central Tokyo. Surrounded by a high stone wall, the embassy's street entrance was guarded by a pair of blue-uniformed Japanese policemen. Only a few blocks away rose the government buildings of the Japanese Diet and ministries.

The driver turned into the long driveway and stopped in front of the main entrance.

Sakai grabbed only his small carry-on bag as he climbed out of the car. "Would you take my other things to the Fairmont, please?"

"Yes, sir. Of course."

The lone U.S. Marine manning the podium inside the foyer checked Sakai's ID. "Welcome back, sir."

"Sergeant Dawson," Sakai responded. "I didn't know you were still here. It was Lance Corporal, wasn't it? Congratulations."

"Thank you, sir."

There didn't seem to be any special security measures in effect, although Sakai remembered that a touch of the red button hidden behind the podium would bring a four-man special fire team to the foyer within seconds. "I'd like an immediate briefing. Anyone available?"

"You're expected, sir. The ambassador's briefing room. Would you like an escort, sir?"

"No, I remember it. Good to see you again, Sergeant."

"You, too, Major."

Sakai smiled in appreciation of the sergeant's addressing him with his reserve marine rank. "Semper fi, Sergeant."

"You bet your ass, sir."

Good man, Dawson. All marine.

In the compact, windowless briefing room, Sakai collapsed in a chair and listened to the update on the car-bombing.

The duty officer, a red-haired thirtyish female who should lay off the sukiyaki, referred to a briefing sheet as she spoke. "We've ID'd the driver. Haruki Yasuda, a rabble-rouser who has some loose ties to the Red Army."

Then it *was* the left-wing radicals. "We thought they were pretty much out of business. Excuse me, it's cold in here. You folks stop paying your heating bill?"

The woman stepped aside and adjusted the wall thermostat. "Sorry. The ambassador is on a budget kick. It'll warm fast."

"Thank you."

"This is the only major incident we've had since 1986. The fact that Yasuda has former ties with the Red Army doesn't necessarily mean he was acting in their behalf."

"You saying he was just a pissed-off individual? I hope I haven't come halfway around the world to learn that."

"No, we're not saying that. There are several possibilities. One, he *was* just a pissed-off individual—as you just so charmingly suggested . . ."

"I apologize."

". . . or, two, he was transporting the bomb or explosives somewhere else and just happened to go kablooie in front of the embassy . . ."

Kablooie?

". . . or, three, he was heading for the embassy gate. At this juncture, take your choice."

"Who's working it?"

"Charlie Porter from the agency desk. The Tokyo police. The Japanese special internal security force. And you, according to the twix we received from the secretary."

Charlie Porter! Sakai should have known who manned the CIA desk at the Tokyo embassy; it had been just one of those facts that had slipped through the cracks as he went about his daily business in D.C. Of course, he had known that Porter was still in Japan, but the last he remembered was that the bastard was just an in-country agent operating out of Kyoto under cover as a free-lance news correspondent. So now Porter was once more part of the diplomatic scene.

That was a switch. Porter had been anything but diplomatic the first time they had met in Saigon in the spring of 1972.

Sakai nodded to the female briefer. "Then I talk to Charlie Porter first."

"He'll be here in about a half hour to brief the ambassador."

I can hardly wait, Sakai thought as his mind flashed back over the eighteen years since he had first met Charlie Porter in Saigon.

. . .

"Shit, that's all we need, another god-damned embassy marine—and a gook at that!" Charlie Porter's outstretched hand certainly didn't mirror his profane welcoming statement. The grasp was warm and friendly although it completely encircled Sakai's fingers. The fullback-shaped CIA deputy chief at the Defense Attaché's Office (DAO) in Saigon towered over Sakai and extended beyond him on both sides, and the only thing wider than his shoulders was his grin. "You just get in-country?"

"No, I've been here a while—since July of '71."

Porter suddenly became very respectful. He leaned forward and ran a hand through his heavy blond hair. "First Marines?"

"On loan from Third Marines. Platoon leader."

"Shit, man, you've been dead for two years and don't know it. You're the first *live* American silver bar I've ever seen in this stinking place."

"It doubles tomorrow."

"Oh? Congratulations, *Captain.* I bet you're wondering how you drew this assignment? You couldn't be a screwup, not with that blue-and-white ribbon on your chest and a pair of railroad tracks in the offing."

Sakai was surprised that Porter would even recognize a Navy Cross.

"How 'bout a scotch?" the big man asked.

Sakai could see that he was going to get one whether he wanted it or not.

"Cheers."

"To the Corps."

"Jesus, you can't even drink with a marine without a propaganda spiel—what the shit, to the Corps."

The scotch was great. Sakai didn't even hesitate to accept a second.

"What's a Jap doing in the Marine Corps?"

Ordinarily, Sakai would have taken offense at such a use of the diminutive, but something about Charlie Porter made his pronunciation of the word seem almost a compliment. Sakai downed the scotch refill and held his hand over the glass as Porter immediately reached again with the bottle. "Native-born American, as I assume you are."

"Little Rock, Arkansas, Captain. Strictly a white Anglo-Saxon Protestant hillbilly. How 'bout you?"

"San Jose."

"Grape picker?"

"San Jose is not vineyard country. My folks ran a bakery called Kuniwada's. That was my mother's family name."

"From the old country?"

"Kyushu. They immigrated in 1939."

"Ah. They were persona non grata a couple years later, I bet."

"Relocated in 1941 to a camp in southern Arizona. Released in 1945."

"I bet that was rough."

"They seldom talked about it. Reopened the bakery in San Jose and I came along in 1948."

"How'd you wind up in the Corps?"

"You ask a lot of questions."

"We're going to be working together. You don't have to answer if you don't want. Just saves me going over your dossier."

"No problem. Graduated from UCLA in '69—political science and prelaw. Beat the draft by joining the Corps. OCS at Newport and then to Quantico. Platoon leader's course and then here."

"Forget my bullshit, Captain. You're okay and I suspect you wielded a mean stick against the Cong. As for this so-called cease-fire we're in now, it's one hundred percent horse puckey. Shit, the NVN regulars are grouping for a big push and the Cong are raising hell all along the Cambodian border. I give it a couple more months at best."

"We've just about pulled out. The ARVN troops are lean and mean."

"And running piss out of everything they need."

"You'll have to speak to Congress about that."

"I don't have a direct line to those fuckers. All I know is Nixon promised increased logistic support to make up for our troop withdrawal and there's been a slowdown of everything."

"There's a new team in, you know."

"Ford? For my money all he gets to do is preside at the wake."

"So, what's my job?"

"You'll work with me here in the main DAO office. You noticed the big building to the east of us? That's the DAO annex. You'll get to know it as well. On the other side of us is Air America—whom you are already familiar with, I'm sure—and just a bit to the south sits the Joint General Staff building, the shrine of South Vietnamese military command. I don't even want to talk about it—until we have to. Our job is to try and make some god-damned sense out of a maze of intelligence reports that come in from the field. You keep track of the military buildup; I try and keep my boss informed of enemy intentions."

"Your boss is?"

"Colonel William LeGro. He reports to Major General Smith, the current defense attaché, and soldier Smith reports to Ambassador Martin. All part of the country team."

"You sound a bit sarcastic."

"Oh? Sorry. More than likely just tired." Porter poured two more scotches despite Sakai's weak protest.

Sakai raised his glass. "Well, I've told you my life's story. What's yours? If we're going to work together, we might as well know all we can about each other."

"Fair enough. Shit, I'm nobody. Out of law school into FBI in 1960. Undercover with all the peaceniks and flower pricks for a while. Lousy job but lots of young ass. As long as the peaceniks were passing it out I was determined to get my share. Job benefits, you know. But I was too right-wing to stay in my place. The poor bastards were so god-damned naive and infiltrated with Soviet agents who worked them like puppets on a string. Typical exploitation tactics. Take a natural dissent and turn it to your own ends. They do it with a masterful touch, you know. Still do. I frosted a few and was instrumental in providing permanent government housing for a few more, but it was a bad scene for a poor old boy from Little Rock who felt the Pledge of Allegiance was right in there with mom and apple pie. I told the feds I wanted out and they fought me at first, but when they found out I just wanted to get closer to the source of things and hit the bad guys where it hurt they even threw me a fucking party! Literally! Assigned here as a junior clerk in 1965. Picked up the language and life-style well enough to be a positive contributor to the war effort. Deputy station chief in '71—and now I've got my own marine to help me wind this mess up. Satisfied?"

"More than. I need to get settled."

"Come on, gyrene, I'll take you to your hotel. This afternoon we have a session with the general and I have a couple of my people scheduled to give you an update on where we stand and what's next. When they are through giving you the bullshit treatment, I'll give you the real skinny and after din-din I'll introduce you to some of the best Saigon pussy you could ever imagine."

"Sounds great—but I'll pass on the social hour. I'm sure you can handle all that's out there."

"I try, God knows I try. But it sure makes me wonder if you really are a Yewnited States gyrene—you aren't a Vietcong infiltrator, by any chance? You sure as hell could pass for one."

Sakai had at least a six-inch height disadvantage, but he swung from the floor and put everything he had in his punch. Porter dropped as if clubbed. Sitting up with his legs crossed, he rubbed the massive jaw that formed the lower half of his silly grin. "Damn, you're touchy."

Sakai had to grin when he thought of their first days together. Their latter days, to the contrary, had been completely devoid of humor. He and Porter had done their thing through the awful times, the demise and complete fall of South Vietnam. Together, they had lived through the resumption of hostilities in late 1973, trying their damnedest to be of some critical assistance to the South Vietnamese military. But the acute shortage of supplies, the mass desertions, and the corruption within the military and political staffs had been too much.

Sitting quietly in the Tokyo embassy, sixteen and a half years after the fall of Saigon, Sakai didn't like remembering that the so-called cease-fire had come to an abrupt end when the provincial capital city of Phuoc Long had fallen to a massive NVA assault in early January 1975, the first of a long string of dominos toppled by the forces of North Vietnam. After Phuoc Long had come Ban Me Thuot, and the first of the endless lines of South Vietnamese refugees. Then, in rapid succession, the fall of Hue to the north, followed by Da Nang, Nha Trang, Xuan Loc, and the climactic Ho Chi Minh campaign, which overran Saigon and had left Sakai scrambling to catch one of the last helicopters away from the DAO compound. His last view of Porter had been one of the profane CIA professional embrawled with a horde of panic-stricken refugees who were determined to force their way onto the American helo airlift.

Once safely aboard the U.S.S. *Blue Ridge*, one of forty Seventh Fleet ships used in the evacuation of U.S. nationals, dependents, and several hundred South Vietnamese refugees, Sakai had vowed that his military career, once his life's ambition, was over. No more.

At that time, he figured he had seen the last of Charlie Porter.

Chapter 5

Within a few minutes' drive of the American Embassy, the Fukadaya enjoyed a reputation as a premier *ryokan* (Japanese-style) hotel.
Situated in Chiyoda, the center ward of Tokyo, the Fukadaya was
almost the lone survivor of the traditional downtown hotels. The
Imperial Hotel, the Palace Hotel, the Hotel New Japan, the
Marunouchi, and a host of others were all Western-style, and Genda
avoided them with a passion.

At the moment when George Sakai was sitting in the briefing
room of the American Embassy, awaiting the return of Charlie
Porter, Saburo Genda was in his room at the Fukadaya, sitting
crosslegged on the familiar reed mats and glaring across the room
at four associates. A small ceramic jar of sake and five serving cups
sat on the low table before him but he made no offer to pour. He
wanted to shout but knew the traditional rice-paper walls would
allow his displeasure to go much farther than the ears of those for
which it would be intended. He was furious at the carelessness that
had cost him his first chance to strike the Americans. Staring back
at him and trying unsuccessfully not to be intimidated were Toshio
Goto, the forty-two-year-old leader of the Red Army cell; Michio
Ohiro, twenty-eight, by coincidence a fellow naval pilot but a de-

serter from the Maritime Self-Defense Force; Nobuo Sakamoki, nineteen-year-old former student at Tokyo University; and Taeko Nikahura, Ohiro's philosophical and sexual partner.

Ohiro was the only one of the four who did not wear glasses. He was also the tallest at five-feet-eleven and had the build of a ball player, lean and hard with eyes that always seemed to be looking for the long ball pitch. While in the JMSDF, his fondness for women and sake had convinced his superiors that he needed some strong discipline. Ohiro had taken exception to their actions and had simply walked away from his obligations. Now his likeness was distributed throughout Japan, a situation that had prompted him to develop a shaggy mustache and let his hair grow.

Despite a two-inch height shortfall, Sakamoki appeared taller than Ohiro until they stood together, mainly because Sakamoki carried only enough flesh on his bones to hold in his other organs. His clothes hung on him as they would on a rack, limp and loose. A shaved head, sharp nose, and large round eyeglasses gave him the look of an owl.

The woman, Taeko, was somewhat better endowed than the average Japanese female and certainly well proportioned. Slightly punk in her choice of clothes, she habitually managed to show enough skin to arouse the curiosity of any passing male. Her generous use of dark eyeliner and deep-red lipstick were carryovers from her early days as a prostitute. Like her three male companions, she was not pleased with Genda's anger.

"Sit," Genda ordered.

The four arranged themselves on cushions and waited.

"Stupidity! Sheer stupidity! How could the fool, Yasuda, blow himself up? The plan was for him to place the car in front of the embassy, get out and away, and then activate the explosive by remote control. Instead, he explodes himself prematurely and kills innocent people! I was not enthusiastic about such a tactic in the first place. I should never have let you idiots talk me into it." Genda paused to regain his composure. "Ohiro, I thought that you knew how to handle explosives."

Ohiro did not appreciate the put-down. He knew more about explosives than Genda had ever known. True, his knowledge was primarily limited to conventional aircraft-delivered ordnance, but it far exceeded that of the old man who had spent his last years in the JMSDF flying a desk.

"We have not worked with plastique before."

"You are a military man. You mean you are that ignorant?"

"I am a pilot."

"You *were* a pilot. Now, you are a deserter. In my day, the time of the great war, we pilots knew how to fight with every weapon available." Genda despised incompetency almost as much as disloyalty. He strongly reasoned that had not Ohiro deserted he would have been forced out of the JMSDF.

Taeko could see that the argument was straying from the subject at hand. She did not want Ohiro to be chastised by Genda in front of the others. She knew of Ohiro's temper. If Genda continued, Ohiro would say things to which Genda would take offense. Such an argument could escalate senselessly and the group could split. Taeko did not want that; she wanted Genda's money first. She was hoping that Goto would intervene; he was their real leader. But she also knew that Goto was not assertive enough to stand up to the older Genda. Perhaps she could steer the discussion another way. "I think we acted too hastily. We need to plan more and get better weapons."

Genda raised his eyebrows. "Ah so, perhaps we should listen to our young friend, the expert on such matters. Maybe, if she had driven the car . . ." Even as he rebuked the girl, Genda admired her spunk. In his day, a female would not even have been allowed to sit in on such a discussion. Even had she been admitted, she would never have been so presumptuous as to venture such an opinion.

Goto could see that Taeko had spoken out of turn. It was time to voice his opinion. "I think we should shoot down an American airliner."

Genda's eyes mirrored his surprise. "You what?"

"Everybody does car bombs. Why don't we shoot down an airliner?"

"A jumbo jet," Sakamoki declared, leaning forward with enthusiasm. "They arrive every afternoon at the same time. We could not miss."

From the beginning, Genda had little respect for Taeko and the equally young Sakamoki. They were superfluous to his needs and he regretted ever allowing them to be part of the personnel package that seemed to come with Goto. Now, Goto seemed to be as irresponsible as they, advocating the senseless destruction of innocent women and children. Yet, the Red Army leader's suggestion could have merit, only the target should be a military aircraft.

Genda turned to Goto. "Are you sincere? It would be a dangerous undertaking."

"It would be a great accomplishment. Or we could plant a bomb."

"No, an attack in broad daylight from the ground would be more dramatic. But we would need a weapon—and our target must be military."

Goto allowed his tongue to reach up and sweep his upper lip. "I know where we can get just the weapon we need, a one-man shoulder-held missile, but we will need more money."

Where would Goto get such a thing, Genda thought. Yet, if what Goto had said was true, Taeko's idea had merit indeed. "How much more?"

"Perhaps—they will want American dollars—fourteen thousand."

"About two million yen. I can get that. How do we go about it?"

Goto raised himself to a kneeling position. "In 1970, I and several of my young comrades took command of an airliner and forced the crew to fly us to North Korea. You must have read about it. At that time, I made contact with a member of the Popular Front for the Liberation of Palestine, a hero of many several such acts who was interested in setting up a multinational network of those of us who could sympathize with the Palestinians. He never achieved his goal, but we have remained in touch, and over the years we have performed small favors for each other. For some time, he has been offering me a wire-guided missile but we have not been in position to acquire such a thing. It is expensive."

"The missile is here?"

"No. Getting it is a bit complicated but only in logistics. A transfer would have to take place on the island of Pohnpei, in the Carolines."

The mention of the Micronesian island brought back sad memories to Genda. His mind flashed back to the day he had been selected as a Thunder God and had carefully placed his fingernail and hair clippings in a small envelope to be passed on to his brother, who was fighting his own war in the Pacific islands. His brother's last duty had been on Ponape, as the island had been called during World War II, and he had never returned, the victim of a munitions accident just five days before the war's end. Genda's envelope had never reached his brother's hands. "Why such an out-of-the-way place? Particularly an island that is under direct American influence."

Goto held up a hand. "I said that it is a bit complicated. Let me explain." He pulled out his wallet and reached inside to pull out a small folded piece of paper. "A ship from the Middle East stops by on a monthly basis to buy copra and Pohnpei pepper—and pure Pacific grass. And, once a month, an ocean fishing vessel belonging to Matsui Canneries makes the same port, for the same reason. My contact can arrange a transfer of cargo to the Matsui vessel—and the first mate is my brother, who has many of the same values as I but is somewhat more conservative. As for Pohnpei being under American influence, remember that it was a former Japanese possession. The Americans have very few of their people on the island; a few Peace Corps workers from time to time, maybe an AID representative. I have friends there who can assist for a price."

Genda appeared puzzled. "Pacific grass?"

Taeko giggled. "Marijuana, old man. The best grass this side of South America."

The short hairs on the back of Genda's neck became rigid at the girl's disrespect. He chose to disregard the remark for the moment. "The people of Pohnpei grow it?"

Goto shook his head. "Only a few, but we have friends there who grow it as a money crop to finance their other activities. Some slips out to the locals, but they get their own high from a drink made from some sort of pounded root. It's perfect. The island is sparsely populated and heavily wooded. An abundance of rain. No one bothers my friends there and they are starting to ship many places."

Genda disliked hearing such a thing. The attitudes and moral values of the youths around him at the moment were part of the reason he had deserted the modern Japanese society. He did not like their present relationship. They seemed to be tolerating him for their own ends. That was not his plan. He was the leader and a leader must command respect. Now was the time to clarify matters. He stood. "We must speak of something. As long as we are together . . ." He looked directly at Taeko. ". . . you will not address me as 'old man.' I am descended from a long line of samurai whose service goes back to the days of the Kamakura period when my ancestors were soldiers of the great shogun, Minimoto Yuritomo. My forebears stood against the Mongols in 1281 and watched the divine wind, the *kamikaze*, destroy the Mongol fleet. I fought in the great war against the Americans. I have served my country for over four decades and have contributed more to the late Emperor than all in this room. We are together because of only one reason: vengeance. You may wish to disrupt relations between Japan and the United States for the purposes of socialism. I merely wish to strike the American military or perhaps government officials in payment for the murder of my parents and the lustful taking of my bride. While we are together, my personal motive transcends your common cause. Nevertheless, we need one another. I need you for your youthful agility and willingness to carry out daring plots. You need me to provide you with the wherewithall and the leadership to keep this mission from becoming like all of your other worthless attacks. We kill for a purpose, my purpose. And when the time arrives, I will lead you in one final moment of glory. Until then, I am Genda-san, your leader and benefactor. If any of you dispute this, I am out of patience."

Genda watched the reactions on the faces of his companions. They were angry at being addressed in such a manner. So be it. They could function as a team only if there was unqualified loyalty and one of the main ingredients of loyalty was respect. If it was not already present, he must demand it. And if this was the time of decision, Genda was prepared.

Ohiro was already smarting under Genda's remarks. He could not let Genda's verbal chastisement of his mistress go unanswered. He slowly stood and challenged Genda. "We have carried out many attacks before you came and can do so without you in the future—*old man.*"

Ohiro's premise that Genda was incapable of any serious physical rebuttal was a gigantic mistake. Genda's body might be six decades old but most of those decades had been filled with a strict regime of martial arts; among other things, Genda had been a master of kendo, the bamboo fencing skill that required quickness and precision of attack. Consequently, Genda's step to close the distance between him and Ohiro was too sudden to be countered and Ohiro never saw the edge of Genda's hand that sliced out from his side. Nor did he brace himself for the blow across the side of his neck that numbed his entire body. Before he could fall to the floor, Genda's left leg chopped forward and the point of his foot drove deep into Ohiro's gut.

The JMSDF deserter remained prone, gagging against the fluid that tried to erupt from his throat and trying to take in air. Genda stood over him, one foot on his throat. Genda's words were measured. "The next time, I will kill you, but not so fast that you fail to feel pain. If you wish to leave us, this is a proper time." Cautiously, Genda removed his foot.

Obviously still in pain, Ohiro forced himself to stand. Goto stepped forward and held an outstretched arm between the two men, his palm facing Ohiro. "No, Michio. Genda-san is right. We must all have respect for one another. It is the only way we can operate."

Ohiro glared at Genda. Those in the room read his flashing eyes as a signal that he was either going to attack or storm out of the room. He did neither. Instead, he took a step backward, placed his hands at his sides and bowed deeply. Keeping his eyes on the floor, he apologized. "I am not worthy, Genda-san."

Genda stretched himself erect. Every joint in his body ached from the sudden movements he had extracted from them. It had been a while. "There, in your inner self, is some remainder of proper conduct. I am glad to see that. Nurture it and I will make you a hero of Nippon."

Ohiro held his bow. "*Hai!* Genda-san."

"Goto, you are the leader of these two. Do you wish to add anything to this discussion?"

Goto answered with a low bow. Sakamoki and the girl, Taeko, matched it.

Genda spread his legs and placed his hands on his hips, triumphant. Except for the Western dress of his companions, the scene might have been taking place in the courts of the great shoguns. The subsequent generations of tradition and exclusive Japanese heritage that had been the hallmark of the Japanese social structure were not lost to Genda's younger companions no matter how much they had tried to embrace the new ways. Their submission was inevitable, ingrained deep into their souls by over eight hundred years of absolute, structured social behavior with first the shoguns and then the Emperor. Such a tradition had inspired a sense of loyalty and devotion beyond the understanding of the Western mind. It had taken only Genda's outburst to trigger that inherent trait in their psychological makeup. They might harbor resentment but they would submit to a greater force: the nature of the Japanese way. And Genda was the personification of that force. For the moment, he was pleased but he would not show it. As their leader, respect was his due. With that matter settled, their discussion could continue.

"What is the weapon?" Genda asked.

"A Dragon missile. I can get a launcher and two missiles for two million yen."

Genda snorted in disgust. "The Dragon is an American antitank weapon, ground-to-ground. It is old technology—wire-guided. For a Dragon, your supplier wants too much."

"Look, it *can* be used ground-to-air. Its ground range is a bit over three thousand feet. We can use it up to an altitude of one thousand feet easily. We hit an airliner when it is landing."

"A military aircraft," Genda corrected. "Where did your friend acquire such a thing?"

"The Iranians acquired ten thousand of the weapons and fifteen hundred launcher-trackers in 1976. They modified a few with proximity fuses to use in their war with Iraq. They worked well. My contact had been able to procure a small number after the fall of the Shah. They can be similarly modified."

Genda was not sure that a Dragon missile would suit their purpose, but it most probably was the only weapon they could obtain in short order. "Then, let us discuss a plan to get the weapon. I can have the money by tonight."

Goto grunted in agreement. "I will make my contact and I am certain that we can expect a shipment on the next vessel to Pohnpei. That will be three weeks from now. We will be required to take custody of the weapon during the period it will be waiting to be taken aboard the cannery ship. I propose that Ohiro and Taeko go to Pohnpei and safeguard the shipment until the cannery ship arrives, usually a week later. They can pose as newlyweds on an excursion from a Guam honeymoon. They will need airfare and expenses."

Genda did not like the delay. A month was a long time when you had only several to live. "We are speaking of four weeks before we can act?"

"I would say so."

"Then we will use the time to select a site near the airport to launch the attack. Make the arrangements."

Alone in his room, Genda felt uncomfortable with his decision. He had little confidence that the Dragon would do the job required of it. Still, it was a beginning, and if something more sophisticated became available, their plan could be adjusted. In the interim, he would use the month to return to his cottage on Hokkaido. It would allow him time for one final period of meditation before embarking on the task that he knew would extend into his final days.

Chapter 6

Charlie Porter, ostensibly the Special Assistant to the Ambassador for Administrative Affairs but in reality the CIA station chief at the Tokyo U.S. Embassy, swung into his reserved parking place in the lot behind the large rectangular main building. Proceeding through the embassy personnel entrance, he flipped open his ID case and held it out toward the marine at the desk. The sentry ignored it and, instead, handed him a pink telephone note form while announcing, "You're logged in at ten-oh-five, Mr. Porter, and you have a visitor in the briefing room."

Porter stopped at his office only long enough to toss his overnight bag on the sofa and hang his coat. Then he walked briskly down the long hall and entered the back entrance to the briefing room. A broad smile spread across his face as he saw Sakai sitting alone in front of the podium. Reaching out with one arm, he greeted Sakai with all of the profane enthusiasm he had shown eighteen years back in Saigon. "Holy shit! It's the Jap gyrene from 'Nam!"

Sakai grabbed his hand. "Hello Charlie."

"I saw the twix that said you were coming. I wanted to meet you at the airport but was all tied up."

Probably with black leather straps and being whipped by a pair of

Japanese transvestites, Sakai thought. Immediately, he felt he was being unkind. Charlie Porter had weathered the years well. A little less of that wavy blond hair, perhaps, and barely hidden in it were batches of dull gray. The big frame was still there and the shoulders and the grin, but there were a few deep lines in the face and there was a lot less taper to the waist.

"Let's go down to my office." As he led Sakai down the long hall, Porter began a barrage of questions.

"Heard you got married—and unmarried."

"Short but sweet. Seven years. We're still friends, you might say."

"White girl?" Porter had lost none of his touch.

"Southern belle. The daughter of John Richards, our ambassador to Australia from 1974 through 1984."

"Kiddies?"

"Two daughters. Angela Joan, nine, and Kristen Anne, three. She has custody."

"Par for the course. A good lay?"

"Damn you, Porter. I would have thought that some couth would have rubbed off on you over the years."

"Hey, I don't mean any offense. I was just curious what kind of girl corraled my old Saigon sidekick. I'm sure she was—is—a lovely lady. I apologize." Porter held open the door while Sakai entered the office and started for the straight chair in front of a very cluttered desk. "Shit, sit on the sofa. Be comfortable." Porter grabbed his overnight bag and dropped it on the floor.

The sofa was, indeed, the only comfortable spot in the office. The chair in front of Porter's desk was a wooden high-back with no padding. The room itself was chilly and quite small and made to look even smaller by the array of green file cabinets and gray metal bookcases and shelves that covered every inch of the walls. There were no windows, but a programmable thermostat was sandwiched in between the two file cabinets behind Porter's desk. He adjusted it and Sakai could hear the low swish of forced heat entering the room. The stained oak desk was overflowing with manila file folders, assorted papers and notepads, and on one corner sat a green three-tiered tray, the individual levels marked IN, OUT, and TO HELL WITH IT.

"Excuse me a moment." Porter pushed aside some papers and punched a a button on his intercom.

"Welcome back." The voice from the speaker was very feminine.

"Mary, I'm due to brief the ambassador in eight minutes. Can you check with him and see if we can let it slide until tomorrow morning? I don't have anything earthshaking."

"Right away."

"So," Porter said, flopping down into his chair, "where were we?"

"How long you been with the embassy?"

"Well, I stayed in Japan after our haul-ass drill out of Saigon. The agency had me slip back in-country a couple times after the dust settled. POW searches, that sort of thing. Even got back to Sin City in '87. But I found out I was still on their shitlist and it was too risky. So I took the first opening at the embassy here, kept my nose clean, learned a little Japanese, and now I'm good for a few more years as my own man—with proper respect to Ambassador Oroku. Damn good man and a Jap-Yank like you. Good to see the president and State giving these spots to the appropriate ethnic groups. Of course, with the megabucks Oroku poured into the presidential campaign coffers, he was owed."

"Were you here at the bombing?"

"No. I understand you'll be with us until we get a handle on it."

"I hope so. It came as a shock. Things have been pretty quiet over here. Where do we start?"

"With a scotch, old buddy, with a scotch." Porter pulled a bottle from his desk and poured a couple fingers in each of two paper cups.

"Charlie, it's just after ten A.M."

"Shit, it's happy hour in California. Cheers."

"To the Corps."

"I shoulda known—to the Corps."

One thing Sakai had to concede big Charlie. He knew how to stock good scotch, but Sakai declined the offered refill.

As Porter raised his glass in a solo toast to thin air, the feminine voice came over the intercom speaker, "Same time tomorrow, Charlie, but the ambassador says your expense account is due today—without fail."

"Fix me up with something, will you, Mary?"

"I need your receipts."

"They're classified."

"Uh-huh. . . ."

"You're a doll, Mary." Porter set down his glass and looked for a moment at the disorderly pile of material on his desk. Then he stood and clapped his hands together. "Okay, Sakai-san. Let's go to work. We start with the files."

Six hours later, Porter tossed the last of a ten-inch pile of manila folders over to George Sakai. "That's the last one. All the known crazies, including the Red Army cell that sporadically uses Tokyo as its base of operations. We're checking on those that we can locate, but most of these files have been inactive for some time, a couple years in several cases."

"I think we've hit a dead end if none of these characters can be tied in to the bombing. Maybe it's a new group," Sakai suggested. "How about the lab people?"

"They've come up with some pieces of the puzzle. The explosive was plastique, as we suspected. There was a remote control device, which puzzles the piss outta me. You would think that the bastard intended to ram the gate from his actions prior to the explosion. A simple impact fuse was all he needed. Whatever, it must have gone off prematurely."

"If we can tie in the driver to any other person we would have a starting point."

"I talked to all of the witnesses who were able to talk. Shit, they didn't even see him. Morning traffic rush. Just all of a sudden: Boom!"

Sakai thumbed through the last folder. "Have you folks been given any details of the Mutual Security Treaty?"

Porter hesitated, perhaps curious at the change of subject, before replying. "Only that it is in the mill and that most of the preliminary work is completed. We have a file of classified briefing sheets from the pissers at State but they don't say much. Some trade provisions and general aims of the treaty. The ambassador is probably quite familiar with it."

"Nothing that reached out and really grabbed you?"

Porter seemed to be evasive despite his ready answer of a question with a question. "Ah . . . no, should there have been?"

"I really sat in on my first briefing just yesterday. It was interrupted by the news of the bombing. But there are a couple of things in it that could generate some opposition."

"From who?"

"That is just it. I don't know who."

Porter pushed the stack of files off to one side. He seemed to be reviewing in his mind whether he wanted to pursue the subject of the new U.S.-Japanese agreement. He apparently decided in the affirmative. "Shit, we're on the same team. We're talking about the resurrection of the Japanese military, right?"

"I thought you didn't know that much about it."

"Just me and the ambassador. My need-to-know covers my primary task at the moment: to be on the lookout for any signs of leaks on this side of the pond."

"No one else in the embassy?"

"No one."

"And have you had any signs?"

"The car-bombing may be related."

"Based on?"

"Purely speculative. Gut feeling."

Sakai shook his head. "I don't know. I suppose that if someone was opposed to the treaty, a bit of terrorism might put a strain on relations. But it wouldn't be a serious threat. Too isolated and not necessarily representative of Japanese public opinion. I would think that the real fight over ratification will come in the Diet between those who see it as a move whose time has come and those who don't want to lose their privileged status with Uncle Sam continuing to pick up most of the tab for western Pacific defense. The buildup of the Japanese military is going to cost money—lots of money."

"That's for shit sure. The ambassador's evaluation here is that most of the old militarists would break out their samurai swords and see it as a return to the grandeur of the Imperial forces. They've been suffering a loss of face for almost half a century. A few who worked with MacArthur on the drafting of the constitution—and there are a couple of the old bastards left—would see it as a repudiation of everything Japan has stood for since its adoption; you know, no aggressive military action, renunciation of war, no nuclear weapons, and so on."

"Are they influential?"

"You are damned right they are, at least a few."

"How about the new generation?"

"Most people think they're too fucking yen oriented. *I* think they would jump at the chance to rearm. Not that they want to go charging all over the western Pacific again; no, they want it as the final step in making Japan a world force. Their attitude is that a real dragon has to breathe fire and shit bricks, and I agree with them."

"So, there could be a fight over ratification?"

"A weak fight, but it will be approved. And the reason that it will be is that Japan is obviously moving into a new age. Hell, she's already there. And she is no longer willing to be thought of as a conquered nation. For the average Japanese, World War II is over the minute she is a self-sustaining nation and that requires a competitive military, not just a token force."

"If there is that kind of popular support in Japan, why have the president and the prime minister been so adamant about keeping the military force and hardware provisions so classified?" Sakai asked.

Ported jabbed a finger into the air. "Politics, Sakai-san. When this treaty is announced, it will be the most significant international agreement since the end of World War II. For one thing, we haven't wanted the Soviets to get a firm whiff of what is going on until it is a fait accompli. The Soviet bear will grab his balls and scream to high heaven about the rearming of the Japanese dragon; you can bet your own family jewels on that. Believe me, no matter how far we have progressed in this era of so-called *glasnost* and disarmament talks, the Soviets are going to raise holy hell. They will orchestrate a UN assault and a program of world propaganda the likes of which we have never seen. For one thing, their dispute with the Japanese over the Kuriles may require some serious reconsideration."

Sakai could not agree more with Porter's thoughts. For all of his outward roughness, Porter had a very firm grasp on the situation—that was perhaps his strongest quality.

Porter continued. "At the same time, the president will be hailed by us as the macho man of the nineties, who has forced Japan to assume her responsibilities in defense of the western Pacific, and Prime Minister Hoikata will be *ichi-ban*—number one—hero to the Japanese, for he will have restored Japan to her prewar status as a military power. So, my man, for us and the Japanese, it's a double-barreled sure thing. And a sudden joint announcement will give it the maximum impact. On the other side of the table, the Soviets are going to be caught with their pants way down below their knees."

Sakai could easily see that. It *would* be a blow to the Soviets. "It's certainly to the Soviets' advantage to disrupt U.S.-Japan relations. Especially if they have learned anything about the rearming provisions of the treaty. Maybe they do have a piece of this."

"I—" Porter never even got into his next sentence. The telephone rang loudly and he picked it up. "Porter."

Sakai reached over and browsed through the file folders while Porter took the call. The embassy CIA resident hurriedly penciled some notes as the party on the other end of the line talked. Hanging up, he clicked his tongue in emphasis. "That was my contact in the Japanese internal affairs division. The driver of the car, Yasuda, was from the Shinjuku ward of Tokyo and was a part-time student at the private Waseda University. A very poor student, mind you, and he had a reputation as a troublemaker, a heavy drinker, and an ardent plower of Japanese pussy. On the day before he blew himself into little pieces, his sleepmate had waited while he met with an older gentleman dressed in traditional Japanese garb. They had talked for the better part of an hour and when Yasuda returned to the girl he had a considerable roll of yen. They partied all night."

"That could have been his contact."

"Let's go."

Sakai marveled at the way Porter held his own against the native drivers, particularly those hell-bent on proving that their taxis were not only supersonic but indestructable as well.

"Lose your horn and you're out of luck in this league," Sakai commented. "I didn't drive a lot when I was here before."

"You just have to close your eyes and boogie, partner. These folks respect a driver with a suicide complex. Mine's faked, of course, but it gets me around town." From the embassy, they had proceeded north to pass by the grounds of the Omna Imperial Palace, formerly the property of the Emperor but open to the public since World War II. Once established on the wide Shinjuku-Dori Avenue, Porter accelerated until they approached its interchange with Meii-Dori Avenue. Slowing only slightly, he leaned on the horn and nosed out two Sentras battling over the right turn lane. A few minutes later he left Meii-Dori and slowed as they entered the grounds of the Waseda University of Science and Engineering and found a parking place.

A Japanese internal affairs officer was waiting in a small conference room in the administrative building. With him was the girl. The officer bowed. "I am Oto Nakai." Nakai could only be described as a round Japanese, almost as wide as tall. In keeping with his station, he wore a black suit, white shirt, and a rather soiled dark-blue tie. He held out his card.

"Charlie Porter—we talked on the phone." The CIA agent took

the card and offered one of his own. "This is George Sakai, from the U.S. State Department."

The three men listened intently as the young woman repeated her story about observing Yasuda with the older man.

"Did he use a name for the other man?" Sakai asked.

"No."

"How old was he?"

The girl wasn't sure whom Sakai meant.

Sakai clarified his question. "The older man, how old was he?"

"I don't know . . . maybe sixty, sixty-five perhaps."

"Did Yasuda say anything that would give any indication as to the man's identity?"

"No."

"Afterwards, you and Yasuda partied?" Porter questioned.

"Yes. We met with some friends and danced for a while."

"And then what?"

"We went to my room and stayed until morning."

"Could you see how much money the man had given to Yasuda?"

"No."

Nakai resumed his questioning. "Was Yasuda a member of the Red Army?"

The girl looked startled. "I do not know such a thing if he were."

"Did he ever make any political statements in your presence?"

"No. We were students and friends."

"What did you talk about?"

"We talked about our studies, and about each other."

Sakai wondered if the girl was lying. If so, she was very good at it. "Do you have anything of Yasuda's in your room?"

"A few clothes and some books."

"You live near here?"

"Walking distance from the campus," Nakai stated.

Sakai nodded. "Can we see them—in your place?"

"Yes."

The short walk took only fifteen minutes. The girl's tiny room was over a book supply store and the air within was heavy with the sickening sweet smell of marijuana. The walls were covered with Western rock star posters. A low table and a higher study one with a chair were the only pieces of furniture. A pair of *futons* were rolled and placed against one wall. A two-burner electric hot plate and some assorted pots and plastic dishes filled one corner. There was a cardboard box with several food items and a plastic container of water. The girl's clothes were in another cardboard box, except for several coats and sweaters that were hung on wall hooks. Another box contained several articles of male clothing, and on the study table were textbooks and a notebook.

Sakai examined the clothes, checking all of the pockets. They were empty except for a roach clip and a book of matches.

"Are these books his?"

"Yes."

The textbooks, obviously on their third or fourth student, were dog-eared and heavily marked with penciled notes. Sakai scanned them and then picked up the notebook. It was unused, but inside the front cover was a name and phone number.

"Saburo Genda," Sakai read. "Do you know the name?"

"No," the girl replied.

Sakai laid the notebook back on the table. "Anything else?"

"No."

"Did Yasuda ever bring any of his friends up here?"

"No."

Sakai started for the door, followed by Porter, Nakai, and the girl, but stopped short. "Can I take the notebook?"

The girl shrugged. Sakai walked back over to the table and pulled out his pen. He copied the name and number from the inside cover onto one of the pages, tore it out and folded it, and stuck it in his wallet. "I'll just take this."

Lieutenant Nakai poured hot tea as Porter and Sakai made themselves comfortable in his office. Sakai sipped his for a minute, then pulled the note from his wallet. "Can we trace this number?"

Nakai took it and picked up his telephone. After a short conversation, he hung up. "Hokkaido exchange—an inn at Urohoro."

"Urohoro?" Sakai had no knowledge of the place.

"A small village on the southern coast," Nakai added.

Porter decided it was time to see where he and Sakai stood politically. "What is our status in this investigation as far as your office is concerned?"

"We are to keep you informed of developments," Nakai replied.

"Would it be out of place for George to track down that number and see if he can contact this Genda?"

"It would be a great help. I would like to speak to the girl some more and then research the man, Genda, in our files. We may have something or there may be something in the central computer. You may wish to wait until I accomplish that. It could save you a trip to Hokkaido. The name may be nothing. However, my superior informed me that your ambassador has requested permission for a liaison person to work with us. If you wish to designate Mr. Sakai, that would be agreeable." Nakai seemed a bit nervous. "Please, I regret I must ask one thing. You are a trained investigator, Mr. Sakai?"

"Yes."

"George used to be with the embassy. He does have investigative experience," Porter added.

"Then, please forgive me for asking. It was necessary."

"Of course," Sakai responded.

"Thank you, Lieutenant Nakai." Porter exchanged bows with the policeman before turning to Sakai. "You've got the ball, George. Stay in contact with Lieutenant Nakai and I will work with the Tokyo police."

"This is interesting." Sakai once more sat in the small office of Oto Nakai. He faced a disproportionately large window that formed a dark frame around a spectacular panorama of the Tokyo skyline to the west and beyond. Just beyond the far horizon, the snow-capped tip of majestic Mount Fuji dominated the landscape. His remark, however, was in reference to the information presented to him on a computer printout. It was a complete dossier on a Saburo Genda.

"It may or may not be the same person that is listed in the notebook. Saburo and Genda are both common names, and it would not be unusual to find a number of people with that combination of names. The central computer did print out that one, however," Nakai reported.

Sakai studied the printout. "Captain, retired, maritime arm of the Japanese Self-Defense Force," he repeated to himself. What relationship could there be between an ill-disciplined and obviously radical, failing college student and a career military officer?

Nakai seemed to read Sakai's thoughts. "We are very fortunate. That is a complete file on Captain Genda."

"I can't imagine the connection."

"I suspect there is none. Even if there is, it may be buried under a mountain of routine facts. You may look afar at Fuji-san for a long time before you finally see the slight flaw in the southern slope."

"I'm sure." Sakai continued to stare out the window in the direction of the sacred mountain, its classic cone unseen but clearly definitive in the eye of his mind. Against it, he was mentally reviewing the content of the dossier. Genda had an honorable record, although he had received some criticism for his relationships with American advisors. He had a reputation of being polite but aloof in his dealings with them. A not uncharacteristic Japanese trait, thought Sakai. Genda's background included service with the old Imperial Navy, 1944 to 1945, and for a while he had been a security guard at Oppama during the American Occupation, then ran a small souvenir shop on the Ginza. Sakai noted that Genda's parents had been among the casualties at Nagasaki and that his wife died during a robbery attempt by two Americans. Under the comments section, Sakai read that Genda had been pretty much a recluse after his retirement from active JMSDF service, remaining at his cottage on Hokkaido except for occasional visits to Nagasaki and Tokyo.

"Oto, there are certainly enough indicators here to arouse suspicion, but like you say, I need to study the mountain. I'll check in with you when I reach Hokkaido."

"I shall look forward to your report, Sakai-san."

The two men exchanged bows and Sakai left. Nakai walked to the window. As always, his gaze was riveted on the western horizon. He liked Sakai. The Japanese-American was very comfortable with the Japanese way, as well he should be. For a moment he had been tempted to tell Sakai of the classified section of Genda's dossier. But perhaps that would not be wise. Not just yet.

Chapter 7

Urohoro had a special charm. The fall season saturated it with a chill that required the people of the village to hurry about their business with deliberate intent, their wool kimonos pulled tightly around their bodies and heads covered with an array of cowls, woolen caps, and for the hearty, coiled headbands. One did not stand and visit when the wind from the north Pacific whipped ashore and snaked through the back alleys and narrow streets of the village. There were few signs of modern Japan. The Western influence was reluctant to force its way into a place where the natives considered the occasional pair of leather oxfords degeneratively progressive. As Sakai drove among the wooden buildings he felt as if he had entered a time warp and instead of late-twentieth-century Japan, he was in medieval Nippon. At any moment a group of growling samurai could burst out from one of the alleys, their eyes flashing and their swords singing the praises of their local shogun. He had never seen such harmony as that of the ancient buildings with the surrounding land and sea scapes. Perhaps he was the first outsider in eight hundred years! So complete was the feeling of yesterday.

The inn was easy to find and parking was no problem. His Mazda was the only automobile in evidence. Once inside, he was immediately greeted by the innkeeper, a one-armed veteran of the great war, judging from the worn brown army cap pulled down over his head, its peak and bill crumpled but still reminiscent of the headgear that had marched triumphantly across most of the Pacific during the years 1941 to 1943.

"You wish a room?" the innkeeper asked anxiously.

"No, thank you, honored one. I am seeking information and the whereabouts of a Captain Saburo Genda. Does he lodge here?"

The innkeeper shook his head. "No."

"I see. I had a telephone number for him and it was registered to your inn. Do you know a Captain Genda?"

"The captain sometimes uses my instrument. He has none of his own."

"Then, he does live here in the village?"

"No."

"Do you know where he does live?"

"Yes."

Sakai did not want to display his irritation, but the old man was trying his patience.

"May I ask where?"

"Ah . . . he has a small cottage on the beach some eight kilometers from here."

"Could you give me directions?"

"Forgive me. One of the reasons most of us live in Urohoro is our desire for privacy. You have business with Captain Genda?"

Sakai studied the old man. Why was he reluctant to give the necessary directions? Or was it simply that the inhabitants of Urohoro did, indeed, value their privacy and not appreciate visits from strangers. "Yes, I do—of a personal nature. I ran into a friend of his in Tokyo who indicated that Captain Genda could assist me in some research I am doing."

"The captain is not very active these days."

"It concerns an operation of the Self-Defense Forces. One in which Captain Genda participated. I am writing a book."

"You have transportation?"

"I am driving."

"Then, you will have no difficulty. Continue on the main highway to the east side of our village; there you will find a coastal road leading south and then east. It is narrow but quite drivable. Within six kilometers you will come to a lake on the ocean side. There is another lake three kilometers farther on. The cottage of Captain Genda is between the two. You will see a turnoff to the left. You will have to walk the last one hundred meters but you will see the cottage from the road."

"*Arigato.*"

"You are welcome." The innkeeper spoke in English, smiling broadly through metal-capped teeth.

"My Japanese is that bad?"

The innkeeper continued speaking in English. "No, it is very good, very natural, but with a slight American accent. You are a nisei?"

You are quite perceptive, old man. "Yes. It is one of the reasons I have been given this assignment."

"He is a great war hero."

"So I understand. He is a friend of yours?"

"We entered the service at the same time. I, the army, Saburo, the navy."

Sakai eyed the stump of the innkeeper's left arm. "I suspect you are a hero also."

The innkeeper shrugged awkwardly. "No. I am still alive."

"Any man who fights for his country is to be honored."

"You are kind, *Amerikajin.*"

"Thank you for the directions."

"*Do itashi mashite.*" The innkeeper's eyes twinkled as he returned to his own tongue with respect for his visitor who shared his race and language if not his nationality.

The directions were precise and accurate, and it took only a few minutes to turn into the road leading toward Genda's cottage. Sakai buttoned his jacket and pulled the collar up as he walked the last meters. So near to the water, the chill was biting.

Sakai was ready to call out, to inquire if anyone was inside, when his gaze was led along a curving black stone path to the rocky bluff overlooking the water. A figure was seated, crosslegged and rigid, facing the sea. Sakai paused and waited.

The chill wore through his jacket and began to caress his skin. He wanted to announce himself but something about the dignity of the seated figure caused him to hold his voice inside. The man was apparently deep in meditation, otherwise the cold sea breeze would have him at least curled tightly into the heavy kimono. It would not be proper to call out.

He had no need to. The figure's voice was swept back to him by the wind.

"You wish to see me?"

"*Konnichi-wa.* Captain Genda?"

"*Hai.*"

Sakai bowed low. The figure could not see him, but his traditional mark of respect would be sensed. "I am George Sakai from the United States Embassy in Tokyo. May I speak with you, please?"

"I am listening."

Sakai bowed again. "Captain Genda, I am quite chilled. Perhaps you would honor me with an invitation to take tea."

The figure stood and turned. "Of course. I apologize for my lack of manners. My meditation sometimes robs me of my obligations. I tend to be offended at interruptions."

Sakai bowed a third time. "Then, it is I who must apologize for my thoughtlessness. It is only that my business is urgent that I intrude upon your private time."

Genda returned the bow but not as deeply, as he established who was the superior in the meeting. "Your skin is my skin and your eyes are my eyes, but your subtle inflections tell me that you are an American."

Sakai remained erect and held out his personal card. "*Hai.* As I said, I am with the U.S. Embassy."

Genda let a thin smile draw his lips aside as he strode strongly towards Sakai. He accepted the card with a slight bow and led the way to the cottage. Sakai removed his shoes and followed Genda inside. They sat on the reed matting and Genda took a small bamboo whisk and stirred pulverized green tea leaves into a pot of hot water. He poured the tea into a handleless porcelain cup and offered it to Sakai, then waited. Sakai bowed slightly before filling Genda's cup. Together, they raised the cups with both hands and let the warmth of the porcelain fight the chill in their bones. Genda leaned over and excited the charcoal embers in the hibachi. They drank in polite silence until they refilled their cups. "I can be of service?" Genda asked.

"Does the name Haruki Yasuda mean anything to you?"

"No, should it?"

"He was a student at the Waseda University. Apparently, he called you at one time."

"I have no telephone."

"Did he ever call you at the inn in Urohoro?"

Sakai studied Genda's face and sipped his tea as the old man replied, "No, I am sorry. Perhaps he was referring to someone else."

"That may be, Captain, but why the inn's phone number? Could there be another Saburo Genda around here?"

Genda chuckled. "I think not. You say you are with the American Embassy. May I ask, in what capacity?"

"I have been asked to assist the Tokyo police in investigating a recent car explosion near the American embassy in Tokyo, Captain Genda. It was driven by Yasuda and carried a bomb of plastique. It appears he was about to make an attack on the embassy when the explosive detonated prematurely."

"I have heard of the incident," Genda said, one hand waving toward his small television set.

"Among the driver's possessions was a study notebook. Inside the cover was penciled your name and the phone number of your friend's inn in Urohoro. You have had no relationship with the young man?"

"Yasuda?" Genda repeated. "I do not recognize the name. I am sorry."

Sakai nodded in acceptance of Genda's reply. "Then, it is not important. It is just strange that he would have your name and a contact phone number."

"What was he studying at the university?"

"I am sorry, Captain. I do not know."

"I am on their list as a consulting professor in military science. Perhaps he was planning to contact me for some assistance. One of the course directors could have given him my name."

"That is possible, of course. But he was not a very highly motivated student. Why would he trouble himself to contact someone as far away as Hokkaido when there are many veterans in and around the Tokyo area?"

Genda raised his hands by way of emphasis. "Perhaps that is why I never heard from him." Smiling at Sakai's empty teacup, he suggested, "Would you like something stronger? The formalities are over. Sake, perhaps?"

"Yes, that would be most pleasant. I am sorry to have troubled you, Captain."

"You are part of the investigative team? That must be very interesting."

"I have been accepted as the liaison contact between the United States Embassy and the Tokyo authorities."

Genda placed a small lacquered tray on the low table. On the tray rested a black sake vase with an enameled white chrysanthemum on its side. He poured the warm sake into the two matching thimble cups and offered one to Sakai.

"*Kampai*—cheers!" Sakai reached out and touched his cup to Genda's.

"*Kampai!*"

The sake warmed Sakai's stomach much more efficiently than had the tea.

Genda set his cup down. "So, you are nisei."

"Yes. My parents migrated to the States in 1939. I was born after the war, in San Jose, California. They were originally from Fukuoka, on Kyushu."

"Very near my parents' home."

"You come from Kyushu also?"

"Nagasaki." Genda spoke the word as if it were a prayer. His eyes remained on his sake cup.

Sakai knew what he must ask next. "They were there during the war?"

"They are still there—in the air over the rebuilt city."

"I am sorry."

"Your parents, I suspect they were sent to a camp?"

"Yes."

Genda smiled. "Then, I am sorry also." Seeing Sakai's embarrassment, he added, "It was a long time ago. War is a series of tragedies, each one compounding the one that comes before it."

"I was a marine—in Vietnam. The wisdom of your words is part of my experience also."

Genda began to like the American who was Japanese. They shared a warrior bond and perhaps a common frustration. The American defeat in Vietnam was not quite the disgrace that World War II was for Japan, but it was a defeat and the nisei must carry some loss of honor. Almost with their first words, Genda had felt a certain *amae* between them—an inherent closeness that most probably was also the result of a shared heritage that Sakai had not lost even though he was an American. As for Genda's long-felt bitterness toward Americans, Sakai and his ancestors certainly had no part in the bombing of Nagasaki or the occupation of Japan. "I am glad you came to see me. I have few visitors."

"This is my first time to Hokkaido. I was with the embassy in Tokyo from 1975 to 1981 but Hokkaido is the one island I did not get the opportunity to visit."

"You must return some time. This is the most beautiful of all Japan. I would like you to see the Ainu, the original Japanese people—you could say that they are the aborigines of Japan. By the eighth century, they had been pushed up to the northern tip of Honshu and began to bleed over into Hokkaido and the small islands farther north. They were completely dominated by the "new" Japanese, those of my—and your—heritage. They are a vanishing race, the Ainu. Very proud. I am afraid we mistreated them in the early days, much as did the Americans with their Indian tribes."

You are friendly, old man, but you get in your licks.

Genda poured more sake.

"I have read of the Ainu," Sakai commented, sipping his sake.

"Then you know that their features and skin coloring more closely approximate those of Caucasians than orientals and they have thick facial hair, which is not a Japanese trait. They are a tall and dignified people. There are less than twenty thousand pure Ainu remaining. I would like to study them some day. Their origin is still hidden, although they may very well have come from Siberia. There is an Ainu village near Sapporo where visitors are most welcome."

"I should look forward to such a visit." Sakai felt very comfortable in the presence of Genda. He began to wonder what was the source of the anti-American entries in Genda's official dossier. The old warrior was certainly cordial at the moment. "Your cottage radiates peace and contentment."

"I am very comfortable here. I am afraid that I am too much the traditionalist to enjoy the more crowded islands."

"Do you travel?"

"Only rarely. An occasional visit to Nagasaki to honor my parents. Tokyo perhaps once a year. I still have good friends in the naval service headquarters." Genda filled their sake cups a third time. "Whom do you suspect to be responsible for the car bomb?"

"Perhaps just the driver. We have made no connections yet with any organized group."

"It sounds like a Red Army tactic."

"That is the main slant of our investigation."

"I wish that I could be of some assistance."

"That is quite all right, Captain. Your name was a lead we had to follow but I did not anticipate finding any connection, not with someone of your professional background and service to Japan."

"I am sorry to be of no assistance."

Sakai refused Genda's offer of another refill. "I've taken enough of your time. You have been most gracious."

"I am honored by your visit. I should look forward to another—perhaps when you wish to see the Ainu."

"Thank you, Captain."

Genda escorted Sakai outside and the two men exchanged bows. Back at his car, Sakai could see that Genda had returned to his meditation, seated and facing the sea.

Arriving at the embassy, Sakai reported on his visit to Hokkaido.

Charlie Porter scratched his head as if it really itched. "Puzzling that the old bastard would treat you with such hospitality knowing that you are American."

"I share his heritage. He may not think of me as an American."

"Well, Genda's name was in that notebook for some reason. I'll check it out with the military science department. Maybe it was there just for the reason he suggested. It's just that Yasuda wasn't that serious a student. He seldom attended classes."

"Can the Japanese put Genda under surveillance? He's our only lead at the moment."

"I don't think we have enough to ask for that. Remember, Genda is an honored war veteran and retired senior military officer. They might even take offense at such a request. However, when it comes time for that—if it comes time for that—Japan's police organization can be very efficient. They have no problems of jurisdiction such as we have in the States. Any policeman can pursue any crime or criminal anywhere and receive nationwide assistance. At the same time, individual policemen are quite area-oriented and people contact them freely. There is outstanding public-police cooperation."

"Well, with respect to Captain Genda, something is not ringing quite true here. The vibes aren't right."

"Vibes? Since when did you start to use your intuition as an investigative tool? I always had you pegged as a facts-and-figures man."

"You know what I mean."

"I'm not sure I do," Porter replied.

"When he and I were talking, at his cottage, I just had the feeling that he was holding back. Maybe it is just that I read him wrong."

"You want to pursue it further?"

"How about his fellow officers? Could you get me some of their names?"

Porter shook his head as if the idea didn't set well with him. "Possibly. They may not take kindly to your inquiries, however. Japanese military officers are tight sons of bitches when it comes to talking about their own—especially the navy types. The discipline and junior-senior relationships of the old Imperial way are still respected. They have a very high code of honor and loyalty among themselves. You will have to be very tactful and use considerable discretion."

"Those are my strong points, spook. Now, get me the name of some old-timey Japs I can talk with."

Porter opened his eyes wide and let his jaw drop in mock disapproval at Sakai's use of the wartime diminutive. "Shit, you never forget, do you?—I'll see what I can do."

It was dark and rainy by the time Sakai returned to the Tokyo Fairmont. The message light was glowing as he entered his room. He called the front desk.

"This is three-oh-two, Sakai. You have a message for me?"

"*Hai*! Excuse a moment, please." The voice was gone only a few seconds. "You have a request to call the Tokyo Hilton Hotel. The party's name is Alicia."

Alicia? Here, in Tokyo? "Arigato."

It took only a moment to dial the Hilton and ask for Alicia's room.

"Alicia, what in God's holy name are you doing here in Tokyo? Where are the children?"

"With mother. Bert Thompson told me where you had flown off to. I called the embassy when I arrived and got your hotel."

"Why didn't you tell the embassy to contact me?"

"I didn't want them to know your ex is chasing you clear across the Pacific. I'm not all hussy. Something important has come up. We need to talk right away."

"Alicia, I'm in the middle of a terrorist incident investigation."

"George, get your ass over here or I'm coming over there. It's immaterial. But either we talk or you'll never see the kids again."

"For God's sake, Alicia, this is crazy—all right, I'll be over as soon as I can grab a cab."

Sakai tried to imagine what could have precipitated Alicia's drastic flight to Tokyo. She had always been impetuous, that was one of the things that had been exciting at first. You never knew what she was going to say, who she was going to shock, where she would want to make love. Their courtship had been a continuous round of exciting social adventures. Parties hosted by her family's Georgetown friends, sailing excursions to Newport and even Bermuda, charity galas where Alicia had shown him off with a pride that he granted was sincere but just a bit too enthusiastic. He had just returned from Vietnam, exhausted and disillusioned and with the Navy Cross to remind him of a place called Soc Trang. The ready access to Alicia's body and the social whirl had clouded his judgment and they had married when she was two months pregnant with their first child.

It had been a living hell since their first married night together, when Alicia had announced she wanted to emigrate to Australia. The summers of her schooling years at Ole Miss had been spent with her father in Sydney at the ambassador's residence and she had been infatuated with the stark beauty of the world's largest island.

"Australia? Whatever are you talking about?" he had said, sitting up in their wedding bed as if she had suggested living on the moon.

"I want our child to grow up in a land where there is still primitive beauty and isolation and a chance to be an individual."

"So, we take him to Yellowstone. For Christ's sake, Alicia, I can't earn a living in Australia. I just got a position with the State Department. I can use my 'Nam experience, my education, my training."

"Daddy has it all fixed. A family friend in Sydney has offered to practically give us a small sheep station."

"I don't believe this. Alicia Jane Richards-Sakai, a sheep station matron?"

"Our children will grow up surrounded by nature."

"How many babies are in there?" Sakai said, patting her still-flat stomach. It was time to lighten the conversation.

"We'll have more."

"Alicia, your sole experience with nature has been as honorary chairperson for a Save-the-Whales fund drive. You don't even own a pair of flat-heeled shoes."

"George . . ." She wrapped her arms around his neck. "We would be like pioneers."

"For God's sake, most of Australia is a modern, progressive, fully developed, sophisticated country. Their pioneers disappeared when the last criminal settler died off a hundred years ago."

"We would be a thousand miles from the nearest city."

Sakai was beginning to get irritated. She was much too serious. "No, Alicia. I have a good, promising position with State. I like this country. I spent four of my best years proving that in a shithole of a place that took a terrible toll on me and way too many of my generation. There is no way I'm going to turn around and walk away from what I'm entitled to in return."

"A pissy-ass civil servant, working sixty hours a week and feeling grateful for a weekend off every few months? We will have no social life at all."

"It's my career choice, Alicia. You knew that before tonight. It's a job with a future."

Sakai remembered almost every word of that conversation, sitting in the back of the cab as it careened across the rain-wetted streets of central Tokyo, more a surfboard than an automobile. It had been the first of so many mixed discussions when they had started out making love and wound up screaming and hating each other. How they had managed to conceive a second child in all that turmoil was beyond him, the only possible explanation being that despite her tantrums over his job with State and her constant insistence that they "go somewhere" and "become something," when they crawled into bed together it was a trip into outer space. Sex was Alicia's strongest suit, and all of their fights and disagreements were like aphrodisiacs to her. Still, she had finally laid down the ultimatum. Leave State or she walked. He didn't and she did.

She was waiting in her room and kissed him lightly on the cheek as he entered. As always, her lips were warm and very moist. She was wearing her auburn hair in a different style. If anything, it was more full than before and framed her face and neck as it rested on her shoulders. Her blouse was fresh and just thin enough to reveal the outline of her bra. The brown leather skirt was completely out of character but it fit well and gave her a new dimension.

Sakai plopped into an overstuffed chair. "What is this all about?"

"Our marriage."

"We don't have a marriage. We're divorced, remember? You have custody of the children. I pay you most of my hard-earned bucks every month, Alicia. Don't say that this is about our marriage."

"Daddy's Australian friend died and the family will be going to Melbourne for the services. Daddy wants me to come and bring the children. I'll need your permission to take them out of the country."

Sakai sagged. *Is that all?* "You have it."

"While we're there, the girls and I will be going to Woomera in South Australia. Daddy shared an investment there with his friend and will be buying out the estate."

Sakai's one-word observation was almost a curse: "Sheep?"

"I've seen pictures. It's a lovely wilderness with a beautiful old ranch house and outbuildings and miles and miles of land."

Sakai sat silent. He should have known.

"We will have no money worries, George. There's a staff and it is a very successful station."

"How many times have we had this conversation? Five? Fifty?"

"It's not the same this time. We won't be tenants. We'll be American settlers."

"Stop using 'we' as if it includes me. Alicia, why are you doing this? It's all over between us."

"Not while there are the children. I love you, George; I just can't share our bed with the State Department."

Sakai studied his ex-wife. Carrying and delivering two children had failed to leave any mark on her figure. Straining the architecture of her blouse and skirt was the same body that she had thrown at him a decade earlier in Georgetown. Even as he sat in anger at her arrogance and persistence, he had to admit that not all of the old fire had died. Sitting in the well-appointed room at the Tokyo Hilton with the night rain playing its erratic rhythm on the big picture window and blurring the multicolored lights of downtown Tokyo, he had to concede a certain romantic ambiance. And it was impossible not to be aroused by the casual crossing of Alicia's legs that emphasized the delicious contour of her thighs and hips. In addition, the thrust of her breasts, caused by her supporting herself on the bed with her elbows, certainly did not help to keep the conversation in the proper perspective.

"Have you forgotten what it was like?" she asked quietly.

"No, I haven't—" Sakai rose and walked over to stand in front of Alicia. She lowered herself and let her arms rest outstretched on the bed, her eyes extending the familiar invitation that was his only pleasant memory of their times together. "—It was pure unadulterated hell, Alicia."

Instantly, her eyes flashed the same message as her lips, "Damn you! You god-damned orientals are impossible!" She started to rise but Sakai leaned over and pinned her to the bed.

"You go to Australia, Alicia, and you live on that sheep station and you play the part of the adventurous American female all you want. But the children stay in Washington, D.C., in the good old U.S. of A."

"Ohhh!"

Sakai kept her pinned as she squirmed and cursed. It was all too familiar. They had played the same scene a thousand times. Angry tears welled in her eyes and were slung aside as she twisted her head in protest and fought to free her arms. Off balance, Sakai fell across her. Immediately, she tried to bite him. Her mouth opened over his, her teeth pressed into his cheeks. Abruptly, her struggles ceased. Then, the sharp feel disappeared and there was only the softness.

"Why does it always turn out this way?" Alicia asked.

"It's the way we are, Alicia. We can't live together and we just can't seem to live away from each other. We're a hopeless mismatch—except for this."

"Then there has to be hope." Alicia kissed Sakai lightly on the lips. He began to unbutton her blouse.

Chapter 8

The Air Micronesia Boeing 727 dropped through the fair-weather cumulus as if it were a shotgunned duck. Free of U.S. air traffic restrictions and picky-ass FAA monitoring, the pilots of Air Mike flew their island-hopping missions with a flair long gone from stateside commercial aviation. With only rare periods of bad weather, and that usually a stubborn thunderstorm that refused to leave its comfortable spot over a western Pacific airstrip until it had laid down a deep layer of rainwater, the Air Mike crews were accustomed to get-'em-on-the-ground, get-'em-off-and-on, and get-up-and-out! With no other traffic and normally light aircraft, such procedures were quite safe and certainly fuel-saving. But to the uninitiated passengers, a swooping steep turn and a plunk down on the numbers at the approach end of a narrow, water-enclosed runway, followed by maximum reverse thrust and a hearty application of the brakes, was a thrill akin to Magic Mountain at Disneyland.

Understandably, such procedures were often quite necessary, for the concrete strips of Johnson Island, Majuro, Kosrei, Pohnpei, and Truk were laid on top of scraped coral with very little excess length and no overrun. You were over water until just before the moment of touchdown, and when you ground to a stop there was water just a few yards in front of you.

Michio Ohiro and Taeko Nikahura leaned into each other for mutual support as their pilot banked steeply onto a short base leg for the runway at Pohnpei. The strip was actually on a small outer island and the proudly named but rather meager Pohnpei International Airport was connected to the main island by a paved causeway.

Taeko squealed with delight. "Look at that rock formation!" Jutting out from the far side of a shipping inlet was a large dark block of rock with an abrupt face that dropped vertically to the water.

"That is Sokehs Rock, Pohnpei's Diamond Head so to speak, and the village down there bordering the harbor is Kolonia, the capital of the Federated States of Micronesia."

"How do you know such things?" Taeko was taken aback at Ohiro's casual description.

"I have flown into here when I was with the defense force. We flew some joint training exercises with the Australians from Guam and Truk and here at Pohnpei. There was not this nice runway, then, but the strip was ample for us."

The aircraft rolled its wings level and began to slow.

Taeko pressed her face against the small window. "I can see nothing outside but water!"

The pilot added a burst of power.

Ohiro felt the nervous squeeze of Taeko's hand over his. "This is standard. We are on final approach. You will see the runway just before we touch down."

"I better!"

Just as it appeared the 727 was going to touch down on the surface of the shallow green water, a momentary strip of surf appeared and then the threshold markings of the runway. Taeko immediately felt the touchdown and was forced forward against her seat belt as the pilot applied full reverse thrust and stomped on his brakes.

It was a good solid landing. Ohiro nodded his head in approval. "*Joto!*"

Taeko raised her hands to cup them over her mouth in relief. "*Mi-ya!*"

A smattering of applause rose from the other passengers and the muu-muu-clothed flight attendant gave a little bow. "Air Micronesia welcomes you to the island that Robert Louis Stevenson called 'the Pearl of the Pacific'—Pohnpei. For your safety, please remain seated until the pilot shuts off the engines."

Their rental Nissan Sentra was waiting as they cleared customs and within minutes Taeko was getting her first look at the former Japanese possession while Ohiro talked of the island.

"Lots of rain forest and no beaches. Mostly mangrove swamps around the main island itself. The harbor is over there by Kolonia."

The two-lane road quickly faded to rough asphalt.

"This is the only road around the island but it gets pretty rough on the far side."

Taeko hid her face and giggled as they passed a native shack with a Pohnpeian grandmother sitting in the door opening, her depleted naked breasts hanging loosely down her chest, the dark nipples resting on her stomach. Three huge hogs were resting in their pen enclosures.

"Pigs are wealth here," Ohiro said. "You don't want to run one down. There, up ahead, is the turnoff to the Village Hotel." Ohiro swung left onto a climbing dirt road. Rainwashes and deep potholes forced him to proceed very cautiously as he nursed the Sentra up the winding path.

"What happens if we meet another car?"

"It depends on how big the driver is." Ohiro pulled the steering wheel quickly left to avoid a bottomless pothole. Up ahead, several thatched roofs came into view, and soon they were passing under an overhead walkway and stopping by the open-air lobby.

As Ohiro checked in, Taeko ambled into the open dining room. The hotel, a main lobby/dining/bar structure and a collection of some twenty individual living huts, was high on a steep hill, and the dining area overlooked the unbelievably blue lagoon and a large outer island. Beyond, the white ribbon of foam crashing over the encircling barrier reef was clearly visible. The dining area was two-level, with a small sunken bar in one corner of the lower level, and the tables were spaciously arranged, most with a quartet of wing-backed wicker chairs. Several overhead fans were turning lazily, keeping the humid air at least circulating. A large, elderly gray wolfhound was sprawled in a far corner, his moist muzzle lying on outstretched forepaws. The reception/registration desk was merely a small closet-sized enclosure off the dining room.

"Come." Ohiro led Taeko out the back of the dining room and across a small footbridge to their hut, one of several sitting on the mountainside among the thick stand of palms and fern trees. Each hut was staggered on the hillside to provide privacy from the others. Easily twenty feet square, they were poised on stilts and screen-enclosed on three sides. Taeko was pleasantly surprised to find a pair of queen-sized water beds and several pieces of white-painted wicker furniture that sat in a compact grouping under an overhead tropical fan.

"Canopies," Taeko observed, looking upward at the two rectangles of flowered cloth stretched over the beds.

Ohiro grinned. "Lizard catchers." He pointed up at the high-peaked thatch roof. Several wiggling green tails were protruding through the woven palm fronds.

Taeko shuddered and cautiously examined the bathroom, which was set off from the main area by a privacy wall. Ohiro was gazing out the screen when she rejoined him.

"Beautiful. . . ." Ohiro pointed toward the white-frothed coral reef that ran loosely around the island.

Taeko moved to place her body lightly against his. "And very romantic. Genda is providing us with a promising holiday."

As if not hearing her, Ohiro remarked, "The delivery will take place tonight, on the far side of the island. The ship will pause opposite a small passage through the reef and one of its boats will deliver the crated missiles to one of the small artificial islands that make up the ruins of Nan Madol. The natives hold it to be a sacred place and will not enter the area after dark. They believe that to do so will result in their death before the night is over. I will arrange for a boat with the hotel and at first high tide tomorrow, we will ride out and retrieve it."

"How do we know exactly where it will be?"

"I have a map identical to the one the ship's crew will use. Goto gave it to me."

"How do we get it aboard the cannery boat?"

"We will be contacted here at the hotel and arrangements made."

"Then, we have no obligations until tomorrow morning." Taeko coyly eyed the water beds while placing an arm around Ohiro's waist.

"True enough." Ohiro's eyes twinkled in response to the unspoken invitation. He protested only lightly as Taeko pulled him toward the bed. "But the second thing we must do is arrange for the boat."

Fortunately, a full moon made recognition of the reef passage less of a problem than the captain of the *Khafji Ajr* had anticipated. The bridge radar showed only an unbroken sea return from the breaking of the waves over the submerged coral. Beyond the reef rose the dark silhouette of mountainous Pohnpei, its rugged natural skyline outlined against a night sky full of countless silver stars. A few clusters of man-made light dotted the coastline where restless natives were still awaiting the arrival of elusive sleep. But they were few and far between. There would be very little activity on the main island and none on the islets within the reef.

"All engines stop," the captain ordered, and the quiet of the night was broken by the clanging of the engine order telegraph.

He walked out on the starboard wing of the bridge and checked to insure that all was in readiness. A clandestine visit to the island was not new to him, but he was not particularly pleased with the cargo he had to transfer. Usually, he stopped only to pick up a covert shipment of the island's marijuana crop. Such a task involved little risk, as Pohnpei had no coastal patrols and the sellers would paddle freely out to his ship. But this time he would be sending three of his crewmen inside the reef and they would have to step on one of the small islets to deliver the package. There was always the chance of a coincidental discovery.

Leaning over the side, he quietly gave his order: "Away, the *Odyssey*." His ship was making only a few knots and slowing. After the rubber boat cleared the side, he would let the *Khafji Ajr* drift unless it began to close the reef.

The coxswain of the *Odyssey* sat at the motor tiller and timed his order to the arrival of the crest of the low swell: "Release all lines."

His two Arab crewmen released their fall lines and pushed against the side of the *Khafji Ajr* to break clear.

The high whining outboard partially masked the sound of the water broken up by the reef, but the ratio of noise began to favor the waves as the coxswain searched ahead for the passage.

"There!" The bow crewman pointed slightly to port.

The coxswain corrected his course and they eased through the narrow break in the reef. Once inside, the water became glassy smooth. Keeping his hand-held compass heading as steady as possible, the coxswain steered the boat towards the right edge of a small islet. The water was extremely shallow. Slowing, he tilted the outboard to raise the propeller clear of the coral that was only inches below the bottom of the rubber boat. No other craft could have even transited the lagoon at low tide.

"That will be it." Arriving on the far side, he guided his craft along a narrow channel, thankful that the bright moon provided enough light to navigate by. Using a light would be to invite detection, and he had heard that the natives of Pohnpei took very poorly to anyone violating the sanctity of the ruins of Nan Madol. The ancients had laid out a complete city around a network of shallow canals sometime around 600 A.D. Natives of unknown origin, they had lived, and fished, and worshiped from their man-made islands until something catastrophic must have happened, for they vanished, leaving only their dwelling places to mark their passing. Over the years, the structures had deteriorated and were now only a jumble of basalt logs, most arranged in erratic low walls that gave rise to wide speculation as to the history of the ruins.

"Look at that!"

Ahead in the moonlight lay the dark silhouette of an aged temple, topless but with the walls of stone logs largely intact. A stone pier jutted out into the canal and the coxswain brought his high-riding craft alongside it. He remained at the tiller as the two other crewmen lifted the crate and carried it into the open courtyard of the temple. Farther on was a small roofed room with a low doorway. The two men entered and placed the crate on the crushed coral floor.

The younger of the two was visibly nervous. "Let's get out of this place. I don't like it here."

"There is a strange feeling," his companion agreed, "but that is only because we have never been here before and the people that built this place are long gone. It is very interesting, is it not?"

"Interesting yes, but not a place to stay."

"Allah is with us this night as on all others. Do not act as a child." The two hurried back to the pier.

The coxswain pushed off as his two crewmen jumped back in the boat. Within a few minutes they cleared the canal, and the return trip across the quiet lagoon calmed the nerves of the one Arab who was very glad to be away from the ruins.

The coxswain leaned forward and strained to pick up the difference in the rhythm of the whitecaps that would mark the channel through the reef. He called out to the bowman, "Can you see the break?"

The bowman shook his head at first, then pointed. "There, a point to port."

The coxswain nodded as he, too, picked up the relative calm stretch of water. Cautiously, he approached it and steered the *Odyssey* out its middle and into the open sea. A half mile away, the *Khafji Ajr* rode easily with only her running lights visible.

It was good to be out of the lagoon and away from the dark ruins.

Taeko watched Ohiro dress. Torrential rains had greeted the dawn and wakened them both. Never ones to waste an opportunity, they had greeted the murky daylight with the same sexual enthusiasm they had displayed under the soft light of the full moon before the thunderstorms came.

"Get up," Ohiro urged. "We have things to do."

Taeko stretched and flung back the sheet. She enjoyed her nakedness almost as much as Ohiro. The thunderstorms were passing but there was still a healthy breeze passing through the screened walls, and her body welcomed the tiny invisible fingers of cooling air. With Ohiro, she had worked up a good sweat.

This was a much better life than she had enjoyed in the dingy hostess bars back in Tokyo. In fact, she was quite pleased with herself. A daughter of *barakumin* parents, the lowest strata of Japanese society, she was a descendant of those who in feudal times were relegated to the more onerous chores, such as the slaughtering of animals and the cleaning of the stables. The *barakumin* still tended to live together in their own communities, away from the mainstream of Japanese progress. Ordinarily, Taeko would have been destined to remain with her own kind, but she had two things going for her. One was a body that drove men to the extremes of sexual conduct, and the other was a stubborn refusal to accept her fate.

It had been easy to bargain her way into Tokyo; a furious romp in the sleeping compartment of a heavy cross-country truck not only paid for her passage to the capital city but placed in her hands sufficient yen to buy her way into one of the sleazy sex bars off the Asakusa district, one of Tokyo's prime entertainment areas. The rest was easy for the *barakumin* girl with the body of a goddess and a complete lack of inhibitions, often finishing her live sex performance by inviting a member of the audience to join her on stage. Overnight, she became a sensation along the "sin strip," and it was during one of her performances that she had met Ohiro. Still in hiding after his defection from the JMSDF, the all-night session of drinking sake and watching Taeko take on a series of paid performers stimulating him almost to the bursting point, he had drunkenly accepted her challenge and they had received a standing ovation after their first public coupling. Taeko had figured at that moment that if he was that capable a lover while thoroughly intoxicated, his sober performance must be something of which she had only dreamed.

They stayed together as lovers while Taeko worked at her profession through the lower class of hostess bars and then to the standing of a private prostitute on call to only the wealthiest of Japanese professionals. Unfortunately, one of the older gentlemen had a massive coronary while trying to match Taeko's enthusiastic services and traces of cocaine had been found in his body. The police took a dim view of drugs of any kind, and to avoid prosecution Taeko joined Ohiro in his underground Red Army endeavors. It was not exactly a match made in heaven, but it was great sex.

"Give me time to take a shower," she said.

"I will wait for you in the dining room. High tide is in three hours. I want to be the first boat to the ruins. It would be awkward recovering the weapons with tourists present."

Taeko entered the bath area and chased away the small green lizards that were nibbling at the dark mold trapped in the moist creases of the shower curtain.

Two other tables were occupied when she joined Ohiro. At one sat four men, two of whom were apparently Americans. A young Japanese couple sat at the other, obviously real honeymooners.

A dark-skinned Pohnpeian girl appeared and offered Taeko a menu board.

"Papaya juice."

"Nothing else?" Ohiro was surprised his mistress ordered so little. She certainly had exercised during the night.

"I feel too good to eat. You have the boat reserved?"

"Yes, a twelve-foot flat-bottomed skiff. Even at high tide, we will have less than three feet of water beneath us. I have rented snorkling gear. As far as the hotel knows, we are going to swim part of the reef."

"They do not require a guide?"

"I showed them our snorkling certificates and they pointed out several areas suitable to our qualifications."

"I have never snorkled in my life. I barely swim."

Ohiro laughed. "You will not today unless the boat sinks. We better take some towels and hats. The sun will be merciless out on the water."

The equatorial sun *was* merciless as Ohiro put full throttle to the thirty-five-horse Mercury and they sped across the lagoon. Once out of sight of the Village Hotel, they continued on around the main island, passing several exposed coral strips where small groups of Pohnpeians were fishing. Taeko snapped several pictures and gave them her best tourist wave. Forty minutes after leaving the boat pier at the foot of the Village Hotel's mountain complex, they were approaching one of Pohnpei's satellite islands. Ohiro throttled back to idle and approached a native hut sitting partially out over the lagoon waters.

"Temwen Island," Ohiro said. "The ruins are on the other side, but we have to make a stop here and pay a fee to the high chief of Madolenihmw. He owns the island and we must have his permission to visit the ruins."

Taeko giggled. "I can't even pronounce the name."

They eased up to the hut. The Nahnmwarki, high chief, was sitting crosslegged, his lava-lava almost hidden under the fold of a great brown stomach. He was leisurely fanning himself and drinking a can of Classic Coke. Ohiro handed him several bills and the old man smiled and nodded his assent.

"Hard work for papa-san." Taeko waved as they backed away.

The old chief removed his teeth and clacked them at Taeko, who fell laughing in the bottom of the boat, completely overcome by the humor of the unexpected gesture.

Ohiro was not amused. The old chief could have taken offense. "Don't be disrespectful."

The canals of Nan Madol ran between a series of stone-log structures, each of which was almost completely overgrown with tropical flora. Taeko began snapping pictures, genuinely impressed by the ruins. "Remarkable." To any observers, she and Ohiro were typical tourists.

Ohiro slowed to bare steerageway. "A lost civilization built these artificial islets. There is a complete city of ruins here. The logs are basalt and come from the main island, transported on bamboo rafts sometime between 1245 and 1445 A.D."

"You make a good tour guide."

"I have been here several times—there, ahead, is where we are going." Ohiro shut off the motor and let the boat ease up to the stone pier, quickly jumping from the bow and securing a line to a segment of the ruins. Taeko followed him and they entered the small room in the center of the topless temple. A wooden crate lay in the shadows of the room. "This is it!"

The crate was about four feet long, two feet wide, and a foot thick. One of the dark stencils on the sides indicated the weight: ninety-eight pounds. Taeko grabbed one end and helped Ohiro carry it to the skiff. Ohiro retrieved the bow line and pushed off from the pier. Once they cleared the canal, they were in open water and he once more gave full throttle to the motor. A school of triangular dark shapes crossed in front of them and then paralleled the speeding boat, remaining just below the surface of the superclear water.

"Rays!" Taeko gleefully shouted. The flat fish were escorting the fast-moving skiff much as porpoises at sea swam off the bows of larger ships. Taeko watched them with awe. Ohiro was more interested in the wooden crate sitting in the bottom of the boat. Stenciled on its four sides in black ink were the words "Diesel parts," and the ends carried the logo of the Ford Motor Company. A plastic-enclosed bill of lading was stapled to the top of the crate.

Ohiro could already visualize the exploding American aircraft.

Soon they had worked themselves back around to the north side of the main island and could see the covey of thatched huts belonging to the Village Hotel. As they approached the small inlet that led to the boat dock, a tiny winged shape appeared over Sokehs Rock. At first, Taeko thought it was a bird, but it quickly grew in size and its identity became obvious. "Look, Michio, an airplane."

Ohiro had already seen the approaching aircraft and was surprised to see it letting down and heading straight for their skiff. Something about its nose-on profile looked hauntingly familiar. "It is an old fighter plane of some kind!" Then a chill climbed his vertebrae and left cold footprints up his back. The aircraft was less than one hundred feet above the water and was banking steeply to avoid flying right over them. It was dark green and on the bottom of the low wing were the red sun insignias of Japan. "I don't believe this! It is a Zero!"

"A what?" Taeko recognized the insignia but had no idea as to the aircraft's identity.

"A Mitsubishi Type Zero fighter! It was our number-one airplane in the great war. Genda flew one!"

The Zero pulled up in steep climb, rolled completely over, and dove back toward the skiff in a Cuban Eight maneuver. Again, it broke to the side just before reaching the boat and the freshly painted metal picked up the sun's rays and flashed them across the water, momentarily blinding Ohiro and his mistress. Another climb, another roll, and the ghost from the past leveled and flew back toward the Pohnpei airport.

Ohiro was a little boy, jabbering at full speed about the Zero and its attributes and status as Japan's premier World War II fighter. He didn't stop talking until they had made the boat dock, carried the heavy crated weapons up to their hut and locked the door as they left. She had never seen Ohiro so excited and had to trot to keep up with him. "Where are we going?"

"To the airport, Taeko, to view a piece of our history."

The Mitsubishi A6M-2 Zero-sen sat to the right of the main terminal, just outside a temporary sheet metal hangar. Ohiro stood a respectable distance away and let his eyes enjoy the feast. The Zero appeared factory-fresh. The bright chromed propeller spinner jutted out from a black cowling that was gracefully curved to provide just the right flow of cooling air around the radial engine. Behind it stretched the fuselage, lean and mean, tapering to a point just aft and below the high triangular fin and rudder. The cockpit was covered over with panels of clear Plexiglas inserted into a teardrop-shaped metal frame, giving the pilot visibility around his entire horizon. Ohiro recalled reading that the American fighters didn't adopt such a canopy until halfway through the war, when the later models of the North American P-51 and the Republic P-47 began to offer their pilots an equally generous view of their battle space.

The resurrected Zero sat at a jaunty angle, its long slim main gear holding its nose high and the tail wheel providing just the right angle to enable the pilot to taxi with some degree of forward visibility. The aircraft was painted Imperial Navy green with gray undersides, and on the wings and afterfuselage were the large red sun insignias of Japan, each outlined in a circle of pure white to provide a clear definition between them and the overall dark green.

A pair of vertical white chevrons were wrapped around the fuselage just aft of the sun insignias, and high on the tail were squadron markings: 653-11, an identifying number of the 653rd navy air corps.

Several men were puttering around the front of the aircraft, one peering inside the engine cowling to find the source of oil dripping from the bottom. Ohiro recognized two of them as the Americans he had noticed at breakfast.

Ohiro bowed. *"Konnichi-wa."*

"Konnichi-wa," replied one of the men, a big shirtless blond with a deep bronze tan.

Ohiro gave two more quick little bows. "You speak Japanese!"

The muscular blond laughed. "Only a few phrases." It was easy for him to understand the Japanese couple's interest. "Would you like to see our airplane?" he asked.

"Oh, yes, very much. *Domo arigato!* Thank you very much!"

The blond made brief introductions and helped Ohiro climb up on the wing. "Sit in it if you'd like."

Ohiro carefully swung a leg over the cockpit rim and settled into the metal bucket seat. Without a parachute or cushion he was almost out of sight to Taeko, who remained beside the airplane, putting on her own show for the other two men.

Ohiro was too fascinated to notice. "Oohhhh, this is beautiful. Where did aircraft come from?"

The blond talked of the first find in 1989 and the subsequent restoration effort. "We plan to take it back to the United States."

Ohiro was enraptured. He was sitting in an actual wartime Zero, looking at a completely restored cockpit, Japanese markings and all. "Was that you in air?"

"Yes."

"We were in small boat."

"Oh, yes. I couldn't resist."

Ohiro laughed. "I could not believe eyes. I have friend who was pilot in war. He flew this type airplane. He will be very excited when I tell him and he will reply that I am great liar!"

"Take some pictures," the blond offered, tapping Ohiro's Minolta, which was slung around his neck.

"Yes, yes, thank you. You will be flying again?"

"As soon as we find that oil leak. It looks like it's from one of the lower cylinder rocker-arm covers. Hopefully, we just need to replace the gasket. If you are around in the morning, we should have it back in the air."

"You will be flying it back to United States?"

"We'll fly it first to Hawaii and participate in the ceremonies commemorating the attack on Pearl Harbor." Even as he finished speaking, the blond felt awkward. The Japanese could be embarrassed.

"Oh."

The American quickly recovered. "There will be several World War II vintage aircraft flown over Pearl Harbor. We thought it only right that our Zero join them. The war is long over."

Ohiro looked up at the American. *Our Zero?* "Yes. That would be very respectful gesture. Our countries are great allies now. You really intend fly all way Hawaii?"

"Yes, we will island-hop."

"That very fantastic."

"Not really. The airplane has been completely rebuilt and we have a state-of-the-art inertia navigational system installed. We will go from here to Kosrae, then we have prearranged permission to refuel at the U.S. facilities at Kwajalein and Johnson Island. The military is even prepositioning aviation gasoline for us."

"That is over much water." Ohiro did not wish to be impolite but he could see the difficulty of such a task.

The blond man explained. "The Kwajalein-to-Johnson leg is the longest: fourteen hundred nautical miles. With the belly tank, we will have ample fuel with probably three hours reserve. Your own pilots during the war flew close to two thousand miles on ferry flights—and they didn't have our sophisticated navigational gear. Also, we will have a chase plane, a twin-engined turboprop Mitsubishi MU-2. It will also carry a supply of aviation gasoline in a special rubber fuselage bladder."

"Ah, you seem to be well prepared." Thanking the Americans profusely, Ohiro led Taeko back to their car. "I am thrilled to see such a relic of the old Imperial Navy, but I am disheartened that it will be flown by Americans. A Japanese hand should wrap itself around the control stick and Japanese feet should rest on those sacred rudder pedals. Genda will be furious."

As Ohiro and Taeko drove away, the big blond reached down and pinched his smaller partner on the buttocks. "I ruv you, G.I."

His partner laughed and bowed deeply. "And I ruv you, too. Did you see the ass on that slant-eyed dolly? I bet her stud hasn't slept in a month."

"Gentlemen," the third man, a Pohnpeian native, said solemnly with an affected English accent, "could we please get back to the task at hand? I saw nothing exceptional in that pleasant young lady from a foreign land." For emphasis, the Pohnpeian bit hard on the knuckles of one hand and let out a low moan of anguish as he grabbed his crotch with the other.

The small refrigerator ship sailed by Matsui Canneries arrived in the Kolonia harbor five days later, and that evening Goto's brother joined Ohiro and Taeko for dinner at the Joy Restaurant in Kolonia. Run by island Japanese, the restaurant was off a side alley, and although it featured Western-style seating, the food was dominantly Japanese.

Ohiro looked around carefully before speaking. The dining room was only sparsely occupied. "When shall we deliver the diesel parts?"

"In the morning. I will have a small boat at the Shell Oil landing. There will be no problem. Customs is not interested in any outgoing cargo."

"How about at the other end?"

"We'll make port at Nagoya. No problem there, either. We will keep the crate on the ship, in the engine room. Our auxiliary generator is a Ford diesel. Customs will not be concerned about it. A few days later I will contact you and you can take delivery."

The three drove up to the Village Hotel after dinner and sat at the sunken bar in the dining room. The two Americans joined them for a while and they all spoke of the Zero and Japan and the United States. After a while, Ohiro offered to drive Goto's brother back to his room in Kolonia and Taeko retired to their hut.

When Ohiro returned, Taeko was lying nude on one of the water beds. There was a sweet smell, instantly recognized by Ohiro. Hurriedly, he stripped and joined Taeko, who offered him the remainder of a moist joint.

"Pure Pacific grass," she muttered dreamily. "It makes our native product taste like the droppings of very sick chickens. . . ."

On the northern horizon, the late-night thunderstorms were approaching Pohnpei.

Genda greeted his companions with the obvious question. "You have the weapons?"

"*Hai*, Genda-san," Goto replied. "There was no difficulty and the transfer went as planned. Ohiro and Taeko returned from Pohnpei and joined me at Nagoya. The Matsui Cannery vessel docked on schedule. After the ship cleared customs, we were able to transfer the weapons to our vehicle, drove here, and have it stored as you directed."

"Excellent. We go ahead with our plan." Genda was pleased. "My brother served on Pohnpei during the war—it was called Ponape then—and on the neighboring atoll of Majuro. I have often wanted to visit those places. Perhaps I shall go there someday."

"Genda-san, Taeko and I have a surprise for you."

"A surprise?"

"Yes. While we were on Pohnpei, on the very morning we took custody of the weapon, we observed a Mitsubishi Type Zero flying around the island."

"A *Reisen*? Impossible."

"No, it is not. Taeko and I went to the airport and saw the airplane. We met two Americans who discovered the Zero on one of Pohnpei's satellite islands. It had been stored there since the day in 1944 it had crash-landed on the beach. The Americans are members of a special restoration group who have rebuilt the airplane and they plan to take it to Hawaii for the fiftieth anniversary commemoration of our attack on Pearl Harbor. There is to be a week-long remembrance. Their president and our prime minister will take part."

Taeko asked, "Can they really do that, Genda-san? Fly that little airplane to Hawaii? It is a long way."

Genda's chest swelled. "The Zero fighter is fully capable. The A6M-2 model could fly two thousand miles nonstop in its ferry configuration. With the proper navigational equipment, the Americans can island-hop all the way to Hawaii. This is most interesting. I had forgotten how close we are to the anniversary of that day. And the fiftieth. That will be special, very special. You are sure, Ohiro, that it was an authentic Zero?"

"*Hai*, Genda-san. A beautiful A6M-2 wearing the colors of the Imperial Navy. I am not mistaken."

For a brief moment, Genda's face softened as he remembered his days in the cockpit of the classic fighter, but the fact that Americans had recovered and restored one and would be flying it over Oahu burned hard into his soul and his eyes narrowed with displeasure. The Zero was a Japanese aerial masterpiece, as much the symbol of the warrior as the sword of the samurai. If there was indeed one flying, and it was to be part of an aerial display, it should not be guided through the sky by the thick hands and large feet of an American. The delicate aerial dance of the Zero should be choreographed by a Japanese.

For the briefest of moments, a startling question flashed through Genda's mind: Could Ohiro's sighting of the resurrected Zero on Pohnpei be a message from the gods urging Genda to stop such a blasphemy?

If so, how? Such a thing was surely impossible. Besides, the instrument of his revenge was more logically the small Red Army cell led by Goto, not a reborn Mitsubishi A6M-2.

Genda dismissed the thought. It was fantasy.

But the human brain is a remarkable organ in many ways. One is that it retains every thought it has ever generated. It only takes an appropriate stimulus for that thought to resurface.

Chapter 9

George Sakai poured himself a cup of coffee and plopped down on one of the recreation room chairs at the American embassy.

"Well, gyrene, how'd it go?" Charlie Porter asked.

"You were right. None of Genda's contemporaries were very receptive to my questions. They're a closed society. But I did talk to several—enough to come up with a disturbing picture."

"Oh?"

"I gather Captain Saburo Genda has never really reconciled himself to being on the losing side of World War II. I get the distinct impression that he still harbors a grudge. It could be even more personal than that. We nuked his parents at Nagasaki."

"And probably saved a million Japanese lives."

"That's true, but I doubt that he thinks of that aspect. I found out that in the closing days of the war he was a seventeen-year-old Zero pilot with the 823rd Ku, that was the 823rd squadron, attached to the Yokohama Kokutai, Naval Air Corps, at Atsugi Air Base—it was a Tokyo air defense wing. He flew thirteen combat missions although he was shot down on the first. Must've been a fast learner. Our pilots were shit-hot good by then. And get this: He was a *kamikaze* selectee on the day the war ended. He missed his big day of glory. Even had his airplane turned up and ready to take off."

"Sounds like someone opened up."

"No one person. Just bits and pieces from several. There's more. The printout on him that Nakai let me read stated that Genda's wife died during a robbery attempt by two Americans. She was actually raped by both men and she considered herself so dishonored she killed herself. She was also pregnant."

"Jesus, no wonder he's pissed! I've read that sort of thing didn't happen very often. Our troops were generally very well behaved."

"Well, all it takes is one time if the victim is your wife."

"George, old buddy, that's one hell of a suspicious profile. But why would he have waited all these years before striking back?"

"Who knows? Really, we don't have anything concrete. My question is, do we have enough for Japanese surveillance?"

"I've some surprising news about that—but go on with what you found out."

"He is a hero among his contemporaries, a traditional samurai type whose code of personal honor and loyalty to the Emperor is of the old school."

"Hirohito is dead," Porter stated flatly.

"No matter. Genda serves until *his* death is the way I read it."

"Even in his retirement years?"

"Well, according to his old shipmates, now that he is out of uniform he has disowned everything Western. When he received me on Hokkaido he was all traditional. He has apparently climbed into a prewar shell and spends his days painting watercolors, mostly battle scenes and landscapes. He has a talent, actually."

Porter considered the contradiction. "Shit, he was open and friendly with you."

"Because if he *is* involved in the bombing, he could very well suspect that I suspect him. Right now he is an enigma, but from what I've learned, my reading is that he may very well feel he has every reason to spend his remaining years taking out his wrath on Americans."

Charlie Porter made some notes in a small spiral pad. "You do good work, *gaijin*, even one whose flesh and blood are Japanese."

"So, I'm a foreigner—technically. But, you know, Charlie, there is a certain affinity here; maybe it is because my blood is Japanese.

I just feel I should know Genda. Think back to 'Nam. Remember how completely devastated we felt pulling out? It wasn't a very good feeling then and it's not a good feeling now. We failed in our country's mission, Charlie. And that failure was not on the grand scale of Genda's. Hell, he *lost* his country—at least, as he knew it; we lost a lousy war we shouldn't have been in in the first place."

"You just said he was an enigma."

"And he is. I just don't feel he should be. I should be able to better figure him out. One voice inside of me says he's a patriot. Another voice says he's a low-scale traitor who is on the verge of some sort of vendetta."

"It may even be worse than that," Porter commented. "While you were gone, I made some inquiries and was referred to a Commander Mikimoto of the Tokyo office of the maritime arm's interior intelligence agency. Mikimoto dropped the other shoe. We're getting into a god-damned sensitive area here, George, so what I say stays between us for the moment."

Sakai nodded.

"Genda spent his thirty years in the JMSDF as a low-level Soviet agent."

That was a side of Genda that Sakai had never suspected. "And the authorities know it?"

"Yes. Here's the kicker. He was deliberately fed inconsequential data as a function of a counterintelligence scam. Practically all of it was information the Soviets had already acquired from NATO sources. The Japanese used him to ferret out Soviet agents. He didn't know it, of course. When it came time for him to hang it up, there was a move to arrest him and put him away but some higher-ups—probably old World War II associates—put the kibosh on that. He was led out to pasture. But naval intelligence wasn't about to call off their dogs and have had him under a routine surveillance ever since. Up to now, he's been clean. But their latest report on him was a follow-up on a visit to Nagasaki where he periodically goes to honor his dead parents. Some days before the car-bombing, a naval intelligence agent working out of the Nagasaki office observed Genda meeting with a Colonel Tsuan, a KGB officer assigned to the Soviet embassy in Tokyo. Why would he do that? Genda doesn't have access to any military information now. A day later, he left Nagasaki and took the hot baths at Takaragawa, north of Tokyo, and returned to Hokkaido."

"Then, in all probability, everything I've uncovered, Japanese naval intelligence already knows." Sakai didn't appreciate his duplication of effort.

"That, and more."

"So where does that leave us?"

"The only thing we have to link the old bastard with the car-bombing is his name in the driver's notebook. Circumstantial."

"Then I think I should go back and see him."

"And really arouse his suspicion?" Porter had some reservations about the possibility of Genda's going silent on them.

"No, he invited me back to see and talk about the Ainu. And I think he thinks of me as more Japanese than American. He could let his guard down."

Porter shrugged. "Well, gyrene, I think it's the chasing of a wild goose. But worth a try."

"I'm off."

Sakai cursed. Genda's cottage was boarded up against the approaching winter seas and winds and the old warrior was gone. The innkeeper at Urohoro was of no help at all.

The one-armed veteran seemed truly surprised. "It is a strange thing for Genda-san to do. He has never left his cottage before except for short trips."

"Did he stop by here and talk to you at all?"

"No. I did not know he was gone."

"You are a close friend."

"As close as anyone gets to Genda-san, perhaps. But all we share are memories of the war. He sometimes visits and we drink for a while, but I really know little of him."

"May I ask a rather private question?"

"Of course."

"In his visits with you, has Captain Genda ever displayed any particular antagonism toward Americans?"

"No."

Sakai studied the innkeeper. He was a master of the oriental inscrutable smile. Did he know more about Genda than he claimed? Every man has to have a confidant. Regardless, the old army fighter was not going to say any more than he had. That was apparent.

"May I use your telephone?" Sakai asked.

"Of course."

Sakai could see a bit of concern come over the man's face. "I will leave money to cover the cost of the call. I must talk to Tokyo."

"It is an incidental cost." Despite the innkeeper's polite reply, he was obviously relieved that he did not have to embarrass himself by asking for reimbursement. "I will be in my room."

Sakai watched the door curtains sway after the man made his withdrawal.

Porter was anything but happy to hear the news. "Oh, shit, he's bugged out? That could be significant."

"Do you think the Japanese have a tail on him?"

"Could be. Why don't you shift into reverse and get on back here? I'll see what I can find out."

"Will do." Drawing back the curtains, Sakai handed a small roll of yen bills to the innkeeper.

"Oh, that is too much!"

"*Dozo.*" Sakai gently forced the man's fingers around the money.

"*Arigato.*" The innkeeper bowed repeatedly. "*Domo arigato!*"

It was amazing how much the man resembled Sakai's father.

The ride back to Sapporo gave Sakai time to think. After all, he was Japanese in mind and body and in his soul was ingrained the pride and sense of family adhesiveness and honor that had been inbred in his people for almost ten thousand years; from the time around 8000 B.C. when his earliest ancestors had worked with their primitive stone axes and knives in the Kanto plain around what was now Tokyo, to the present day when the year 2000 was less than a decade away. Even though a native-born American, Sakai would always remember the overwhelming sense of belonging that came over him when, assigned to the American Embassy, he first set foot on the land of his ancestors. Only a few days later, unexplainable tears bled down his cheeks as he first viewed Fuji-san, the soul of Nippon. That same feeling had returned on this visit while the embassy car was driving him from the Narita airport. And again, the view of Fuji-san from Lieutenant Nakai's Tokyo office window awakened in him a yearning he could not even explain to himself. It had not been just déjà vu.

Perhaps it was not so strange. His genes would always be thousands-of-years-old pure Japanese genes, and he had to wonder if those genes could affect his beliefs and actions even though he might not be consciously aware of their influence. If so, only his children, their blood and flesh diluted by those of Alicia, would begin to evolve out of the Japanese mold. Then their children, his grandchildren, would most probably be further mixed with some other culture, and finally, perhaps even as soon as the appearance of his great-grandchildren, the soul of Sakai would be gone.

But for the moment, his soul was akin to the soul of Genda and he could understand the anguish and even the hate of the old man for the people who had cost him so much. And Sakai intended to use that inherent insight to anticipate the thoughts of Genda. All he needed was to regain contact. And if his premonitions were correct, there would be another incident.

Chapter 10

Colonel Bob Taylor, USAFR, sighed with relief. The seven-and-a-half-hour flight from San Francisco was down to the last seven miles. Not that the flight time was that much different from his usual experience, it was just that the gigantic Lockheed C-5 logistic transport was not the easy-riding mount to which he was accustomed. In his civilian capacity as the captain of a Northwest Airlines Boeing 747, he regularly flew the San Francisco–Tokyo route and the procedures were as familiar to him as the deep lines that etched his cheeks and tried to give his brow a look of concentration much deeper than was his norm. But his Air Force Reserve crew did not pamper him quite as much as the Northwest flight attendants. Still, the monthly stint of active duty was a welcome change from the routine chauffeuring of four hundred chattering and demanding tourists and businesspersons across the broad Pacific. In the big belly of the C-5, 200,000 pounds of inanimate objects rode silently and uncomplainingly, lashed to the cargo deck by a strong spiderweb of nylon strapping, and in the upper aft passenger compartment a smattering of men and women were raising their seat backs and checking their seat belts in anticipation of their Tokyo arrival. Most were service personnel returning from leave or reporting for Japanese duty; a few were DOD personnel on official business; the rest were military retirees and their wives bumming their way across the pond.

Taylor downed the last dregs of his cold coffee and handed the empty cup back to the flight engineer. Dead ahead, stretched out like a long white welcome mat, was the duty runway of the international airport at Narita, thirty-seven miles northeast of Tokyo.

"Cleared to land," his copilot reported, parroting the Nakita tower operator's latest transmission.

"Gear down." Taylor backed up his order with a thumb-down hand motion.

His copilot grabbed the gear handle. "Comin' down." Even those back in the passenger compartment felt the soft vibration of the great doors on the bottom of the C-5 as they swung open. From within the recesses of the bomb bay–sized wheel wells, four giant axle assemblies, each with six mammoth wheels and wide, low-profile tires, began their articulated journey to their down-and-locked position. Simultaneously, from under the bulbous nose of the Galaxy, a smaller but still sizable four-wheeled assembly swung down and locked into position.

Taylor adjusted his elevator trim tab as the three green gear-down lights announced all was in order with the twenty-eight-wheel ensemble now hanging locked below his airplane.

On each side of the runway ahead, a few yards beyond the runway threshhold, the green visual glide path lights confirmed that he was on the proper descent path.

The copilot gave Taylor a thumbs-up. "Landing checklist complete."

Taylor drove the gigantic military transport down the invisible glide path with all of the nonchalant professionalism ingrained within the thirty-five-year career aviator, confident in his ability to gently place 597,000 pounds of aluminum and human flesh on the long concrete strip with less impact than the average Honda driver experienced turning into his own driveway.

The sudden black blur that flashed upward directly in front of him was a complete surprise.

"What the hell was that?" His mouth remained open after he spoke.

An instant later, an unseen explosion above the C-5 caused him to instinctively push forward on the control column. The Galaxy dropped rapidly.

The copilot was already on the tower circuit. "Narita Tower, Air Force two-five-one, two miles out. We just observed what appeared to be a missile pass in front of us and am executing an emergency descent. The object exploded above us."

"Are you declaring an emergency, two-five-one?"

The copilot took his cue from the negative shake of Taylor's head. "Negative emergency. We are clear of the area, one mile from touchdown."

Nakita Tower was taking no chances. "Roger, two-five-one, cleared for immediate landing. We're holding all other traffic and we have emergency equipment alerted. Are you reporting any damage?"

"Negative, Nakita."

Taylor drug the Galaxy across the end of the runway and let it settle just beyond the numbers. Thick puffs of white smoke erupted at the touch of the tires with the concrete and the massive logistic carrier rolled down the runway with three bright yellow fire trucks and a covey of small red-and-white vehicles chasing it. They continued following the C-5 as it wallowed onto the taxiway.

Taylor pulled off his headset and ran a hand through his sweat-soaked hair. "Hell, for a moment there I thought I was back in 'Nam. Did you get a look at that thing?"

"It was too fast for me. Wasn't very large, that's for sure, just a black streak. You really think someone was firing something at us?" asked the copilot.

"You bet your sweet ass I do." Replacing his headset, Taylor angrily repeated his assessment to the airport authorities. "Tower, some son of a bitch fired a missile at us. What's going on?"

"We have personnel proceeding to the area, two-five-one. Follow the taxi vehicle ahead. We will park you in a secure area." The monotone of the tower's reply irritated Taylor even further. As his copilot rogered the tower's instruction, Taylor looked back down his approach path. *Someone* was back out there somewhere and probably all pissed off that they had failed to bag a mighty big bird. "Bastards," he muttered.

. . .

"You missed!" Toshio Goto was almost as angry as Colonel Taylor as he and Michio Ohiro raced toward the waiting Nissan Pathfinder. Ohiro slung his Dragon launcher in the open rear and dove in behind it. Goto leaped into the front seat as Taeko floored the accelerator and the small hybrid truck spun and slid its way across the slick grass.

"Watch it!" Goto yelled as Taeko momentarily lost control and then regained sufficient traction to steer toward a break in the high wire fence ahead.

"Ayyyy!" Taeko's exclamation was both relief that she had regained control of the vehicle and alarm as the gap in the fence was filled with a pair of black-and-white police cars, one at less than a car's length behind the other, their red lights flashing and sirens wailing.

"Turn around!" Ohiro ordered.

Taeko spun the steering wheel. The Pathfinder swapped ends and she gunned it toward the far end of the field, driving with a fury that surprised both Ohiro and Goto.

"Head for that housing area!"

Taeko kept the engine roaring at maximum power as they bounced and careened across the rough terrain. Misjudging her speed, she applied her brakes a moment too late and the Pathfinder turned sideways and slid hard into the chain link fence. Goto and Ohiro leaped from the truck. Goto slung the Dragon launcher over the fence and clawed his way up the heavy wire. Ohiro was already dropping over the other side. Taeko tried to follow but her body would not respond to the urging of her brain. After a few moments, she could hear excited voices approaching and then several pairs of hands reached inside the truck and jerked her from behind the steering wheel. Everything faded to black.

George Sakai and Charlie Porter watched the special report on the embassy television set.

The Japanese TV reporter, obviously inspired by his impression of American journalists, almost struck Bob Taylor on the chin with the microphone as he aggressively edged out his competitors and shouted his question in heavily accented English. "When did you first see missile, Colonel Tayror?"

"We were about six miles out on final and had just lowered our landing gear. It just erupted right in front of us. How it missed, I'll never know."

"Was aircraft damaged?"

"We didn't think so at the time, although we did feel the force of the explosion. The airplane flew fine. But once we got on the ground and took a walkaround there were a couple bad wrinkles in our horizontal stabilizer. The thing must have gone off right above us as we passed underneath. Everyone was already strapped in for landing so there were no injuries."

Porter reached over and turned the volume down. "You thinking what I'm thinking?"

"I don't know. Would Genda go this far?"

"You know the old bastard better than I."

"Well, it was a military target. They could have taken a shot at a civilian transport. Or maybe it was just a target of opportunity," Sakai speculated. "Could be coincidental—some other group."

"You don't want to believe it was Genda, do you?"

Sakai shrugged. "No, I don't want to. I admit the old man has a possible profile for something like this. But he's military. I would expect him to go after a combatant airplane or a base, not a C-5 with passengers. I don't like to think of him as a terrorist."

"The airplane carried military cargo. Shit, it's a military target. Besides, what was the car-bombing but an act of terrorism?"

"We don't know for sure that he was in on that."

"Bullshit. I think he's gone over the edge."

"Wonder what kind of missile it was."

"Not too fucking sophisticated if they missed a C-5 at a thousand feet."

The door to Porter's office swung open and Ambassador Oroku stuck in his head. "They've got one of them—a girl. I've requested representation. You've got it, Chuck, and take Sakai with you. They're taking the girl to headquarters, Chiyoda ward."

"What was it, sir?" Sakai asked.

"Something wire-guided. They found the wire and some propellant debris. The wire apparently broke short of the aircraft's altitude and the missile was free-flying."

Porter cast his eyes upward. "Thank God for small favors. We're on our way, Mr. Ambassador."

The drive across central Tokyo to the police headquarters of the Chiyoda ward took only ten minutes, and Sakai was impressed by the uniformed driver, who seemed reluctant to admit that the car was equipped with brakes and kept a steady pressure on the horn although the high-pitched beeping was completely overshadowed by the loud undulating wail of the baritone siren. The other drivers seemed to accept the police car's approach as some sort of challenge to be met with increased speed and a noticeable propensity for absolute failure to give way. The police driver, on the other hand, was equally determined that he would have the right of way even if it meant a suicidal refusal to give any quarter to his fellow motorists. Fortunately, his bluffing tactics were infallible, perhaps because in the long run a collision would invariably result in the civilian car's being charged with the responsibility for the accident. The Tokyo drivers might seem to be obsessed with a death wish but they were not quite that crazy.

Porter and Sakai identified themselves and were led to a small observation room where they were able to observe the interrogation through a one-way mirror. Two detectives were in the middle of questioning a young-woman. Her black hair was clipped short, almost in a bob, and she had a body that would drive a monk to self-abuse. Both her black blouse and matching skirt were dangerously overstressed as she sat on a straight-backed chair.

Their escort identified the suspect. "Taeko Nikahura. She was driving the getaway car. We have been talking to her for about ten minutes."

"What do we know so far?" Sakai asked.

"She is from Nagoya but has no permanent Tokyo address. Claims to be a drifter. Has a mother still in Nagoya. No other relatives. Twenty-three years old. Supports herself by odd jobs, probably prostitution."

The younger of two detectives upended the girl's tummy purse and ran his fingers among the contents. Keys, makeup, pen, earrings, a few coins, and several bills. He searched in the purse and pulled an envelope from an inside pocket. After glancing at the address, he handed it to his partner. The older man pulled out the single letter sheet and scanned it. He was almost fatherly in the way he asked the question. "Is this your mother's address?"

"Yes."

"Why did you fire the missile?" asked the younger man.

The girl met the sudden change of subject matter without any visible change in her expression. "I do not know anything about any missile." Then she turned angrily toward the older man. "What is this? I am the injured party here."

"You were with the men who fired the missile. Is that not true?" The older detective's voice had abruptly lost its fatherly tone.

"I told you, I do not know anything about any missile. I was being attacked."

The older man was careful not to let his expression betray his skepticism at the girl's answer. "The two men that ran from your car—they fired the missile."

"They could not have. They were too busy trying to rip my clothes off when the police cars interrupted them."

"Your clothes are not torn."

"I was fighting them."

Showing some slight exasperation, the younger detective insisted, "You *were* in the field with them."

"Not by choice. They commandeered my car and forced me to drive to the field."

"The car is registered to Tanaka Taro. Why were you driving it?"

"He is my friend and I borrowed the car to run some errands."

Behind the mirror, Sakai watched the girl respond to the questions. "She is one cool young lady. Those two have their work cut out for them."

Porter chuckled. "She had her story all ready, that's for sure."

The older man sat down opposite the girl. "Where were you when the men, as you say, commandeered you and the car?"

"In Tokyo on Sakurada-Dori. I was leaving the Konpira shrine after burning prayer sticks for the peace of my father's soul."

The older man lit a cigarette and blew a thin stream of gray smoke into the air. "You expect us to believe such a thing? That you were taken captive and forced to drive fifty-six kilometers to the field south of Narita Airport and yet you did not observe that they had with them a missile-launching device and a missile? A blind woman does not drive an automobile!"

"They wanted me to have sex with them!"

"In the middle of the day in clear view of a housing area?"

"Yes."

The older detective sighed, asking the next question with a complete lack of enthusiasm. "Did you have sex with them?"

"No; the police arrived in time to save me."

"Then your virtue is intact." The younger detective let his raised eyebrows provide the sarcasm to his statement.

Taeko smiled sweetly at the man and nodded her head. "May I have one of your cigarettes? I am quite nervous."

"I bet she is," the police escort commented to Porter and Sakai.

"She's lying through her teeth," Sakai said.

Porter agreed. "It's a good story if she sticks with it. Anything in the car to counter her story?"

Their escort shook his head. "Nothing, but the registered owner is either an alias or there is a mistake in the address. It is a sushi bar just off the Ginza and there is no Tanaka Taro known there."

"Figures."

The younger detective had left the interrogation room and now joined the three men in the small observation annex. As he introduced himself, he presented his card, "Jiroh Kaneyama." Tall and slim by Japanese standards, Kaneyama had the easy bearing of a play-for-fun second baseman with long arms and relaxed dangling hands that were naturals for making double plays. His hair had probably never been combed.

"How long can you hold her?" Porter asked.

"As long as we wish. Our system is a bit different from yours. This is a matter for the district court and the prosecutor has considerable flexibility in how he wishes to handle the case."

"Have you charged her yet?"

Kaneyama smiled. "With what? Defending her honor?"

"You know she is as guilty as sin," Sakai declared.

Kaneyama's smile remained. "Ah, so, but perhaps the Japanese and American definitions of sin are a bit different."

"What is that supposed to mean?"

"Certainly, we know she is the driver of the car that carried two men away from our police cars which were in hot pursuit—to use an American term—but she claims they threatened to kill her if she did not make a maximum effort to escape the police."

"Which she certainly did."

Kaneyama threw up his hands in frustration.

The interrogation was still proceeding. "Did you see anyone else in the field?" the older detective asked.

"No."

"And you saw no one fire a ground-to-air missile?"

"No."

"Were you aware of the air traffic passing directly over the field?"

"No. I was only aware that I was going to be raped."

Sakai turned to Kaneyama. "Do you think the prosecutor and the court could be persuaded to let her go?"

Kaneyama nodded. "I have been pondering the same question. She has a good story and we have little to counter it except circumstantial evidence. We are canvassing the housing area for possible witnesses but have nothing as yet. There is no doubt in my mind that she and the two men fired the missile, but unless we come up with an eyewitness, the court may believe her story. If we had your jury system, we might have a stronger case. But there is a good chance she will eventually be released if she can stick to her story."

"So, we buy her story—and let her lead us to the others," Porter concluded.

"Exactly. That would be my recommendation—at the prosecutor's discretion, of course. But I should be able to convince him and the judge who will be trying the case. She is handling herself well, but I do not believe that she is a very smart woman. This has all been rehearsed. I think her story was canned before they ever drove into the field. If we had caught all three, the men could have collaborated her excuse and the prosecutor might have a difficult case. She could even drop the charges once the rape offense was accepted. In any case, they would all probably be released and disappear. I would rather go after the leaders or the organization behind this."

A faint wrinkle formed on Porter's brow. "One thing bothers me. They *were* out in an open field in plain view. Does that make sense? They were sure to be spotted."

"You forget," Kaneyama replied, "that if they had hit the aircraft, the explosion and crash would have overshadowed any activity in the field—or anywhere else for that matter. All eyes would have been on the disaster. Human nature. There is also a more sinister aspect to this. They acquired the missile somewhere. Who supplied it? How did it get here in Japan? Are there more? I should tell you also that we know she is Red Army."

"She admitted that?" Sakai asked.

"She did not have to. She was strip-searched. On the inside of her left thigh is a one-inch butterfly tattoo. It is their mark. They place it on their women. They like to think they are as hard to catch as a butterfly as long as they keep moving."

"But why have they resurfaced now?" Porter wondered aloud.

Sakai sat silent, rerunning the girl's testimony through his head. At the same time, he was puzzling over Genda's abrupt departure from his home on Hokkaido. If he accepted the premise that Genda was connected to the car-bombing then he should not overlook the possibility that the old warrior was involved in the attempt on the C-5. Perhaps it was time to bring that aspect up with Kaneyama. Porter seemed to be reading Sakai's thoughts and gave a slight shake of his head. To him, it was not quite time to mention Genda. It appeared that the United States was the sole target of the attacks, not the Japanese. Thus, it might not be the best course of action to have the Japanese authorities catch those responsible before the reason—and force—behind the actions of the terrorists were known.

The other detective having left the room, the girl deliberately swung around to face the mirror and hiked her skirt in defiance at the unknown observers she knew were behind the glass. If they wanted a show, she could give them one. But her performance was interrupted by a uniformed matron who appeared and led her from the room.

Porter spoke over his shoulder to Kaneyama. "Will you let us know what you decide?"

"Certainly. I have your number at the embassy."

Sakai and Porter sat silent during the ride back across the city.

Only when they were within the embassy walls did they try to decide upon the next course of action.

"What's the next play, boss?" Sakai asked.

"I'm going to talk to the ambassador and get him to use what influence he can to get the girl released. I think our only chance is to have the Japanese put a tail on her, or better still, let us run the tail, and try for the biggies. Shit, she's in on it all, but I doubt that, even if she were willing to talk, she would know enough for us to close in on the others."

"You think they would let us in on the action to that extent?"

"You, they would. You slant-eyes all look alike—you'd blend right in. There would be no evidence of any obvious American interference in their affairs. They are touchy about that. But you're Japanese in everything but citizenship. A big plus. They won't let you go off by yourself. You'll have a partner or at least a tail. But you're the most recent contact with Genda. That may be a factor. I'd like to present it to the ambassador. Any objections?"

"No. In fact, I'd like to be in on the apprehension of Genda. I do have a personal situation, however."

"What's that?"

"My ex-wife. She's off to Australia with my kids. I'm not sure she's coming back."

"She the woman at the Hilton?"

Sakai should have known. Porter would have routinely put surveillance on him. The spooks liked to cover all angles. "I'm not sure I like that."

"Hey, nothing personal. Standard ops, George. That, you know."

"You bastards didn't have anything in the room?"

"No. We just checked out the identity. No bedsprings audio. We have some vestiges of decency left."

"I doubt it."

Porter laughed. "Shit, it's been a long day. I'll buy the drinks—as long as it isn't sake."

"You're damned right you'll buy."

Fifteen minutes later they were seated in the lounge of the Tokyo Fairmont, sipping scotches.

"Lighten up. George. You look like you're carrying the weight of all the sins of mankind on your shoulders."

Sakai forced a smile. "I just don't like the idea that somewhere out there Genda may be deciding what his next move will be."

"Hey, we still haven't made the connection, remember?"

"True. You know, I really didn't think he could be in on it until I went back and his cottage was boarded up. After all, he invited me back—but that was probably just a courtesy."

Porter signaled the waiter for another round.

"I'll tell you something, Charlie, I was real excited when my boss sprung me out of the office to help on this thing. The timing wasn't so hot—the situation with Alicia being what it is—but I needed to get out in the field. That cubbyhole back in D.C. was getting to me. I was getting lazy. But now that I'm here and being jerked around by circumstances, this is bigger than I anticipated."

"Well, Sakai-san, old man, maybe we need to fall back and regroup. Why don't we take the rest of the night off and go get laid? I'm real close to a couple of embassy round-eyes who like to party."

"No thanks, Charlie. I need to sort some things out. You go ahead."

"You sure? I can promise you a night that will be all italics when you write your memoirs. A little lighthearted fucking can do wonders for the blahs."

"No, really. You go ahead."

Charlie Porter downed the rest of his drink. "I'll leave a number with the duty officer if you need me."

"Have fun."

"Indubitably, George, indubitably."

A four-man combo from Kyoto was rendering a very good big band imitation of "Stardust," their two synthesizers creating an entire orchestra backup for the lead horns played by the other two. Sakai sipped his scotch, unable to shake off a feeling of impending disaster.

Chapter II

Once more Saburo Genda was beside himself with anger and disappointment. "We paid two million yen for a defective missile? I will not stand for this! That's two failures in a row! I want the other one checked out thoroughly."

Goto was uncomfortable being on the defensive. "For two missiles. I bargained for *two*. Besides, we are not armament specialists."

Genda's eyebrows slid quickly upward. "Ohiro, you were military. Do not tell me you know nothing about weapons."

"I am not a technician."

"Ah so! But you said the weapon would work!" Genda's early misgivings had come back to haunt him, and he did not like the feeling.

"It *will* work," Goto retorted. "In this instance, the guidance wire broke short of the airplane's altitude. Ohiro had the C-5 in his sights and the missile was running true. When he lost guidance, the missile swerved ahead of the airplane and exploded above it. It is that simple."

Genda shook his head. "The Dragon was never intended to track a fast-moving target. I am not sure it is the weapon we need."

"It is the only weapon we have—and it *will* work."

Genda was not appeased, but Goto's point was certainly correct. Since time was such a critical factor with respect to his health, they might as well use the remaining missile. But it must be thoroughly checked. "The next one *must* work. And you will go with the others to insure it."

"We will do what we can, Genda-san. I will personally check the entire length of the wire."

"Good. Now, there is a more urgent problem. Taeko. We must get her free from the police before she tells anything."

Goto waved a hand in protest. "We have no control over that situation at the present time. Despite her youth, she is a strong woman and her cover story is good. There is no physical evidence to identify us. Nothing was left in the car and we escaped with the launcher. They will have to let her go."

"I am not that confident. Someone has to talk to her."

Ohiro did not appreciate the tone in Genda's words. "What do you mean?"

"I mean that she must be fully aware of what will happen to her if she betrays us. If they work on her long enough, she may very well break. It is the nature of a woman. But our threat may be just the added incentive to keep her strong."

"We are not in medieval Nippon, Genda-san. The police do not torture prisoners." Ohiro knew that Genda had every intention of killing Taeko if in his mind that was necessary. Ohiro's obsession with the girl was primarily physical, but he would raise a strong objection if it came to that.

Genda ignored his comment. "You will go to the Chiyoda ward station. Say that you are her older brother. Talk to her. If they refuse her visitors, that will mean they still maintain a strong suspicion of her role in the attack."

"I am a JMSDF deserter. My face has been circulated all over this land. I cannot march in and present myself for arrest. That is what I will be doing."

Genda knew that Ohiro was right. His anger had generated that proposal, not his logic. "Then, I will go."

"Do you think it wise?" Goto asked.

"The police have no reason to suspect me of anything."

Ohiro was not so sure. "What about the nisei that visited you— from the United States State Department?"

"A routine investigation. I gained his confidence in a matter of minutes."

Goto continued to protest. "I am against this. Even if you are allowed to talk to Taeko, the conversation can be monitored. What can you say to her that will change things? Either we have her thoroughly indoctrinated or we do not. Your visit will be after the fact."

Genda wanted to continue the discussion but Goto was making sense, as much as Genda hated to admit it. "I do not like sitting and doing nothing." He turned to Goto. "Could the police have seen your face?"

"No, Genda-san. We were over the fence while they were still seventy meters away. But they have a file on me—with photographs."

"Then Sakamoki must be the one to regain contact with Taeko." Anticipating further protest from Ohiro, Genda hurriedly continued. "All right. We will take no action against the girl but she must be contacted and told of our concern. While in custody if necessary. We will wait overnight. Nobuo, you will set up surveillance of the Chiyoda station. Be very careful and discreet. If Taeko is released, you will contact her, go to a safe place, and get word to us. We will give instructions. From this moment on, if she is released, we must assume she will be used to find us. The police know she did not act alone and that there are at least two others."

"What if she is not released?" Nobuo Sakamoki asked.

"Then, we will proceed without her."

"*Hai*, Genda-san."

"Finally, we have one other problem. We cannot return to Narita for our next attack. Ohiro-san, you will find us another target location."

Ohiro was pleased that Genda addressed him with respect for the first time.

"The only prerequisite is that it must be an airport where American military aircraft operate. The weapon may stay where it is for the moment—and check the wire."

"*Hai.*"

"I will sanitize this place so there will be no trace of our presence. Meanwhile, Nobuo will take up his surveillance. Have our target location for us by this evening, Ohiro-san. Go to the library at Hibaya Park and ask the reference person for the *International*

Airline Guide, the English version. Write the target airport in the lower left-hand corner of the inside of the back cover. This will enable me to establish a new base of operations. Now, we will all go about our appointed tasks and meet four days from now at Ueno Park, at the Saiyokan restaurant. I have been there often and we will have privacy for our dinner at the hour of seven. When you arrive, inform the hostess you are to join Captain Genda. In the interim, any messages may be left for me at this number." Genda handed out small cards.

Genda remained seated while the others rose and took their leave. He was very tired. The death disease in his veins was strengthening and his final plan was still incomplete. True, they would strike the Americans, but vengeance called for more than just random attacks. Such moves would generate little sympathy for his cause. There must be some identifiable significance, some tie-in with the psychological injuries he had suffered during the final days of the war. And the final blow must be of such magnitude that the world would take notice of Captain Saburo Genda—no, the world must take notice of Flight Petty Officer Genda of the Imperial Japanese Navy. That would be the proper way for a samurai to die.

What was the date? November tenth. If his physician had been right, another month would be all that was left for a life with any strength.

Genda lay back on the *futon*. Life had been so much more simple for Flight Petty Officer Genda. Everything was black and white in those days. You served your Emperor. You died for your Emperor. He recalled the celebrations when the news of the successful attack on Pearl Harbor had been announced and his determination at that moment to join the fight when he was of age. Even in the futile closing days of the war, it had been the best time of his life.

His eyes were heavy with fatigue. His stamina was being eroded rapidly by the curse that flowed through every part of his body.

There was no hurry to sanitize the room. He could rest for a short while. His consciousness faded, and from the deep recesses of his memory a dark-blue Hellcat hurled down from its advantageous position up-sun.

Genda caught a glimpse of reflection and immediately pulled his Zero into a vertical bank and stomped on the top rudder. The fighter slipped violently downward and the Hellcat, taking its lead from the direction that the Zero's nose was pointing, loosened the fury of its six wing guns. But the Zero was not going in that direction, and the fire missed Genda by yards. As the Hellcat flashed by, Genda reversed his bank and swooped after the diving American. But the American had too much lead on him, and as the Zero's airspeed passed 240 knots, Genda felt his ailerons stiffen. His one advantage, maneuverability, was now lost, and he knew that at around 330 knots he would begin to experience wing buffeting. The engineers had placed too thin an aluminum skin on the wings of the Zero in the interest of saving weight. He would dare not let his speed build any faster. The Hellcat was easily passing 400 knots and pulling away. Genda was helpless as the Hellcat outdived the Zero and used its superior speed to zoom high for another position of altitude advantage.

Genda climbed as well as he could and waited. The Hellcat swept down for another pass, but Genda pulled sharply upward and turned toward the Hellcat. There was not an aerial fighter built that could turn inside a dash-two Zero. The American tried, but was sucked to the outside, and Genda knew that if he could hold the Hellcat during two complete horizontal circles, he could reverse positions with the Hellcat and become the attacker. But the American knew that also, and after some three hundred degrees of turn nosed down and opened the distance between them. Genda once more followed, his engine screaming at full power, but again the Zero entered the high-speed range where it was ineffective. Still, the excitement of the engagement carried Genda to the peak of his alertness and skill. This was not like his first fight, where the pair of Hellcats had made short issue of him. This was a one-on-one encounter. He knew he lacked experience but aggressiveness could make up for some of that. He would just have to keep the words of his instructors uppermost in his tactics. *Never, never, try to outdive or outclimb the American fighters. The Hellcat and Corsair are much more powerful and more heavily armored. Remember the tactics of the samurai when encountering a larger opponent. Parry and thrust, dart in and turn away. Dance around your foe, do not stand toe to toe with him. His arm is longer and his sword heavier.*

The Hellcat was pulling powerfully up into a wide loop. That, Genda could counter. He pulled up inside the Hellcat, still too far away for effective fire, however. But on the downside of the loop, he would close the distance! Whoops! There was no downside. The

American simply turned his loop into an Immelmann maneuver and rolled out on top of his vertical circle.

Genda rolled level also and paralleled the Hellcat's course, directly below but with more than a thousand-foot altitude disadvantage.

The American had apparently lost sight of the Zero and started a series of steep banks. Genda could imagine the American straining to look back over his shoulder, searching for the Zero. To make the American's job harder, Genda attempted to match the Hellcat's weave.

The American was good. Unable to see Genda directly below him, he simply rolled over on his back. Now, Genda was in plain view, and the Hellcat's nose pulled through and roared right at the Zero. Genda had been suckered. A head-to-head encounter was no contest, the lightly armored Zero no match for the Hellcat's superior armor and concentration of firepower. Genda pulled up to shorten the Hellcat's firing opportunity and waited until the last possible moment before once more stomping left rudder and using aileron to keep the Zero from rolling and giving away his tactic. His cross-control maneuver again slid him sideways and the six streams of fifty-caliber steel walked along only one wingtip instead of pouring into Genda's engine and forward fuselage. The two aircraft passed within a dozen yards of each other, the Hellcat at 400 knots straight down and the Zero staggering nose-high at less than 70. Genda used the hammerhead stall to reverse his direction, but the Hellcat was long gone. Genda continued his dive but could not regain visual contact. The Hellcat should have had him on that pass, but it didn't. Genda was straining at his cockpit straps, every muscle in his body rigid with anticipation of a kill. They were equals, the American and he.

Rolling the Zero once more into a vertical bank, he began a tight circle. As his nose came around toward the sun, he held up his left hand and covered the brilliant orange marble with his thumb. Immediately, he saw the black nose-on profile of the Hellcat diving once again! Even though hampered by the altitude disadvantage, he must not allow the American to get a proper lead.

The Hellcat was almost within firing range. Genda waited one more agonizing second, then pulled the Zero into a high-speed stall while holding top rudder. The Zero rolled violently over the top of its tight circular path, reversing direction. Genda allowed the horizontal spin to continue through a full turn, then broke the stall with a sharp forward stick movement. The desperate maneuver had thrown off the American's initial volley, but now Genda felt his rudder pedals jerk as streams of fifty-caliber rounds pounded into his empennage. Fortunately, the American closed too rapidly and roared back and behind Genda. That was what the Japanese wanted. Now, there was no way the American could pull sharply enough to get his nose ahead of Genda's, and without that aspect, he had no firing solution. Genda tightened the turn until the Zero fairly groaned with agony at the g-force thrust upon it. Looking back over his inside shoulder, Genda could see the Hellcat being forced farther and farther toward the outside of the turn.

Why didn't the American break it off? Another complete circle and Genda would be closing into firing position. Already the two snarling antagonists were on opposite sides of the circle. Genda saw the Hellcat's flaps drop from the trailing edge of its wing. The American was determined to turn inside the Zero. Genda already had his flaps partially down; it took him only a second to lower them all of the way. He turned even tighter, flew even slower.

The Hellcat shuddered and started to stall, but the American relaxed some of his back pressure and flew out of the near-catastrophic situation. Genda cursed! If the American had lost control, before he could have recovered, Genda would have had him. Instead, the American did the smart thing. He rolled over on his back and dove for the water.

"Come back!" Genda shouted. "Come back!" Eagerly, he kept the Zero on one wing and searched the sky below and around him, keeping a minimum of 150 knots airspeed. From such a turn, the Zero could enter any combat maneuver, its slow-speed capability giving it a definite edge over the American fighters. But there was no sign of the dark-blue Hellcat. The American had broken off the engagement.

A drip of phlegm down his throat caused Genda to cough and brought back his conscious thoughts. It was all a daydream! A wonderful, satisfying intrusion of his subconscious, bringing back his last combat mission.

If only he could say some magic words or drink a secret potion that would take him back to the heady days of the early forties. But that was impossible. Maybe he was being foolish in trying to relive them, even in his dreams. Yet, those were such glorious days. And it was a great comfort to lie there and relive them, to imagine himself once more wearing the headband of a samurai and, though hopelessly outnumbered, carrying the fight to the enemy with boldness and— In an instant, it came to him! The realization of how he would accomplish his final act! The thought was so unexpectedly powerful he sat bolt upright on the *futon*! No need to abandon his dream! In but a speck of time, an ingenious and most daring plan had burst forth from his mind, a perfect melding of his past experiences and the results of the past weeks with Goto and his people. No, there was no reason at all now to abandon his hopes! None at all!

But first, he would meet with Goto and Ohiro and Sakamoki and perhaps the woman, Taeko, as planned and they would carry out their next action. The car-bombing had been a mistake; it never had any possibility of furthering his goal. The downing of an American military aircraft would be more appropriate, but only the second act of his grand scheme. Now, he knew exactly what they would do for a finale!

Nobuo Sakamoki looked through the wire mesh at Taeko Nikahura. Unknown to either of them, a small microphone imbedded in the counter was carrying their conversation via a small wire into an anteroom where Detective Jiroh Kaneyama was monitoring their conversation. The two terrorists were not stupid, however, and kept up the facade initially introduced by Taeko during her interrogation.

"Who were the men?" Sakamoki asked, feigning ignorance.

"I don't know, Nobuo. They jumped in the car and forced me to drive to Nakita."

"Why are the police holding you? You have done nothing."

"There was an attempt to shoot down an American airplane from the same field. The police think the men did it."

The microphone could not pick up the slight twinkle in the eyes of Taeko and Sakamoki as they carried out their charade.

"Then, they cannot hold you, Taeko. You are innocent. They should be trying to catch the men who attacked you. Perhaps, if I talked to them."

"If I cannot convince them, how can you?"

"I am your friend. I can testify as to your character."

Taeko shook her head. "No, it would do no good. Just inform my mother in Nagoya and tell her I am all right."

"I will do that, Taeko. And I will come and visit you tomorrow. By then, perhaps this nightmare will pass."

"Come tomorrow, Nobuo. Do not abandon me."

"I will, I promise."

In the listening room, Kaneyama took off his earphones. The two were play-acting quite well. The young man, Sakamoki, could very well be one of the group. On the other hand, the detective had to admit, there was a possibility he was as he said, a friend of Nikahura's. If so, the visit had revealed nothing. Still, Sakamoki's picture was now on file, his countenance having been recorded routinely by the camera in the visiting room. Kaneyama would run it through a routine check, as he would do with the fingerprints that were splattered all over the counter that had separated the two. Something could turn up.

Michio Ohiro had the taxi drop him at the southeast corner of Hibaya Park. He walked northwest on Uchi Sawai-cho past the T-shaped Hibaya Hall. Ahead, just beyond the park boundaries, were most of the government ministry buildings, but he would stop short of those. Turning right, he walked up the steps to the library that sat on the edge of the park just opposite the Nippon Press Center and proceeded directly to the reference section.

"May I see the *International Airlines Guide*? The English copy?"

The young woman apparently considered his request routine. After the customary bow of respect, she selected the thick volume from a full shelf behind her desk and handed it to him.

"*Arigato.*" Ohiro took a seat at a nearby table.

It took only a moment to find a suitable airfield. Following Genda's instructions, he wrote down the name of the airport in the lower left corner of the inside back cover: Itami International Airport, Osaka. It would be perfect. Before he returned the book, he also thumbed to another page, and after studying the schedule for a few minutes made a personal note, which he folded and stuck into his card case. He had not forgotten the humiliation Genda had handed him at their initial meeting. The old man needed to be taught a lesson.

. . .

Detective Kaneyama dialed the number of the American Embassy and asked for George Sakai.

Sakai recognized Kaneyama's voice. "Hello, Jiroh."

"Sakai-san, I think we are going to let her go."

"The prosecutor agrees?"

"With reservations. However, the district judge feels we do not have enough evidence, witnesses, or testimony to make a strong case. Since the aircraft was not downed, and really not damaged seriously, the consensus is to let Nikahura go, put a tail on her, and hope for a break. The argument I used with the prosecutor is that if we keep her, the terrorists might go ahead with another attack. At least, this way we have something to work on."

"I agree."

"The final decision will be the prosecutor's but I know him well. He will come around. He knows he has a weak case."

"I would like the tail."

"All right. You and I, Sakai-san. I will inform you when the decision is made."

"I will be here or at the Fairmont."

"We might make a good team. I've never worked with a *gaijin* before."

Sakai smiled at the good-natured reference to him as a foreigner. "Nor I with a Godzilla fan."

"How did you know that? In the closet at my home, I have a Godzilla tie!"

"Do not wear it, Jiroh."

"*Hai*, Sakai-san," Kaneyama replied in his best gutteral voice. "I will wear paisley like you Americans." Laughing, he hung up the phone. George Sakai should be convinced to stay in Japan. He would be a valuable asset to the Tokyo police force with his American background and Japanese blood. Tokyo was becoming more and more like New York, complete with the *yakuza* thugs and a noticeable increase in drug-related crime. There were some things American that Kaneyama would not like to see Japan adopt. Sakai could provide valuable insight. Kaneyama made a mental note. After this was over, he and the nisei would talk.

The next day, Sakamoki returned to the Chiyoda ward police station. Taeko greeted him with exciting news.

"I am being released! The papers are being signed now by the district judge upon the recommendation of the prosecutor."

"That is as it should be. They should concentrate their efforts on catching your assailants."

Unseen in the listening room, Kaneyama and Sakai waited for the two terrorists to play out the scene.

Kaneyama spoke softly even though they were in a soundproof room. "The girl knows me too well from the interrogation. You will have to do the tail alone, George. Report to me frequently and as soon as you detect a meet, I will join you."

"Sounds good."

Detective Kaneyama handed Sakai a small hand radio. "You can reach me anywhere within Tokyo with this. If they start to leave the city, I will join you. Remember, we want Genda."

"Or whoever is at the bottom of all this."

"It will be the old warrior."

"I keep hoping not. If you could have seen him sitting there outside his cottage on the harsh coast of Hokkaido, so full of dignity and tradition . . ."

"Do not be too easily impressed, George. I smell the foul odor of deceit."

"Perhaps. It is just that I know he was also a man who was once willing to give his life for his country—more than that. He actually was on the way to his death when the war ended. Say what you will, he was once a man of great honor."

"Strange words coming from a *gaijin*, especially an American."

"I just hate to see him end up like this."

"He must have made quite an impression on you."

Sakai looked hard into Kaneyama's eyes. "He did. I am an American and I love my country. But, I'm not one hundred percent *gaijin*—if my parents had not migrated and my nationality matched my blood, I wonder how I would see Genda."

"Just as I do, Sakai-san. A potential mass murderer."

Chapter 12

Genda stood on the highest observation platform of the Tokyo Tower, 795 feet above Shiba Park, on the southern edge of central Tokyo. Around him lay the 831 square miles that made up the Tokyo Prefecture, and below him, driving, walking, working, and living among the multithousands of hovels, homes, and buildings, were over twelve million people. The vast complex of the capital city included twenty-three districts, twenty-six separate cities, seven urban districts, and eight villages.

Tokyo City, itself, was much more definable, and Genda studied the personality and character of the world's great metropolis. To the north of his high vantage point lay the Imperial Palace and the surrounding grounds, a green oasis bordered by the dark waters of a series of man-made moats. One, the Hibija Moat, bordered the park of the same name. He would be meeting Goto and the others at the Saiyokan restaurant near there later on in the early evening.

To the east, and even closer than the palace grounds, was the winding Sumida River, its southern end widened to form the turning basins and piers for the international shipping traffic that made Tokyo its destination. At the moment, Genda could not see a single unoccupied pier, and several large freighters seemed to be anchored back toward the Tokyo Bay entrance, undoubtedly waiting their turn for an offloading berth.

Even closer, to the west and almost at the base of the tower, was the embassy of the Soviet Union. He had never been there, but he knew his name had been known inside the buildings for over thirty years. Just a short distance to the north, less than a thousand yards actually, was the embassy of the United States of America, and he could even see the spot on the street leading to it where the idiot Yasuda had met a slightly untimely death when his car bomb malfunctioned.

This was his first time in the tower. On a whim he had decided to enter it. After all, he owed it to himself to make a visit and take a last look at the city that traced its heritage back to the time it was known as Edo and even as early as 1758 was the largest city in the world, with one million, four hundred thousand people. There were no tall buildings back then and the ward of Chuo-ku, just off to the northeast of where he was standing, had been just another heavily concentrated living area. Now, it enclosed the gaudy Ginza district, which at night was illuminated with a thousand different neon colors, most of them moving or merging or turning on and off in an obscene kaleidoscope of Western-inspired decorative decadence unrivaled in any other city of the world.

It was hard for Genda not to think of Tokyo City as a scab on the wounded body of ancient Nippon. Certainly, when the great feudal lord, Ota Dokan, built the first fortress in 1457 on what was to become the palace grounds, he had no way of foreseeing that his initiative would spawn such a great metropolis. Nor could he have imagined that from his fortress there would expand outwards the greatest concentration of urban living ever to develop. Fortunately, those who followed him had the foresight to set aside areas of natural beauty, from the tiny block gardens only a few yards square to the manicured parks of Hibaya and Yoyogi and Ueno and all the other gardens and shrine grounds.

Genda had no love for Tokyo, but he could not deny it its symbolism as the home of the Emperor—and its practical worth as the seat of the national government. And he remembered the days and nights forty-six years back when the city burned, the result of the American air raids during the closing months of the war. The long-winged B-29s, practically unopposed by what was left of the Japanese air forces, were every-night visitors in those final days.

The flames could even be seen from his air base forty miles south-west of the city, and he and his companions had watched them in silent horror, knowing that thousands of their fellow citizens were dying from the flames and oxygen starvation created by the gigan-tic firestorms. Many more of his countrymen had died in the Tokyo fires than in both the Hiroshima and Nagasaki single bomb attacks, but the awesome atomic attacks were much more promi-nent within Genda's tortured memory.

Somehow, the Americans had spared the Imperial Palace. Genda had never seen *tenno heiko*—Hirohito. Before the war, he would never even have spoken his name. Even now, as he fixed his gaze on the palace grounds, he felt a sense of destiny in his continued service to the late divine one, even though he realized that the palace, indeed the country, could no longer be the same with Akihito now its occupant.

He stayed on the top viewing level for several hours, reviewing his life and at times attempting to meditate. But there was a constant flow of pedestrian traffic and his concentration was too often inter-rupted. For the first time, he found his mental recollections slow to form. It could be the same death disease that was slowing his physi-cal body.

As the afternoon wore on, the blue haze seemed to thin, and finally to the west faintly appeared the perfect cone, Fuji-san, a purple mound of inspiration capped by its perennial white mantle of snow. Generations of Japanese had been stirred by that sacred sight, and Genda bowed in silent reverence as the lowering red sun grew larger and faded to deep orange, finally disappearing with incredible dignity behind the dormant volcano. It would be the last time he would see it so.

Both the owner and number-one hostess of the Saiyokan restaurant greeted Genda warmly and ushered him down the spartan rice-paper-and-polished-wood hall to a private dining room. Sake and a geisha with a lilting samisen were waiting.

The first to join him was Toshio Goto. Genda poured the warm rice wine and handed a full thimble-cup to Goto.

"*Kampai!* Cheers!"

"*Kampai!*"

Genda wanted to express his concern before the others arrived. "Goto-san, we have been together for some days now and I am troubled about the ability of our companions. Sakamoki, for example. He is quite young."

"I consider that an asset, Genda-san. The youthful ones are so full of fervor and have yet to learn of the futility of certain actions. Their ideals have yet to be tarnished. So, we can use them better. Ohiro, on the other hand, has a more realistic view of the situation. Ohiro will not go charging about before making his own evaluation of the matter. In that respect, they compliment one another."

"And the girl, Taeko? I am also uneasy with her. She is Ohiro's mistress but I have seen her deliberately flaunting herself in front of Sakamoki, and even you. If a rivalry would develop, it could destroy our ability to work together."

"She has already proved her worth as far as I am concerned. She held up well under the police interrogation. She is a flirt, yes, but that is just her nature. I have no interest in her. True, Sakamoki is full of masculine juices, but I have seen no signs that he wishes to challenge Ohiro."

"But the stupid mistake in failing to bring down the C-5 bothers me. Could there have been any tension that affected their performance?"

"It was material failure. The weapons we have procured are old. And Ohiro assures me that he has given our second weapon a thorough check and it is ready."

Genda nodded. "Yes, I suppose I am just impatient." He turned and waved the geisha away before unfolding a small piece of paper. He laid it on the table between them. On it were the words "Itami International Airport, Osaka." He had copied them from the notation Ohiro had made in the airline guide.

Goto grunted in approval as he refilled the sake cups.

Genda continued. "This is our next target location. Ohiro tells me that there is a weekly American military cargo jet transit and there is suitable access to the airport perimeter. I have used part of the days since we last met to arrange accommodations at a nearby inn."

Both men looked around as the *fusuma* slid open and Ohiro, Sakamoki, and Taeko entered.

"It is good to see you," Genda said to the girl. "We are very proud of your conduct."

"*Domo arigato*, Genda-san."

"Was there any difficulty?" Genda asked of the young Sakamoki.

"No, Genda-san. Taeko was released three days ago. We stayed at my apartment until now."

"You all came in together." Genda's statement was spoken with some concern.

"We met as you suggested—by prearrangement and only a few hours ago," Ohiro responded.

Genda nodded. "I think we must assume that the authorities did not buy Taeko's story in its entirety. They could be following her—and you."

"We took special precautions. I am certain we were not followed."

Several rooms away, George Sakai and Detective Kaneyama were being ushered into their private dining area. It was near the main entrance as they had requested. They were not close enough to Ohiro's party to hear any conversation, but they could monitor the hall and would know when the three conspirators left. Just before they entered their dining area, Kaneyama flashed his badge and identification to the hostess. "The three who preceded us, two men and a young woman, they are by themselves?"

"They joined another party."

"Who?" Kaneyama asked.

"They joined a Captain Genda and another man." The hostess's unexpected reply caused both men to stop in their tracks.

Bingo!

The hostess was uncomfortable with the questions. She was not accustomed to such an interrogation and answering personal questions ran contrary to her training.

Kaneyama waited until she had left before speaking further. "This certainly links Genda with the terrorists who tried to shoot down the C-5 aircraft."

Sakai had to agree. "I am disappointed."

"It was inevitable after the briefing you and Porter-san gave me."

"So, what do we do now?"

Kaneyama smiled. "We enjoy a good meal. I have instructed the owner to advise me when they are ready to leave. We have identification on four of them now: Genda, the woman Nikahura, the young man Sakamoki, and Ohiro, the deserter. We must get a look at the fifth person. It has to be Toshio Goto. He is Red Army and possibly the leader of the cell. I would like another check made for prints after they leave—in case it is not the same man."

"You do not intend to apprehend them?"

"No. Not yet. My plan is to track their movements for the next few days and let them commit themselves. If need be, we can always pick them up, of course. That is satisfactory to you?"

"Yes. There may be others."

The *fusuma* slid open and a hostess appeared with their beers.

During the meal, Genda kept quiet and the others followed his lead. Only after the hostesses left did he resume the conversation. "Goto-san, you and Sakamoki will retrieve the remaining weapon tonight and proceed by automobile to Osaka. Here is the address. Ohiro-san, you and Taeko will wait twenty-four hours, then proceed by train. I will join you a day later. My plan is that we strike again, then proceed immediately to board the flights indicated in these envelopes. There is one for each of you. Inside are travel tickets, passports, sufficient funds, and new identifications for us all."

"Where are we going?" Ohiro asked.

"You do not need to know that information at this moment. Your airline tickets are in sealed envelopes. They are not to be opened until you are inside the airport terminal. Take only carry-on luggage. This way, if any one of us is apprehended by the police, the person apprehended will not know the destination of the others. I will contact you and give you the information on when and where our next rendezvous will be.

"It is necessary for us to leave Japan to carry out the remainder of my plan. When we down the American aircraft, there will be an immediate manhunt. We must be prepared to move instantly—and we are. We will depart from Osaka."

Goto was not sure that he agreed. "I would think that a better plan would be to go underground in a remote area of Honshu, or perhaps Kyushu, and wait until things cool down. We have contacts who will hide us. The airport seems the least likely place to go. It will be clouded with police."

Genda could not consider such a move. His body would afford him no time to wait. The days were already getting more tiring and he had ample medication for only a few more weeks. "No. There will be confusion and it will take time to set up any type of concentrated search—but you must waste no time, absolutely. There will be an initial period of panic and confusion. The runways will be immediately closed, but there will be no increased terminal surveillance until someone in authority remembers to direct it. As for the airport being the least likely place for us to go, it is the ideal place— for that is the last place they would expect us to be. Which brings me to a very important point. Ohiro, you have provided me with both the arrival time and departure time of our target aircraft. Are the times reliable?"

"Yes, Genda-san. I have personal knowledge of their schedule and I suspect they are habitually on time."

"They had better be, for our escape tickets reflect the schedule you provided me. However, they are based on the requirement that we shoot at a *departing* aircraft. If we hit an aircraft as it approaches the field, it may very well crash on the airport itself. That would close the airport for hours, maybe days. Destroy it as it departs and we know it will go down well outside the airport boundary. And with the volume of traffic the Itami airport handles, they will want to reopen it as soon as possible and that is what we want also. It is a key factor in our escape." Fixing Goto with his eyes, he continued. "Our arrangement, as we agreed in our initial meeting at Takaragawa, was that I will direct our operations. So, you will follow my plan exactly. I will make one provision, however. After our last attack, the one after this one, I will turn over to you fifteen million yen and you and your comrades may go about your business. My goal will have been achieved."

Goto nodded. Fifteen million yen would provide him with several options, even an opportunity to take a sabbatical with Taeko back at Pohnpei. From the way she and Ohiro had described it, the island would be an excellent place to ride out the storm that was sure to erupt once their tasks with Genda were executed. Sakamoki could be disposed of when the time came, and even Ohiro would present no obstacle—he could simply be turned over to the authorities and face his desertion trial. A woman such as Taeko would readily adjust to a new lover. As Genda had noted, Goto had already detected signs of her interest in him. She could be tiring of Ohiro.

Their conversation was interrupted by the owner of the Saiyokan, who apologized as he entered and then spoke quietly to Genda. "Captain Genda, there are two policemen here who have asked me to inform them when you and your friends are about to leave. I thought I should mention this to you."

Genda glared at the others. "Fools! I told you the authorities would not believe the woman! You have led them here." *Fools!* If he were seen in the presence of Taeko, Ohiro, and Sakamoki, he could be tied in to the shootdown attempt on the C-5. Until this moment, he had no idea the police were on to him. He was tempted to give his companions a severe tongue-lashing but that could come later. The damage was done and there was the immediate problem of what to do about it. Only his long-standing friendship with the owner of the restaurant had prevented his careful plans from being stopped this very night. "There is a back way out?" he inquired.

"Yes, Captain Genda."

"There are only two?"

"Yes, Captain Genda."

"They intend to follow us. Otherwise there has been plenty of time for them to call for additional police and take us into custody. The fact that they asked to be informed when we leave supports that. Goto-san, you and Sakamoki will leave now. One of the men will follow you. Do what you must. Ohiro-san, you and Taeko will leave shortly after. The other will follow you. Evade him and carry on with our plan. I will meet you all in Osaka as we have discussed."

The restaurant owner quickly left the room and Genda nodded to Goto and Sakamoki, who rose and left.

Sakai and Kaneyama thanked the owner of the Saiyokan for informing them that Genda's party was leaving.

"I'll take the first two," Kaneyama said, sliding aside the *fusuma.* "Keep in touch through precinct headquarters." He disappeared into the outer hall.

Sakai allowed Ohiro and Taeko to leave, preferring to wait for Genda, but quickly became impatient. Why was not the old man leaving? Suspicious, he cornered the owner. "Genda? Is he still in the room?"

"I assume he left with the others."

"Liar!" Sakai rushed outside. There was no sign of Genda or any of his companions. Reentering the Saiyokan, Sakai hurried into the room used by Genda and his people. He carefully placed the five sake cups into his coat pockets.

Detective Kaneyama kept his black Stanza a respectable distance behind Goto and Sakamoki as they led him east through the Setagaya district and on into the suburbs of Tokyo City. He thanked his foresight in having Sakai man a separate car. He picked up his radio microphone and called his district headquarters. "This is Kaneyama, following two suspects east on expressway number three. Agent Sakai will be contacting you with amplifying information. Keep me informed." The car with Goto and Sakamoki moved over into the left lane of the freeway. Kaneyama followed.

"Is he still back there?" Goto asked.

"Yes. He is keeping several cars between us but he is still there."

Goto swung the small Toyota van off the expressway and began winding among the myriad narrow streets that haphazardly criss-crossed the high-density residential district of eastern Tokyo. Turning finally down one just wide enough to allow passage of single-lane traffic he stopped beside a deserted shed.

"Goto-san, you have taken him right to our weapon!"

Goto could see the lights of Kaneyama's vehicle disappear some distance behind them. "Get inside the shed. Move around and make some light noise, but not enough to arouse the neighborhood." Goto disappeared into the night.

Leaving his car, Kaneyama threaded his way among the shacks and sheds of the low-income residential area, taking care to avoid the sewage and debris strewn around the few open areas. He passed the back of the shed where the two terrorists had parked and approached it from the opposite direction. Carefully sliding along one wall, he reached the front corner of the shed and stopped. Inside, someone was moving around. Drawing his service revolver, he slowly inched his way toward the door. A faint light inside was his last glimpse of the mortal world. The unheard bullet entered the back of his head at the precise junction of his brain stem and his brain, instantaneously introducing him to eternity.

Goto flung open the shed door and helped Sakamoki carry the remaining Dragon missile and its launcher to the car. They sped away, their right front fender grazing an old man who had stepped outside to investigate the noise.

Goto wheeled the car through the maze of narrow streets. "We will return to the expressway. We must assume that the others took care of the second policeman. This one was not overly bright."

Laughing and very much pleased with himself, Goto found an on-ramp and joined the four lanes of traffic rushing bumper-to-bumper along the expressway.

Back at the Chiyoda ward precinct headquarters, Sakai sat and dejectedly relived the events of the night. If it were physically possible he would be kicking his rear all around the police station. Letting Genda slip away was a major blunder. Now there was no telling where the old man had gone. Kaneyama was the only hope at the moment. As soon as the Japanese detective reported in, Sakai could at least rejoin him in the surveillance effort—provided Kaneyama still had confidence in his *gaijin* partner.

Thoughts of Alicia and the children returned. His brief encounter with his ex-wife at the Hilton had reminded him of how it had been. If she just wasn't such a daddy's girl. Every word the old man muttered was swallowed by Alicia, hook, line, and sinker. And the Australian thing, that had been a burr between them from the very beginning. Now, she and the children were actually in-country and, knowing how she was impressed with her own imagined spirit of adventure, Sakai reasoned that her visit to the sheep station would convince her to follow her father's crazy wishes. And if she did, thought Sakai, trying to remain objective, what could he do about it? Probably nothing. If it was not for the children, he could not care less, but the children were the main issue. He would *have* to do something about them.

He was still fuming a half hour later when one of the precinct officers entered the room. Sakai knew the man carried bad news, for the officer didn't even bow, just stood and shook his head before speaking. "Detective Kaneyama has been killed."

Sakai stood. "How? Where?"

"On the east side. A bullet to the head."

That was it. Genda and his group were now alerted to a tail and would be taking steps to see that they were not picked up again. But how had they taken Kaneyama? He was an experienced law officer. For some strange reason, Sakai could still see the cheerful officer's face, and around his shirt collar a Godzilla tie. It was very hard to keep his eyes from flickering.

What should he do now? The terrorists knew that they were under surveillance—or, at least, had been. Would they scatter? Or would they proceed to their next task? He spent the next hour trying to second-guess Genda. It was a useless exercise. Finally, he walked slowly into the operations room and approached the officer in charge of the shift.

"There was a possible unknown with the suspects at the Saiyokan restaurant earlier this evening. The five sake cups I turned in earlier may help us identify him. Are we checking them for prints?"

"Yes, Sakai-san. The laboratory is lifting any that appear even at this moment and we can have them researched. I will coordinate it with the officer in charge of the investigation."

"As soon as possible?"

"It will take several hours to get a reply back from Central ID."

"I'll wait here."

Four hours later, Sakai was roused from a fitful sleep in one of the chairs in Kaneyama's office.

The watch officer had the report. "Each cup had at least one good print. We have identified them as belonging to Captain Saburo Genda, a retired JMSDF officer; Michio Ohiro, a JMSDF deserter; Taeko Nikahura, the girl we interrogated on the C-5 incident; Nobuo Sakamoki, who visited her while she was being held and later met her when she was released; and Toshio Goto, a known member of the Red Army group."

"Excellent!" Sakai was particularly pleased with the confirmation of Goto. Such knowledge was almost a certain indicator that Genda had access to a Red Army cell. "Can we get photographs of each?"

"You may have what we have in our files."

"If the detective in charge agrees, I think we should send copies to all major city air, bus, and sea terminals."

"We can telefax them."

"*Domo arigato.* I will be at my hotel in the meantime."

Sakai used the cab ride to the Fairmont to recap the events of the previous evening, trying very hard not to let the death of Kaneyama muddle his thinking. The Japanese authorities would immediately assign another detective to the case. But there seemed to be little he—or Sakai—could do until the terrorists surfaced again. Sakai would have the photographs, but to whom could he show them? Bus, rail, and air terminals, perhaps, but that was a long shot. Genda and his companions could very well be traveling by car, or maybe not traveling at all. Above all else, Sakai could not shake a terrible premonition that the next time he heard of the terrorists, there would be dead Americans involved.

Chapter 13

The Daikokuyu, in the northern Osaka precinct of Kita, was a small *ryokan* hotel by Tokyo standards but certainly ample for Genda and his companions. They would be using it only a short while.

Osaka, itself, was a good choice for their second attack. Both American military and civil aircraft routinely flew into the nearby Itami International Airport. The second largest city in Japan, Osaka sat majestically on the southern coast of western Honshu, where the River Yodo poured its waters into the wide sweep of Osaka Bay. The industrial, commercial, and administrative center of western Japan, Osaka was a major seaport in its own right. Threaded by the delta waterways of the Yodo, it boasted a thousand bridges and laid claim to the title of "Venice of the East." More than one Western European tourist claimed it to be the Leningrad of Japan.

Toshio Goto and Sakamoki were the first to arrive at the Daikokuyu, just eight hours after Goto had put the single bullet into the base of Detective Kaneyama's skull. Ohiro and Taeko joined them the next day, having ridden the Shinkansen bullet train from Tokyo to Kyoto and then a local line south to Osaka. Finally, a day later, Genda arrived.

"All is in readiness?" Genda queried.

Goto seemed very pleased with himself. "*Hai*, Genda-san. The weekly American military C-141 courier flight from Kaneda via Tokyo arrives in two days. It will be a perfect opportunity. Ohiro and Sakamoki have the weapon readied and I propose to conduct the attack in a similar fashion as we did the one at Narita."

"Access to the airport?"

Ohiro spoke before Goto could answer. "A bit more difficult. We do not have the wide field available but we have reliable information on the prevailing winds, thus the normal duty runway. We have selected two spots, each of which gives us some protection, but once the missile is launched we must quickly leave the scene."

Genda nodded agreement. "I must repeat myself. You will proceed directly to the international terminal after the attack. In the confusion, providing you clear the launch area safely, your entry into your respective departure compound will not arouse any suspicion.

"One final order. We must all make our departure flights. Thus, timing is very critical. If the American aircraft does not depart on time, we have only a thirty-minute cushion. After that, you will abort your attack, for there may be insufficient time remaining to get back to the terminal and catch your flights. In that event, we will reschedule the operation. And I remind you. If one or more of us is caught, the rest will continue with their own departures."

"And if *you* are apprehended?" Goto asked.

"Then our association is over. You may use your travel documents and funds as you desire. But do not waste a moment in getting to the terminal. There most probably will be many emergency vehicles moving and traffic confusion. You could get stuck outside and may consequently miss your flights. That would be bad."

Ohiro certainly shared that thought. "We will not even bother to retain the launcher once the target is struck. A short distance away, we will abandon the van for a prepositioned airport rental vehicle. We return the vehicle to the airport as a normal evolution of departing passengers. It will work beautifully."

"I have transferred our funds to our ultimate destination," Genda announced. "We will have no more ties to Japan until after our final attack, at which time we will separate, you with your fifteen million yen and I with much satisfaction."

"What is the final attack, Genda-san?" Taeko asked.

"Patience. I am still working on the details. But it will be a bold stroke, I assure you. Our names will be long remembered."

Goto looked sternly at the others before replying to Genda's boast. "You may have all the credit, Genda-san. We will still have our own work to do."

The female clerk at the Nippon Auto Rental desk near the baggage claim section of the Itami International Airport terminal needed only one other bit of information. "How long will you need the automobile?"

"Just overnight," Ohiro replied, passing his Soviet-supplied driver's license and credit card across the counter. "I will return it here in the morning."

"That will be fine . . . ah . . . Kamisu-san." Bowing, the clerk handed a copy of the paperwork to Ohiro. "Your automobile is being brought to the Nippon area just outside the first door to your right. Thank you for driving Nippon."

As Ohiro walked away, the clerk pulled a single sheet of paper from under the counter. On it were five photographs—four men and one woman—arranged under a proclamation: "Wanted for Suspicion of Terrorist Activities." Her last customer, Kamisu, had a face very similar to the one identified as Michio Ohiro. The paper was issued by the Chiyoda substation of the Tokyo Police Authority. The clerk again studied the picture but still wasn't sure. Nevertheless, she picked up her telephone and punched in the airport security number.

Ohiro followed Taeko and Sakamoki from the airport, keeping the 1992 Maxima several car lengths behind the van. Working their way around the east side of the airfield, the two vehicles reached an out-of-the-way alley. Sakamoki jumped from the van and removed the No Parking/Airport Authority sign, and Ohiro drove the Maxima into the spot. Their switch vehicle was in position.

It was just a few minutes after 9:00 P.M. when they reported to Genda. Goto was also waiting.

Ohiro answered Goto's unasked question. "It is done."

"You drove the route?" Goto asked.

"Yes," Taeko answered. "It is not complicated."

Genda poured bourbon whiskey for all. "Our two-day wait has tried my patience, but now it is time. I thought tonight we should toast the arriving American airmen with their own drink. A gesture of our concern that they have a smooth flight into the great city of Osaka—the last stop on their itinerary."

The five touched glasses and drank.

"Now, to rest. We have a full day tomorrow." Genda was very tired.

Goto spoke for the others as well as himself. "Sleep well, Genda-san." The old man was not looking well.

Taeko was removing her blouse even as she and Ohiro entered their room. "*We* can sleep on the airplane," she coyly announced. "It is early."

George Sakai threw back the bed cover at the first irritating sound of the telephone. The softly glowing numbers of the clock radio read 11:07 P.M. "Yes?"

"Sakai-san . . ." Sakai recognized the voice of Detective Shiganori Kami, Kaneyama's replacement. ". . . we have a possible sighting."

"Where?"

"Osaka. Auto rental desk at Itami International Airport. The clerk thinks Ohiro has rented a car."

"Can we get out tonight?"

"There is a direct flight—I think you Americans call it a red-eye—from Haneda at twelve-oh-five. Can you make it?"

"I'm on the way. Meet you there?"

"I have the district watch until morning and it is a madhouse here. We're short two regulars. I will join you first flight tomorrow. Check in at police headquarters in the Higashi district."

"See you there, Kami-san!"

"You got it, *gaijin*."

By 9:45 A.M., Ohiro and Sakamoki were sitting in the van with Taeko just outside the airport fence. The tightly packed perimeter shacks provided some cover from those passing down the street behind them. A Japan Air Lines Boeing 707 passed overhead, its engines screaming and its wheels folding up into the waiting cavities of the fuselage.

"I have seen little military traffic," Taeko commented.

Ohiro and Sakamoki both laughed before Ohiro replied, "No, little one of my heart, but this is exactly where we want to be."

"I do not understand."

Ohiro leaned over and spoke slowly. "There is no weekly C-141 military courier flight into Itami—but there is a daily American jumbo jet departure at ten thirty for San Francisco."

Taeko's face paled. "No. We cannot shoot down a civilian aircraft. There will be women and children—Japanese as well as American . . ." Taeko felt her stomach tighten; there were too many innocents involved.

"Shut up! Genda needs to learn a lesson. If you want to kill Americans, it does little good to target a few military personnel. This will get their attention much more thoroughly."

"Genda will not approve of this," Taeko insisted.

"Goto approves. And I have planned it. By the time Genda even learns of the switch, we will all be on our way out of Japan. It will be too late for him to do anything about it."

Three minutes late, United Flight 809 lifted from Itami International Airport and started its climb. The huge Boeing 747SP carried a load of 372 passengers and 15 crew members.

"Okay, Bo, gear coming up and we're cleared to climb out on runway heading to five—" The copilot never completed his sentence. The Boeing rocked violently as an explosion took off fourteen feet of its left wingtip.

"Jesus!" Captain Bo Collins instinctively cranked in full right aileron and shoved hard on his right rudder pedal in a frantic attempt to counter the left roll.

His copilot was on the controls with him and triggered the tower radio circuit. "Itami. United eight-oh-nine, mayday! In-flight explosion! Mayday!"

"Roger, United eight-oh-nine," came back the tower's instant reply. "You are cleared to return to Itami, cleared to land any runway. Emergency equipment is being alerted."

"Engine overtemp, number one!" the flight engineer reported over the cockpit intercom. Almost immediately, he followed with, "Engine fire, number one!"

"Shut down number one!" Collins ordered. He was no stranger to such sudden emergencies, having had two F-4s blown apart around him in Southeast Asia, but his instantaneous gut feeling of impending disaster was almost overridden by his astonishment that it was happening again and he was at the controls of a civilian airliner. For a brief moment, the fact that he was not strapped into a sturdy rocket-propelled ejection seat carried him to near panic but he quickly overcame the feeling. There were 386 other souls on board United 809 who were his responsibility. "What the fuck's happened?" he yelled.

His outburst actually calmed him. They still had some measure of control, and as long as they had control and the big metal son of a bitch wasn't on fire, they would take it back to Itami. The roll slowed but the giant Boeing was still trying to creep over onto its back. Collins cut back the power on the two right engines and the roll stopped, but so did the climb. With movements more character- istic of a thin-framed neurosurgeon than a slightly pudgy ex-fighter pilot, he cautiously adjusted his control pressures and engine power settings to reverse the roll. He was holding full right aileron to force that wing back down. Ever so slowly, the 747 eased itself back towards a level flight attitude.

Bo fought to maintain a level attitude. "I think I can hold it but we're not going to be able to climb. Inform Itami."

The copilot called the tower a second time. "Itami, we have control but are unable to climb. United eight-oh-nine will attempt to return Itami!"

"Roger, United eight-oh-nine, you are cleared any altitude. All other traffic held clear. Emergency equipment has been alerted. Itami standing by."

A scan of his instruments told Collins that the situation was even worse than not being able to climb. With maximum controllable power, he was descending at thirty to forty feet per minute! At the present radar altitude of 768 feet, he and his crew and passengers would have only another twenty or so minutes of life left. He would have to risk an increase in engine power. He eased the power levers forward, taking some comfort from the fact that his three remaining engines were burning fuel at an incredible rate and for each one hundred gallons burned his airplane was six hundred pounds lighter. At five hundred feet he reached a balance and could hold his altitude.

Bo knew what he must do. "We've got to get it headed back to the field. I'll stay on this heading for another few minutes, then we have to start back." With some aerodynamic stability returning he could devote some of his thinking as to how such a thing could have happened.

As if his thoughts were being read, the senior flight attendant came up on the intercom, her voice reflecting remarkable compo-sure. "We've lost a big chunk of our left wing, Captain, about ten or twelve feet off the tip. There was an explosion."

"Any other damage?" Collins asked anxiously.

"None that I can tell. We're working with the passengers. They are all right."

All right? Collins could imagine the initial terror in the passenger compartments. Panic, to be sure. Some would be screaming out of control, many stunned into immobility, others praying, a few join-ing the flight attendants in restoring order and confidence.

The copilot transmitted amplifying information. "Itami Tower, we've lost a portion of our left wing. Am holding altitude five hundred feet on heading two-six-five. Will attempt to return to Itami."

"Roger, United eight-oh-nine, we have you in sight. Airport is in your seven o'clock position."

Ohiro jumped into the van ahead of Sakamoki. "We almost missed again!"

Taeko, thoroughly disgusted with their attack, floored the accel-erator and the boxlike vehicle sped back out into the street and headed east around the airport.

Sakamoki shook a fist. "But we did not! He is done for!"

Bo Collins began to regain some authority over his breathing and heart rate. He was still holding their precious altitude and soon should be able to start a very gentle and wide turn back toward the airport. With so much of the left wingtip gone, he was forced to use full power on the lone left engine and unable to use all the power of his right engines. The result was a dangerous yaw, a partial sideways passage of the 747 through the air. The landing gear was fully retracted but the wing configuration was still in its takeoff mode, with flaps partially down and the leading edge camber slats extended. Three-engined operation normally would not have pre-sented any problem, but without full power on the right engines, it was an entirely different situation. In addition, the near-maximum deflection of his right aileron and rudder was creating too much drag and his airspeed was too marginal to risk changing the wing flap setting. Any movement of the wing lift surfaces could result in a sink before airspeed acceleration could give a climb. He could not afford any sink.

"Jesus," he said, half praying and half cursing, "it's going to be close."

Very close, thought his copilot. "You've got it, Bo. Just hang in there and nurse this baby right back to home plate. Lots of time, Bo. Let's just think this out as we go."

"Okay. I want a few more knots before I start the turn. This altitude's okay if we can hold it."

The 747 was feeling more stable and the airspeed was slowly creeping up. They could convert it to additional altitude by a grad-ual climb or they could use it as insurance for their turn. As soon as they lowered one wing, the lift-drag-thrust equation would change and they would have to trade airspeed for maintaining alti-tude. That was normal. Collins just needed a few more knots for a safe tradeoff.

The control column started to vibrate.

"Now what?" Collins asked. "Perry, get back there and take a look!"

The flight engineer hurriedly unstrapped and disappeared aft into the passenger cabin.

Collins began a mental review of the outer left wing construction. There were undoubtedly hydraulic lines severed, but there were two other backup systems. Apparently, the lost portion was out-board of the wing fuel tanks. The flight engineer had not reported any fuel loss. Obviously, the aileron and outboard leading edge slat were gone. Debris from the explosion must have been the cause for the number-one engine malfunction. There must be mangled metal and the slipstream could be tearing it farther. That could cause the vibration, but it felt like it was more in the control activating system. Whatever it was, the shaking was at a constant level.

The flight engineer returned and spoke immediately over the intercom. "Nothing other than what's been reported, skipper. Can't really see much except that a large part of the tip is gone. The passengers are in good shape."

"How are your hydraulic pressures?" Collins asked.

"Some fluctuation in main flight control system but backups are steady."

"United eight-oh-nine, what is your position?" For the first time, there was anxiety in Itami Tower's call. The 747 was so low and far away from the field, the controller had lost visual contact.

Collins checked his DME reading. The distance measuring equipment indicated that they were twenty-three miles out. His copilot said basically that as he responded to the tower call, then added, "We're still holding altitude and should be able to start a turn momentarily. Has radar got us?"

"Intermittently, eight-oh-nine. They report a distance of twenty-three miles, bearing two-six-eight true."

It might as well be twenty-three hundred, Collins thought.

Taeko braked the van to a solid halt and followed Ohiro and Sakamoki into the Maxima. Ohiro slid under the steering wheel and quickly guided the Nissan back out onto the airport approach road. He dropped Taeko and Sakamoki at the departure terminal. "Get over to your gates. If you see Genda tell him that I will be there in a few minutes!"

Instead of returning the car to the rental area, Ohiro made a quick circuit of the airport approach and departure roadway and stopped in front of the JAL arrival area. Leaving the engine running and driver's door open, he casually walked inside and started for the escalator leading up to the ticketing and gate areas, not even noticing the two plainsclothes detectives who were standing near the Nippon Auto Rental counter waiting for the clerk to give them the signal that customer Kamisu had returned.

What he did notice was that the terminal was alive with concerned chatter. Obviously, the news of the distress of the United aircraft had spread rapidly through the building. He paused to open his ticket envelope and check the gate number for his flight. His destination was a complete surprise.

Ohiro passed through the security post as an inconspicuous member of a steady stream of departing passengers and proceeded casually to his JAL departure gate. He checked in and received his seat assignment. As he turned away from the counter he was startled to see Genda sitting in the same area. They made brief eye contact before Ohiro looked for a place to wait for the boarding call. There was Sakamoki! And Taeko and Goto!

Ohiro looked back at Genda, who was allowing himself a slight smile. The crafty old man had arranged tickets to the same destination for all of them but had given them the impression that each was going to a separate place. Had one of them been apprehended they would have carried that impression into the police interrogation room. Clever. It could have compounded the search, to be sure. It would not be necessary for Genda to tell them to board separately; that was an obvious ploy. And since they had checked in separately, each had an individual seat assignment. The flight information board indicated that their departure was still on time. Ohiro looked through the large glass windows at the surrounding terrain. There were no columns of dark smoke within his view. But the aircraft had been hit. It had to have crashed. A glance at Genda triggered raised eyebrows, nothing more.

"Coming right," Collins said. It would be slow going but he dared not turn left into his damaged wing.

His copilot realized that and also the uncomfortable fact that a right turn would take them directly back over central Osaka. "Roger right. All clear."

Collins watched his heading indicator swing. Two degrees per second. Not bad, almost a standard rate. It would take roughly ninety seconds to reverse his course.

As they passed through a heading of northeast, both pilots strained to sight the airport. The copilot saw it first. "There!" He pointed with his hand.

Collins caught the alternating green and white flashing light of Itami International Airport. "Got it!" He stopped his turn with the light on the horizon dead ahead. Passing underneath them were the outskirts of Osaka. Much of the central city was dead ahead.

The uniformed schoolchildren looked up in alarm at the massive shape passing overhead. The noise was deafening and the ground was actually shaking. One of the older students shouted, "Look!" He could see the jagged edge of the shortened left wing. A thin trail of black smoke was streaming from one of the engines.

Bo's copilot tried very hard to keep his voice from cracking. "Itami, we have the airport in sight, approximately fifteen miles out."

The vibration was worsening.

"Something's happening," Collins declared. "I'll slow it a bit."

"God, not too much, Bo. We're just hanging in the air now." They were over downtown Osaka, and the copilot could see the frightened movements of people on the ground. The radar altimeter was reading four hundred and twenty feet. A number of office buildings were higher than that! In just a few moments Collins would have to actually divert their course to miss several of the high-rise structures.

"Shit!" Collins shook his head as if he could somehow make the situation go away. "We're not going to make it!"

"To the right, Bo! It's clearer. Let it drop if you have to in order to keep your airspeed!"

"Coming right! I've got to add power! Let's go up!"

The copilot kept his backup hand over Collins's grip on the thrust levers and felt them ease forward. The 747 began to climb but their shallow turn had placed the airport back over to their eleven o'clock position. Amazingly enough, the airplane continued to slowly gain altitude. At six hundred feet, Collins realized that in order to head back to the airport he was going to have to turn left into his damaged wing and shutdown engine. He simply had no other choice. The control yoke was almost shaking loose from his hand and the instrument panel was vibrating with such intensity that the instruments were a blurred mass of unreadable dials.

A violent jerk pulled the nose farther to the left and upward. As one, Collins and his copilot pushed forward on the control column in a desperate attempt to stop the alarming rise of the nose.

"We have to get the nose down!" Collins shouted, knowing full well that his copilot was already making a maximum effort to help him do just that. The aircraft was buffeting badly and the shrill tone of the stall warning horn told them what they already knew. They were on the verge of a stall. Collins had no choice. He slammed the thrust levers forward in a futile attempt to let thrust carry him out of the edge of the unsafe flight envelope. The decision, while the only one available to him, was fatal.

The increased power caused the big Boeing to steepen its left turn, the right wing consequently moving even faster through the air but the left one losing airspeed until it stalled and the 747 began an irreversible roll over onto its back.

The copilot froze, unable to speak.

"Oh, dear God, help—" The flight engineer's last words were cut off by his rising stomach contents.

Bo Collins tried to roll the airplane completely around to at least hit the ground right side up, but it was too late. The 747 had insufficient altitude for that last panic-inspired maneuver. "Brace yourselves..." he instinctively cried out despite his horrified recognition of the inevitable.

Upside down, United Flight 809 plowed into a high-density business area just to the east of Osaka's central district, cutting a wide swath of death and destruction for a quarter mile before its disintegration was complete. In the grip of the infallible law of physics that proclaimed energy can neither be created nor destroyed, the metal, fluids, human bodies, fabrics, rubber, wire, and plastics that once were passing through the air in an orderly fashion were transformed into a huge expanding ball of orange fire, much of their substance rising rapidly skyward as part of a thick cloud of black smoke.

George Sakai had been at the Higashi headquarters station only a few minutes when the report of the crash of the 747 came in. He rode with two uniformed policeman as they, along with a dozen other teams, drove furiously toward the scene.

The smoke was visible almost immediately, and as the police car approached the crash site Sakai could see that there was absolutely no chance of any survivors. More so, there had to be a great number of ground casualties. There was complete devastation and a number of buildings were burning along each side of the death swath. He jumped out as soon as the car stopped. Already, hundreds of people were at the scene, most cooperating with the increasing influx of fire fighters and police who were making a heroic effort to rescue the scores of injured from the wide expanse of burning and smoking debris.

Sakai ran and joined two men who were digging through smashed concrete sections toward a protruding arm. They grabbed it and pulled and immediately became ill when all they extracted was the arm. Sakai took a moment to stand erect and swallow in an attempt to coat his throat with some moisture. A feeble cry off to his left alerted him, and he ran over to join one of the firemen who was throwing aside boards and glass and chunks of unrecognizable material.

The small girl was burned and badly crushed. As soon as Sakai touched her she screamed in agony, her eyes wide with terror and pain. Sakai hesitated. To move her might not be wise. He looked up at the fireman, who obviously had the same doubt. "I'll get a board," the fireman said.

Abruptly the child's screaming stopped and her face froze, eyes and mouth wide open.

"We won't need it." Helpless, Sakai watched the little girl die. He tried to clear his vision by blinking the moisture from his eyes. It didn't work. Tenderly, he lifted the mashed little body and handed it to the fireman.

The scene was now alive with rescuers and the police had established a measure of security around the area. Sakai recognized that he was not needed. There were ample rescue personnel for survivors of what had to be the worst single aircraft disaster in history. There was little doubt that the ground casualties would be in the hundreds. Like most on the scene, he was almost overcome by the magnitude and horror of the tragedy. The carnage was unbelievable. The big jet had cleared away buildings, vehicles, and people as if it had been a giant bulldozer. Anything remaining was burning. Strewn luggage and shattered cargo cluttered the entire area of the initial impact. Ripped articles of clothing were barely distinguishable from pitiful parts of bodies. As Sakai tried unsuccessfully to tear his eyes away from the scene, the horror drained him emotionally and he was on the verge of physical sickness. He could not see how many of the victims could ever be identified from such pitiful remains. Still, amazingly, a very few were relatively whole. The stench of burning fuel, materials, and human flesh forced him to work farther upwind in a desperate attempt to learn from eyewitnesses what had happened. Several described the missing tip of the left wing and the smoke trailing from one of the aircraft's engines. With the initial police report that the aircraft had been hit by a missile ringing still in his ears, he wanted to scream out against such a mindless attack. Instead, he walked out to the perimeter of the crash site and stood resting against one of the police vehicles. He no longer had any sympathy for Genda. The man had to be mad to be a part of this. And he would have to be stopped. An overhead noise caused Sakai to look up. It was the slightly muffled noise of the fanjets on a climbing jumbo jet, a JAL Boeing 747 sister aircraft of the one now strewn across downtown Osaka. Itami International Airport had resumed operations.

Genda could see the ugly black pillar of smoke rising from central Osaka as the 747 climbed over the city. His body was rigid with anger; he had overheard one of the flight attendants telling another that the destroyed airplane was a United Airlines Boeing 747. Goto and Ohiro had double-crossed him! They had used him for their own purposes, and now in the eyes of the world, Captain Saburo Genda, a true patriot of Japan, would be seen only as a mass murderer. Despair caused him to keep his eyes diverted toward the window by his seat even though the JAL 747 was high above the clouds and moving farther away from the disaster with the passing of every moment.

As furious as he might be, he could not let the evil act of his compatriots deter him from his ultimate goal. His motivation was still the same. The downing of the United flight, as horrible as it was, had no bearing on his determination to avenge the murder of his parents and the rape of his beloved Emiko. The world would know when he struck that blow. He made a promise to himself that he would deal with Goto, Ohiro, Sakamoki, and Taeko in due time, but for the moment he needed them. His final plan was coming into focus and he would need help to carry out a scheme so diabolically clever that the name of Saburo Genda would be long remembered. The newspaper on his lap had filled in certain blanks that had remained in his mind. He flipped it open and again read the feature story.

In just over a week, the president of the United States and Prime Minister Hoikata would be meeting in Honolulu to sign a most significant treaty, one that would establish a vibrant new trading relationship between the two countries and establish Japan as a new full partner with the United States in maintaining the security of the western Pacific. The details would be announced at a special press conference preceding a historic signing of the agreement. Later on, there would be a special ceremony on the *Arizona* Memorial in Pearl Harbor. It would be a symbolic ceremony that proclaimed to all the world that the Pacific war of 1941 through 1945 was now a part of history, an era for the scholars, and Japan would be unreservedly welcomed to the community of Western nations as a premier ally. A half century of penance was over.

That fact, alone, gave renewed purpose to Genda's intent to avenge his dishonor. Japan did not need such a patronizing display of forgiveness. Could not the whole country see the disgrace of the direct representative of Emperor Akihito being paraded out to the sunken battleship *Arizona* in order that Japan could symbolically apologize for the attack on Pearl Harbor? The war had been Roosevelt's doing, not Imperial Japan's. If the United States had recognized the inevitable, the leadership of Japan in the southeastern Asian sphere of oriental dominance, there would have been no war. Genda shook his head as if to physically reinforce his thoughts. No, Roosevelt wanted that war; he needed a war to complete the pull of America from the Depression and he needed an excuse to enter the European war. So, he had issued an ultimatum, a revoking of the trade agreement that had been providing Japan with precious refined oil products and high-grade scrap steel. Such a blow to the lifeblood of the samurai nation could only generate a response in the way of Bushido. For Japan not to have replied as she did would have doomed her to a subordinate role in the growth of Southeast Asia. Japan had given her blood for the desperately needed assets of Indochina and the resources of Manchuria. The United States had wanted her to give them up. Japan could not have survived without oil and steel. She had been forced to go to war.

Genda knew that the new generation had no feel for why their grandfathers had fought so brilliantly in a spectacular display of military prowess, conquering most of the Pacific basin in less than six months. It was a military feat even greater than the march of Hitler across Europe. *That* was the glory of Nippon. Now, the modern Japanese saw only the yen and its power. And the idiot prime minister, Hoikata, had even publicly stated that the "samurai nature of the Japanese mind-set was no longer applicable to the modern world of high technology and international finance." Those words had caused Genda to seriously consider the assassination of Hoikata. He had harbored the thought for several days before deciding he would not want to make a martyr of the man. Let the fool renounce his heritage. Perhaps someone would charge him with treason. But now, because of a most fortunate set of circumstances, Genda would accomplish a blow much greater than just the assassination of a foolish politician. That thought gave him a feeling of incredible peace.

Several rows back and on the opposite side of the cabin, Taeko was fighting back tears of shame and anger. Goto's decision to down the 747 rather than a military jet was more than she could handle. When they arrived in Guam, she would tell him so—and maybe even leave the cell.

Chapter 14

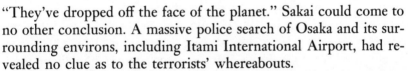

"They've dropped off the face of the planet." Sakai could come to no other conclusion. A massive police search of Osaka and its surrounding environs, including Itami International Airport, had revealed no clue as to the terrorists' whereabouts.

The abandoned rental car had been discovered, as had the escape van. The Dragon launching mechanism had been found at the site of the attack. The lab people were going over the vehicles and the weapon.

There were two witnesses to the firing of the missile, but each had failed to identify any of the three people involved.

Detective Kami had arrived from Tokyo and was sitting with Sakai beside the precinct chief's desk in the Higashi ward headquarters in Osaka. All looked up as a fourth figure entered the room.

"Charlie," Sakai said. "I was hoping you would come."

The big man grabbed a chair from the outer office and pulled it in as Sakai made the introductions.

"So, what've we got?" Porter asked.

"The getaway vehicles and the weapons launcher," Sakai stated flatly.

"What did they use?"

"A Dragon."

"Shit, the Dragon's for land targets, ground-to-ground. It's old, outdated. Where in hell did they get a Dragon? And how in bejesus did they bag an airplane with it?"

"We don't know where they got it. I suppose they just pointed it up and fired away. They probably used the same weapon back at Nakita when they tried to bring down the C-5."

"Prints?"

"The lab people are running them now. It had to be Genda's group. Ohiro was ID'd earlier."

"Roadblocks?"

"Set up within a half hour of the crash."

"Probably too late." Porter picked an infinitesimal something from his lower lip, examined it curiously, and wiped it on his pants leg. "The airport should have been closed shit-tight right away."

Detective Kami shrugged. "It was, but they reopened it without consulting us within the next half hour. The crash was several miles away and constituted no threat to airport operations."

Sakai voiced the thought that had plagued him ever since he had left the crash site and returned to the station. "I dropped the ball on that. I was too caught up in the crash scene."

The Hibashi ward chief, Haruki Aoi, held up a hand. "Do not blame yourself. Many things were happening. We had almost twenty minutes after the aircraft was struck before it finally crashed. We immediately dispatched units to the site of the attack and set up checkpoints at all of the airline boarding gates. Of course, we did not know who we were looking for except suspicious-acting persons. The ID of Ohiro had not been circulated to my people in the field. Looking back, we should have closed the airport. But we do not know for a fact that they left through there. They could have continued on by vehicle, or separate vehicles, or even stayed in the area at one of the hotels. As soon as we get some positive ID, it will confirm who we are looking for."

"There is no doubt, is there?" Sakai asked. "The auto rental clerk made Ohiro and you've found the car he rented—abandoned at the terminal."

"And we have your flyers out to all law officers with pictures. I did not mean to imply we do not have suspects."

"Chief Aoi, if I may suggest," Porter said, "we should be canvassing every boarding gate attendant who was on duty at the time and for several hours after the attack."

"We have our plainclothes division doing just that. What success they will have depends upon two factors: one, how much attention the boarding attendants paid to the passengers as opposed to just the boarding passes; and, two, if one or more of the terrorists actually boarded an aircraft. With two variables, our chances of success diminish. Many people passed before the eyes of the airline employees, and a number, I would venture, did not even receive a cursory glance from the busy gate attendants."

"Jesus," Porter said aside to Sakai, "if you damn people spent less time bowing to one another, you'd know who was passing in front of you."

"Stuff it, Charlie. It would have been the same at Dulles or JFK. We just have to wait and see."

"*Gomen'nasai*—I'm sorry. I agree."

Chief Aoi stood. "Gentlemen, I assure you we are doing all within our power. If the suspects have not left the area then we will find them. You are welcome to join our forces in any way you deem appropriate, but I would suggest that there is nothing you can do that is not already being done." The chief paused to answer his phone, listened for a moment, gave a curt "*Hai!*" and hung up. "That was the crime laboratory. Prints on the vehicles and the weapons launcher have verified the suspects to be Ohiro, Sakamoki, and the woman, Nikahura—as you already knew."

"Genda?" Sakai asked.

"Nothing. And nothing on Goto. But there is no doubt now."

Sakai knew the confirmation was redundant. And the shrewd old Genda had kept himself clear of any incriminating evidence by letting his lackeys do all of the dirty work. "I could use a cup of tea," he said aside to Porter.

"Tea?"

"Tea. Chief, we'll be at our hotel. If we come up with any ideas, I'll give a call. Kami-san, will you join us?"

Detective Kami shook his head. "I am well rested. You are the one who was up all night. I think I will go down to the crash site and nose around."

"You won't stay long." Every horrible detail of the tragedy was still present in Sakai's mind.

"I am sure. But you never know. There are times when the criminal cannot resist the urge to return to the scene of his crime. A very long shot as you would say, but I have to do something."

"We will see you later in the day."

The coffee shop at the Western-style International Hotel Osaka was all but empty, mid-morning being the slack time of the day. Only two other tables were occupied, both obviously by American tourists who were pouring over maps and brochures.

Sakai sipped his tea while Porter laced his coffee with scotch from a small hip flask.

"Scotch and coffee?" Sakai could only imagine the taste of such a mixture.

"You look like shit, gyrene. Why don't you go up to your room and log some z's?"

"I will in a bit. I just can't get the crash scene out of my mind." Sakai's color was bad and his breathing was irregular. He seemed to want to say more but just couldn't bring it out.

Porter knew it would come. He sat still and waited.

"You okay?"

"No."

"Wanna talk about it?"

The clear fluid in Sakai's eyes was threatening to overflow. "There was a little girl, Charlie; God, she could not have been more than three years old—about the age of Kristen. All I saw at first was a piece of her ripped and burned dress. One of the firemen and I dug her out and she died right there as I tried to hold her. If I live to be two hundred years old, I'll hear that last pitiful cry. She was in such extreme pain; God, her little body was rigid with it. I hear her and feel her every time I close my eyes. She was burned alive, Charlie. God help me, I prayed she would die—she was almost solid bloody crust—but when she did, I was suddenly back in 'Nam near Soc Trang. I held . . . a burning little girl . . . there, too. The Cong torched her, Charlie. The fuckers incinerated the whole godforsaken village—just kids and old people who had committed the capital crime of giving my troops some water the day before. There in Osaka, at the crash site, holding that pitiful little burned-up child, it all came back and suddenly I was on my knees in the piss-saturated Vietnam dust and everything around me was on fire and the little girl just kept screaming. What was left of her flesh was coming off on my hands and arms. Long ragged strips that stuck to me, glued in place by her body fluids. Every breath that she took was a raw swallow of hellfire and brimstone. She had to be burned inside as well. I don't know why she was still alive, Charlie. I remembered shouting and pleading, 'Please die . . . please die.' I actually had my sidearm next to her head when she beat me to it . . . she was in such terrible, terrible pain, Charlie. I couldn't have let it go on. And then when she did go, her eyes stayed open and tears kept oozing out. They were brown tears, Charlie; even her little eyes had been on fire. A man shouldn't have to go through that twice, Charlie. . . ."

Porter reached over and placed his cup in Sakai's hand. "Let it go, George. Shit, cry a flood if you want. Get it out of your system."

Sakai downed the spiked coffee between sobs and slung the empty cup across the coffee shop. The tourists looked up, startled and confused. What was the crazed Japanese going to do next?

Porter helped Sakai stand and spoke to the alarmed Americans. "It's all right, folks. He just needs a little sleep. No problem. Please, excuse us." He pressed two small-denomination bills into the waitress's hand as she approached, and led Sakai out the door to the elevators.

Chapter 15

It was late afternoon when Alicia and her two daughters settled themselves in the Sydney Hilton. The long plane ride back from the sheep station near Woomera had been pleasant enough at first, but the small, twin-engined Cessna's pressurization system had died midway through the flight and the pilot had to stay below ten thousand feet because of the oxygen requirements. It was still quite hot at that altitude and the air that flowed through the cabin carried the fine ocher dust of the outback. She felt as if she were caked in an inch of it. And the two girls as well.

Stripping off the small one's clothes, Alicia had Angela take her into the shower and together the sisters giggled and played and washed themselves until their skin glistened with the natural beauty of childhood and their dark hair was plastered to their heads.

Alicia dried the smaller Kristen and the two girls plopped on one of the beds in the suite.

"Can we watch television?" asked Angela.

"Yes. But watch your sister, too."

Alicia wiggled out of her bush blouse and thick riding breeches, cursing herself for not changing before they left the main house. She had to peel off her sweat-soaked bra and even inside her panties there were little moist cakes of the fine gritty dirt that had filtered through her outer garments. Most of it was along the elastic and down the center of the back. Shuddering in disgust and discomfort, she turned on the cold water and stepped into the shower, squealing with delight and shivering at the impact of the water that turned light brown as it ran down her body and carried away the dirt. The initial rinsing completed, she fed in just the right amount of hot water and adjusted the shower head to take away the sting.

As usual, the girls had left the soap on the floor, and she stooped to retrieve it. Still squatting, she spread herself sufficiently to soap the inside of her thighs and the valleys of her crotch, using the fingers to reach all of the crevices and the palms of her hands to massage away the remainder of the dirt. Then she did her buttocks and lower back. Raising herself into a crouch, she soaped her legs and feet and let the wide stream of water pound her pelvic area before it ran down and rinsed her lower extremities.

Fully erect, she soaped her upper body, rubbing the bar hard into her armpits and in the deep creases under her breasts, thinking all the while that she was doing everything backwards. She should have started at the top and worked down.

Her hair came next, and she used the hotel shampoo and conditioner. She would get a proper rewash and set in the hotel shop later. All she wanted now was to be clean. And it took a while. When she finally completed her final rinse and wrapped herself in the deep pile bath towel, Kristen was asleep and Angela was watching the news.

"They had a airplane crash in Japan, Mama."

Alicia sat on the bed and started to vigorously rub her hair with one end of the towel. Her heart skipped a beat when the reported announced that it was a United Airlines jumbo jet.

"Was it American, Mama?"

"Yes . . . hush and let's listen."

". . . Osaka authorities have identified the terrorists as a small Red Army cell led by a retired officer of the Japanese Self Defense Force . . ."

Terrorists?

". . . however, the motivation for the attack is still not known as the investigation enters its second day. The fatality count is now up to four hundred and forty-seven . . ."

Oh, my god.

". . . and expected to rise as a number of the injured on the ground are in critical condition. Osaka authorities are being aided in their search for the terrorists by Detective Shiganori Kami of the Tokyo police force and two Americans from the embassy in Tokyo, Charlie Porter, an aide to the U.S. ambassador to Japan, and George Sakai, an antiterrorist specialist from the United States State Depart ment . . ."

"Mama, they said Daddy's name. . . ."

"Yes, dear—shhhh—please be quiet."

". . . The Osaka police have roadblocks set up on all roads leading from the city and have special details stationed at all public intranational and international transportation ports in the city and expect to apprehend those responsible within hours . . ."

Alicia sat back farther on the bed. Until this moment, her husband's job had been unimaginably boring to her. Even the car-bombing incident and the few that had happened before in Sakai's area of responsibility had failed to stimulate much appreciation for the nature of Sakai's work. But the televised pictures of the crash scene and the realization that in one moment the terrorists had wiped out the equivalent of a small town's population sobered her thoughts. Sakai was in the middle of a great tragedy, and knowing his workaholic nature so well, she realized the drain the task would take of him.

"Mama, is Daddy in Japan?"

"Yes, dear, and he is very busy."

Maybe this would be the perfect time to hit him again with her Australian plan. For a moment, a trace of guilt flitted through her mind. Using the shock of the plane crash to make her point was not something she would be proud of—but it could certainly strengthen her argument.

There was no way she could tell how long Sakai would be in Japan. Bert Thompson might know. If only there was some way she could get Sakai to come to Australia before he returned to the States. If he could just see the land and the house and the range and the sheep. Even the outback had a special weird sort of beauty. But there was little chance Sakai would travel down under. There was a better chance that she could meet him somewhere, and the ideal place would be Hawaii. Ordinarily, she knew, when he finished with his work in Japan he would return by way of the great circle route via Seattle.

She had plenty of business to keep her in Sydney for several weeks. Perhaps if she called Thompson. Yes, that would be the first step. Find out what Thompson knew of Sakai's progress in his terrorist investigation and eventual return to the States.

Kristen began to channel the TV, looking for something more interesting now that the news was over.

Alicia reached down and touched the remote control. "Turn the TV down a bit, sweetheart, Mama has to make a phone call."

Chapter 16

George Kohji Sakai slept the sleep of the drugged, as well he should. In a way, he *was* drugged, overdosed with senseless tragedy and mindless horror.

He had not wanted to sleep, for he knew what would come. One could not witness an event such as the crash scene of the Osaka 747 and not know what would come when despair and fatigue finally forced the eyes shut. But his body—and Charlie Porter—had insisted.

Sakai had other disturbing memories stored in that part of his mind reserved for such things, memories that in times past had stayed with him too long but had eventually faded from his consciousness. Now, his surrender to the subconscious in the room at the International Hotel allowed all of the past horror to return.

First came the casualties his platoon had taken in 'Nam, some with their feet and legs blown off by land mines, others with bodies ripped apart by primitive but deadly accurate artillery, still others with heads and torsos shattered by fire from the Cong. They led the parade of death that marched forth from the dark parts of his mind.

Next came the pitiful Vietnamese themselves, innocent and guilty alike, all twisted and broken. They lay in their blood-soaked black pajamas along the roadways, in the burned villages, in the trampled rice fields—in the clearing near Soc Trang.

There, in his disturbing dream, the little village girl materialized and climbed into Sakai's arms, her fragile body almost stripped of flesh by the fire. She screamed and jerked in the most intense agony Sakai had ever seen. "Die!" Sakai pleaded. "Please, die. . . ." He held his automatic to her head and squeezed the trigger but the bullet only caused her more anguish. He fired again and again, until the clip was empty, and she just kept screaming. Suddenly, her face was that of his Kristen, and Sakai screamed even louder than the child.

Then she was still, her flesh stuck to his.

There were other children, two hundred and thirty-seven of them, lying in the mud only eighteen miles out of Saigon. The huge C-5 Operation Babylift had lifted off from Ton Son Nhut only thirty minutes before. The aft pressure door had failed, damaging the Galaxy's elevators and blowing some of the infants out into the sky while others died from lack of oxygen. The rest, all but a pitiful few, died in the resultant crash along with sixty-one of the sixty-two adults who were on board as attendants. Thirty-seven of them had been female employees from the Defense Attaché's Office where Sakai and Charlie Porter worked. Coincidentally, Sakai had been airborne in an Army recon chopper on that April 1975 day and was one of the first on the scene. For hours, he and the others wandered the deep mud trying to separate the bodies from the debris. Miraculously, some of the infants survived, their tiny bodies sprinkled among the dead. Sakai's deep sleep allowed the scene to resurface in living color.

Finally, there was the crushed and burned little girl lying in the 747 debris at Osaka. A raw skin-sack full of broken bones and mashed organs, so tiny, so much in pain. Once more she died with her eyes and mouth open.

Sakai was asleep but he knew he was in the middle of a hellish nightmare. Angry and horrified, he fought the terrible dream, yelling in anguish and despair at the small ripped and burned creatures marching through his mind. He convulsed repeatedly on the bed and gripped the covers until his fingernails pierced the cloth and cut into the palms of his hands. He had to wake. He had to wake. He had to wake. He *had* to wake!

He did. Immediately, he sat up, sweating and gasping for clean air.

Fuck sleep. There was no way he would lie back down.

Chapter 17

"Guam?" Sakai's entire face expressed his astonishment.

"Exactly," Detective Kami replied. "We have a positive ID on Genda from one of the Itami boarding agents. She initially noticed him because he was the only one on the whole flight in traditional dress. When we showed her the flyer, she picked him out right away. We also have a possible on the girl, and I think we can assume the whole lot of them were on the flight."

"God in heaven, they've already been in Guam for over forty-eight hours. They could be anywhere on the island. But why Guam?"

Kami chuckled. "Why not? For all practical purposes, it is a Japanese island. Our people vacation there, they honeymoon there, they invest there. It is the gateway to our memorials on Saipan. Genda and his people will not even be noticed."

"I still don't see why in hell Itami didn't cease flight operations."

"We know that they did initially. But the crash site was miles from the airport. Once recovery operations were under control, they saw no reason to remain closed, I am sure. Whatever, it is history. In any event, we are booked on the next flight out."

Tired and discouraged, Sakai shook his head in disbelief. Genda and his gang were once more just a step ahead of him. There was a faint glimmer of good fortune, however. Guam was a confined space. Genda might have gotten on the island undetected—but it would be another matter for him to get off. "We have to alert the Guam authorities."

"Already done, and they have been informed that we will be on the next flight. I guess our positions are reversed, Sakai-san. Guam falls within your jurisdiction; I will represent the Japanese interests in the case."

"Why didn't they go underground here? On Guam, they're isolated. We'll get them."

"First of all, they did not expect to be identified. They counted on the confusion of the crash to mask their movements. They carried false ID, of course, and boarded the aircraft separately. We traced the seat assignments of Genda and the girl—they were not related so we can assume each boarded independently of the others, not that it is important." Kami paused before continuing. "And I think they have another operation planned."

"Christ! No!"

"Face it, Sakai-san. That would be the only reason for proceeding to Guam. They could have remained hidden here indefinitely. We might never have found them. The Guam police and military have photos and descriptions and are starting an island-wide search. It is just a matter of time."

"Would that it were. Genda has the gods running with him."

"A strange philosophy from a *gaijin*." Kami seemed to have the same sense of humor as the murdered Kaneyama.

Sakai shrugged. "When in Rome, think as Romans."

Charlie Porter walked in while Sakai was packing his bag. "Shitters made it to Guam. A bit out of my jurisdiction."

"You going back to Tokyo?"

"Might as well. I guess you're on your own, gyrene."

Sakai paused and held out his hand. "Kami's going with me. It's been good seeing you again, Charlie, even under these circumstances. Thanks for everything."

"Yeah. Don't let the bastards get any farther." Porter's grasp was warm and firm.

"You can count on it."

"I'll keep in touch with the Japanese police in Tokyo. If there is anything I can do . . ."

"Thanks, Charlie."

"Semper fi, little buddy."

"Semper fi."

Sakai could see the whole 212-square-mile peanut-shaped island of Guam as the airliner descended and positioned itself for landing. To the north glistened the raised limestone plateau that was largely occupied by Andersen Air Force Base; below, the pinched central district featured the main townships of Agana and Tamuning and the U.S. Naval Station; and to the south the high volcanic hills were interwoven with numerous waterfalls and rivers. Roughly 30 miles long and 9 miles wide, the largest island in Micronesia was geographically the southernmost of the 200-mile-long chain of the Northern Marianas and only two and a half hours jet flight time from Tokyo.

Originally the land of the ancient Chamarros, themselves probably of Filipino and Indonesian descent, the island had seen very influential occupations by the Spanish, the Americans, the Japanese during World War II, and again the returning Americans. An Unincorporated Territory of the United States, Guam was fast becoming the Japanese Oahu, a popular vacation and honeymoon resort and a gateway to the historic battle sites on Saipan and in the western Pacific. The luxurious hotel row along Tumon Bay was evolving into an Asiatic Waikiki, and the expansive white-sand beaches were the playgrounds of bodies already tanned, and playful new age spirits, their inhibitions released by the mores of the new Japan.

A Guam police staff car was waiting for Sakai and Kami and carried them swiftly into central Agana.

Captain Jose Chimananshe was a mountain of a man, easily three hundred pounds and a good hand-width above six feet, the type of *Homo sapiens* who would pick his teeth with an ax handle. He waved Sakai and Kami to the two chairs in his office without rising, but his smile was welcome enough. Obviously of Chamarro heritage, his ancestors had probably included Japanese as well, and the mixture produced a strikingly handsome man despite his self-indulgent size. "We have all of the island forces alerted," he began. "My people are canvassing hotels and inns—on a low-key basis. We don't want to create a panic here. The military will provide whatever assistance we need. Since we read your alert, all air and sea departures have received our closest scrutiny. This man, Genda, and his companions cannot leave this island without detection. I can assure you of that."

"It is possible they plan an operation here," Kami said.

Chimananshe nodded. "If so, we are ready for them. I have taken personal charge of the operation, subject to the approval of you, Mr. Sakai. Federal authorities have requested from the governor that we report to you as the direct representative of the State Department. At first, I was a bit disturbed by such an arrangement, but as I understand it, you are an expert in such matters and we certainly bow to your expertise."

"Chief Chimananshe, I do not wish to place you and your people in any awkward position. You know your own area much better than I. I am at *your* disposal. Let the bureaucrats set up whatever paper organization they like."

Chimananshe roared. "I like that! We will work good together and soon apprehend these devils. Detective Kami, I am deputizing you at this moment as the official representative of the Japanese government. You have full authority to carry out whatever police procedures you deem appropriate under the laws of the Territory of Guam."

"Do I get one of those T-shirts?" Kami asked, smiling.

The chief was very casually dressed in the official uniform of the Guam police, tropical khaki shorts and a blue T-shirt upon which was stenciled a silver police badge. Around his ample waist was a black leather gunbelt laden with several pouches containing handcuffs, mace, and other law enforcement paraphernalia.

"Ha! Of course, of course, if you wish! Now, to the task at hand. I have set up an office for you and any leads or apprehensions will be immediately reported. If you prefer to work the streets, I have a car available. That may be the wisest choice, Sakai, since I understand you have met and talked with this Genda and would more readily recognize him on sight."

"That sounds fine. I would prefer to move about. Detective Kami and I would like to follow up on leads personally, using your forces as backup."

"Good. We have hit the large hotels and checked the papers of arrivals since the alert. A good place for you and Detective Kami to start would be the down-class Japanese hotels along the northern edge of Tumon Bay: the Fujita, the Terraza Tumon Villa, and so forth. I have a list here with locations. There are any number of smaller hotels on the island, even a few bed-and-breakfast places. If the terrorists split up and have any ability to alter their appearances, they could hide out for a while, but I feel we will eventually uncover them."

"How about deserted beach areas?" Kami had seen many on their landing approach.

"They might decide to rough it, but I think they would be even more conspicuous than if they stayed to the crowded hotels where a mass of people would surround them."

"The southern end of the island looked pretty remote from the air."

"The hills? Yes, they could hide there and we would have some difficulty. But they would need food and the farmers and fishermen would notice strangers. We will cover all areas, of course. I don't have a large force. We can ask the military for assistance."

"Let's do that," Sakai suggested. "Just enough augmentation to provide a thorough area search. I don't think we have to turn the island into an armed camp. And the terrorists won't want to call attention to themselves. It might be a better course if we kept the search at such a level that they would not know an extensive man-hunt was on. They may not even know that we know they are here. No sense in giving ourselves away and forcing them into deeper cover."

"I would agree with that," Chimananshe added. "Let them think they are safe and that we are not suspicious."

Sakai nudged the Japanese detective. "How's that sound to you, Kami-san?"

"In good order. I suggest we get a place to stay and join the hunt—"

Chief Chimananshe interrupted. "I have taken the liberty of arranging space at Andersen Air Force Base. They have quarters set aside for federal use and you will have all the communications you need. If you would rather be nearer to my office, we have a duty room available. It is rather basic, but comfortable."

Sakai was pleased to see that the Guamanian was on top of things. "That would do fine, Chief. I would rather we become a part of your

M. E. MORRIS 198

effort. We can stay right here and keep in close contact with you and your people, which I believe would be the best course for now."

"Then it is done. I will have one of my men show you where you can put your gear. Here are the keys to your car. Your radio call is on the dash. Incidentally, I should issue you one caution about our island roads. Because of the composition of their surface, they get quite slippery when wet. Now, if you will keep the desk sergeant informed of your plans, we can insure you are kept informed of our progress and avoid duplication of effort."

"Thank you. Let's dump our gear, Shiganori, and go to work."

Saburo Genda stood a safe distance from the open window on the third floor of the Terraza Tumon Villa Hotel and gazed out at the Fujita Tumon Beach Hotel just across the side street of the northern end of the Tumon Beach area. Ohiro, Taeko, and Sagamoki were there in separate rooms as a honeymooning couple and a vacationing student. Goto was in the room down the hall from Genda. Separated, yet within a workable distance from each other, the five had taken steps since arrival to avoid one another and further disguise themselves. It was apparent from the police activity on the island that some sort of search was being undertaken. While Genda was reasonably sure that their departure from Osaka had been undetected, he could not be certain. Discarding his traditional garments, he had Goto purchase Western-style clothing for him. There was little else he could do other than change his glasses and now wore ones with oversized lenses and heavy black frames. He had also applied some dark tint to his hair, leaving sufficient gray to avoid the appearance of an obvious dye job. Goto had adopted the guise of a business executive with the purchase of a dark suit, white shirts, and a variety of dull ties. An ever-present briefcase was his adopted accessory, and as soon as a room was available at the crowded Hilton International Guam hotel, he would be taking a room there—at the opposite end of the beach area.

Ohiro and Taeko made sure they were always in the company of other vacationing couples and seldom allowed themselves to be out alone. A Do Not Disturb sign was constantly on their hotel door. Taeko had achieved some measure of figure alteration by padding her bra and hips when in street clothes and fixing her hair in a completely different manner.

Overnight, Sakamoki had become one of the Japanese cowboy

enthusiasts. Dressed in Western style, he kept a Walkman earphone plugged in when outside and had become a regular among the single male crowd who spent most of their time at the popular Island Shooting Gallery, one of the many gun clubs in the area.

Thus, the five terrorists had melded in with the mass of Japanese working and playing in Guam, their false identities well supported by their passports and personal papers provided by the Soviet Mongol back in Tokyo.

Genda was anxious to get his people together, and at the moment he considered a rendezvous with Goto most important. Time could be of the essence. He dialed Goto's room. "I think we should meet."

"Your room?"

"Yes."

"*Hai*, Genda-san." Goto's acknowledgment was overly solicitous.

Genda knew his companion would figure a severe tongue-lashing would be forthcoming as a result of the 747 downing, and there was a strong urge in Genda's heart to do just that—it was overdue—but this was a time for more objective reasoning. Checking his appearance, Genda uttered a grunt of disapproval at the dark-blue cotton pants and flowery sport shirt. How could he project the dignity of a samurai in such clothes?

Within minutes, Goto arrived and Genda motioned him inside. "Sit in the chair. I'll sit on the bed."

Goto sat and waited.

Keeping his voice low, Genda spoke. "I've changed my mind. I think we should all meet soon."

"I thought we were a bit concerned about all of the police presence."

"I am inclined to think it is more of a local search for an island criminal."

Goto was not so sure. "I do not know."

"In any event, while this is a good place for us for the moment, we must make plans for continuing on to our next objective." Genda rose and walked to the window to gaze at the area in front of the hotel. "We are certainly among our own kind. Where do so many of our youth get such money to come here?"

"Ha! It is cheaper than staying in Tokyo and having their parties!"

Genda sighed. "True, enough, I suppose. I will never become accustomed to such wealth among children."

"These children, Genda-san, are for the most part very successful capitalists—our American mentors have taught us well. They are not executives, necessarily—their kind stay at the Hilton or Pacific Star—but these young people are climbing the ladder toward corporate positions. You are looking at exactly the type countrymen we socialists oppose. They live well by the sweat of others, and that has never been the Japanese way. It is economic oppression. That is why we fight."

Genda took a long sip of his beer. "Fight? I haven't heard of much fighting by the Red Army. Shooting down unarmed airliners seems to be more your style."

Goto did not appreciate the sarcasm of the remark but did not wish to give Genda the chance to pursue the subject. He continued with his own thought. "The times have not been too ripe. The workers need to be more discontented. That will come as we see the gulf between the corporate executives and the workers widen. When they are ready to do something about the situation, the Red Army will be there."

Genda grunted. "Huumff." Goto's traditional Party argument seemed tired and dated. As much as he disliked the reason behind the new prosperity of Japan, Genda knew that the man in the street recognized his slice of the pie as being quite attainable. True, the average Tokyoan might live in an unbelievably cramped space and face an everyday fight with the maddening traffic and population crush within the city, but he had more material possessions than ever before. More important, he had opportunity. Revolutionaries were never those with opportunity. The rural Japanese were even more well off, when one considered their relatively spacious farm homes and their increasing ability to provide themselves with an improved standard of living. Goto was living in his own narrow world. There would be no national labor-management discontent for a very long time. The Red Army would slowly die off with its dreams, its only political philosophy, revolution, being completely alien to the Japanese, whose life was built around a generations-ingrained respect for authority. The pitiful cell now employed by Genda was a good case in point. Goto was a ne'er-do-well at best; Ohiro was a deserter from his country's armed forces; Sakamoki was an immature ex-student; and Taeko an oversexed ex-bar hostess. If he didn't need such fools, he would drop them without a second thought. But they would be useful to him. Still, he would not allow them another opportunity to double-cross him.

Genda put his doubts aside. "I don't think we should delay. Alert the others. We will meet on the beach in an hour, the stretch directly behind the Fujita. There is usually a crowd milling around just before the afternoon ends."

"Why not here in your room?"

"Because I have decided to meet on the beach!" Immediately, Genda regretted letting Goto's questioning irritate him. Meeting in the room would be safer, but he would not admit that now. *He* would decide when and where to do things.

"What is your plan?"

"I will discuss it then."

"In an hour," Goto repeated as he left.

Genda pulled off his shoes and lay back on the bed. He felt lightheaded and extremely tired. There was no pain, but he knew that the disease within him was progressing. He had no stamina. He glanced at the calendar: December 3, 1991. It would be a day earlier in Honolulu. He tried to formulate his last action but his mind refused to follow any logical sequence of thought. He should rest. He dialed the front desk.

"This is three-thirty-one. Please give me a call in one hour."

It felt good to lie down. Within a few minutes, he was asleep.

Taeko was too close to her orgasm to tolerate interruption by the ringing telephone. "Don't . . . answer . . . it," she gasped, pulling Ohiro harder against her. As for Ohiro, he was already exhausted to the point of pain and an excuse for even a brief respite from the demands of his mistress was most welcome.

"I have to, it could be Genda."

"Fuck Genda!"

Ohiro flashed a look of amusement at Taeko. "I will ask him over." He rolled off Taeko and reached for the phone. "Yes?"

"Goto. We meet on the beach in an hour, directly behind the Fujita. Tell Sakamoki."

"In an hour."

Taeko pulled him back to her before he could replace the phone in its cradle.

Ohiro resigned himself to his fate. *In an hour I will be a thoroughly drained corpse.*

Sakai and Kami sipped coffee and studied the map of Guam on the wall of Chief Chimananshe's office.

"I didn't know Japanese drank coffee," Sakai commented.

"You are Japanese," Kami reminded him.

"Once removed."

"I like coffee on occasion and on this occasion there is no tea. I am not sure that Guamanians are a civilized people."

Sakai turned his thoughts back to the case at hand. "This is not a big island."

"No. Chimananshe says they have checked the larger hotels and have people at the airport and at the boat docks. I don't think Genda would be that stupid—to try and leave right away."

"I agree. They'll hide out, perhaps try and change their appearance. Stay apart. But if they're planning an operation they'll have to expose themselves. What do you figure they will do?"

"Hit another American target, perhaps one of the military installations."

"What with? They couldn't have brought any more missiles with them."

Kami agreed. "They have small arms, you can count on that, and there are explosives on the island and people who respond to yen— or dollars."

"They'll need a vehicle."

"That is just what I was thinking, Sakai-san. Maybe that should be our starting point. Our first lead in Osaka was the car rental agency."

"The airport first and then local rental offices."

"Then the small hotels along Tumon Beach as the Chief suggested?"

"Exactly." To Sakai, it was almost eerie working with Kami; he was practically a clone of Kaneyama both in appearance and in his thought processes. Sakai had rapidly warmed to Kaneyama's easygoing professionalism and give-and-take banter. When one of the terrorists put a bullet in the Tokyo detective's head, Sakai had felt deep grief, as if he had lost a longtime friend. Now he was becoming just as attached to Shiganori Kami. Sakai wasn't sure that was a good thing.

. . .

Genda and his people stood casually in a small group amid the chatter and excited activities of the larger beach crowd.

"We cannot stay on this island much longer," Genda began. "There is a critical time element to our last action. I believe we all feel comfortable among our countrymen here. We rarely even see any of the islanders. Still, I think it is time to consider our departure."

"But, Genda-san," protested Taeko, "Michio and I have observed considerable police activity, as have Goto and Sakamoki. They are looking for someone."

"As I stated earlier, I am confident they are searching for a local individual. Have they not been to your hotel? And have they inquired about any of us? If we are the objects of their search, they must have photographs of at least Goto and Ohiro and even me. No. Even if we are the ones they seek, our changes in appearance are good."

"Where will we be going?" Taeko asked, her voice nervous.

"I will tell you in due time. For the moment, I want someone to go to the airport and look around. See if departures are being scrutinized and how thoroughly, if they are. We will leave by air."

"I should do that," Goto announced. "It calls for experience."

"Good. Tomorrow, I will go to the South Pacific Memorial Park to pray for the spirit of my brother. When I return, you will report to me, Goto."

"*Hai*, Genda-san."

"The rest of you remain in your hotel. We should disperse now."

Genda walked off, then Sakamoki. Taeko waited for Ohiro.

"Taeko," Goto said, "you go ahead. I need to talk to Michio for a moment."

After the girl left, Goto spoke softly to Ohiro. "I am worried about Taeko. She seems very nervous."

"She is very upset about the 747."

"What has she been saying?"

"She says we are murderers. She just seems to have lost her enthusiasm for any further operations."

"Do you think she wants out?"

"I know she does. But where would she go?"

"Even if there were a place, we could not allow it. You know that."

"Yes."

"I think we must get rid of her."

"No—she will be all right."

"You are confident of that?"

"Goto-san, Taeko stood up under the rigid interrogation back in Tokyo. She is strong." Even as he spoke, Ohiro knew he had doubts.

"I do not deny that, but that was before the 747. Forget for a moment that she is your mistress. Being good in bed is not a substitute for the motivation we must have to accomplish our tasks."

"We have been together for three years. Why not just send her back to Japan?"

"Fool. She is the one of us whom the police have already interrogated and undoubtedly are looking for. She would be picked up the instant she set foot on Japanese soil. And what is to prevent her from going to the authorities here?"

"I can control her."

"We cannot take that chance. She must be dealt with. I will do it. I have no emotional attachment."

"Genda might not approve."

"He has no say in this. She belongs to our cell and she is on the verge of leaving—maybe betraying—us."

Ohiro knew Goto was right. When Taeko was not pulling him onto the bed with her she was complaining about being looked down upon by Genda. She was upset with the Osaka attack and getting impatient and anxious to be done with Genda and in possession of the promised payment. There was another factor: With Taeko gone, Genda's payment would be split three ways instead of four. And there was the deciding factor: Since arriving in Guam, Ohiro had discovered that he was tired of Taeko. She was becoming too demanding and much too assertive about her role in the cell. There was not another body on earth such as hers, but Ohiro was all too familiar with it and the excitement was not the same.

"You will have to do it. I cannot," Ohiro declared.

"I said I would."

"When?"

"I think tonight."

Genda lay in his room trying to recoup some of his energy. His need for rest was coming more frequently. His appetite was gone. After the beach meeting he had rested until dinnertime, then picked at his

meal and eaten little. He had been in his bed by nine in the evening—the sky was still light—and he had lain awake trying desperately to get to sleep until almost two in the morning, when his
phone had rung.

"Taeko is no longer with us."

Genda had recognized the voice as Goto's. "What do you mean?"

"She was threatening to go to the police."

"You have killed her?"

"There was no other choice."

"Why did you not contact me? Why was I not consulted?"

"You direct our operations. I handle my people when there are
internal conflicts. Believe me, it was necessary."

The fact that Goto had murdered the girl was disturbing to
Genda, but if she had been considering turning them in he could
not fault Goto for such action. In fact, he should applaud it. Still,
the action weighed heavily on his considerations of just what he was
becoming. Was he by association a murderer? Was he becoming as
callous as the terrorists? If he truly thought so, he would have drawn
a knife across his stomach this very morning. Still, the possibility
deeply troubled him. He tried to excuse himself from the downing
of the 747. He had given no such order. That had been Goto's doing.
Genda recognized that he would have to share the guilt, but he
refused to take the blame. He had played no part in the murder of
the girl, but he knew he condoned it. His one consolation was that
his final act would be indeed one of great achievement and honor.
Until then, he would have to tolerate his companions and try to be
content with the thought that the end justified the means. And at
some point, he would need only Ohiro. Then, eliminating Goto and
the fool, Sakamoki, would be an act of samurai justice, and such a
deed would in some measure cleanse him of the guilt in the tragedy
of United Flight 809.

The early-morning call had aggravated his inability to go to sleep.
He had managed to drift in and out of the state, but disturbed by
a dream that seemed to pick up where it left off each time he closed
his eyes. At first it was a pleasant dream, for he was back in the
cockpit of his Zero and fighting skillfully with a trio of blue Hellcats. He shot down two, but as he closed to make his third kill he
could see the pilot's helmet in the cockpit. Just as he squeezed his
gun trigger the helmet turned and the face was that of Emiko.
"No!" he screamed, trying in vain to release the pressure on the

button. But he could not and his tracers entered the Hellcat cockpit. Emiko's face disappeared in a burst of blood and flesh.

Genda sat up, once more awake. Even as he had dreamed, he had known that the nightmare was only in his subconscious, but he awoke wet with sweat and completely spent from the feeling of guilt generated by the trick of his mind. He calmed himself. He had not killed Emiko. The Americans had done that. Still, he refused to try for rest again.

It was just as well. Wearily, he realized that it was time for him to get up and go to the South Pacific Memorial Park.

"Well, good morning, how goes the search?" Chief Chimananshe entered his office with his cheeks full of fresh apple. He tossed the core into his wastebasket.

Sakai and Kami were waiting for him. "No leads. Kami-san and I hit the car rental agencies and a number of the low-end hotels. We'll start off the day with those on the north end of Tumon Beach. Your people have any luck?"

Chimananshe shrugged. "Several leads. None checked out. But the search is narrowing. We at least know where they are not."

A police clerk entered after a polite knock and laid a folder on Chimananshe's desk. "Preliminary coroner's report," the officer said as he left.

"Life goes on," Kami tilted his head toward the folder.

Chimananshe picked it up. "And so does death." Thumbing through the folder, he continued: "Young woman. Beach patrol found her last night, face beaten beyond recognition, fingertips mutilated. No ID. Just a tattoo."

At the mention of the tattoo, Kami leaned forward. "Tattoo? Where? What kind?"

Chimananshe looked up at the Japanese detective. "Butterfly— inside left thigh."

Sakai rose from his chair. "Taeko Nikahura! Didn't the ID flyers mention the tattoo?"

Chimananshe shook his head. "No."

"It has to be her. No random killer would beat away the face and destroy the fingertips. What's her description?"

Chimananshe read from the report. "Female, early twenties, one hundred and one pounds, five feet, three inches, sexual activity within past twenty-four hours. No scars or marks other than the tattoo. Time of death, approximately midnight. Cause of death, severe head trauma."

Kami snapped his fingers. "That will be Taeko. The question is why. And so brutally."

"To keep her from being identified." Chimananshe swallowed the last of his apple.

"Then the idiots left the butterfly tattoo."

"You can look at her if you like."

"Yes. I need to see the tattoo for confirmation. A photo record was sent to us at Osaka when the girl was being interrogated concerning the car-bombing incident. It is a standard Red Army mark they put on their women."

Fifteen minutes later, Sakai and Kami were gazing down at the sheet covering the female as she lay in the cooler drawer in the coroner's laboratory. Sakai pulled back the cover to view the face but there was none, just a mass of mashed bone and contusions. Kami lifted the cloth and folded it back over the left thigh. Pulling the flesh gently, he rolled the leg outward.

"That's it."

"Taeko Nikahura." Sakai spoke as if he expected the girl to answer. "Why would they do this?"

"I can think of several possibilities," Kami ventured.

"Jealousy?"

"Possibly. Or maybe she had outlived her usefulness."

"She was a strong member of the group."

"Things change, Sakai-san. It is of little importance to us as to why they did it."

"Assuming it was one of Genda's group, that could mean they are here on this side of the island."

Kami replaced the cloth and the attendant rolled Taeko back into the refrigerated unit. Kami offered another opinion. "There was evidence of sexual activity. It could have been rape."

"I doubt that, not with her background. And not with the thorough attempt to remove her identity. Maybe some unanswered questions, Kami-san, but I think maybe time is shortening for Genda."

Back in Chimananshe's office, the three sat around the chief's desk and reviewed the situation.

After a while, Chimananshe mused, "So, we have a vengeful old man who hates Americans—and has a good reason for that hate, I would agree—and is determined to strike back. Does he feel he will regain his lost honor by that?"

Sakai felt certain that was a factor in the mind of the troubled Genda. "I believe that is the key. Genda is old school, traditional Japanese. He thinks of himself as a warrior, perhaps even as a samurai. I could see that when I first met him at his cottage on Hokkaido. In his mind, he is acting honorably, seeking to strike those who struck his nation and his Emperor. To Genda, the act of killing Americans—as long as they are military or at least governmental—is proper repayment for the killing of his innocent parents and the rape of his wife by those Americans. He has never given up the World War II fight; he merely set it aside until he gained the wherewithall and the mind-set to resume hostilities. He could have no other motivation. The man is intelligent and a career naval officer."

"I would carry your analysis one step further," Kami added. "There are many veterans of World War II living still in Japan. Many of them suffered similar atrocities as did Genda and are as bitter. But they have recognized that what happened fifty years ago was the result of a terrible war and have adjusted to that. Genda simply has not adjusted. Something in his mind just never snapped back into place. Despite his considerable accomplishments in the JMSDF, he has never entered the modern world. In that sense, he is mentally flawed."

"Insane?" Chimananshe asked.

"That is not my field, but I would say some sort of delayed psychological disorder, created by his extreme grief at the loss of his parents and wife and the dishonor of being a defeated—but still living—samurai. He may even be out of touch with reality."

Sakai knew Kami had a point. "And that is what bothers me. I have read that a person in such a mental state is capable of doing things not considered attainable by the normal mind, simply because that person does not recognize the limitations of a given goal. Genda may have something in mind that goes far beyond the destruction of the United flight, and he may even have a chance at carrying it out."

Sakai and Kami walked away from the Terraza Tumon Villa Hotel and climbed back into their patrol car.

"That's the last one," Sakai said.

"We still have the Mai' Ana and a couple of the sleezy pads over near the airport."

Sakai checked his watch. It was almost noon. "Let's head over to the Tumon substation. I want to call Chimananshe and let him know we've finished the beach area."

"Why not use the car radio?"

"I need to ask him several things. No need to tie up the radio circuit that long. The substation is just a few blocks back. We need a sandwich break, anyhow."

"What a poor representative of the honorable race of Japanese you are. A sandwich break with excellent *ryokan* dining rooms all around us. Where do you want to go? *McDonald's?*

Sakai turned the needle around and gave it back. "No, you are right. A good dish of fish entrails and seaweed would be much more nutritional."

"I do not eat fish entrails."

"Let's compromise—we stop at a deli."

"Now you are talking, Sakai-san!" Kami guided the car back onto the beach highway and headed west. Once in the substation, Sakai dialed Chief Chimananshe's office.

"We're finished with the beach area. Nothing. I was wondering—"

"Just a moment! I was just trying to call you, Sakai. We may have an ID on Genda!"

"What? Great! What's the story?"

"We have flyers out to all the cab drivers. One says he took a man answering to Genda's general description to the South Pacific Memorial Park on the north end of the island and waited while the man went into the temple there. A half hour later he returned the man to his hotel."

"The name of the hotel?"

"The Terraza Tumon Villa."

"For Christ's sake! We just left there! The desk clerk could not make any of the photos."

"Well, the cab driver isn't positive, but suspicious enough to give us a call. You want to check it out or shall we?"

"Kami and I will take it. We'll get back to you."

Sakai hung up the phone and looked at Kami, his face still reflecting the astonishment of having been right where Genda might have been. "The Terraza Tumon Villa. A cab driver says he dropped a man answering Genda's description there less than an hour ago."

The equally surprised Osaka detective grabbed his head with both hands. "He was there when we were checking!"

Both hurried out the door. Kami roared off before Sakai could close his car door and drove back east on the beach highway. Within minutes they were at the Terraza Tumon Villa Hotel. A number of the occupants of the small three-story hotel were milling around in front of it, probably trying to decide on their day's activities.

Sakai and Kami entered a side door. "You give the desk clerk another chance to look at the pictures," Sakai suggested. "I will ask around the lobby area."

He walked first into the small lounge area.

Saburo Genda was at a window table sipping hot tea and watching the activity outside.

Chapter 18

"Captain Genda."

Genda immediately recognized the voice and inflection. His shoulders dropped and he leaned back in his chair to look up at Sakai. "The nisei from the U.S. State Department," he muttered, his voice full of resignation. He nodded. "I am surprised."

"Yes, Captain, and you are under arrest for conspiracy to murder and the first-degree murder of over five hundred persons killed in the United crash at Osaka and those killed by the car-bombing attack upon the American Embassy in Tokyo." Even as he spoke, Sakai was shocked to see how much thinner Genda had become since their meeting back on Hokkaido. The old man's cheeks were shallow and his eyes set back into his head. He had the gaunt look of a seriously ill man. It was no wonder that the desk clerk had failed to ID him from the wanted photo.

"You are mistaken. I know nothing of what you speak."

Sakai sat down across from Genda and studied the old man's face. Despite its reflection of a sickness, it was calm. "Why? Why have you done such terrible things?"

"You are indeed out of your mind. I am here on my way to Pohnpei to visit my brother's grave. This very morning, I visited the

South Pacific Memorial Park and prayed for the eternal peace of his soul. It is a pilgrimage."

"It is over, Captain Genda. You are here as the leader of a group of Red Army terrorists. We have identified the body of Taeko Nikahura. You will be charged with her murder also."

Genda's expression did not change. "I know nothing of what you speak."

"Captain Genda, I know that you feel you are an honorable man, but I have no respect for you now. You have let your hatred make you a terrorist and a murderer. I do not believe that was your intent but it has happened. Where are your companions?"

Genda's eyes narrowed. "I did not order the destruction of the American airplane."

"If that is true, Captain, help me catch those who did."

"You must understand. I am a samurai. I owe allegiance only to my Emperor. I must fight his enemies until my own death in battle releases my spirit and I join my companions at the Yasakuni Shrine." Genda stared directly into Sakai's eyes. "You are not my enemy, nisei, but the Americans who killed my parents and raped my beloved Emiko are."

"They are long dead, Captain. The passage of time has revenged your loss."

Detective Kami had entered and was standing quietly behind Genda. Sakai glanced up and shook his head sadly. Then he looked back at Genda. "You must come with me, Captain Genda."

"May I finish my tea?"

"Of course." Sakai looked back up at Kami and mouthed a call for a backup unit. Kami walked outside to their car to relay the request.

The tea seemed to revitalize the old warrior. His look softened and he smiled for the first time. "You must understand me, nisei. Can you at all?"

"I don't know, Captain. I would like to."

Genda sat erect. "I was a pilot with the Imperial Japanese Navy—a Thunder God. Are you familiar with the Thunder Gods, nisei?"

"No, Captain, I am afraid not."

"We were special. Hand-picked for a sacred mission, the most elite of the elite. Many of us flew the *Ohka*, the Exploding Cherry

Blossom. It was the ultimate weapon. Some of us flew the great Mitsubishi Type Zero. Are you familiar with it?"

"I have heard of it, of course."

"It was the world's best fighter aircraft. Nothing could touch it in a dogfight. Nothing. Our pilots flew eight-hour missions. Ten-hour missions! *Ten hours* in a fighter plane. I was selected to fly it to my death—and in a way I have been dead since that time. It was a glorious time, nisei, and I was a Thunder God. Seventeen years old . . ." Genda's words trailed off.

Sakai leaned forward and placed a hand on Genda's arm. "Captain, it is time to go." Outside, Kami was waiting with two Guamanian police officers who had arrived in a backup car.

Genda nodded. "Yes, yes. You are a good person, nisei, but do not ever forget your heritage. You understand me. I will tell you everything that you need to know."

"Thank you, Captain." Sakai took Genda's arm and guided him out toward the waiting car. The two policemen met them at the lobby door, one of them with open handcuffs.

Genda looked plaintively at Sakai. "Must I wear those?"

Sakai indicated to the policeman that he should put the cuffs away. "No, Captain. I will ride with you."

Most of the people outside began to approach the police activity at the entrance to the Terraza Tumon Villa Hotel, curious about the arrest of an old man. Kami walked out to hold them back, as did one of the uniformed policemen. Neither saw the rapid approach of a gray Nissan sedan that burst out from the far side of the Fujita and roared up the street between the two hotels. The automobile announced its intentions with a shattering volley of gunfire.

The policeman walking in front of Kami dropped, a fountain of blood erupting through his punctured uniform T-shirt, and Kami dove for cover behind his car. The policeman with Sakai and Genda flung himself against the hood of the black-and-white police car and began returning fire but was immediately hit in the head and tumbled backward onto the ground. Sakai had pulled his weapon, but the panic-stricken crowd was running across his line of fire. He pressed himself against the police car and twisted around to help Genda, whom he had thown to the ground at the first sound of the attack. The Thunder God was gone.

The intense gunfire from the Nissan forced Sakai to keep low.

When he finally felt he had a chance, he rose to return the fire, but the Nissan was speeding away, the left rear door still ajar. Genda's legs were thrashing outside the car but the accomplice in the backseat had a firm grip and began to pull him inside.

Grabbing the police car mike, Sakai called for help. "Police officer down! Terraza Tumon Villa Hotel! Request assistance. Armed terrorist suspects are heading east on beachfront road in a gray Nissan four-door sedan. Armed and dangerous!" He sprinted over to Kami, who was sliding into the driver's seat of their car. "Let's go!" the Osaka detective yelled.

Kami drove as if the devil were chasing him with a nonstop ticket to the deepest, darkest reaches of Hell, but the Nissan stayed a steady distance ahead. Doggedly, he followed it into a hard right turn onto a street leading away from the beach, his tires squealing in protest and threatening to roll off the rims. "They're heading for the main highway!"

Sakai relayed the information over the radio and tried to steady himself as Kami passed a slow pickup truck with opposite traffic closing fast. Another coat of paint, thought Sakai, and it would have been crash city!

The Nissan fishtailed to the left onto Highway One. "They're heading east on One!" Sakai reported. He leaned out his window and fired but with no apparent results. There was not a lot of traffic, but he could see that his shooting opportunities would be hampered. The terrorists had no such restraint. A volley of gunfire forced him to duck back inside the car as Kami swerved back and forth to present a difficult target. The maneuvering also cost Sakai a chance at getting a steady shot. "Damn it, Kami, hold this thing steady!"

"Keep down, Sakai-san! They have us outgunned. I am going to back off until some other unit can cut them off . . . oh, shit!"

A white contrail of steam erupted from the front of the car and cascaded back over the hood and windshield.

"They have punctured our radiator!" Kami turned on the windshield wipers but the steam continued to cover most of his field of vision. The wipers furiously swept back and forth but were completely overcome by the volume of hot moisture escaping from the radiator.

Sakai unfolded the car's road map, trying to keep track of where they were heading. "Suspects swinging southeast on Highway One, proceeding toward . . . Dadedo!"

A violent grinding sound preceded a sudden grabbing of the rear wheels and then the transmission began to come apart as the engine seized. The breakdown caused a sharp swerve to the right. Kami fought skillfully to keep the car from rolling over but could not prevent it from smashing through a wire fence bordering a small manufacturing building. He stomped on the brakes and they skidded to a halt. "Dog shit!" he cursed, thoroughly disgusted.

"Chase terminated . . . we're out of it," Sakai reported. "Suspects last seen continuing southeast on Highway One toward Dadedo."

Thoroughly winded, Genda lay half on the floor and half on the backseat of the speeding Nissan.

"They are gone." Ohiro was still holding onto him.

Relieved of pressure of the chase, the driver, Goto, half turned and spoke to Genda. "We're very lucky. Ohiro and I were talking in his room at the Fujita and he just happened to look out and see the police car pull up in front of your hotel. What happened back there?"

"I was recognized by a Japanese-American who works for the U.S. State Department. He just walked right up to me and sat down." Genda made his way fully onto the rear seat. "There will be roadblocks everywhere; head for the east side of the island."

"What is over there?"

"It is what is not over there that matters. It is mostly open road. We may have to swap this car. There! Up ahead is Highway Twenty-six."

The Nissan was just leaving Dadedo.

"Take a right!" Genda ordered.

"There are no markings," Goto protested.

"It is the correct highway. I have studied the map of the island just in case something like this arose. It will take us over to the east coast road and then we can go south toward the hills."

There was no sign of any police cars, but Genda knew that units were being dispatched all over the island and rushing to blockade critical intersections. He and his companions would have to encounter one sooner or later. If they could reach the intersection of the coastal highway and Highway Ten before the police could react they might reach the small town of Mangilao safely. Possibly, they could commandeer another car there. They were probably seven or eight miles from Mangilao—about five minutes providing their speeding Nissan did not attract a local cop.

Goto hit the outskirts of Mangilao doing fifty. He slowed and looked for a side street.

Genda tapped him on the shoulder. "No! Even if we get another car, there will be too many places they can intercept us. We have to get off the island."

"Off the island?" As far as Goto was concerned, Genda might as well have suggested they go to the moon. "How in the hell do we do that? All of the port facilities are on the other side and that is a hornet nest of police by now."

"Keep going ahead—we have a way."

Goto shrugged. What other course had he other than to keep going?

"There!" Genda exclaimed. "That sign. Take the left turn."

They had just passed through Mangilao and the sign ahead read UNIVERSITY OF GUAM. The entry road led into a cluster of inconspicuous university buildings scattered across a neatly manicured green lawn. Only a few persons were present walking across the campus.

Genda waved his hand ahead. "They have a school of oceanography here. That means boats."

Ahead, a smaller sign indicated that the oceanography school lay dead ahead. The pavement ended but the road remained smooth.

Goto began to have a real appreciation for Genda's thoroughness. The old man seemed to always be a step ahead of the situation. A slight bend in the road led to a small parking area only fifty or so yards from the cliffs bordering the Pacific. A greenhouse-type building squatted amid the heavy foliage, and behind it a steep flight of wooden steps led down to the water and a wooden boat pier.

The only occupant of the pier, a young man, most probably a graduate student or associate professor, was tying up a cabin cruiser. Goto judged it to be an eighteen-footer.

"Hello!" the young man said. "Can I help you?"

Goto and Ohiro approached him. "*Dozo*, we are looking for Professor Akuni."

The young man pursed his lips while his mind tried to place the name. "Akuni? I don't know if we have anyone by that name; not in the oceanography department, anyhow. Could he be in—"

Goto's fist interrupted the reply and the young man fell heavily backward. Ohiro drove his shoe into the side of the man's head. Quickly, he and Goto placed their hands across the unconscious man's mouth and nose and held them there while Sakamoki searched the man's pockets for the keys to the boat. There were none.

"Here!" Genda shouted. "The key is in the ignition." He jumped on board as his three companions dragged the man into the thick brush, all the while keeping his mouth and nose blocked. He was apparently dead from suffocation by the time they released their grip. They started covering him with loose foliage.

Goto grabbed Ohiro's arm. "Wait, we have to be sure." He scooped up a handful of loose dirt and began packing it into the man's nose and mouth. "It will be days before they find him. I want to make certain that he stays here."

The boat was a new inboard research craft, and in addition to the instrumentation it featured an ample galley and a supply of fresh water and packaged food. If necessary, they could lay off the coast of Guam for days, although Genda was hoping that such a tactic would not be their best of options. Ohiro had the engine started by the time Goto and Sakamoki cast off the lines.

Sakai and Detective Kami sat in Chief Chimananshe's office, thoroughly disgusted with their performance. "Sometimes," Sakai said, "I think I would screw up a two-car funeral."

"We will get them, Sakai-san. This island is a finite piece of land."

Chimananshe returned carrying a Diet Coke. "Nothing. Our roadblocks are in place and we have military units supplementing our patrols. They have slipped away for the moment. But it is only a matter of time."

"Your men?" Kami was concerned about the two shot policemen.

"Sergeant Keno was DOA. Sergeant Murray died on the operating table."

"I am sorry."

"Keno was a bachelor but Murray has three kids. Four months from retirement."

All three looked up as a clerk entered the office and placed a file folder on Chimananshe's desk. Sakai started to get out of the chief's chair.

"Keep it," Chimananshe said, stooping to pick up the folder.

"The routine goes on." He thumbed through the few pages in the folder. "We're not a big crime area compared to the States but we have our problems."

Sakai walked over and peered across Chimananshe's shoulder at the folder.

"Twenty-four-hour summary for yesterday," Chimananshe explained. "One homicide. One domestic quarrel. Three burglaries, one convenience store holdup, a fight that cost a good cop a broken nose when he tried to break it up. A car theft."

"Not at all bad compared to D.C.," Sakai commented, reading from the file.

"I can imagine."

Chimananshe placed the folder on his desk. "Don't understand the homicide. The guy was a high school teacher from Ohio—here on an organized tour. Killed in his hotel room. Nothing stolen. Oh, well. The homicide boys can handle it. We've got more serious problems."

Kami lifted a soaked tea bag from his cup and dropped it into the wastebasket. "I am surprised none of the patrols over on the east side have made any sightings. We radioed their location and direction."

The chief nodded. "Yes. That means the devils have left the main roads. Maybe a side road and a place to hole up. It'll take a while to search all of those but we will."

"They really surprised me at the Terraza," Sakai observed.

"Me, also," Kami added. "They really burst out from the back of the Fujita. They must have been staying there and saw us come out or the arrival of the patrol car could have alerted them."

"Maybe I should have been driving, Kami-san. I am not much of a shot with a handgun. You may have been able to hit them."

"I believe the expression is 'spilled milk' is it not?"

"Ha! That is right. An old American expression. Do not cry over spilled milk."

"Besides, Sakai-san, I am not the best shot on the force either. I would have done no better."

The squawk box on the chief's desk came alive. "Chief, Agent Tonishi is here."

Both Sakai and Kami looked questioningly at the chief as the Japanese name was announced.

Chimananshe explained: "Japanese naval intelligence. One of the agents assigned to routine surveillance of Genda after he retired.

Tokyo called and filled me in and said they were sending him in the event he could be of any service."

Kami felt a slight embarrassment at not having been previously informed, but another law officer was certainly welcome, especially one with a thorough knowledge of their principal quarry.

Chimananshe walked to his door to greet the arrival. Kami stood to one side as the man walked in, looking past Chimananshe and smiling directly at Sakai. "Special Agent Tonishi, Japanese Maritime Self-Defense Force Intelligence," the man said, bowing to Chimananshe but letting his eyes twinkle at Sakai.

Sakai had the feeling that he had a lot to learn about the fine points of the Japanese intelligence network. The man bowing to Chief Chimananshe was the one-armed innkeeper from Urohoro.

Genda stood in the rear of the boat well aft of the cabin, looking seaward and estimating the amount of daylight left. Too much. The sun was still thirty degrees above the horizon. They were out in open water, several hundred yards off the shoreline and proceeding south in plain view of anyone along the southeast coast of Guam. From the beach, the white research boat on the deep-blue water must be as conspicuous as a wart on a nun's face. However, unless the theft of the boat had been detected or the body of the young man uncovered, a small boat cruising offshore should not be of any special interest to anyone. He could see several craft sailing the same water, another powerboat several miles to the southwest, a sloop under full sail to the north, probably returning to Pago Bay just to the south of the University of Guam. A small freighter was far to seaward, also steaming north.

He scanned the skies. No signs of any aircraft or helicopters. That would be the first indication; the American military must have search-and-rescue helicopters on alert, and one would surely be scrambled if the boat or body were found.

Goto was at the helm. "Where will we go? We can't stay out here forever."

"We should make for an inlet and lay to until nightfall," Genda suggested. "The coastal road is a mile or so inland. After dark, we can continue south. There is a place we may be able to hide for at least a while. Cocos Island—there, just about two points off the starboard bow. It looks like a good place."

Goto had no idea what "two points off the starboard bow" meant, so he sighted in the direction of Genda's raised arm.

"Ohiro, take the helm," Genda ordered. "Steer for the inlet. Goto, we need to talk."

Goto joined Genda. He could see that Genda was exhausted. "If you are looking for a plan, I have none," Goto said.

"No. I have the plan. But it may be only a temporary thing. There is a massive dragnet set up by now. I am afraid our chances of continuing our mission are diminishing rapidly."

It was the first time Goto had heard the old man even speak of not carrying out his final task—whatever that was. But he could understand. From his standpoint their situation was only a whisker away from complete hopelessness. Why had the old fool brought them to Guam—and why had they not resisted and stayed in Japan?

Genda fixed his eyes on the faraway freighter as he continued. "I think we have to consider the possibility of imminent capture."

"But you said you had some sort of plan."

"I do, but I am not sure it will buy us anything but time."

"Then I say we try it, regardless."

"Perhaps. On the other hand, there is an honorable way out for us."

Goto did not like the inference. He was not a traditionalist. Nor had he any real appreciation for a custom that had all but disappeared in modern Japan. "I will not kill myself."

"We have accomplished much. If we can do no more, why give the authorities the opportunity to place us on public trial? The spectacle will cause the ashes of our ancestors to writhe in shame. By our own hand we can die with dignity. In the end, it may be the only way."

"Not for me, fool." Goto no longer had any fear of offending Genda. The old man was obviously ill. Even if he were not, Goto would not be caught by surprise, as had Ohiro. If Genda attempted to strike him, he was ready. He tensed, awaiting Genda's response.

Genda merely shrugged. "We will talk again later. For now, I will guide us in the plan I spoke of."

Goto turned and went forward, furious at finding himself in such a position. He had allowed Genda too much leeway in his leadership. Goto was the experienced terrorist. He might never have been a markedly successful one, but neither had he ever backed himself and his people into such a corner. He would not kill himself, but for the first time he considered killing Genda. That would provide him some satisfaction before they were finally caught.

Genda was not at all surprised by Goto's response to his suggestion of ritual suicide. The man was a thug without any sense of personal honor and certainly had no appreciation for his ancestors or national heritage. He was of a different generation. And Sakamoki was even of another. It would not be necessary to question him. In his youth, Sakamoki was undoubtedly living in that frame of mind that all young people harbored. Death was a very faraway thing and he would undoubtedly choose capture and trial.

That left Ohiro. He had been military and must at one time have had a sense of personal honor and duty to country. Before Genda made his decision he must question Ohiro and now was the time.

"Forgive me for staring," Sakai apologized.

Agent Tonishi nodded, amused. "Of course. I can understand your surprise."

"Beautiful cover."

"A natural. I am of Genda's generation. After I was captured at Okinawa, I spent some time in your medical facilities before being repatriated to Japan. A number of your occupational doctors were consultants at the time as our medical resources had been depleted by the war. They saved my life. I managed to get some education after the occupation ended and went to work for the maritime arm of the JSDF as a clerk in the intelligence section. My career years paralleled Genda's. We both retired about the same time—he as a senior officer, I as a minor investigative agent. We wanted to continue surveillance on him due to his association with the Soviets, but he was not considered worthy of a full-time agent. So, the inn at Urohoro was purchased and I installed as the innkeeper. It gave me a more secure retirement and Genda and I naturally came together and became friends, although no one gets close to the man."

"We are very glad you are here."

"I do not know what I can contribute, but Genda is, as I said, my friend and he was once a man of great honor. I do not understand why he has become involved in such terrible activities."

"You indicated at our last meeting in Urohoro that you had no idea that Genda was gone from his cottage. Was that true or was that part of your innkeeper role?"

"It was true. I knew nothing. He had given me no indications of leaving."

Tonishi accepted tea from Chimananshe. "How may I be of assistance?"

Chimananshe took his chair while Sakai leaned against the wall. "We have the whole island covered. Unless you can offer some insight into what Genda may do next, I think we can only wait."

"I will tell you this. Genda is a master tactician. He would have risen further within the JMSDF had not his attitude toward Americans been so embarrassing. And I can tell you that whatever he is doing at this moment, it is not standing still. He is planning and plotting and making every effort to avoid capture. He will not give up. That is not his nature."

"Nor is it mine," Chief Chimananshe replied quietly.

Genda watched while the others covered the boat with foliage. The inlet was well protected by steep canyon walls overgrown with the thick flora of southern Guam. They had food and water. It would be unlikely that anyone would wander down from the coastal road above; the terrain was too rugged and passage through the brush would be almost impossible. They could hide for days provided the theft of the boat were not discovered. But that was inevitable. A coastal search would result and every indentation in the island would be searched. So safe time was limited.

He rested and listened to the soft lap of the water against the boat and the shoreline. For him, there was a special essence to the island of Guam. It had been the first territory taken from the Americans at the outbreak of the war and one of the last to be given up. His brother had first fought on Guam before being assigned to Ponape. Ironically, Guam was now a Japanese playground and for all practical purposes a Japanese possession. Hotel row along Tumon Bay represented considerable Japanese investments. The entertainment and restaurant communities catered primarily to the Japanese and the rare American tourist was hard-pressed to find even a menu in English. Even the typical American franchise, Tony Roma's Ribs, served rice with its delicious pork. The tourist road map of the island was in Japanese script.

The yen had succeeded where blood had failed.

Genda sat in the stern of the boat and studied the changing colors of the setting sun. The evening insect noises were beginning and there was just the hint of a cool sea breeze. The moist green foliage rising up the canyon walls was giving off a medley of sweet odors.

There could be some satisfaction in dying in such a place.

Chapter 19

The early December snow cascaded onto the District of Columbia with a vengeance. The previous falls of the season had been spotty and light but now the evening automobile traffic was fighting foot-deep drifts as the winds behind the slow-moving cold front swept through the capital and drove the large flakes across central D.C. with a fury that foretold a long night ahead.

The beltway was an immobile river of stalled cars, only a few lucky ones mushing ahead to take whatever off-ramp was available. Even those efforts were futile, for the streets off the beltway were equally crowded. Snowplows tried, their operators cursing and waving at stalled vehicles as if the trapped cars could respond, but they could do little except take their place in the jumble of traffic.

The mall was by contrast a thing of beauty, the heavy white blanket from the Capitol to the Washington Monument adding even more dignity to the monuments and buildings that were so precious to the people of the United States.

Occasionally, a snow-enshrouded airliner would make it off the embattled Washington National Airport and soar skyward to meld almost immediately into the low gray clouds over the Potomac, the flight crews undoubtedly thinking of another winter day, years back, when one of their number had roared down the runway laden with wing ice and had made it only as far as the 14th Street bridge before crashing into the ice-covered water. That would not happen again, the captains now insisting that a complete deicing be performed within a few minutes of takeoff. There were delays—but no deaths.

The president watched the snow fall from inside the warm confines of the oval office. A few days in Hawaii would be a welcome change. For a few minutes he had some time to himself, a very unusual occurrence. He must remember to bring back some macadamia nuts. He stood quietly and enjoyed the calm of the moment.

But such a luxury was a fleeting thing. A knock on the door preceded his chief of staff's entrance.

"The secretary is here, Mr. President."

The president remained facing the window. "Jack, do you like macadamia nuts?"

"Why—yes, Mr. President."

"They're my main weakness. I want to pick up some while we're in Honolulu."

The chief of staff smiled at the incongruity of the request. Why should the president of the United States have to pick up his own macadamia nuts? "I'll see to it, sir."

"Good." The president smiled to himself. Along with all of the eighteen-hour days and constant stress over international and national crises and bouts with the press and kissing all the asses that had put him in the oval office there were some very pleasant perks. He only had to mention macadamia nuts, for example, and when he returned from Hawaii, they would be there in the little white porcelain dish on his desk whenever he wanted them. Of course, even at this very moment, he could have one of his White House staff fight through the blizzard and pick up some at one of a hundred places in the District that sold macadamia nuts, but that would not be the same. Macadamia nuts should be personally brought back from Hawaii in your carry-on luggage, not bought at a nearby store after having ridden across the Pacific in the dark hold of a ship. And pineapples. He had never tasted a Stateside-purchased pineapple as good and fresh as he had brought back with him from Oahu, despite the fact that they all came from the same fields.

It was hard not to recall his first taste of macadamia nuts and fresh pineapple. Forty-seven years ago, as a nineteen-year-old crew-cutted ensign on his way to the South Pacific battle area, he had used those precious few days in the Territory of Hawaii to sit in the wide comfortable rattan chairs under the banyan tree at the army's Fort DeRussey on Waikiki Beach and sample the Mai Tai–soaked fresh fruit and down dozens of the large round nuts. He had become an instant addict. Now, in the autumn of his life, they tasted even better—as long as he brought them back himself from the fifty-first state. That was a prerequisite. And the opportunities were fewer and fewer. But one was coming up.

"Let's get to work," the president said. His rare reverie was over.

The secretary of state strolled into the oval office trailing a small entourage of assistants. His primary action officer on the U.S.-Japanese Mutual Defense Treaty carried several copies of the final draft. Bert Thompson, the chief of the Special Directorate for Terrorist Affairs, carried a clipboard that held a small collection of dispatches and memos. Jesse Simmons, the head of the CIA State Department liaison group, carried only a black notebook, and Murray Franklin, the Treasury Department head of the presidential security detail, gripped a white folder containing the approaching trip's security plan.

The men arranged themselves comfortably about the president's desk, the chief of staff taking the seat immediately to the right of the president.

"Real pisser of a storm," the president commented. "I'll try and not keep you all too long. Are we all set?"

Secretary Baldwin led off. "The smooth copies of the treaty will be ready by tomorrow morning. I will hand-carry them, of course. Prime Minister Hoikata's request for the change in the appropriation section pertaining to the transfer of the carriers and air wings has been signed off by the Chairman of the Joint Chiefs, the CNO, and SecNav and incorporated in the final draft."

"That was the last item pending, was it not?" the president asked.

"Yes, sir."

"How about the itinerary?"

"We depart at eight, Thursday morning. That'll be the fifth. Arrive Honolulu at eleven thirty-five. Arrival ceremonies at Hickam, lunch at the Royal Hawaiian with Governor Kaheke and representatives of the Republic of the Marshall Islands, the Federated States of Micronesia, the Republic of Palau, the Commonwealth of the Northern Marianas, and the governor of Guam. Your luncheon speech will be in your briefing folder on Air Force One. Fifteen minutes on the effect the treaty has on the security of the western Pacific."

"My changes incorporated?"

"Yes, sir."

"Go on."

"Afternoon at leisure in your suite at the Royal Hawaiian. Dinner at the Hale Koa with local dignitaries and the members of the Survivors of Pearl Harbor Association. Also selected members of the armed forces stationed in Hawaii.

"Not all officers. I want the enlisted there—with their wives."

"Already arranged, sir."

"Women members and minorities."

"Yes, sir, a complete cross section of the armed forces."

"Japanese guests?"

"Selected by the prime minister."

"All right—I'll feel better when that one is over. At the risk of repeating myself, I do not want any disturbances from a few kooks who might decide to protest."

Bert Thompson interjected. "We don't anticipate anything, Mr. President, but we will have people on hand."

"I don't want a word of bad press on this."

"You have my word, Mr. President."

"No, Bert, I have your *ass* and it is to be hung high on the Washington Monument if anything goes wrong."

Thompson let a helpless smile convey his response.

Keeping his eyes on Thompson, the president asked, "What is the latest on the Osaka shootdown?"

"The suspects have all been identified and tracked to Guam and apprehension is just a matter of hours."

"Thank God for that. It could not have come at a worse time. Minimize press coverage as much as you can."

Secretary Baldwin continued with the briefing. "Prime Minister Hoikata and his party arrive at Honolulu International the following morning at eight. Military honors at Hickam and breakfast with Commander-in-Chief, Pacific Command, and Admiral DeHart will host breakfast for you and the prime minister at his quarters."

"That isn't rubbing it in a bit?"

"Certainly not, Mr. President. CINCPAC stands to benefit most among our military commands from the treaty. It gives him the opportunity to welcome Japan into the Western military community without too much public fanfare. Admiral Togakagi, the chief-designate of Japan's new armed forces, will be a member of the prime minister's party. The admiral will have a private meeting with CINCPAC after the breakfast."

"The Imperial Navy still calls the shots, eh?"

"Your words, Mr. President."

"Well, I can still see the bastards steaming around after they bagged my ass off Iwo Jima in '44. They didn't take any prisoners in those days. If old Chugger Downs hadn't kept his Hellcats around to scare 'em off, I'd have been fish food. Oh well, that's a long time ago."

"I didn't realize that you had been shot down during the war, Mr. President," Murray Franklin said, then immediately realized he should have kept his ignorance to himself.

The president gave his chief of security a look that plainly agreed with Franklin's after-the-fact assessment of the remark. "Yes, I took the nylon escalator down to the water and swam like hell until the *Sharkfin* picked me up right under the nips' noses. Rode that boat all the way into Tokyo Bay and back to Pearl Harbor. Went through depth charge attacks and the whole bit. But that's another story. I'm sorry, go ahead, Don."

"Ceremonies at Punchbowl at noon with Prime Minister Hoikata. Private meeting with him in the afternoon—also the two staffs will meet to cover the December seventh ceremonies in detail. State dinner at the Royal Hawaiian, where you and the prime minister will jointly announce the full provisions of the treaty."

"And the shitski hits the fanski. . . ."

"Perhaps not, Mr. President. I think everyone is ready for this."

"Except for the liberal press. Okay, Don, how about the Pearl Harbor ceremony?"

"On the morning of the seventh, as you requested, you and the first lady will attend church services at six. Prime Minister and Mrs. Hoikata will attend a Buddhist service somewhat earlier. There will be a brief joint TV press conference at six-thirty; arrive at Memorial Park at seven; ceremony to start on the *Arizona* Memorial at seven-thirty with Prime Minister Hoikata's remarks. You will follow with yours and during the Navy Hymn, the World War II dive bomber will make its flybys. As previously discussed, we plan to have a restored Zero join the SBD on its last pass as a gesture to the

Japanese. Afterwards, you and the prime minister place the lei on the water and we have the national anthems.

"At approximately eight-fifteen, aircraft of our three services will conduct a flyby in company with aircraft from the JSDF. Nonsectarian benediction and that's it."

"The Zero will have a Japanese pilot?" The president was not sure that was the best idea in the world.

"No, sir. Both pilots will be Americans and each has been involved in the restoration of the aircraft."

"That's better. But, it would be a kick to find an old nip bastard to fly the thing, wouldn't it? Hell, why can't I fly the Dauntless?" The president asked, referring to the SBD by its World War II nickname.

The laughter almost drowned out the secretary's response. "I'm certain that you could, Mr. President!"

"*You* can stand on the memorial with Hoikata. Have the navy rustle me up some old World War II flight gear and I'll do it!"

"Is that an order, Mr. President?"

The president sighed. "I'm sure as hell tempted. Are we certain that having the Zero is a smart move? Some older Hawaiians could object. They still remember that morning."

"We've made some informal inquiries. I think everyone understands. It is a conciliatory gesture to the Japanese government: the immortal Zero flying number-two position on the American SBD. Very symbolic. They will take great pride in it."

"And some *kanaka* might well shoot the god-damned thing down!"

"We can scrub it, Mr. President, if you feel it is inflammatory."

"No. I like it. It's a proper thing to do. Japan's young men didn't create the war, they just fought it along with ours. Sorry for the sidetrack. What's after the ceremony?"

"You have a meeting with the governor on island considerations. The briefing sheets are in your folder. The first lady visits the Pali and some local day-care centers. At eight, Prime Minister Hoikata hosts a formal dinner at the Hawaiian Hanami Hotel. It's Japanese owned and staffed. The next morning you see the prime minister and his party off and leave for the mainland."

The president looked squarely at his chief of staff. "When do I get time to buy my macadamia nuts and pineapple?"

"There will be time, sir. We'll work it in."

"We better."

The five subordinates instinctively knew that the briefing was over. Standing, each offered his congratulations to the president and they filed out of the oval office. The president returned to the window.

The snow was just as heavy, perhaps even more so, and the lights around the White House illuminated the torrents of white flakes that were streaking down from the night sky and rapidly overpowering all of the winter foliage in the Rose Garden.

The president could only imagine the chaos on the beltway and city streets. That was another perk for him. At the end of his day in the oval office, he could just walk upstairs to his quarters.

His mind feasted on the treaty. It would be truly historic, for with its main provision restoring Japanese armed forces it returned complete sovereignty to the island nation. Fifty years after the two countries had engaged in mortal combat, they would be linking arms in friendship and mutual dependence. The past would finally be behind them.

It would also be a two-edged financial coup for the president of the United States. It would enable him to insist on further NATO support cuts and continue the reduction of the nation's military budget while the financing of her own military force would provide some check to Japan's ever-expanding economy. Even a slight slowdown would bolster the dollar's value vis-à-vis the yen. Add the considerable payments for the lease of the naval units and the trade provisions of the treaty and the financial returns to the United States would far outweigh the slight bit of political criticism that was sure to rise from those in Congress whose vision was limited to the tip of their own partisan noses.

The president was very pleased with himself, even more than he had been after his triumphant trip to Poland and Hungary in '89. With the dramatic developments within the Soviet Union and their effect on the Soviet sphere of influence, the world was beginning to be more in balance. His administration was firmly entrenching itself as one that renewed U.S. prestige and influence in Eastern Europe, a feat considered impossible only a few years back. And now there would be a new relationship with Japan and more money for domestic programs. The year 1992 should be a great reelection year.

Chapter 20

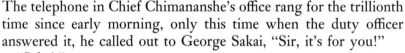

The telephone in Chief Chimananshe's office rang for the trillionth time since early morning, only this time when the duty officer answered it, he called out to George Sakai, "Sir, it's for you!"

"Sakai."

"This is Captain Genda."

Genda? Sakai almost fell out of the chair while frantically motioning to Detective Kami. Kami carefully picked up an extension as Chief Chimananshe hurried in from the outer office.

"It's Genda!" Sakai mouthed.

Chimananshe immediately picked up another line and ordered a tracer.

"Where are you, Captain?" Sakai asked.

"It is not important at the moment. I would like to talk to you."

"Go ahead." Sakai raised his hands in a now-what? gesture.

"No. Face-to-face. Just you and me, nisei."

"Where?"

"First, you must agree to come alone."

Despite Kami's frown and vigorous head shaking, Sakai replied, "I can do that."

"And I must have your word that you will not arrest me—you must not be armed."

"I don't know about that, Captain. I am obligated to apprehend you."

"Keep him talking!" Chimananshe whispered, keeping one hand tightly over the mouthpiece of his handset.

"I am prepared to give myself up but I want a guarantee first," Genda stated.

"What kind of guarantee?"

"A release from any accountability for the United crash at Osaka. It was not of my doing. I am prepared to accept responsibility for the other incidents."

Sakai looked at the others. Kami shook his head. Sakai agreed. "I don't have the authority to do that, Captain."

"Then we cannot meet. That is a nonnegotiable prerequisite."

Chimananshe gave a cranking motion with one hand. The tracing operation needed more time.

"Captain, there is no way you can escape now. The island is sealed."

"There is always another way out, nisei."

"Are you with the others?"

"I am."

"Are they willing to give themselves up?"

"With some conditions. That is why I wished to talk to you."

Chimananshe scribbled a note and passed it over to Sakai:

> He's on a boat! We can only trace as far as the marine operator. He can be anywhere around the island.

Shit! Sakai covered his mouthpiece and spoke to Chimananshe. "The marine operator; does she have a direction finder? Air force—Coast Guard? Can they help us?"

Chimananshe shrugged but immediately selected another line and dialed.

Sakai uncovered his mouthpiece. "Captain, let me speak with the authorities here. Will you hold for that?"

"No. Time is up. You most probably already have this call traced to the marine operator. To no avail, of course. I can give you no more time. . . . It is over, nisei."

"Wait! Genda!" The line went dead. Sakai slammed down the handset. "He's on the water somewhere!"

Kami glanced at the wall map of Guam. "We have checked all the marinas. Nothing is missing and all of the rentals are legitimate. But if he is on the water, we have him. Choppers! We need choppers!"

"I have one available," Chimananshe declared. "The Coast Guard will have one, maybe two. Possibly, the air force at Andersen and the navy at Agana. They've already assisted on the land search. I'll start calling."

Sakai was out of his chair and standing next to Kami. "All right, each of us takes a different area. Have the choppers pick us up on the police pad. We can concentrate on the coastal waters. In the unlikely event that they've gone to sea—and that's suicide unless they have a large boat—let's get the air force and navy to start a search farther out. What in hell can they have in mind?"

"They are desperate," Kami replied. "Nevertheless, while they are on a boat, that does not mean they are out on the water. We must expand the search to seaward but they could still be holed up on the island."

"Where? They are trapped, even if we have to start the island search all over again." Even as he spoke, Sakai found himself confused. Genda was too crafty to have made a sucker call. "We *have* to search seaward. Yet, why would Genda call if he knew we could trace him to a boat at sea? There's no place to hide out there."

"Oh, I think he was sincere in wanting to talk," Kami said. "It was a last desperate grasp at compromise. He knows it is over now."

"Okay, we have the marinas checked again. They could have broken into a boat tied up to a pier and are attempting to mislead us."

"Not very smart of them," Chimananshe offered, "but we'll get right on it. I've got two choppers available immediately; ours and one of the Coast Guard's. It's on the way in."

"I'll take the police chopper. Kami, you take the other. I'll go southeast; Kami, southwest. Where's Tonishi?"

"On road patrol with my deputy. Shall I have him recalled?" Chimananshe asked.

"No, he's probably just as valuable where he is. Chief, can you check the northern coasts when a third chopper becomes available? Most of the north coast is military, anyhow. That okay?"

"Certainly . . ." Chief Chimananshe paused and grabbed the phone before the first ring died. "Great! Thank you, thank you very much." He hung up before announcing, "The air force has given us two C-130s. They'll search around the island between twenty-five and fifty miles out."

The *wop-wop* of an approaching helicopter bled into the building. "Okay," Sakai said, "let's do it!"

"We've got maybe forty-five minutes of good daylight left. . . ." Pausing to let the small two-man Bell Model 47 chopper drop another hundred feet, Chief Chimananshe's police pilot looked to the left seat for instructions from Sakai.

Sakai had his eyes riveted along the southeast coastline of Guam. The setting sun made it difficult for him to get much definition within the shaded coastline, and in most areas the foliage grew right down to the water's edge although there were some small stretches of sandy beach. Genda and company would not be along those and they didn't appear to be farther out to sea. Only a few boats were off the coast and each had been accounted for by a check with the marinas and local owners.

Kami and the Coast Guard chopper were over on the southwest coast, sweeping the area for any signs of the Japanese. The northern coastlines were less suspect since most of that area was within the confines of the island's military establishments. Hopefully, by now, Chief Chimananshe would be looking in that area. The USAF C-130s were most probably on station farther out, in the twenty-five to fifty-mile range from shore, but it was doubtful that Genda and his people would venture out that far. It was all open ocean. And the nearest land, Rota, was fifty miles northeast. Possibly, they might make a run for that island, but the intervening water had been under surveillance since the early period of the search.

"Let's get in close, say, twenty-five yards out, and stay at fifty feet or so. There are all kinds of narrow inlets over there. Depending upon the size of the boat, they could very well be holed up in one and we'll never see them unless we're down at their level."

The pilot nodded and slid the Bell down and over to where the chopper's downwash was rippling the surface of the water. He slowed to twenty knots.

Sakai was still having trouble understanding why Genda had made such a stupid mistake, giving away the fact he was on a boat. That wasn't like him. Maybe it *was* a decoy call. *Wait! What was that?* "Turn around! Back at that inlet! I think I saw something."

The pilot tilted the chopper until the plane of its rotor blades was almost vertical and reversed course.

"There! Over there! Take it slow."

Transitioning to a slow forward hover, the pilot eased down to where the skids of the chopper were almost dragging in the water. Sakai strained to see up the inlet. The slight contortion of the Plexiglas bubble around him and the up-sun view made him uncertain as to what he could see. He leaned forward as if the additional inches could help. Without warning, a covey of orange flashes appeared from within the dark foliage, the chopper's Plexiglas bubble disintegrated, the pilot yelled and grabbed his chest, and the uncontrolled chopper reared up and tossed over on its side. Sakai reached around frantically for additional support, his knees weak from the knowledge that sudden death had erupted from the inlet.

The impact with the water was surprisingly soft, yet Sakai felt himself forced hard against the metal doorframe. A sharp pain knifed through his left shoulder and then he was under water. He jerked up the release of his safety harness and clawed his way forward, but the bubble frame pinned him to the bottom. Panic-striken, he kicked and squirmed, trying to nurse the last gasp of air he had gulped as the chopper hit. Slowly, he began to extricate himself, but his air ran out first and he tasted the first awful swallow of warm seawater. Everything faded to black although he began to hear voices and then hands were pulling at him. Vomiting briefly and then retching with the dry heaves, he felt the hands lifting him but abruptly his senses stopped working. How long he was out, he had no idea, but as he slowly returned to reality he found himself stretched out on a single narrow bunk inside an underway cabin cruiser. A blurred figure was seated opposite him and as its outline began to come into focus he heard an all-too-familiar voice.

"Nisei. You are all right. Do you hear me? It looks like we have the chance for our talk after all."

Chapter 21

Chief Chimananshe waited impatiently in his office, alternately pacing back and forth and sitting briefly to fumble through the piles of papers on his weathered executive-sized oaken desk. A third chopper had not been available and he had not been able to participate in the search. It was an irritating problem, although not necessarily a critical one, for either Sakai or Kami could check the northern coasts at the conclusion of their southeast and southwest sweeps. Provided, of course, there was sufficient daylight left. If not, the north coasts would have to wait until morning. Chimananshe checked his watch. "How long can the choppers stay out?" he yelled to the outer office.

"Ours should be almost out of fuel by now. It should be back any minute. The Coast Guard chopper has plenty."

"Let's start a communications check," Chimananshe directed his dispatcher. "Maybe they've sat down somewhere else."

An hour later it was dark.

The heavy *whump-whump* beat of chopper blades signaled the return of the larger Coast Guard helicopter. A moment later, Kami walked into the office. "Nothing. Did Sakai find anything?"

"We don't know. He's still out."

"He will not see anything in this darkness—" Kami could see the concerned expression on Chimananshe's broad face. "Is there something wrong?"

"Sakai's chopper has to be out of fuel by now. We've made a comm check to see if he landed at one of the island airports. Nobody's seen him. He might be down in a field somewhere but it doesn't look good."

Kami dropped a tea bag into a paper cup and poured in hot water. "If they had gotten into trouble, they would have called. Is that not correct?"

"I would think so. We have the road patrols alerted."

Kami dipped his tea bag several times in the hot water. "We talked to him once, early in the search. Everything was normal. If the pilot used the same tactics we did, he probably hugged the coast and was very low. If anything did happen, it might have gone unseen. The bluffs are quite high and the road sets back some distance."

"That's what bothers me. I notified the Coast Guard at their zero fuel time. They are already over an hour past that."

Kami stopped in mid-sip. "I have a bad feeling."

Chimananshe stepped to his office door. "Sergeant Endiro, check again with the FAA and the Coast Guard. Ask the hooligans if we can get a surface search of the southeast shoreline."

"Hooligans?" Kami was not familiar with the term.

"A slang name for the Coast Guard; really, not very flattering, but I use it in a respectful way. I probably should watch myself. An old navy habit."

"You were in the navy?"

"Eight years when I was just a kid."

"How come you got out?"

"Missed my island— Well, I guess we wait."

Kami dropped himself heavily onto the office chair. "I hope nothing is wrong."

"God, I do, too."

Sakai bent his left arm at the elbow and held the numb forearm across his chest with his other arm. It eased the pain. There was a good possibility the shoulder was dislocated as there was a large hard bulge at the shoulder joint.

"I am sorry you are in such pain," Genda said. "I think we can find something to make a sling."

"That would help."

Genda found several large towels in a compartment just aft of the door to the tiny head. He took one, folded it, placed it around the lower arm, and tied the ends behind Sakai's neck. It did ease the pressure on the shoulder.

The cabin was dimly lit by one of the side lights, and by the sound of the engine and the feel of the ride, Sakai estimated they were cruising at around ten knots. In what direction, he had no idea. He could hear heavy rain on the cabin roof.

Genda had no weapon but one was unnecessary. With his injury and overall weakness, there was no way Sakai could try to escape. Besides, the other three men were in the well deck aft of the cabin.

"Since you refuse to bargain for my immunity to the Osaka attack, my associates will insist that you remain as our hostage."

"It doesn't make any difference, Captain. You cannot get away from the island. It is over. The best action you can take is to give yourselves up. I can testify to your aid in my rescue."

"After we shot down the helicopter! I doubt that we would get any consideration."

"Using me as a hostage will not work. Your crimes are too serious. No one is going to let you get away—even if you threaten to kill me. It just will not happen. This is my job. I am expendable."

Genda knew that Sakai was right. Besides, he had no urge to kill the American. There was some hauntingly familiar yet elusive quality about the nisei that he had first detected during their initial meeting in his cottage on Hokkaido. Perhaps it was the eyes; they had the same softness he had known so well in Emiko. In her, they had been fitting, but in a nisei investigative officer they were totally out of place. Abruptly, Genda asked, "How old are you?"

Sakai could not imagine the reason for such a question. "Forty-three."

That would be the age of my son had he lived. "Your birth month?"

"September. September eighteenth."

Emiko had opened her stomach on September 3, 1948. Genda looked hard into Sakai's eyes as if even in the deep light he could see into the younger man's soul. At that moment, he realized that he would not see Sakai killed. "Nisei, I wish you no harm. Do you think you can swim?"

"I cannot get much use out of my left arm. Swim how far? What are you saying?"

"Patience. If you stay with us, you will die. That rain—we are in a storm."

Sakai nodded and waited for Genda to continue.

"I will have the boat taken within twenty meters of the coastline. Forward, through that bulkhead hatch, there is the bow gear locker and in the overhead there is an access hatch to the forward deck. It is small but large enough for you. When I return to the well deck, I will leave the hatch ajar. When I push it shut, you will go through the bulkhead, up on the bow, and roll into the water. I will have the others distracted and in this storm they should not hear your splash if you are careful. You will have a hard climb when you reach the shoreline and the perimeter road is about one half mile inland. There, you can hail a car. Get your arm taken care of. As for your report to the authorities, it will accomplish nothing. We will be gone by the time they can react. Do you think you can make it?"

"Considering the alternative, I have to. You know that the military have sea patrols, Captain. There is nowhere you can go."

Genda's faint smile was in strange contrast to the sadness in his eyes. "But there is, nisei—are you ready?"

"Yes—why are you doing this?"

"As I said, I wish you no harm—any more than I wished harm on those innocent souls aboard the Osaka 747. Perhaps you will believe me someday. Good luck, nisei. I think we will meet no more."

Even though he was seated, Sakai bowed with respect for the old warrior's attempt to salvage what he could of his honor. Genda started up the three steps to the well deck. Sakai reached down and removed his shoes. His left shoulder was on fire, and when he tried to move the arm a thousand machetes began slicing through the muscles and flesh. Twenty meters, Genda had said—about sixty-five feet. Sakai regularly swam a mile in the gym pool back at State, but that was with two good arms and a healthy body.

Genda stood for a moment in the well deck, letting his eyes adjust to the night. Ohiro and Sakamoki were curled up on the transom seat and covered with a piece of canvas. Goto was manning the helm. The heavy rain from the overhead thunderstorm was masking much of the engine noise. The cloud, itself, was obscuring the moon, and since they were running without any outside lights, it was very dark. Genda reached into a small stowage compartment beside the throttle quadrant and extracted a 9-mm automatic.

"You are going to take care of our guest?" Goto inquired.

"I may have to. He does not want to cooperate."

"Where are we headed?"

"According to the chart, there is another series of inlets and a small cove coming up, We may want to move closer to the shore."

"No one can see us in this downpour."

"It is a local thunderstorm. The rain will pass shortly. Move in closer, maybe twenty meters or so. I need to be able to see the inlets."

Goto spun the wheel and they closed the shoreline. Genda peered out into the wet night. Suddenly, he cocked his head.

"Listen."

"What is it?" Goto asked.

"Throttle back a little. I thought I heard engine noise."

Goto reduced the boat's speed to five knots.

"Out there!" Genda loudly whispered. "Do you hear it?" He pointed one arm off the boat's starboard quarter. Goto turned and searched in the direction Genda indicated. Genda leaned back and closed the hatch to the cabin.

Sakai scrambled through the forward bulkhead hatch and opened the bow deck access hatch. The rain was coming in sheets and he was instantly soaked. With considerable effort, he managed to pull himself up on deck. Staying low, he swung his legs over the side and pushed away with his good arm as he fell into the water. There was an audible splash. He dove as deep as he dared.

"What was that?" Goto exclaimed, turning toward the bow.

Genda pulled open the hatch to the cabin and rushed inside. He immediately returned. "He is gone! He went out through the forward deck hatch!"

Goto spun the wheel. There was practically no visibility but he could make out the shoreline. "He will head for the land!"

"I think I have him!" Genda shouted. "Maintain this heading!" He emptied the automatic into the night. "I hit him. I do not see him anymore."

Ohiro and Sakamoki had jumped up at the first shot and joined Genda at the rail of the well deck.

"We will search up ahead for only a moment; we must continue

south while we have this cover," Genda directed. "I am quite sure
I got him." *Good job, nisei, you are well behind us now.*

"What if you did not?" Ohiro asked.

"It is of no matter. We have lost a hostage but the end will be the
same. I still have a plan."

Sakai swam mostly beneath the surface, grabbing quick gulps of
air between submersions. The pleasantly warm water actually
seemed to ease his shoulder pain and although he couldn't use the
arm, his good-arm side stroke carried him along well toward the
beach. The soaked towel sling was heavy, but he did not wish to
discard it as he would need it for support once he was on land.
Within minutes, he crawled onto the sandy shore and watched until
the barely discernable profile of the boat disappeared several hundred yards out. Then he started the hard climb up the side of the
hill.

Forty minutes later, soaked and exhausted and weak from the
sharp pain that had returned to his shoulder, he stood on the perimeter road, breathing heavily and shivering from the effects of his
exposure to the rain and cool night temperatures. A few minutes
later, headlights appeared and an elderly Chamarro stopped his
pickup in response to Sakai's frantic waving.

"You are hurt," the old man exclaimed.

"Take me quickly to the nearest telephone. I am a police officer."

"There is no need for that. There is a police blockade just a mile
back. It will only take a few minutes."

"They have found Sakai!"

Chief Chimananshe clapped his hands in satisfaction at the call
from his duty sergeant. Kami followed him from his office.
"Where?" Chimananshe demanded.

The sergeant listened on his headset for a moment before replying. "He just showed up at the Highway Four roadblock south of
Talofofo Bay. They have a car bringing him in. Wait—I'll put him
on the speaker."

"Chief, this is Sakai. Genda and his people are in an eighteen-foot
cabin cruiser just off the southeast coast."

"Alert the Coast Guard chopper," ordered Chimananshe.
"Where have you been?"

"We found them just before nightfall in a narrow inlet north of here but they saw us first and shot the pilot. We went in and they pulled me out of the wreckage. Genda wanted a deal but when I wouldn't make it, he let me go. He knows they are in the short strokes—it's almost over. They disappeared out to sea."

"We'll have a Coast Guard chopper there within minutes."

"It'll be rough. There's a hell of a line of thunderstorms and they won't be able to see anything underneath them."

"Where do you figure they are heading?"

"I don't know. Genda said they had one more act to perform. Maybe they're going to try and reach Rota."

"We'll take care of it. Come on in."

"I may have a busted shoulder. Have a medic handy."

"No, have the car take you to the hospital."

"No way. Have someone come to the station. I want to be in on this."

"Where will we go?" shouted Goto above the rain noise.

"Continue south like I said, and stay near the shoreline," Genda ordered.

"You fool!" Ohiro shook his fist in anger. "You should have watched him."

"It makes no difference," Genda retorted. "We have only one course of action now. Let us go about it in an honorable way."

Ohiro was only a breath away from rushing Genda and throwing him over the side, but the rain in his face tempered his anger and brought back his reason. For all of Genda's mistakes, he had kept them free despite impossible odds. Maybe the old man had one more trump card left, after all.

Chapter 22

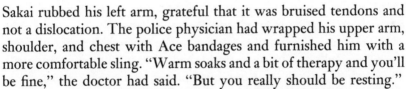

Sakai rubbed his left arm, grateful that it was bruised tendons and not a dislocation. The police physician had wrapped his upper arm, shoulder, and chest with Ace bandages and furnished him with a more comfortable sling. "Warm soaks and a bit of therapy and you'll be fine," the doctor had said. "But you really should be resting."

"Thank you, doctor, but I need to be here," Sakai had insisted. Chimananshe had suggested he lie on the office sofa but sitting upright was more comfortable. A dull rainy dawn came before he was able to doze. It seemed like only a moment when the outer office radio crackled; his watch said 9:33 A.M.

"We've found them!" The duty sergeant's voice rang throughout the headquarters station at Agana. In Chief Chimananshe's office, the Guamanian raised his head from his desk in disbelief. Sakai, instantly wide awake, rose from his chair beside the chief's desk. Detective Kami was already through the door.

"Where?" Chimananshe and Sakai asked simultaneously.

"On the southeast shoreline just north of Inarajen. All dead!"

"Advise we're on the way!" Chimananshe led the rush out of his office. Sakai, Kami, and the one-armed Tonishi piled into Chimananshe's car and they roared away across Agana. Within moments

Chimananshe had picked up Highway Four and with siren screaming and lights flashing sped east across the thin waist of the island.

A voice over the car radio began filling in details. "We have a
charred cabin cruiser and four bodies. Two are burned beyond
recognition, the other two positively identified as Toshio Goto and
Nobuo Sakamoki. One of the charred bodies has signs of ritual
suicide, tentatively identified as Saburo Genda, the other most probably Michio Ohiro."

"Great!" Chimananshe knew that the terrorists' days had been
numbered. His disappointment at having lost them at the Terraza
Tumon Villa Hotel vanished behind a massive grin. He kept his car
at sixty as they passed through the small coastal village of Yona, one
of his patrol cars on the scene having halted all traffic.

"They must have reasoned that they could hold out no longer. I
just wish the bastards had lived so they could stand trial and then
hang—or whatever."

Agent Tonishi had been very quiet until now. "It was the only
way out for Genda. He had to do it. I think that is why he let you
go, Sakai-san. It is tragic, but I also would have preferred for him
to stand trial. The man made some serious mistakes while in the
JMSDF and never had to pay until now due to a special status as
a war hero. Justice is an elusive thing, is it not?"

For the next fifteen miles, Chimananshe pushed his staff car across
the rolling hills as if he were afraid the bodies might get up and walk
away before he arrived. Rounding the top of a rise, he stomped on
the brakes and the car fishtailed to a halt amid a cluster of police
vehicles overlooking the high bluffs of the southeastern shoreline. A
traffic control officer waved them to a clear spot on the shoulder of
the road and one of Chimananshe's deputy chiefs met them as they
climbed out of the car.

"Where are they?" Chimananshe demanded.

"Down at the bottom of the bluff in an inlet. It's rough going.
Follow me."

As the five men made their way down the slope, thrashing their
way through the thick foliage and struggling to keep their balance
on the irregular soft surface, the deputy filled in a few more of the
details. "One of our patrol cars spotted smoke and the officer came
down to investigate. He tried to keep the bodies from burning any
further with his car extinguisher but the boat burned to the water-
line."

Sakai and the others caught their first glimpse of the scene. The unburned portion of the boat was resting on the bottom of the shallow inlet. Remnants of the charred cabin jutted above the water and two blackened bodies were half floating within the confines of what was left of the still-smoldering boat. Neither was recognizable as even male or female, much less as individuals. Two other bodies, fully clothed and untouched by the fire, were sprawled on the grass some twenty feet from the boat. Both were facedown and each had a single bullet wound in the back of the head. Sakai and the others stopped beside them. Kami knelt and examined the faces.

"Goto and Sakamoki. No doubt about it. Executed, I would say."

Sakai agreed, as did Chimananshe with a one word epitaph: "Bastards."

"God, look at that," Tonishi declared, pointing with the stump of his arm. He was on the bank looking down at the two bodies floating in the debris-filled water confined by the charred gunwales of the boat. Both grotesque cadavers were in the classic burned position with arms curled inward across their chests until what had been hands were only a foot or so apart. Their legs were spread, raised, and bent at the knees, the feet apparently the last parts extinguished as the boat sank. Only charred stumps remained.

The body on the right had a large slash across its abdomen and the protruding entrails were black and crusted. Another stretched cut was in the left side of the throat where the carotid artery would have been.

"Genda," Tonishi said.

Ohiro had no visible signs of injury other than by the fire, although it was apparent there would be a bullet wound somewhere. A large-caliber revolver was still clasped in his right hand.

"That's unusual," Chimananshe commented, giving the scene another thorough overview.

"What is?" Sakai asked.

"The fact that he still holds the gun."

"What do you figure happened?"

"Oh, it's obvious, I think. Either Genda or Ohiro—maybe both— shot the two on the grass. Then Ohiro assisted Genda in hara-kiri and poured gasoline on them both. Probably set the fire with one hand and simultaneously put a bullet into his head with the other. He and Genda had enough traditional background—being military—to want just their ashes to remain."

"Chief, you want to look at this?"

Chimananshe followed the officer over to a small pile of rocks. There were four, each about the size of a baseball. A white envelope was under the top one.

"We didn't want to disturb this until you got here," said the officer.

Chimananshe stooped and carefully slid out the envelope, holding it by the edges to protect any fingerprints. It was sealed and had only a one-word addressee. "It's addressed to 'Nisei.' "

"That's me," Sakai exclaimed. "Genda kept referring to me as 'nisei.' "

Chimananshe ran the blade of his small pocketknife inside the top edge and held the opened side toward Sakai, who pulled out the single sheet of paper. The text was in English. After silently reading it, he shook his head while handing it back to Chimananshe. "Not me, Genda," Sakai said bitterly. "It isn't my forgiveness you need."

Chimananshe read it aloud:

Nisei:

At one time, in my search for peace of mind, I studied the Western Roman religion. Reading one of the prayers of repentance, I was struck by the Latin phrase "mea culpa, mea culpa, mea maxima culpa"—through my fault, through my fault, through my most grievous fault.

It is that phrase now that comes to mind as I apologize for my role in the destruction of the American airliner at Osaka. I repeat, it was not my decision but was my responsibility.

Now, I realize that my intense desire to avenge the dishonoring of my parents and my wife has overshadowed my own sense of honor and civilized conduct. Therefore I make amends by the traditional act of self-sacrifice.

In that way, I shall join with the spirits of the Thunder Gods at Yasukuni Shrine. May my decision reinforce your appreciation of the heritage we both share and generate in your own soul some measure of forgiveness.

> Saburo Genda
> Flight Petty Officer
> Imperial Japanese Navy
> Captain, JMSDF

. . .

"He had no right to address such hypocrisy to me." Sakai leaned over the bank to examine the cut in Genda's abdomen. It was horizontal and the stretching of the skin and flesh upon burning had pulled it widely open. The remains of the internal organs were mere lumps of water-soaked charcoal. The wound on the neck was equally stretched, and everything was burned away to expose the neck vertebrae.

"We'll find the knife probably somewhere under the bodies in the bottom of the boat." Chimananshe took a long stick and moved Ohiro's corpse slightly to view the sides of the head. "There, there's the entry wound." A burned plug of black brain matter protruded from a dark hole in Ohiro's right temple as if a large worm had been trying to escape.

"You commented that holding the gun is unusual," Sakai prompted.

"Yes. Ordinarily, the hand would release it upon firing the weapon. I suspect his timing was off. The gasoline undoubtedly flared immediately and he felt the sudden burst of pain just as he pulled the trigger. Reflex would clench his hand and it just cooked that way before the muscles could relax."

Sakai had none of the sour-stomach feeling he had experienced walking among the bodies of the plane crash at Osaka. The horror of the scene before him was, at worst, poetic justice. He was very glad that it was over, and any compassion he had felt for Genda had long ago disappeared despite the fact that he owed the old man his life. There was some remorse that the old man had beaten the hangman but his spirit would most assuredly not make its way to the Yasukuni Shrine. The heroes there would deny it any entry. Perhaps that would be Genda's most severe punishment.

Chimananshe's men continued prowling the scene, carefully looking for any other evidence that might add detail to the obvious. The big Guamanian barked out some instructions. "All right, let's collect them—but photographs of the scene first. I want all angles and overall shots from the four cardinal points. Raise the boat and find the hara-kiri knife. If it isn't in the hull, drag the inlet and search the surrounding terrain." He turned to Sakai, Kami, and Tonishi. "Okay with you?"

The three nodded. Sakai walked back to the bodies of Goto and Sakamoki and started going through their pockets. Then, realizing that he might be overstepping his jurisdiction, he looked up at Chimananshe. "Okay?"

"Sure. See what you can find."

Outside of loose change, wallets, and passports, he found nothing. The passports were in the names of aliases, but the pictures matched the two dead faces. "Sophisticated work. They had help from somewhere."

Kami examined the passports. "The Mongol from the Soviet embassy that met with Genda in Nagasaki. He would be capable of providing such things. I will see that he gets a one-way ticket back to Moscow when I return. That is about all we can do."

The remains of Genda and Ohiro had been placed inside black rubber body bags, and one of the patrol officers was in the water feeling around in the submerged hull. He came up with an Uzi, a 9-mm automatic, then another handgun, and finally a second Israeli-made machine gun.

"Where in hell did they get those?" Chimananshe asked. "They didn't bring them in on the airplane."

Sakai shook his head. He had no idea, but reasoned that Guam with its proliferation of indoor shooting clubs would be as good a source for such illegal weapons as any other piece of American territory. They were run mostly by and for the gun-happy ersatz Japanese cowboys. There were probably dark little rooms in the backs of some of them and all it took was yen. Genda and his companions probably had plenty of that. The guns were undoubtedly the weapons that had been used in Genda's rescue back at Tumon Bay.

Chimananshe yelled back at the officer in the water as he led the way back up the hill. "Keep at it until you find the knife!" The officer responded by slipping under the surface of the warm water.

The drive back to Agana was at a more leisurely pace. Chimananshe knew that his companions were wondering what the follow-on action would be. "We'll make a preliminary coroner's report before we ship the bodies back to Japan. I guess we'll include the girl, also. They sure raised hell while they lasted."

"Your people did good work, Chief," Kami commented.

Chimananshe laughed, his ample belly bouncing against the bottom of the steering wheel. "Thank you, but if they hadn't set fire to themselves they probably could have hidden out in that inlet for several more days. We did okay. I've got some good troops. This thing has been a step above our usual crime in Guam. I'm just glad it's over."

Sakai accompanied Detective Kami and Agent Tonishi to the airport to see them off.

At their boarding gate, both extended their hands to Sakai, using the Western form of taking departure as a concession to Sakai's American nationality. Kami then bowed. "It has been good working with you, Sakai-san. Any time you want to return to the land of your ancestors I am sure we can find a spot for you on our force in Tokyo."

Sakai chuckled. "I might like that." With a more serious face, he added, "I am very sorry about Kaneyama."

"Yes, a good man. But that is the nature of our business, is it not?"

"That it is. *Sayonara*."

"*Sayonara*, my nisei friend." Kami's use of the term triggered a slight distaste for the first time. Genda had seemed too fond of it.

"Tonishi-san, I suppose it will be back to the inn."

Agent Tonishi returned Sakai's deep bow. "That is possible. The agency owns it. Perhaps one day we will even make a profit. *Sayonara*, Sakai-san. It has been an honor."

The three again exchanged bows before Kami and Tonishi disappeared into the boarding tunnel.

Sakai turned and walked away. The crowds in the terminal were light, and although most were quite aware of the drama that had been played out in the narrow inlet on the southeast coast of the island, he doubted that few had let the incident interfere with their visit. A great number were vacationing Japanese—they should feel some shame, he reasoned, for the crimes of their fellow nationals had been so cruel and senseless, yet their excited and generally happy chattering indicated just the opposite. Perhaps it was because they were mainly among their own kind that their embarrassment could be coped with. Undoubtedly, they had been inconvenienced by the roadblocks and extensive search. He also suspected a few had been genuinely frightened. Terrorism was the most unpredictable and nondiscriminating of crimes. Whatever. The extensive police and military presence had been short-lived and things had returned to normal once Chief Chimananshe terminated the manhunt.

Most of the travelers were young, although there was a smattering of senior men and women. They would be the ones traveling on to

Saipan to stand in reverence at the top of Banzai Cliff and reflect upon the circumstances that near the end of World War II caused hundreds of civilian Japanese families to choose the long leap over submission to the conquering American troops. Entire families had lined up by age, with each child pushing or throwing over the sibling younger than he. Then the mothers had thrown over their oldest and the husbands their wives. Finally, in order not to lose their nerves, the men had run backwards over the rim to join their families below while American troops had dropped leaflets and used loudspeakers to beg them not to die and promised they would not be harmed. Sakai could not understand such a thing, nor did he wish to. Yet, a haunting thought lingered: Would his parents have done such a thing to him?

As he walked out the exit leading to the space where he had parked his car, he studied the faces of those with whom he shared a common heritage. He was at once so alike them—and yet so different. One old man, walking with some effort and carrying only a small bag, was entering the far departure entrance, and for a moment Sakai saw Genda, ill but still determined to avenge his honor just as he had been back at the Terraza Tumon Villa Hotel. Sakai shook his head as if to remove a bad dream. He must forget Saburo Genda. The man had been too much of an enigma.

Chimananshe had been kind enough to arrange for a room at the Hilton International Guam, and Sakai settled down on the side of the bed with a scotch and water. He could thank the old reprobate, Charlie Porter, for having kindled that taste. His arm was feeling much better although he still used the sling during the day. He glanced at his watch. It might be an inopportune time to call Bert Thompson—it was shortly after midnight in D.C.—but it should be a good time to catch him. He placed his call and after five rings, Thompson answered.

"Sorry I woke you," Sakai said.

"I was going to try and reach you tomorrow. I figured you were still busy tying up loose ends. We are all relieved back here. Was it bad?"

"Yes."

"I can imagine. When do you want to come home?"

"I'm ready now."

"Okay. But I want you to take a few days off. Stay in Honolulu until after the ceremonies. It'll be a historic occasion, something to tell your girls about."

"I'd just as soon come on back to D.C. . . ."

"I insist. Look, contact Murray Franklin, the head of the president's security detail. After Thursday morning, the president and his party will be at the Royal Hawaiian. I have you a room there. That gives you three days of beach and grab-ass time at Waikiki before they arrive. I've been bumped but Murray will make you part of the security force and you can attend all the festivities. There's a good public atmosphere about the treaty and the president will be in his glory. You'll get caught up in things and maybe forget a little of what you've been through. It's an order, George."

"I really need to get with Alicia . . ."

"She called me a few days ago. She and the girls are fine and she asked about you. Call her when you get to Honolulu. You need a number?"

"No, I have it."

"Okay, so it's done. Have fun, George. I don't want to see you before the tenth."

The click on the other end indicated that Thompson didn't consider his order subject to any further discussion.

Sakai called the hotel travel desk. "I'd like a ticket on the next flight to Honolulu."

Seventy-nine-hundred miles away, Bert Thompson placed his phone back in its cradle. He would like to have been included in the presidential party, if for no other reason than to see George Sakai's face when he realized that the adjoining room at the Royal Hawaiian was occupied by Alicia Jane Richards-Sakai, recently of the outback, Australia. Since her call from Sydney, he had kept her informed as to Sakai's whereabouts and progress in the hunt for the terrorists. Her request to have Sakai return home via Honolulu was easy to honor once Guam was in the picture. Continental Airlines had a nonstop Guam-to-Honolulu flight. In the morning he would call Alicia at the Royal Hawaiian and tell her Sakai was on the way. It felt good to be an aging, overweight cupid. He snuggled back under the covers and placed his rear against that of his wife. She moved slightly and reached back to pat his hand.

"You awake?" he asked.

"Not awake enough, Bert. Go back to sleep."

Thompson dozed off with the smile still on his face. Sometimes his job could be downright fun.

Chief Jose Chimananshe was munching a chocolate-frosted raised doughnut and sipping on a Diet Coke when Sakai walked into his office to say good-bye.

"Well, Chief, I won't say that it has been pleasant, but I have enjoyed our short relationship."

"Me, too, George. It was a pleasure meeting you. Kami and Tonishi, too. We don't get a lot of temporary help but I guess this case was unique."

"Frightening is the word that comes to my mind. If we had not discovered they had come to Guam there could have been hell to pay, perhaps even as far back as the States."

Chimananshe tapped a folder on his desk. "Tied up a few loose ends. One of the university people found a dead graduate student at the oceanography boat pier—that's where the bastards got the boat. They apparently clubbed the kid and stuffed his mouth and nose with dirt. He choked to death on it.

"We recovered the knife Genda used for his suicide. It was from the boat's galley and had Genda's and Ohiro's prints on it, so Ohiro must have assisted. I understand that's the traditional way. How's your arm?"

Sakai removed it from the sling and gingerly moved it about. "The two sessions of therapy have really helped. The sling still feels good, though."

Chimananshe smiled. "I'm glad. You were very lucky. The coroner has determined that the two burned bodies were Japanese males and the ages and sex coincide with Genda and Ohiro, so as far as I'm concerned, it's over. We'll box them up and send them and their dead dolly back to the land of the cherry blossoms."

"Thank you, Chief, for your hospitality." Sakai extended his right hand across the desk. Chimananshe stood and grabbed it.

"Have a safe flight home."

"I'll stop in Honolulu for a couple days."

"We'd be happy to have you stay here with us. We have a nice island. There is much I would like to show you."

"Thanks, but I have commitments."

"Then, next time maybe."

"Next time—good-bye."

Actually, on the drive to the airport, Sakai did look at the surrounding terrain for the first time. He had been too preoccupied before. Now at leisure and looking forward to his days in Honolulu, he could see that Guam was indeed a beautiful island, not too much unlike the islands of Hawaii.

Looking down from his steep-climbing Continental DC-10, he surveyed the resort hotels lining Tumon Bay. The ultraluxurious Pacific Star dominated the array of high rises and was symbolic of the growing foreign investment in the beach area. With rooms starting at eight hundred dollars a night, the Nuaru-owned Pacific Star was exclusively Japanese when it came to clientele.

As Guam disappeared behind the jumbo jet, the flight attendants began taking drink orders and Sakai ordered a Bloody Mary. *To hell with you, Charlie Porter. Man does not live by scotch alone.*

The small group of natives at the Pohnpei International Airport leaned over the waist-high wire fence and watched the restored Japanese Zero roll out gracefully onto its final approach and settle toward the runway until it touched down on the white concrete with the impact of a feather. The tail lowered and it slowed to a stop before reaching even the midway mark of the runway, reversed its direction, and came taxiing back toward the terminal. The big Nakajima radial engine shook the cowling as it idled, its breathing at such a low power setting an awkward thing. Reciprocating aircraft engines were not made to idle; they were made to roar, and only then did the violent explosions within their air-cooled cylinders fall into a mirror-smooth sequence of intake, compression, firing, and exhaust.

The natural element of the airplane was the air, and for the past forty-five minutes the American in the cockpit of the Japanese classic had skillfully demonstrated the ability of the World War II fighter to twist and turn and flip and whirl in a series of maneuvers that had tested the restoration work to the ultimate. The engine had operated flawlessly and the airframe had taken the high g's without any sign of undue stress or strain. The Zero was as perfect as the day it had rolled out of the Mitsubishi factory and it was ready for its long flight across the Pacific to Hawaii.

There were some concessions to modern-day technology. The teardrop belly tank strapped to the bottom of the fuselage was aluminum rather than the original wood, and the cockpit was updated to include modern radio gear, an automatic pilot, and an inertia navigational system. The pilot would merely have to monitor its island-hopping transit, his only obligation to see that the proper position coordinates were set in at the beginning of each leg. In return, the Zero would give him a flight path that never varied more than thirty feet on one side or the other from its desired track over the earth. He could eat and even nap in relative comfort, the bucket seat being lined with virgin wool from New Zealand. There was a compact liquid oxygen system, a built-in thermos for his intake of water, and a funnel-shaped relief tube for his discharge. His parachute seat pack held a steerable winglike canopy and attached to it was a compact raft capsule complete with an initial supply of fresh water, a solar still, NASA food packets, and a hand-sized floatable radio that could transmit and receive on all international distress frequencies. As if such precautions were not enough, another Mitsubishi, this time a modern 1990 MU-2B twin-turboprop executive transport, would accompany the Zero and carry not only droppable water survival equipment but a large cabin tank filled with hard-to-find aviation gasoline for the fighter and a small supply of critical spare parts including a complete set of tires.

Patrick McMahon, Jr., cut the engine and applied left brake to swing the long-legged Zero around to a crisp stop beside the MU-2. He gave a hearty thumbs-up to the other American and several Pohnpeians who were waiting for him. Pulling off his helmet, he climbed out of the cockpit and jumped off the wing.

"She's ready!"

Clapping his hands in excitement, he walked around the resting fighter. No oil leaks. No fuel leaks. No oil-canned skin. No loose inspection panels. No low tires. No hydraulic leaks from the brake system. The exhaust residue along the sides of the fuselage was a pale gray, indicative of a lean fuel-air mixture that would give him maximum range. The only sound was the snapping of the contracting metal as the engine cooled.

"Smooth as a baby's ass." He stretched up and kissed the cowling, then snapped his head back, embarrassed. "Oops, hot!"

The Pohnpeians laughed, and his partner, Terry Simpson, popped open a bottle of champagne, aiming the cork into the side of the hangar and holding the spouting mouth of the bottle away from the airplane. The two Americans took long swigs and passed the bottle to their native assistants. The Pohnpeians tipped up the bottle in turn and giggled as the frothy liquid spilled out the corners of their mouths. One made a furious face and exclaimed, "Sakau more better!" referencing their native drink.

"All right, guys," McMahon announced, "let's gas her up and put her to bed. You're all invited to the Village Hotel for our going-away party."

After supervising the refueling and making sure that both aircraft were secure, the Zero locked in the temporary hangar, the two Americans drove through the outskirts of Kolonia and held on for dear life as one of them steered the battered Toyota up the winding, climbing single-lane dirt road back to the Village Hotel.

"Have you seen the handbook for the MU-2?" asked Simpson, who was driving.

"No. It should be in the airplane."

"I looked and couldn't find it. I wanted to check on some of the takeoff performance charts. I'll be pretty heavy going out Thursday morning with that internal tank full."

McMahon shook his head in disagreement. "Shit, there's plenty of runway and it'll still be cool when we leave. Someone must have borrowed it."

"Who? Our Pohnpeians are the only ones with access besides us. They'd have no use for it."

"Don't sweat it. You're as familiar with that airplane as you are with your wife's ass."

"And they both give me a great ride—God, it'll be great to get back home." Simpson slapped the steering wheel with excitement.

"Listen, if there is any problem, I'll give you a tow with the Zero!"

"Oh, she's sweet, isn't she?"

"That she is. Stomp on it, ole buddy. I need a co-o-o-old beer. Ayyeeeeeeeeeee!" McMahon was ecstatic.

It had been thirteen months since they had first torn their way into the hut on the out island and found the Zero. Thirteen hot, humid, ball-breaking months. Tonight, their hardworking team would feast on mangrove crab and make a maximum effort to drink every drop of liquor and beer in the open-air bar at the Village Hotel. Then, tomorrow they would sleep late and recuperate by one last dive in the lagoon. The afternoon would be spent in final aircraft checks, paperwork, and flight planning. Then, early to bed and a good night's sleep before the dawn takeoff on Thursday—it would be Wednesday, December 4, in Hawaii. Barring any unforeseen discrepancies, they would arrive on Maui on Friday, the sixth. A bit close in timing, but the Zero was in tip-top shape and there should not be any in-flight delays. And if there were any remnants of the massive hangover they both knew the evening's celebration would cause, each could suck on that revitalizing oxygen until they reached Kwajalein.

"More wine, sir?"

Sakai opened his eyes with some difficulty. The nap had been quite good and undisturbed by bad dreams. Bert Thompson would probably nibble on his posterior for a while because he was riding first-class from Guam to Honolulu, but everything else was sold out. He could have waited for a later flight, he supposed, but Thompson had been very insistent that he relax, and the wide reclining seats in the forward cabin of the big Douglas had helped him do just that. He had remained awake for the first hour and gotten by two Bloody Marys, a half bottle of chablis, and what Continental called a Polynesian snack, a tray of fruit and delicious small sandwiches that were probably twice as much in substance than the tourist-class passengers in the rear of the airplane would see during the entire seven hours of the flight. Now there was more wine, and he could see that dinner was also being served.

"Where are we?" he asked, feeling sort of silly. They were obviously well out over the central Pacific. His watch indicated four hours out. Other than that, how could the pretty young thing pouring his wine be more definitive about the specific spot of ocean they were over. She surprised him.

"We're just about at the international date line. In, let's see . . . just twenty-three more minutes, you will gain back the day you lost coming west. We passed almost directly over Wake Island just an hour or so back. We're cruising at thirty-three thousand feet and our ETA at Honolulu still looks good. Would you like the trout or the filet?"

She had filled his wineglass with a claret. "I guess I'm having the filet."

Catching his inference, she reached for his wine goblet. "We have some chablis if you would prefer the trout."

Sakai placed his hand over hers. It was soft and smooth and warm and she made no attempt to remove it. "The filet will be fine—if it's medium-rare."

"I will see to it, myself." She left the wine and disappeared back into the galley area.

It was a very dry claret. Sakai decided to save it for his meat. Surprisingly, he could see the deep-blue Pacific. There were only a few scattered cumulus clouds well below their flight altitude. He supposed the pilots up forward were sitting back in their seats and enjoying their own dinner while the black boxes and electrical switches and hydraulic controls in the big jet carried them and their passengers unerringly toward Oahu.

They shouldn't feel too smug, thought Sakai. The Polynesians were sailing the waters below before Columbus discovered America or the Vikings ever thought about forays to the west. Modern man might feel quite complacent about his technological achievements but the ancient people of the Pacific had thrown a few breadfruit into a hollowed-out log and covered the entire Polynesian triangle from the central islands southwest to New Zealand, north to Hawaii, and even east as far as Easter Island.

They had fastened outriggers to the big canoes with twine rolled on old men's thighs from coconut fibers. Their sails were made by their women, who would take strips of pandanus leaves and plait them into a fabric almost as fine as cotton.

They didn't have to subsist just on breadfruit, either. They had nuts and fruit and roots and baskets of dried fish. Fresh water was stored in yellow gourds and they usually had a few chickens and even dogs. The dogs provided comic relief on the long voyages and could always be eaten if the food supply got too low.

Most of the early sailors needed neither instruments nor charts, although some of the Marshall Islanders fashioned elaborate and amazingly accurate stick charts that enabled them to follow the stars. The most experienced native would stand in the bow and *feel* the ocean swells and judge the direction of the secondary systems. He would watch the sun's path across the heavens and watch for birds or stationary clouds that were the sure sign of nearby land.

The people of the Pacific had always held a special fascination for Sakai. One day he would give them serious study.

"Your steak, sir."

Well, the Polynesians had to do without filet, medium-rare, and crispy golden fried potatoes, so there were some advantages to modern times.

The Pohnpeian sunset, watched in respectful silence from the open dining and bar area of the Village Hotel, was spectacular—as usual. Every Pohnpeian sunset was spectacular, the moist evening sky taking the primary red color of the sun and the blue of the western Pacific sky and breaking them up into an unbelievable array of yellows and oranges and blues and indigos and even greens where the near sides of the horizon clouds provided shadow. There was no brush that could duplicate such beauty, no eye that could capture for longer than a fleeting moment the brief daily appearance of God.

McMahon and Simpson watched this particular sunset with a special contentment. They would see only one more on Pohnpei. Then, at the next dawn, they would be climbing into their aircraft and Simpson would lead the way off the sea-level strip that sat at the end of the causeway from Kolonia. McMahon in the Zero would follow and they would fly together in a loose formation until they reached Kwajalein atoll. There they would land, refuel, and depart for Johnson Island. They had special Department of Defense clearance to remain overnight at Johnson, despite the limited transit space on the highly classified Pacific Missile Range facility. The next day would see their longest leg, to Maui, where they would land and prepare for the flyby on the seventh. The appearance of the Zero would be unannounced to the public and a special surprise for the thousands of Americans and Japanese who would be gathered around Pearl Harbor.

When he and Simpson had met the old Pohnpeian native on their scuba-diving trip and been led to the stored Zero, he had dropped everything and led the restoration project. Now he was going to fly it over Pearl Harbor on the fiftieth anniversary of the appearance of the first Zeros to fly over Oahu. His only regret was that his father would not be there.

Simpson was every bit as elated as McMahon. He, too, had spent all but a few days over the past thirteen months on Pohnpei. On their long flight to Maui, he would fly the MU-2 escort for the Zero. The sleek little Japanese-built transport was McMahon's Buick dealership airplane.

Next to the two Americans at the sunken dining room bar sat their four native employees, all in their early twenties and dressed in clean shirts and long wash pants for the special night. They would miss the tall blond McMahon and the smaller but also thin Simpson.

"I would toast the Zero," said one.

All raised their glasses and drank. McMahon ordered refills.

"I'll miss this place," Simpson said, "although I didn't think I would ever say that. I'm going to miss all of you."

The four natives smiled shyly and sipped from their glasses.

The six men of two different cultures silently sat together and drank. Words were not necessary to describe the strong bond among them. They were too full to talk much, anyhow, having consumed thirteen of the thick-shelled mangrove crabs, the meat somewhat sparse in each but sweet and tender. Dinner had given way to the sunset watch at the bar, and although none of them would admit it, they were dog-tired and all a little bit drunk.

The night outside became as dark as it was going to get and the evening rainstorms moved in. All of the other hotel guests had left the dining room.

"I think it is time to put the cork in the bottle," McMahon said. He was at that mellow point that just preceded losing contact with the real world.

Simpson was several drinks up on him, and as the two men said good-bye to their companions and staggered in the rain down the dark trail to their hut on the side of the steep hill, they clung to each other both out of friendship and a need for mutual support.

"God-damn it, Terry. I love you, you little shit. You are the best friend a man could have."

"We did it, Patrick. We've got our Zero and we're going home."

The two men managed to navigate across the short plank platform leading to their hut without falling onto the railing, and after considerable fumbling to get the door open, stepped inside.

Across the room stood two dark figures.

"Who's that?" McMahon sputtered. "Shit, Terry, we're in the wrong fucking hut."

But they weren't.

One of the figures muttered something in Japanese and the two dark forms quickly and quietly crossed over to the two confused Americans and slid thin blades of steel through their rib cages and into their hearts.

Chapter 23

Native Pohnpeian Sam Nikisi puffed and grunted as he forced his pants up and over his massive stomach. Inhaling, he managed to slip the top button through the eye and pulled the zipper up and around the bulge that remained below the too-tight waistband. No sooner had he done so than the button flew off, a victim of the considerable pressure exerted by the largest part of his body. Cursing quietly, he ripped off the pants and slung them outside his hut. Stumbling around in the dark, he found his lava-lava balled up in one corner. He wrapped the dirty but still colorful cloth around his waist and securely tucked in the top edges. That was much better. His only shirt, a short-sleeved tropical print that was so soaked from the night's humidity one could probably wring a cup of water from it, was draped across a string that ran the width of the single room. He slipped it on and fastened the only button. Gingerly stepping around his wife, who liked to sleep in the exact center of the hut, he searched for his thongs. They were nowhere to be found. No matter, he seldom wore them, but he did like them when he worked at the Pohnpei airport. The concrete hurt his bare feet.

It was still not light outside, but he wanted to get his chore done early, for he and several of the men were going out to the reef for fishing. Tall tales and beer drinking actually, but they wouldn't tell the women. Besides, the women knew anyhow. And the men *would* bring back some fish. Out by the reef you could hand-catch them if you weren't blind staggering drunk.

Ordinarily, he wouldn't go to the airport until almost noon, just an hour or so before the daily Air Micronesian jet transport arrived. But yesterday's pompous aircraft captain had complained about the rate of fuel flow from the refueling hose and just about had a baby when one of the underground tanks ran dry. And a black man at that. One black man should not talk to another black man the way the airline pilot had talked to Sam. The uppity aviator, of course, was African, not Micronesian, and probably felt he was superior. But to make certain that it didn't happen again, Sam would check out the pump and insure that it was drawing from the full tank.

He dropped out of his hut and walked across his yard, being careful to keep his unprotected feet away from the proliferation of soft drink cans and odd pieces of wood and rusty tin that were left over from the last time he repaired the sides. He didn't really like to get up this early. Hell, his two sows were still asleep, sprawled nose-to-ass in their mud wallow.

Yawning until he thought his mouth was going to split at the sides, he stood by the side of the road scratching himself. For the last two days, his groin had been itching as if a thousand sand fleas had taken up residence around his private parts. At least, he *hoped* they were sand fleas. If his woman had given him something, there would be a reckoning when he got home from the day's "fishing."

He waited almost a half hour before an irregular series of rattles and coughs and sputters signaled that his ride was approaching. The small road-weary Japanese pickup truck stopped and he swung easily into the cab. There were no doors. "I thought you had forgotten to get up."

The driver spit a thick brown blob out the open side and banged on the dashboard with his fist to see if he could unstick the speedometer needle. Instead, one of the headlights went out. He banged again and it came back on.

"That pump better not be broke or we'll be there all day putting in a new one," the driver complained.

"It just needs checking. The fuel flow looked good to me but it stalled a bit after the tank ran dry."

"I hope so."

"Who's bringing the beer?"

"Jack Henry."

"God, it will be that island stuff. He always buys the cheapest he can get. I'd just as soon drink pig piss."

"That's what it is."

The two Pohnpeians laughed until both developed fits of coughing and the driver offered his companion a cigarette.

They passed the crude road leading up to the Village Hotel and wound through the outskirts of Kolonia. They were still a mile away from the airport causeway when the faraway roar of an aircraft engine wafted through the still of the night.

"That sounds like the Americans and their Zero," said the driver.

"I thought they were leaving tomorrow morning."

"Me, too. Maybe they've decided to fly it one more time. I sure would. It's a long way to Kwajalein. I'd want it to be perfect."

"Listen."

The rough staccato of the Zero's reciprocating engine was joined by the smoother spooling up of a turboprop engine.

"They must be checking both airplanes."

"It's not very light yet," Sam said.

The driver guided the pickup across the causeway, slowing to a crawl as he encountered the three six-inch speed bumps just outside the airport perimeter. As he pulled over into the vacant parking lot, the Zero was taxiing out, its white, green, and red running lights bright in the predawn darkness. A moment later, the MU-2 followed it.

Both men quickly walked through the deserted open-air terminal and stood behind the waist-high concrete block fence.

The Zero took its position at the head of the runway and began a high-power runup. On the horizon behind it, the first rays of the morning sun were reaching over to cast an eerie orange hue across the airstrip.

"He's checking his engines," Sam said with some authority.

A cloud of white coral dust flowed back from the Zero and billowed over the blue-green water of the lagoon. The airplane was straining against its brakes, the roar of its engine now smooth and powerful. Abruptly, the sound changed as the pilot throttled back to idle.

"Looks like he's going to go."

The pilot looked over at the MU-2 waiting patiently in the

warmup spot and waved. Then he hunched over and the Zero began to move down the runway, its engine clearing its throat with a couple of healthy coughs before settling down into a smooth powerful rhythm. As the airplane gathered speed it swerved suddenly to the left and then just as abruptly straightened out. The tail came up and the Zero swerved again but not as violently.

"Looks sloppy to me," Sam observed. He had worked at the airport for over a year and knew a lot about airplanes. "Look at that!"

The Zero tipped precariously over on one wing and then leaped off at a steep angle just before it crossed the side of the runway. The pilot pushed the nose over and seemed to regain control, for the fighter assumed a more moderate climb attitude and started a gentle left-hand turn. Its wheels were still down.

The fat, high-winged MU-2 raced down the runway, its two turboprop engines humming like a pair of giant bees, and lifted easily into the Pohnpeian dawn. By the time the Zero had completed its turn and was heading southeast, the MU-2 had caught up with it and was flying behind and slightly out to one side. The Zero's wheels swung inboard into the bottom of its wing.

Sam and his friend watched the two airplanes shrink to just mere specks and then disappear into the sunrise.

"They weren't supposed to leave until tomorrow," Sam said. "That's a pretty shitty trick, leaving a day early. Everybody wanted to watch them take off."

"Maybe they're just doing some more tests."

"No, they're too far away for that. They always stay around the island. They're going to Kwajalein."

"Well, they better check their compasses. They're going the wrong way."

"Let's go look at the pump. That really makes me mad. After everything we all did to help them and they sneak out a day early. I didn't think they'd do something like that."

George Sakai swung his legs across the side of the bed and padded into the bathroom, his bladder about to burst. He must have consumed a gallon of liquid from the time he had left Guam to the early-morning moment he had flopped onto the bed in his room at the Royal Hawaiian feeling completely relaxed. Having slept only a short time on the plane, he had dropped off instantly in the hotel.

He hadn't even dreamed, which was a blessing. Thank goodness his mind was weaning itself from the Osaka crash scene.

It was only seven o'clock. There was nothing he had to do. Trying to keep himself from waking up any further, he ambled back toward the bed and accidentally brushed against the dresser.

"Damn!" He rubbed the right side of his waist where it had encountered the sharp corner.

The dresser rapped back several times in response. The dresser? Dressers didn't rap or make noises. There it was again, a low series of knocks. *Don't tell me the Royal Hawaiian has rats.* The rapping returned a third time. It was coming from the door that adjoined the next room. Whoever was over there must have opened the door in their wall and was lightly knocking on his.

"Hey, I'm sorry. I bumped myself on the dresser."

The occupant must be supersensitive for Sakai's mild expletive to have bothered him.

The rapping continued, insistent but polite. Maybe the guy wanted a personal apology. Sakai unlocked the door and pulled it open.

"Good morning, George."

Alicia?

His ex-wife stepped forward, obviously pleased with her little surprise. She was still in her nightgown, and before Sakai could adjust to the unexpected sight she reached up and slid the straps off her shoulders. The white nylon slithered down her body and pooled itself around her bare feet. Her suntan was exquisite, marred only by a thin white border around her pubic hair. She must have lain on a very private beach.

Alicia reached out and grabbed his undershirt. Sakai resisted her tug on his arms. "I've got a bad shoulder—" His ex-wife apologized with puckered lips and followed his lead as he raised his arms. Carefully, she pulled his undershirt up and off. Placing her arms around his waist, she kissed his chest, his neck, and then his mouth.

As soon as Sakai wrapped his own arms around her middle his body sounded the clarion call to action and he lifted her by the buttocks onto the bed.

"Your shoulder—"

"I'll watch it."

Alicia placed her hands on his temples and pulled him to her. "Enjoy your breakfast, George."

. . .

"I feel like I should be smoking a cigarette."

"You've never smoked, George."

Sakai ran one hand across Alicia's belly. It was as flat and firm as the first time he had felt it. Her head was on his chest so he spoke into her hair. "What are you doing here?"

"Bert Thompson arranged it."

Now, that's a boss. "Where are the kids?"

"They went on to mother's."

"I would have liked to have seen them."

"You didn't seem to be missing them a few moments ago."

"Man is an animal. Once the basic urges are satisfied, he thinks of more important things."

"Are your basic urges satisfied, George?"

"Why this sudden solicitation for my welfare?"

"I saw the Osaka crash on television and for the first time I think I realized what your job is all about."

"I sure as hell didn't do it very well."

"If that is true, it's the only thing you haven't done well." Alicia twisted her head and pressed her lips onto Sakai's. His hand slid up to her breast.

Alicia giggled. "It's almost better—not being married, I mean."

"I'm not going to Australia, Alicia."

"Yes, you will. We have two whole days before the president and his party arrive. I'm going to keep you right here in this bed until then and you will ask me to marry you again and I will say yes. And when I tell you about our sheep station and the people who will be our friends and neighbors and how enthused the girls are about a completely new environment you will tell Bert Thompson you don't want to investigate any more terrorist acts and chase all over the world just to find horror and tragedy and frustration. Life is too short, George."

Sakai pulled himself up into a sitting position. "We always wind up saying the same words, Alicia."

"Then, let's don't talk—for a while longer."

She leaned over and ran her tongue lightly down his stomach and onto the inside of his thighs.

Even if he had been a smoker, Sakai knew it was too late for a cigarette.

. . .

The chalky ring of coral that was Majuro lay some seven hundred and fifty miles west of Pohnpei and the atoll enclosed an oblong lagoon some twenty miles along its east-west axis and about six miles wide. The chain of islets that made up its southern curve were joined by solid fill-ins of crushed and packed coral to form the main living area, and one section of the narrow strip was widened and paved with coral concrete to provide the airstrip.

The MU-2, paced by the much slower, fuel-conscious Zero, had taken over five hours to cover the distance, and the two aircraft approached in trail, the MU-2 in the lead. After a preliminary pass to examine the airstrip, the MU-2 touched down and taxied out of the way. The Zero made a long straight-in approach and landed two-point on its main gear, the tires throwing up a pair of tiny gray clouds as they screeched onto the concrete. The tail of the Zero remained high for a moment and then settled, and the aircraft swerved only slightly before coming to a stop. With a burst of power it turned around and taxied back to the refueling area where the MU-2 sat waiting.

Majuro had been selected for the first stop for several very special reasons. One was that in addition to a normal supply of jet fuel, there was still on hand a small supply of military-grade aviation gasoline, left over from the fairly recent days when the Lockheed P2Vs of Japan operated with the Australians out of Majuro on coordinated ASW and patrol exercises. The fuel was in fifty-five-gallon drums, unfortunately, so refueling would be by hand pump and strainer.

The other factor was equally important. Majuro had no tower or any other aviation control facility. The commercial airliners made their routine stops known by voice reports to the Pacific air route controller handling their flights. There was no radar coverage and aircraft transiting Majuro could do so completely anonymously if they so desired.

The dark Micronesian native in charge of the refueling crew had only a limited knowledge of commercial and military flight procedures, his main aeronautical education having been a short fixed-base operator's school run by Continental Airlines in Honolulu. Thus, the fact that the MU-2 and the Zero had arrived without a flight plan was of no interest to him—or anyone else on Majuro for that matter. Except for a brief entry in his fuel log, there would be no record of their visit, and the cheerful Majuron was only concerned that the refueling went safely and smoothly and that the

Shell credit card tendered in payment by the pilot of the MU-2 was as valid as the company plastic used by Air Micronesia.

The news of the arrival of the World War II Japanese fighter spread over the atoll in minutes and most of the natives migrated to the airport to be a part of the unusual event. Several towed tall white refreshment stands behind their pickups and made a killing on soda pop and candy while the aircraft were being refueled.

Replenishing the Zero by hand pump took almost two hours, although the aircraft only required the contents of two of the fifty-five-gallon AvGas drums.

The crowd was in a festive mood and shouted friendly comments at the two pilots, who stayed beside their aircraft and returned a few of the waves. Several of the natives laughed at the ill fit of the Zero pilot's flight suit. Several sizes too large, it had the sleeves and pants legs rolled up. When the aviators finally manned their aircraft for departure, almost the entire population of Majuro was on hand to send them off with cheers and handclaps. A number held their small children up for a better view. Some of the older ones stood with a faraway look in their eyes, remembering similar airplanes that over-flew the islands on almost a daily basis back during the big war when they operated from the big flat-topped ships far at sea.

The MU-2 lifted off first and started a wide low circle, and by the time it came back around the Zero started down the runway. Its tail rose, then the pilot pulled it from the airstrip and retracted the landing gear, almost in one movement. The MU-2 took its position off the right wing of the Zero and the two aircraft climbed away to the southeast.

The crowd lingered for a while and drank more of the cold soda pop while the native station manager supervised the stowing of the refueling gear. It had been a premier event in the lives of the people of Majuro, one that they would talk about and relive for the next few weeks.

As for the pilots of the Zero and its escort, they were already looking ahead to their next stop at Funafuti Atoll in the Tuvalu Islands that lay twelve hundred nautical miles to the southeast. Funafuti had been selected as carefully as had Majuro and for the same reasons. The Zero and the MU-2 could land, refuel, spend the night, and take off the next morning with no one outside of the island inhabitants knowing they had been there.

The long distance from Majuro to Funafuti would be a test for the range and endurance of both the Zero and its pilot. The many islands and atolls of the Gilberts were strung along most of the route and would provide a visual check on their flight path while the pilots grew accustomed to the inertial navigating systems installed in both aircraft. If that flight were made without incident, the short third leg to Canton Island could be easily made. However, Canton was a British-owned island and had a full-fledged air traffic control facility that was used occasionally by short-ranged jets as a refueling stop on the Hawaii-to-Fiji and Pago Pago routes. The pilots would have to explain why they arrived without a filed flight plan, but they had their story ready and were confident it would be believed. Once out of Canton, the remainder of their long transit across the Pacific could be made with very little risk of detection.

The logistics, including the reserve supply of aviation gasoline carried inside the fuselage of the MU-2, worked out by the two Americans who had planned to take the Kwajalein–Johnson Island route to Hawaii, would suit the purposes of the replacement pilots quite well. They could not have planned better themselves. It was as if the gods, themselves, were smiling on their unique mission.

The pilot of the Zero looked idly down upon the low-flying seabirds as the two planes cruised in the early-afternoon sun, the feathered creatures going about their hunt for fish undisturbed and with no concern over their two inferior metal cousins high overhead.

Chapter 24

The Chief of Forensic Medicine of the Tokyo Police Department stared at the two charred corpses lying on the tables in the coroner's autopsy laboratory. He agreed with the Guam coroner's report on the race, sex, and cause of death of the two, but their identity was a mystery. Over the tables were two backlighted sets of dental X rays provided by the medical records section of the maritime arm of the JSDF. One was labeled "Genda, Saburo, Captain, Maritime Arm, JSDF," and the other "Ohiro, Michio, Lieutenant, Maritime Arm, JSDF." The teeth portrayed in the two X rays resembled in no way the teeth in the two cadavers.

"I am afraid we are going to have some very upset authorities both here and on Guam," the forensic doctor muttered.

"I suggest we get off the information right away," the Tokyo coroner commented. "Perhaps the police at Guam have some missing persons. We may be able to use that information for identification."

"Yes. Of course, this means that Genda and Ohiro are still alive. A clever switch, but I suspect that even they knew their ruse would be discovered."

The coroner nodded. "All they wanted was to buy some time and they have done that. The trail may now have been lost."

"That is not our concern—but we better notify the others immediately."

The coroner took down the X rays and placed them in two manila envelopes. "Shall I or you?"

"I will do it."

Chief Jose Chimananshe glared across the podium at the oncoming eight-to-four shift of his officers. He was not happy and more than a little bit alarmed. A mistake had been made and it could be a very bad one.

"Attention to this. The Tokyo police have advised me that the two burned bodies we shipped are *not* the terrorists Genda and Ohiro. Who they are remains to be seen, but I strongly suspect they are the two missing tourists who were vacationing at the resort on our Cocos Island. They were known to have come across by ferry and had a rental car for sight-seeing. They could very well have gone north on Highway Four and right into the hands of Genda and his group, who undoubtedly selected them because of their nationality, sex, and age compatability. The bastards have pulled off one hell of a well-executed switch on us, and if they are still on the island— which I seriously doubt—I want their asses but *bad*.

"I don't intend to reinstate the maximum-effort manhunt. But I do expect to assign additional personnel starting with this shift. You all have IDs on the two. Keep your eyes open. Be curious. Snoop around. Ask. If you come up with *anything*, do nothing until you have a backup and I am informed—unless to wait would allow them to escape again."

The briefing sergeant took over as Chimananshe walked angrily back to his office. He should have known the death scene was too pat and kept the manhunt going until Tokyo confirmed the IDs. But he hadn't. The obese chief wondered if the Tokyo people had notified George Sakai. Probably not directly, but they would have certainly passed the information immediately to the American Embassy.

He slumped in his chair. There was little chance that the two Japanese were still on Guam; the manhunt had been lifted several days ago. They could have easily left, which was just as well for the people of Guam. But they sure as hell would strike again. The question was: where?

Detective Shiganori Kami accepted Charlie Porter's offer of a scotch. The two men sat in Porter's embassy office.

"Ain't this a shit of a development," Porter spat out. "I thought it was all over."

"I wish we could have run the dental checks right away, before we ceased the hunt."

"Hindsight, Kami-san, the one infallible police technique."

"Well, they have gone somewhere. They will not have stayed on Guam."

"I agree. The question is fucking where? Back here?"

"I doubt it. But we will act as if it were a possibility."

"Genda's Hokkaido beach cottage—staked out?"

"Tonishi is back at the inn and we have several people there to help him. We have alerts out to all transportation terminals. But he and Ohiro could already have returned if they were coming back. Incidentally, we have learned a bit more about him. We located his physician in Sapporo. Genda is dying of leukemia. He will be dead within weeks."

"How in the hell is he still walking around?"

"Medication. But even the doctor is amazed that he is still active. He should be extremely weak and experiencing some pain by now, although the medication will help forestall it some. He refused conventional treatment."

"Then, I'd say the tough old bastard plans to go out in style. One more operation."

"In all probability."

The tall, thin American owner of the Village Hotel was cussin' mad. His two countrymen had flown off in their airplanes a day early and had left an unpaid bill of over fifteen hundred dollars. That was not like them; they had always given him monthly checks right on schedule, drawn on the local branch of the Bank of Guam, and payment had always been honored. They must have slipped out that morning quite early. The maid had not reported anything unusual the first day, even though their clothes and gear were gone. It was not her concern to wonder about such things. But she had asked on the third day since their hut was still on her cleaning schedule and it obviously was not being used. That's when the owner of the Village Hotel had learned they were gone, apparently for good. From now on, such adventurers would pay in advance.

He was preparing letters to the aviators' stateside addresses when the portly chief of the small Pohnpeian police force walked into his tiny office behind the reception desk.

"We found McMahon and Simpson," the chief said.

"Found?"

"Dead. Murdered. They were buried over on the far side near the Agricultural Trade School. Two of the boys there stumbled onto the graves. Their clothes and possessions were buried with them."

The hotel owner was completely confused. "Then, who flew the airplanes out?"

"I would say the killers."

"We have to have help. Your force isn't capable of a complicated murder investigation."

"Since the victims are Americans, the governor has contacted the Micronesian Affairs Office in Honolulu. Your federal authority is going to send someone."

"Stolen airplanes should be easy to trace."

"Maybe so. Maybe not. There are many islands in the Pacific. Our people alone are on over a hundred of them."

"But relatively few have airstrips."

"That is true. We do have some information. I asked the Air Micronesian office to contact their representatives on the island route. The two airplanes landed and refueled at Majuro five hours after leaving here. The pilots were Japanese."

"Japanese? Where did they go from there?"

"We don't know. It will take more sophisticated resources than we have here on Pohnpei to search for them."

"The Honolulu people can do that. They have the FAA and ocean route information."

"I hope so."

Chapter 25

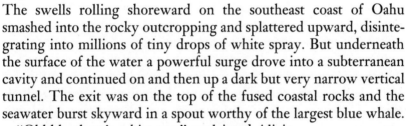

The swells rolling shoreward on the southeast coast of Oahu smashed into the rocky outcropping and splattered upward, disintegrating into millions of tiny drops of white spray. But underneath the surface of the water a powerful surge drove into a subterranean cavity and continued on and then up a dark but very narrow vertical tunnel. The exit was on the top of the fused coastal rocks and the seawater burst skyward in a spout worthy of the largest blue whale.

"Ohhhh, there's a big one," exclaimed Alicia.

Sakai watched the spray from the landmark blowhole dissipate in the strong sea breeze. What had happened to Alicia? Her personality was more relaxed; she was more solicitous of his opinions. She still was dead set on convincing him that they should resume their life together on the Australian sheep farm, but her arguments were not as bullheaded and several of the points she had made were very well thought out and carried with them a surprising amount of logic.

The drive around Oahu had been his idea, and once they left Honolulu and wound along the east shoreline she seemed to become a little girl, oohing and aahing at the windsurfers and the swift catamarans and now the performance of the blowhole.

The sea breeze carried a chill even though it was only early afternoon, and Alicia backed into the protection of his arms. She seemed to be content and at peace with herself as she stood and waited for the next geyser of seawater.

"Alicia?"

"Yes, George?"

"You're different."

"Different?"

"Yes. You're more like you were when we first met."

"I've always been the same person, George."

"Maybe it's me. It's been a long time since I've had this kind of time to myself. It's kind of nice."

"Do I detect a slight weakening of your position?"

"No, not that. Well, maybe I do have a bit more tolerance for your stubborn insistence that we can still get together. But one of us would have to give up a major goal."

"George, last night when you described the scene of the United crash and then related it to the little girl in Vietnam, I saw a side of you I had never seen before, or at least I had never tried to see. I saw a man who is very gentle and loving and who carries a great deal of guilt about things that he has had no control over. I thought of Angela Joan and especially Kristen Anne, and how the death of the little girl in Osaka must have hit you. I would have gone all to pieces but you went on with what you had to do. I don't see how you could love your job, George, but I do see how you respect it. There is a lot of evil and you are directly involved in combating that evil. I suppose the point I want to make is that you can't do it all. Even if you are the best antiterrorist specialist in the world, you can't do it all."

"That doesn't mean I can't carry my share."

"No, it doesn't. But where does your share stop? You did your share by your service in Vietnam. You have done a big share in State—you even lost your family doing that share. How much do you owe your country, George? Your whole life? Your daughters?"

Sakai didn't like the return of the familiar bitterness to Alicia's words. She recognized his reaction immediately.

"Forgive me, I didn't mean that like it sounded. I just want you to weigh your priorities. I know you love those two more than life itself and I have to assume my share of the blame for taking them from you. I don't want them away from you, George. I don't want you away from me. It's just that I want us to be together in an environment where we're a family and we do family things like sit around after dinner and talk to each other about our problems and the day's happenings. I want to go on weekend picnics and watch you teach the girls to swim and watch them grow and have their first dates."

"I want all those things, too, Alicia."

Alicia squeezed his hands. "I know you do. But working at State you got home barely in time to put the girls to bed and you were gone before they woke up. We were lucky to have a Sunday, much less a whole weekend, and even then that damned beeper was always clipped to your belt. It even went off when we were making love, George—usually before you did." The humor in Alicia's last statement failed to mask the exasperation that prompted her words.

Sakai knew that she was speaking the truth but that was the nature of his work. Man was supposed to extend himself. The woman was supposed to provide him a home and care for his children while he provided for their welfare. It was a traditional exchange, but for the first time, hearing Alicia's words spoken in love rather than anger, he began to wonder if it was a fair exchange.

"I know you don't like the idea of accepting any of Daddy's money. But, George, I am his only daughter and the girls are his only grandchildren. He worships them, but he wants to do this for all of us. He doesn't want us to wait until he and Mother are gone. The papers for the sheep station are all prepared—and they are in your name, George, not mine. It was Daddy's idea. He knows it won't work if it's just me and the girls. Please let him do this for us."

Sakai knew he was weakening. He just didn't like the feeling that somehow he would be relinquishing part of his responsibilities, part of his obligation to be the provider. Not that heading a sheep station would be the life of a gentleman farmer. He had met enough Australians to know that one of their national characteristics was hard work. But that same factor was a Japanese trait and had at one time been an American trait. For some unexplainable reason, he felt that accepting Alicia's father's offer was the easy way out. And he had never taken the easy way out of anything. At that particular moment, standing with his arms around Alicia and watching the periodic eruptions of the blowhole, to say that he was confused would be a gross understatement.

"I will do this, Alicia. I will think about it. I will try very hard to understand your feelings because for the first time I think you understand mine. I will seriously think about it."

"That's all I'm asking, George, except for one thing. We will be here until after the ceremonies on the seventh. We have to decide by then. I won't mention it again. Just kiss me and hold me for a moment and then let's go. By dinner, I'll be very hungry and you can wine me and dine me and we can at the very least have these days together."

Sakai had the uncomfortable feeling that he had already made his decision.

It was close to midnight when Sakai and Alicia returned to the Royal Hawaiian. He saw her into her room, entered his and opened his connecting door, and then noticed that the message light on his telephone was blinking. As he called the front desk, Alicia opened her connecting door and stood in the opening.

"George, would you . . . excuse me, I didn't know you were on the phone."

"This is eight-oh-three, I have a message?"

Pause.

"Yes, thank you."

"Important?" Alicia asked.

"I have to call Charlie Porter. He's the CIA rep at the Tokyo embassy. I didn't realize that he knew what hotel I'm in."

"You have to call him tonight?"

"The message he left said yes—regardless of the time."

Sakai took a small black notebook out of his briefcase and flipped the pages until he found the special embassy number. It should be a little after eight there and Porter should still be in his office if the call was as urgent as his request indicated.

There was some sort of mixup with the automatic dialing sequence, and he had to talk to the Tokyo operator for a moment, but Porter answered on the first ring of his phone.

"Charlie, what's up?"

"Take a deep breath, gyrene. The two pieces of charcoal that Guam shipped us along with Goto and the rest are not Genda and Ohiro."

"My God, are they sure?"

"Fucking-A sure, Sakai-san. Confirmed by JMSDF dental records."

"What a frame. I had no suspicion at all."

"I don't think anyone did at the time. Probably so relieved that the bastards had gotten their fucking due."

"I'll have to call Bert Thompson right away."

"State has the word, so I suspect he's trying to reach you or is waiting for a call. Sorry, ole buddy. I personally don't see no sense in you coming back out here. Kami tells me the Japanese police have gone to a national alert—on the quiet side, of course. I talked to Chief Chimananshe in Guam and they've gone back to a full surveillance, but he doesn't feel they're still in Guam. Any ideas?"

"No, I'm still in shock here. Alicia and I—"

"Alicia? Hey, back in the sack with the ex? Drive one home for the Gipper, you shifty old bastard."

"Porter, you're an ass."

"Have a nice day, Sakai-san—call me if there's anything I should know later."

"Will do. You likewise."

Sakai replaced the phone in its cradle and sat back in the bedside chair.

"What was that all about?" Alicia asked.

"Would you believe that two of the terrorists are still alive?"

"I thought they were all dead."

"So did we. But two of the bodies were ringers. Saburo Genda, the main one, and one by the name of Ohiro are still out there. Shit. I have to call Bert Thompson."

"I'm sorry, George. I know how you must feel. I'll be in the other room when you know what you have to do."

"Thanks, Alicia. I'll be with you in a bit."

Sakai felt that his shoulders had sagged almost to his knees. It would be early morning in D.C. He dialed Thompson's home number.

"Yes?"

"George. I just heard. Sorry to wake you."

"Hell, I'm up. Due at the office shortly. I thought we were through with this one."

"I figure I'll get back out to Guam and start from there."

"No. No, George. That's why I haven't tried to reach you. Let the Guamanians and the Japanese have it from here. I think the two bastards will go underground and stay there. You stay in Honolulu and check in with Murray Franklin as I suggested. If anything develops, you can still head west."

"Whatever you say."

"How's Alicia?"

"Great—thanks to you."

"Well, enjoy. I have to run. I figured you would call but I really don't see that there is any great urgency for you to get back in the picture. They're running scared."

"I'll stay in touch."

" 'Bye, George."

Sakai could not agree with Thompson's assessment of what Genda and Ohiro would do. Genda would not crawl under the bushes and curl up to die. But he had to admit that returning to Guam made little sense. Strangely enough, he was glad. For the first time since he had gone to work for State, he was glad he had been pulled off a case.

Alicia was in bed by the time he walked into her room.

"Everything all right?" she asked.

"I don't have to leave. But I have some thinking to do. I think I'll go down to the bar for a nightcap. Want to go?"

"No, sweetheart. You go ahead. I'll be here when you get sleepy."

Alicia's forehead tasted almost as good as her lips. More surprising was her attitude. She knew that his work had once more entered their bedroom but this time she seemed to understand.

"I'll be back shortly."

Chapter 26

For the first time in over forty-six years, Saburo Genda was happy—genuinely happy. Not since his time with Emiko had he experienced that unfamiliar emotion. True, he had enjoyed a certain degree of contentment during many of his years in the JMSDF, particularly when he had been exercising his skills as an aviator, but his other duties had been tainted with the realization that he was, in a very real way, a fraud. Only when he had been in the air and preoccupied with the safe, efficient operation of a highly technical flying machine had his mind ever been at ease. But even that had not been true happiness, the kind of feeling that so overpowers one with a sense of precious well-being that everything else ceases to be of any concern.

The single joy that was now his drove him toward his final task. Strapped in the seat of his beloved Mitsubishi Type Zero-sen, holding it on course and altitude with the same delicate touch that he had learned in his days with the *Tokkotai*, special attack corps of the Imperial Navy, Genda was once more a Thunder God.

Now he could put aside the events of the past weeks: the undesirable but necessary association with Goto and his completely immoral associates; the shame in his role in the downing of the

American passenger jet; the embarrassment of being apprehended as a common criminal at the hands of the nisei in Guam; the necessity to murder the young man at the university, the two innocent tourists on southern Guam, and the two Americans on Pohnpei. He could also ignore the fear that he felt as the gradual weakening of his body reminded him of the thinning fluid within, an impotent solution that was not quite able to carry sufficient oxygen to his body or remove sufficient waste. Even the physical pain that had become almost intolerable the past days was of secondary importance. In fact, all of those things were immaterial.

After the near-catastrophic takeoff from Pohnpei, where he had failed to remember the effect of the terrific torque of the Zero's Nakajima engine and almost went crashing off the side of the runway, he had settled down, and his landing at Majuro and the subsequent takeoff had been much more skillfully accomplished. The instruments and controls of the cockpit were as though he had never been away from them, his aviator's cockpit scan returning as easily as a swim stroke returns to the swimmer after he has been away from the water for many years. Swimming, sex, and flying, thought Genda, are the skills that once learned are never forgotten.

His landing at Funafuti had been even better than the one at Majuro, and the operators of the small airfield had been so excited over the appearance of the Zero that they had readily accepted Ohiro's claim that he had filed their flight plan—and closed it—while airborne. The natives had hardly even questioned the reason for the transit, Genda explaining that he and Ohiro were making a documentary of airfields formerly used as Zero operating bases in the great war. The people of Funafuti had fed and housed the two Japanese as if they had been conquering heroes and spread flowers on the runway prior to their takeoff.

Now, three hours out of Funafuti on his way to Canton, Genda was back in the world he had so loved. Glancing over his right shoulder, he could see the MU-2 riding a loose wing position in a pronounced nose-high attitude. Genda was cruising the Zero at a very low speed to save fuel, and the small executive turboprop was designed to cruise at a much faster speed. Staying with the Zero required Ohiro to reduce his power and increase his angle of attack—the angle between the chord of his wing and the relative wind—to a higher than usual setting. This caused him to constantly monitor the controls.

Genda was becoming accustomed to the Zero's autopilot and navigational systems, luxuries that would have been invaluable during the long combat patrols of the early forties. The miniaturized autopilot was simple and straightforward; however, until he tired he preferred to hand-fly the airplane. The inertial navigation system was similar to those he had encountered during his last active duty days with the JMSDF, but it was more compact and had required a bit of study while they remained overnight at Funafuti. Fortunately, he and Ohiro had made certain they were in possession of the INS manual and the MU-2's flight operations manual before they had left Pohnpei. As for Ohiro, he was a more current aviator than Genda and at home in the MU-2, having considerable prior turboprop experience in the JMSDF's Lockheed P-3 patrol aircraft.

The day itself was typically Pacific. Crisp blue sky, even bluer water. A few morning cumuli billowed upward, their tops growing through only twelve thousand feet and easily flown around. By late afternoon they would be giants topping fifty thousand and would have undergone a severe personality change to become angry and violent. But they would not be a problem for Genda and his wingman. Both would have arrived at the tiny British-administered island of Canton, the second-to-last stop before his final flight.

Providing the bodies of the two Americans had not been discovered back on Pohnpei, there would be a good chance that the theft of the two Mitsubishis was still undetected and their arrival at Canton, while a surprise, would have no special significance to the occupants of the island. If the theft had been discovered, there was the possibility that the caretaker and the few natives on Canton would have received an international aviation alert. Then, he and Ohiro might have a problem. Genda doubted that the inhabitants of Canton were armed but it was a possibility. If they were, well, that was a chance he and Ohiro had to take.

Ohiro's voice crackled in his headset. "How are you doing, Genda-san?"

"Well, very well."

"Why not put on the autopilot? You need to rest."

"I am fine."

"You are all over the sky, Genda-san. It is making my job difficult. This airplane was not designed to cruise comfortably at this slow speed."

Genda had not even noticed that fatigue was affecting his pressure on the controls. The airplane could be wandering a bit. "I will do so." He held his heading and attitude steady and punched on the autopilot. His seat would not tilt, but he adjusted the height to provide a different set of pressures on his buttocks and back. The air vents were open and cool air was directed over his upper body and the soft sheepskin cradled him in relative comfort. His seat-pack parachute was hard and lumpy, however. He would not wear it on the last leg. It would be redundant.

Ohiro watched the Zero steady. He had a new admiration for Genda. The old man at the controls was remarkable. Sixty-three years old, he had jumped—well, climbed—into the Zero back at Pohnpei and except for the sloppy takeoff had flown it out as though he had never been away from it. Ohiro knew that the long ten-hour flight from Majuro south to Funafuti had been a terrible strain for Genda. After landing, Ohiro had to help him from the cockpit and Genda's legs had barely held him up. But with a nourishing meal and a good night's sleep, the old warrior had been ready to go by morning.

Ohiro allowed the MU-2 to back off a bit, then he adjusted the power and controls to match the speed and heading of the MU-2 as well as he could with that of the Zero and reengaged his own autopilot.

They were over a very remote section of the central Pacific ocean, approximately halfway between the Tuvalu and Phoenix islands, and their passage would almost certainly be undetected. They were off the major air traffic routes and they had not even seen another aircraft in the air since leaving Pohnpei. That was fine with Ohiro. The sighting of a Zero winging along at ten thousand feet would be an event passed over every radio frequency available. The isolation and quiet of their present passage was much more desired.

He could only marvel at the boldness and ingenuity of Genda's plan. Ohiro would never have undertaken such a task on his own initative. There were too many things that could go wrong. One was the Zero, itself. Even modern airplanes could expect minor discrepancies to crop up when flying over forty-five hundred miles of ocean with four enroute stops. Yet, as of this moment, the forty-eight-year-old Zero was trouble-free.

There was also the matter of Genda's competence. He had almost lost the airplane on his initial takeoff from Pohnpei. His landings had been good, but the two he had made were under ideal conditions with light winds down long, wide, smooth runways. How would Genda handle a severe, gusting crosswind? What about the runway at Palmyra Island, the final layover after Canton? Palmyra had been abandoned long ago as an airfield. There remained a World War II strip, but it had to be in disrepair, with tropical growth pushing up through the aged surface. There could even be serious cracks and most probably potholes. There would be no services and certainly no fuel. Ohiro would have to top off the Zero with aviation gas at Canton and be unable to accompany Genda any farther, for there was no refueling facility at Palmyra.

Thus, when Genda made his landing at Palmyra, he would be alone. If he blew a tire or nicked a prop, it would be all over. There was no way he could carry any of the spare parts stored in the MU-2 and the tools to use them. They had been for the first legs only.

And as if that were not enough, the old man was ill. Ohiro could see that. He tired quickly and much of his physical strength had disappeared since their early days together in Tokyo and Osaka. If the old warrior became incapacitated while in the air, his end could very well take place over some unknown spot of the vast Pacific. Perhaps, that is what kept Genda going. He was either going to accomplish what he had set out to do or die in the attempt. And even though Ohiro was of the new generation, he could see the honor in that. And Genda, if nothing else, seemed obsessed with being a man of honor.

Ohiro saw it first, the intermittent reflection of a white coral ring flickering below the scattered puffs of low clouds. He judged it to be a scant twenty miles dead ahead.

"Canton, Genda-san. Dead ahead."

"Ah, yes. I see it. Let us descend."

As they approached, they could see the atoll's string-thin substance wound around in an irregular, elongated loop. The white ribbon was broken only on its west side by what appeared to be a narrow and treacherous ship entrance channel that led through the ring into the blue-green lagoon. The airstrip lay on the northernmost segment of the curve, a single concrete runway aligned with the prevailing winds. The ocean clipped off both ends. If you undershot or overshot at Canton, you swam the rest of the way.

They made an exploratory low pass across the airstrip and Ohiro could see the sides as well as most of the main island were thick with palms and low tropical brush. A wide-spanned aircraft would have little clearance but it should be ample for both the MU-2 and the Zero. Looking at the surface of the water around Canton, he could see that the windstreaks and the whitecaps frosting the tips of the wind-driven waves indicated a healthy breeze, probably twelve to fifteen knots but aligned right down the runway. There would be no crosswind and Genda should have little trouble with his landing.

A few people ran out from a group of shacks beside a small aircraft parking area and waved. Ohiro dipped his wings in salute and as usual began his approach ahead of Genda. The wind was strong but steady and he touched down easily on the first third of the runway. The surface was smooth. Quickly, he taxied out of the way and watched the Zero approach.

Genda started a long straight final, his landing gear lowered and the wing flaps all the way down.

"You really will not need full flaps," Ohiro radioed to Genda. "There is a strong steady wind." He watched the Zero settle a bit as Genda took his advice and retracted the flaps a notch. A burst of power corrected the Zero's sink and it came down its glide path in a beautiful nose-high landing attitude. Genda brought it across the end of the runway and started his flare as he simultaneously reduced his power. The Zero rotated slightly and touched down three-point. It rolled straight ahead; a perfect landing. Ohiro watched with considerable pride. In his youth, the Imperial Navy's Flight Petty Officer Saburo Genda must have been one hell of a pilot.

Ohiro resumed his taxi with the Zero following. They swung onto the parking ramp and shut down their engines. The few on-lookers, including a Caucasian who must be the station manager, ignored the MU-2 and crowded around the Zero, obviously excited and curious.

Genda waved them away from the front of the aircraft. The engine was still hot and could accidentally diesel, the swing of the propeller easily fatal to anyone in its path. He shut off the fuel selector and the ignition and unbuckled his safety harness. The white man was on his left wing, reaching in to grab and pump his hand.

"Welcome to Canton! What a bloody thrill! Where in hell did you chaps come from? You speak English, right?"

Genda smiled wearily. "Yes. *Dozo*—please. Help me out."

The British station manager was astounded to see the age of the Japanese pilot. He looked seventy or more and obviously was very weak. He grabbed Genda under the arms and helped him to stand on the seat pan. Genda dropped his chute inside the cockpit and smiled at the relief of getting rid of the weight. He managed to lift one leg over the side of the cockpit by the time Ohiro climbed up to assist. The two men held him and guided him off the wing. Standing in the sea breeze, Genda regained some of his energy and bowed repeatedly to those around him.

The small group walked into the shade provided by one of the three open-sided clapboard buildings beside the airstrip. Someone produced a cold can of Pepsi-Cola and Genda upended it immediately. Ohiro received an identical welcoming present.

"I don't have any flight plan on you chaps. We had no idea you were coming," the Brit said.

Ohiro waved the protest away with a friendly hand and replied slowly in heavily accented English. "We are operating out of Funafuti Island, making documentary of World War II airstrips. My friend flew Zero in those days. I am flying camera plane with our equipment."

The Brit could understand that. Funafuti was a little over six hundred miles to the southwest and had a complete terminal and aircraft servicing facility, being used regularly by Air Tungaru. That would be a long overwater flight for the ancient Zero but of course the modern MU-2 had the navigational capability. "I'll send your arrival report," he offered.

"I closed out in air," Ohiro added hastily. "Please, I am sorry you did not get flight plan."

"Not unusual. The blokes over there forget we even exist sometimes. All we get is an occasional resupply flight. There are plans to update us, however."

Ohiro made a show of looking around the island while he sat and drank his soda. "We would like to shoot footage early tomorrow morning. Can you put us up overnight?"

The Brit laughed. "We can feed you and scare up a few beers as long as you don't mind sleeping under the stars. I'm afraid we're a wee bit short on the amenities."

"No problem. My companion and I apologize for inconvenience."

"No inconvenience at all! We're just proud to have some guests. We've had a good bit of rain lately. If you would like to take a shower, we have plenty of fresh water."

Genda bowed in appreciation as he handed his empty soda can to one of the natives. "Cold water! That would be very welcome." The native dashed away and returned with a full plastic jug he had retrieved from a small refrigerator.

Genda reached for it and fell forward onto his face.

When he next opened his eyes, he was lying on a single metal frame bed and a slowly rotating tropical fan was directly overhead. He tried to sit up but a pair of hands gently prevented it. The station manager and Ohiro were sitting by the bed. Genda eagerly accepted the jug of cold water that he had failed to grasp before he fainted.

"Not too much, old chap. Just sip it for a while."

"I am sorry," Genda said. "I was very hot."

"Maybe a touch dehydrated, I'd say. You look a bit like death warmed over."

"I am fine. Just overextended, I think."

"Well, you rest here. Take my bed for the night. Your friend can bunk here on the floor with you. I'll sleep outside."

Genda struggled to rise but thought better of it. He was extremely weak. "No, I can manage. I do not want you to give up own comfort."

"I won't hear of it. You rest. We'll bring you some dinner." With his eyes, the station manager invited Ohiro outside.

"Your friend doesn't look well. He's a bit along in years for this sort of thing, is he not?"

"He is older, yes, but insists on participation. He is financing documentary so I can say little."

"Well, you flamin' well better. He is in no shape to fly."

"We will rest the night. He may be just tired as he says."

"I'll have someone bring him some food later. I can call Funafuti for assistance if you like."

"No! He will be all right, I am certain. Thank you."

"As you wish."

Ohiro watched the station manager walk off toward what appeared to be the cooking shack. It might be that Genda's illness was about to peak. If so, Ohiro needed to come up with a suitable contingency plan. They could leave the Zero and return to Funafuti and start making their way back across the Pacific—but to where? There was a good chance that the authorities back at Pohnpei had become suspicious of the sudden departure of the two airplanes. The bodies could even have been found.

Ohiro ambled out on the ramp and began a slow walk around the airplanes, trying to put together his next move as he examined them. The Zero was still dry, although there was just a touch of oil around the rocker-arm cover seal of one of the bottom cylinders. He would have to refuel the airplane. That meant turning up one engine of the MU-2 for electrical power. The cabin tank that held the supply of aviation gasoline was equipped with an electric transfer pump and refueling the Zero would be a simple matter. Even as the airplanes now sat, the hose should reach. But why refuel if Genda would not be able to continue?

Ohiro knew that Genda would never give himself over to the authorities. Still, if the old man was indeed seriously ill, they should take the MU-2 back to Funafuti and obtain medical assistance. There was a possibility that the theft of the two airplanes was still un-detected—but it was a very slim one. The more he considered the situation, the more confused he became about the right course of action.

While he connected the refueling rig from the MU-2 to the Zero, he continued to ponder the situation, but by the time he had finished and began stowing the hose back in the light transport, he had decided that, for the moment, he had to assume Genda would re-cover. The plan could always be aborted at the last minute if need be.

Ohiro spent the remainder of the evening walking the beach and reviewing his own situation. His continued participation in the Red Army cause seemed of little importance. He had lost his enthusiasm, and returning to the cockpit of the MU-2 had reminded him of the few happy times he had spent in the JMSDF, the flying times.

With some surprise, he also realized that his exposure to Genda's samurai sense of duty and honor had caused him to rethink his own goals in life, and for the first time he began to experience pangs of guilt.

By the time he returned to the shack, Genda was sleeping soundly and Ohiro lay down on the mattress provided by the station man-ager. The rain from a late-evening thunderstorm began to play across the tin roof of the shack and the air over Canton stirred and cooled.

As Ohiro forced his eyes to close and tried to adjust to the hard floor, he knew that soon he, too, would have a very important decision to make. A strange calm came over him. It was as if he had always been destined to spend this particular night on Canton.

Chapter 27

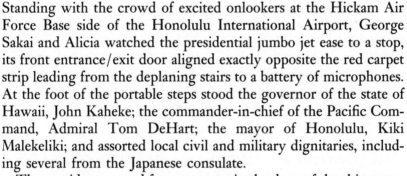

Standing with the crowd of excited onlookers at the Hickam Air Force Base side of the Honolulu International Airport, George Sakai and Alicia watched the presidential jumbo jet ease to a stop, its front entrance/exit door aligned exactly opposite the red carpet strip leading from the deplaning stairs to a battery of microphones. At the foot of the portable steps stood the governor of the state of Hawaii, John Kaheke; the commander-in-chief of the Pacific Command, Admiral Tom DeHart; the mayor of Honolulu, Kiki Malekeliki; and assorted local civil and military dignitaries, including several from the Japanese consulate.

The president paused for a moment in the door of the shiny new silver, white, and blue Boeing 747 assigned as Air Force One since late 1990 and waved before offering his arm to his wife and leading her down the stairs. A pair of twelve-year-old Polynesian beauties shyly placed vanda orchid leis around the president's and first lady's necks as Governor Kaheke welcomed them and passed them on down the receiving line.

"She's a lovely first lady," Alicia commented, "with a special grace that almost any woman can relate to. Certainly not pretentious, just down-to-earth and sincere. Main Street Americana—it's about time we went back to that image, don't you think, George? Back to the days of Bess Truman."

Sakai laughed. "Bess Truman? You weren't even a gleam in your father's eye back in those days. This Australian kick of yours is really making you a woman of the soil, isn't it?"

Alicia pouted. "Well, my values have changed."

The president stopped behind the cluster of microphones, one hand casually resting on the waist-high podium, the other pulling off his glasses and holding them aside. "*Aloha.* My wife and I appreciate the warmth of this island welcome and look forward not only to the historical events that shortly will be taking place here but to a renewal of our love for the beautiful state of Hawaii. To those of you who enjoy this place as your permanent residence, we will not try to hide our envy; to those of you who are temporary residents, we feel the same elation and sense of tranquillity that these islands always offer the visitor; and to our friends from across the seas, we invite you to join us in the prayer that this land that half a century ago saw the beginning of a tragic war now be the site of the beginning of a new era of Pacific progress. We return your *alohas* with enthusiasm and appreciation for this great show of hospitality toward a couple of *haoles* from the mainland. *Aloha nui lua—mahala!*"

The crowd howled with delight as the president mistakenly substituted the Hawaiian word for toilet for the proper word, "loa," in the expression for "much love." The president, unaware of his gaffe, continued to smile and wave as he and his party were quickly ushered into waiting limousines.

"That was quick," Sakai commented.

"And very sweet.

"I believe 'political' is the word."

"No! You're a cynic. I think his remarks were just perfect: informal, brief, and with a touch of humility."

"A humble president? That's a contradiction of terms. Let's see if we can beat the crowd and get back to the hotel. I want to check in with Murray Franklin as soon as possible."

The suite set aside for the presidential security detachment was crammed with extra furniture, mostly desks and long tables. In one room, the new arrivals were checking out the various communications channels and establishing watch and duty schedules according to the planned events published by the president's chief of staff. In another, an entire arsenal of automatic weapons was being issued and signed for and various agents were voicing concern as to how they could conceal their weapons wearing only slacks and aloha shirts.

Murray Franklin had taken refuge in the master bedroom and was sitting on the bed rubbing his stocking feet when Sakai found him. Tall and thin, he had his legs crossed Indian fashion. When he bent forward to massage his feet, the bald spot in the middle of an otherwise healthy stand of dark brown hair gave him the look of a modern Caesar. All he needed was a toga rather than an open-necked white shirt and gray poplin trousers. He was still wearing his shoulder holster. A twenty-year veteran of the Secret Service and a fellow former marine, he was a close friend of Sakai, and they mixed socially whenever their schedules permitted. As with Sakai, Franklin's demanding hours had cost him a wife. "George, good to see you. Bert told me you'd be joining us. Sit down."

Sakai took a chair opposite Franklin.

"Damned feet. Arthritis in the major big toe joints. Imagine that; forty-two years old and damn near crippled with arthritis. Shoes hurt like hell. So, two of your terrorists still at large, huh?"

"Yes. They pulled a switch on us at Guam. God only knows where they are now."

Franklin, looking concerned, stopped rubbing his feet. "Any chance they could be coming this way? We got several reports on the one called Genda from Porter back at the Tokyo embassy. He sounds like quite a character."

"I'll be frank, Murray. They could be anywhere—but I suspect they have gone back to Japan. It's easier to hide there and Genda is a dying man. Leukemia. He can't have much strength left."

"Okay. For the moment, that's your responsibility. Just try and use your own sources to monitor that operation. You can use our comm facilities if you need to. They're reliable and worldwide. Bert told me this is sort of a short sabbatical for you so we'll handle all of the routine security. We don't figure your suspects are any threat, but we do have the usual number of kooks to watch out for. Stop outside at the credentials desk; your ID card and badge are ready. You have your own piece?"

"Yes."

"Then, welcome aboard. In your packet are passes for all of the events—incidentally, the president wants you with him on the Memorial Saturday. Bring a guest to the dinners. You, as well as our regular people, will be assigned seating at random with the invited attendees. Spot anything suspicious, let us handle it unless there's not time. You know the drill. Damn these feet! I may have to get a couple cortisone shots. I hate shots, but that usually does it."

"Thanks, Murray. I'll keep your duty officer advised of my whereabouts and activities."

"Have fun, George."

Sakai returned to his own room. Alicia was in her room, lying on her bed and browsing through the *Honolulu Advertiser*. Sakai walked through the connecting doors and plopped down beside her.

"What would you like to do this morning?" he asked.

"What are your obligations?"

"None for the moment. We can skip the noon lunch, although I think we should attend the dinner at the Hale Koa. The president's remarks might be interesting since he'll have an audience that's predominantly military."

"We're invited?"

"Murray gave me passes to everything. I'll need a date for the dinners. It's our decision, really, although a couple are mandatory by nature. At least, for me."

"Why don't we go out to the beach. I've a new suit. The morning sun should feel good. We can just relax for a couple of hours."

"Sounds great."

"I'll change." Alicia rolled off the bed. Sakai knew he could delay for several minutes and still have to wait for Alicia to be sure her face and body were ready. He stuffed a pillow behind his head and picked up the main section of the newspaper. On page 2, an article caught his eye and produced a temporary quickness of his heartbeat. The heading read: JAPANESE HIJACK RESTORED WORLD WAR II AIRCRAFT. It was an Associated Press report, dateline Pohnpei, December 5. That would be December 4, Honolulu time, he thought—yesterday.

> A spokesman for the Federated States of Micronesia announced today the theft of two aircraft on the island of Pohnpei in the western Pacific. One was a rare World War II Mitsubishi Zero type aircraft, just recently restored, and the other a small executive transport. Both aircraft were the property of American aviation enthusiast Patrick McMahon, a prominent automobile dealer from Omaha, Nebraska.

McMahon and his partner were apparently murdered by the thieves, who were reported to be Japanese.

FSM authorities at the Pohnpei capital city, Kolonia, have asked for U.S. assistance in the investigation, and the FAA and the International Civil Aeronautics Organization are directing inquiries to all Pacific islands with landing strips for possible information as to the aircrafts' whereabouts.

The two airplanes were reportedly refueled at Majuro, an atoll several hundred miles east of Pohnpei and later they were sighted passing through Funafuti.

"Oh, my God! Alicia! I have to run back up to the command post! I'll catch you later!"

"What is it, George?" Alicia had on only the bottom of her swimming suit as she stepped around the bathroom door. Sakai could only hope that there were no nuns, monks, Quakers, or little boy children down on the beach.

Murray Franklin was still in his room.

"Murray, look at this."

Franklin quickly scanned the article on the theft of the Zero. "Pohnpei? Where in hell is Pohnpei?"

"Caroline Islands. Genda and Ohiro could easily have made it there from Guam."

"You think they stole the airplanes?"

"Genda and Ohiro, my friend, are professional military aviators; Genda retired after a thirty-year career with the JMSDF and Ohiro is a recent deserter. It just fits."

"Where's Funafuti?"

"I don't know. I'll have to check."

"Wait a minute." Franklin cocked his head slightly. The mention of the Zero had triggered an alarm. "Have you seen the complete schedule of events?"

"No."

"There's one in your packet. On the seventh, there's to be a flyby by a World War II dive bomber, sort of in the president's honor since he flew one in the war—got his ass pegged, too—and a Zero. Let me call the chief of staff."

Franklin finally reached the president's chief aide in the president's suite.

"Sir, this is Murray Franklin. The flyby on the seventh by the two World War II airplanes. Where are they coming from?"

"Hi, Murray—ah, the dive bomber was shipped out last month by the Confederate Air Force and they'll be flying it from Hickam. The Zero is coming up from an island in the Pacific where it has been restored by a couple of Americans. A fellow by the name of McMahon is one; he's a major campaign contributor and personal acquaintance of the president. They should be over at Maui, but as far as I know no one has talked to them, yet."

"They won't. McMahon is dead, murdered on Pohnpei."

"That's the island—*murdered?*"

"Murdered—and the Zero and another airplane were stolen by two Japanese who were probably the killers."

"Well, I guess that shoots down the flyby." The chief of staff did not sound overly concerned. "No problem. I won't tell the president the reason until after the ceremonies. We'll just use the dive bomber. The Zero was an iffy proposition anyhow, a sort of concession to Prime Minister Hoikata. You know, all is forgiven—that sort of thing—and a little political payback to McMahon."

"Thanks, sir." Hanging up the phone, Franklin turned to Sakai. "That was to be our flyby Zero. This is weird. You really think it could be your terrorists?"

"Who else?"

"Maybe some Japs got pissed off that we had restored the airplane and not them."

"No, too coincidental. I really have a feeling about this."

"Well, the first thing is to find out where they've gone. Hell, you can't fly around the Pacific without some sort of flight plan or recognition. A World War II Zero is bound to attract a lot of attention. They must be crazy to even attempt such a thing."

"Look, Murray, I'm off to the FAA. They should be able to expedite their search. They have communications with all of the flight-following stations and airfields, probably phone lines or satellite comm with most of them."

"All right. As soon as you find out where those airplanes are, I want to know. But I really don't see them as any kind of threat to us here. They can't fly them to Hawaii, surely."

"*Bakatada!* You are crazy!" Ohiro was standing with Genda at the side of the Zero.

Genda shook his head at Ohiro's rebuff. "No, I am determined. I feel well. I have my strength back. I am ready."

"Once you leave here, Genda-san, you are alone. What happens if you mess up your landing on Palmyra? The station manager says that it has been completely deserted since the first of the year."

"That is exactly the way I want it and I will not mess up the landing. The technique for flying the Mitsubishi Zero-sen has completely returned. If my body were younger, I could do everything with it I did in the old days when I took on the best of the American navy pilots."

"And got shot from the sky?"

"Ha! One time! Then, I learned." Reaching up, Genda patted the fuselage of his Zero.

"At least, let me fly to Palmyra with you."

"You do not have enough fuel to return. We have already discussed it."

"So, my service to you is ended."

"I go alone from here. It is my plan."

Ohiro lifted his arms in surrender to his companion's stubbornness. "I will waste no more time talking to a madman. I have food and water in the cockpit containers. There is sake, also, that I picked up on Pohnpei. It is useless to try and store any replacement parts since there is no place for a toolbox. Your chances are slim, Genda-san. It is only a matter of time before the airplane will have need for some repair."

"But my rewards are the rewards of the samurai and you share in my glory, Ohiro-san." Genda placed a hand on Ohiro's shoulder. "I am in your debt. Without your assistance I could never have done this."

"I speak to you freely, old man." Ohiro smiled broadly as he used the dangerous term. "When we first started operations, I was ready to use you, to take your money and run when our task was done. That is why I, along with Goto, switched targets back at Osaka. We wished to disgrace you and pull you down from your lofty pedestal. I had little respect for you."

"And until we started on this leg of our mission, I was planning to slide my knife between your ribs when *your* use to me was finished."

Ohiro bowed. "I apologize, Captain Genda. I ask your forgiveness and plead for your mercy in recognizing me as your friend. In a way, I almost consider you as my lord samurai."

Genda stood erect, not returning the bow. "I am honored."

"I salute you and will light prayer sticks in your memory when I return to Japan."

"You have my forgiveness, Michio, and as you accept it, my friendship, but you also have one thing of honor to do. That is one reason why you must not accompany me to Palmyra. You must give yourself back to the JMSDF. It should be some comfort that together we have accomplished a great thing, an achievement that is yet to be completed. But, when it is, history will tell of Saburo Genda and his friend, Michio Ohiro. I shall place my *haiku* on Palmyra. In it, I will speak of your loyalty and devotion. We have made some serious mistakes, you and I. Each of us must redeem himself; I by my mission, you by atonement. Now, it is time. We must carry out the last scene of our charade and bid our good-bye and appreciation to the station manager."

Together, the two walked into the station manager's shack. Ohiro handed him their flight plan.

"Ah, returning to Funafuti. I understood you were going to do your photography first."

"We will do it in the air. That will be sufficient."

"Well, jolly good, then. Are you certain you feel up to flying?" the Brit said to Genda.

"Yes, I am quite well. It was just temporary thing. I should pace myself. Your hospitality is appreciated."

"My bloody pleasure."

The station manager and most of the natives on Canton stood aside as Genda climbed into the Zero and Ohiro helped him strap in.

Ohiro stood on the wing by the cockpit and bowed. Genda lowered his head in return, then slipped on his helmet.

"*Banzai!*" called out Ohiro, slapping Genda lightly on the back, his eyes moist.

Genda looked up at him. "*Banzai!*—It continues!"

On the ground, the station manager chuckled and spoke aside to one of the natives. "Bloody playacting. They take their work with some seriousness, eh?" He was a bit confused as to why the two Japanese seemed so somber and weren't photographing the manning of the Zero. It seemed like an appropriate part of the documentary they were working on. Maybe they had already captured that particular scene. Crazy nips.

Ohiro stood by with a fire bottle while Genda started up the Zero, its Nakajima engine puffing out globs of gray smoke as the sparks within the cylinders set fire to the rich fuel-air mixture. He then manned the MU-2 and started its engines. Both pilots returned the waves of the small group as they taxied away.

Genda roared down the runway and lifted off just prior to the midway point. Now very confident, he rolled smartly into a left bank and came around to pick up Ohiro, who left the runway with equal ease and grace. Together, they made a low pass across the ramp, wagged their wings, and pulled up to climb among the morning cumulus clouds. Tiny Canton fell away beneath them.

Ten miles out Genda looked back at Ohiro and saluted a final time. Ohiro nodded and returned the salute as Genda pulled away from the MU-2 and took up his heading for Palmyra. Ohiro made a lazy circle to keep the Zero in sight as long as he could but soon the tiny dot disappeared. For a moment, he was tempted to follow, but realized that Genda would not approve. Instead, he pointed the MU-2 eastward toward open ocean, determined to fly until the last fumes in his tanks passed through the engines. He would atone for his dishonorable deeds by riding the stubby turboprop to a last landing. *In a way*, thought Ohiro, *it has always been my destiny*. He had often fantasized about dying at sea, although he could not recall why. Perhaps it was because millions of years ago his ancestors had crawled from it, dripping and straining to take in oxygen from their new environment, and in the brain of every man there was a vestigial subconscious urge to return. His spirit would most certainly not precede Genda's to the Yasukuni Shrine—he had no entry qualifications. But as he flew east away from any land he had a strong personal sense of achievement. That was enough—until the next life.

Genda tried to reposition himself in the seat. During the three hours since he had left Canton he had become stiff and there was a particularly irritating spot on his right buttock where it felt as if that portion of his pelvic bone was going to burst through the skin. He did manage to obtain some relief by lowering his seat and adjusting the tension on his seat belt and shoulder harness. He cracked open his canopy just a bit to allow more cooling in the cockpit and took several refreshing swallows of his water. His INS had indicated an average groundspeed of one hundred and forty-seven knots since leaving Canton, and his distance to destination read one hundred and ninety-nine miles. About eighty minutes to go. Fuel consumption was down to seventeen gallons per hour and the quantity gauges indicated he had burned fifty-seven gallons since liftoff. The aluminum drop tank fashioned by the Americans had carried more than one hundred and twenty gallons, almost twice as much as the original Mitsubishi design. Once it was empty, he would drop it and eliminate its drag. If he could use less than twenty gallons for the remainder of his leg to Palmyra, he would have slightly over one hundred gallons left. That did not sound right. He went over the calculations a second time and came to the same conclusion. *That would not be enough!* He would need almost one hundred and fifteen gallons. Could his original computations have been in error? No, it had to be an unexpected headwind or excessive fuel used in the climb out.

With some regret he completely closed the canopy. He could not afford even the slight drag with it open even an inch.

His flight from Palmyra would have to cover nine hundred and eighty miles. If he could average one hundred and fifty-five knots, that would be six and a half hours. At seventeen gallons per hour, he would be about ten gallons shy: forty minutes flight time in round numbers!

He would be slightly over a hundred miles short of his destination—unless he could pick up an additional tailwind. That would be possible although not too likely. He had enjoyed fifteen knots since leaving Canton. He could save some fuel by a gradual glide into Palmyra and a bit more by a cruise climb out on Saturday. Maybe a total of ten to fifteen gallons, maybe not. He would just have to wait and see.

For the most part, he would leave the Zero on automatic pilot. The device could do a more precise job of holding altitude and airspeed than the man. Desperately, he searched his mind for other ways to increase his range. Lighten the airplane, that was one way. He would take only one bottle of water out of Palmyra. And no chute—he could leave his chute. In fact, there was no use for it now. Carefully unbuckling his safety harness, he wiggled out of the arm and leg straps. The life raft snapped to the bottom could be removed. He would use that as a cushion. Opening the canopy, he halfway stood and pulled the parachute from underneath him. Wrapping the arm and leg straps around it, he threw it over the side and refastened his harness. He was sitting too low in the cockpit so he raised his seat to the full up position. He wasn't as high as before, but he was high enough. At least he was fifteen or twenty pounds lighter. Quickly, he closed the canopy to smooth out the airflow over the fuselage. Finally, he reset the mixture control as precisely as he could. The fuel flow dropped to just a thin line over sixteen gallons per hour. In eight and a half hours that would save him almost nine gallons! Now he was less than a half hour shy of the necessary flight time. But he could get by on less tailwind! He would have to closely monitor the cylinder head temperatures. With such a lean fuel-air mixture, they would tend to run hot. He would have to make sure they did not.

Seventy-five minutes later, he sighted tiny Palmyra dead ahead. He waited until he was fifteen miles out and throttled back, adjusting his power to just that necessary to reach the island. At eight miles, he could see the strip but not its condition. He would like to make a low inspection pass but that would cost him precious fuel. Instead, he kept up the gradual glide and lined up with the runway. He waited until the last moment to drop his landing gear and half-flaps and guided the Zero across the threshhold with less than twenty feet of altitude. Instantly, he recognized that the runway was cracked and potted over its entire width and length! He lowered full flaps and slowed the airplane as much as he dared, using power to keep a nose-high drag down the runway. The left side of the airstrip seemed in slightly better shape than the right or the middle and he eased over to touch down. With a textbook stall, he dropped the airplane onto the weathered surface and cut his engine, keeping the stick full back in his lap. He must save every precious drop of fuel.

The Zero shook and clattered as if he had landed on a corrugated washboard, but his runout was short and he came to a halt without any blown tires or strained landing gear components. He opened the canopy—a safety check he had forgotten when on his final approach—and climbed out on the wing. The island was deserted and only a few dilapidated clapboard shacks stood off to one side of the airstrip. Climbing out, he placed heavy chunks of coral around his tires as chocks.

A steady sea breeze was blowing, easily fifteen knots. He walked over to the shacks and searched them. Broken office furniture. Empty file cabinets. He could use some of the furniture padding to enable him to sit higher in the cockpit. The water collectors were almost full. There had been rain and he would have plenty of fresh water for his two-night stay on the island.

The abundance of palm trees would give him coconuts if he was still hungry after eating the food Ohiro had provided. In fact, with the seabirds flying all about and the fish in the small lagoon, a younger man could survive for many days. That was not Genda's problem. His was to rest and ask the gods for favorable winds. It was only early afternoon. He would sit in the shade of one of the shacks and drink water. No unnecessary exertion. Making himself comfortable, he sat and listened to the few noises present. The palm fronds were rustling under the steady force of the wind and the waves were crashing onto the shores. The gulls were squealing. The combination of sounds was not at all unlike those of the seashore by his cottage on the southern coast of Hokkaido.

One thing for sure: he was safe. There was no one to report him and his flight could not have been detected. If nothing else, he could stay through the next day with only the gulls and the wind and the sea as his companions.

He would leave the Zero where it was until he walked the remainder of the runway. If the last half was no more corroded than the first half, he could take off from his present position. That would save taxi fuel. His last leg was going to take every bit of his flying and fuel-management skills. In the end, he would have flown 1,720 miles on full tanks. The book figure for extended cruise was 1,930 miles; he remembered that and had often quoted it, rounding off the figure to 2,000 miles.

His comrades had flown many ten-hour missions during the war, including a half-hour of combat at near full power. His total enroute time on full tanks would be close to eleven. He *should* be able to do it. But at that moment, he still had the longest leg ahead of him and he had burned more fuel since leaving Canton than he had anticipated.

There were many variables, of course. His flight techniques could well affect fuel consumption per hour. The restoration of the airplane could have involved a significant weight change, although it flew as he remembered it. Certainly, the addition of the autopilot and the INS added weight. But it was useless to contemplate unknowns. His problem boiled down to the simple task of flying the distance he had to fly with the fuel he had remaining on board.

There was one final plus. Once he neared his empty fuel state, probably during the last two hours or so, his fuel consumption should dramatically decrease as the Zero neared its empty weight.

The margin for error was slim, perhaps nonexistent, but Genda looked upon that as a challenge worthy of a samurai. It was what had made the Japanese pilot superior early in the war, his ability to coax unbelievable performance out of his airplane. Genda could do no less.

Sakai found that the FAA at Honolulu was a step ahead of him. The stolen MU-2 carried a U.S. registry number, as did the Zero actually, and the agency had been notified of the murders of McMahon and Simpson. Consequently, there had been a sense of urgency to their communications search for the two aircraft.

Sakai was handed over to a Sammy Lee, who was the senior assistant to the Honolulu administrator of the FAA office. Lee, a mixed Hawaiian and Chinese perfectionist, already had a handle on the movement of the Zero and the MU-2, but was completely in the dark with reference to who the hijackers were. He sat shaking his head in disgust as Sakai filled him in on the background and activities of Genda and Ohiro.

"It has to be them, I agree," Lee said. "The station manager at Canton Island gave a description when we finally contacted him this morning. We only missed them by an hour! They filed for a return to Funafuti but there has been no arrival. I suspect their actual destination is somewhere else."

Sakai studied the map of Pacific air routes that Lee had on his wall. "There aren't an awful lot of places they can go, are there, before landing to refuel?"

"No. The station manager said the MU-2 pilot refueled the Zero from a cabin tank carried in his aircraft—aviation gasoline has been phased out of many places—but there are no refueling capabilities at Canton so the MU-2 had to go out with what fuel he had left. He could have made it back to Funafuti or the Samoas, possibly the Gilberts, but not much farther. And there is no report of any sightings since Canton."

"How long ago did they take off?"

"Shortly after dawn this morning, so they have to be someplace by now. There isn't an island airstrip within two thousand miles of Canton that hasn't been issued an alert."

"Then, why haven't we received some report?"

"It's possible they have set down on an abandoned strip some-where; there are literally hundreds within that radius."

"I doubt if they had any preplanning that would allow them to benefit from that."

"Then, they may have decided to put the airplanes down wher-ever they could and make their way back to Guam or Japan. The Japanese are all over the Pacific. If they have papers and some money, it could be done."

"But they knew when they took the airplanes that it would only be a matter of time before the theft and the murders would be discovered. Why would they steal an airplane with such high visibil-ity as the Zero? It would attract attention wherever they took it. There's something here I'm missing."

"I wish I could be of further assistance, but our main concern is locating the airplanes. We have an excellent communications net-work but very little investigative expertise of the nature you require. We will do everything we can, of course."

"The abandoned strips. Is there any way of searching them?"

"Only by actual physical examination from the air. Obviously, that's a time-consuming and expensive operation. We can have the scheduled airline runs make visual passes on any strips along their routes, but we will have to reimburse the airlines for any extra fuel expenditures. We have an airplane at Tarawa on a navigational aids check mission and can use it, but it will take weeks before we can look at all possibilities, provided DOT will give us the money. Our budget won't handle a full-scale search."

"I understand. I'll call my superior in State and maybe he can expedite the process by personal liaison with DOT. I don't think we have any choice. Those people out there are not just airplane thieves, they're international terrorists with the blood of over five hundred people on their hands."

"We certainly agree, and I repeat, we will do everything we can and a few things we ordinarily could not."

"I appreciate that, Mr. Lee. You have my hotel number and I'll check with you on a daily basis."

"That will be fine. I will notify you immediately of any develop-ments."

Sakai briefed Murray Franklin before searching out Alicia. She was on the beach, under a brightly colored shade umbrella and sipping a tall red drink.

"Rum punch?" Sakai inquired, lowering himself to the sand beside her beach chair.

"Want a sip?"

Sakai shook his head. She was in her new swimsuit, three tiny triangles of white cloth strategically held into position by tied string. She would have been much less provocative buck naked.

She leaned over. "Want to talk?"

"No. I've got as many angles covered as I can. Let's plan on the dinner at the Hale Koa this evening. Maybe something will come up by then."

"Want to go up to the room?"

"No, it's nice out here. I'll just sit with you for a while and study a map I bummed off the FAA."

Leaning against Alicia's raised legs, Sakai unfolded the *National Geographic* map of the Pacific. Highly detailed, it showed every island of the Pacific, although not all the airfields were marked. He looked at each speck of land in turn and tried to second-guess the latest strategy of Genda and Ohiro.

Genda sat on the white coral overlooking the northern section of the group of tiny islands collectively known as Palmyra. Altogether, they only stretched for five miles east and west, two north and south, and enclosed a central lagoon and several much smaller patches of coral. He had removed his clothes and was letting the cooling sea breeze bathe his body. He would not stay too long in the sun but the outcropping where he sat was the perfect spot for meditation. He pulled his legs into the lotus position and closed his eyes. There was not another human within six hundred and fifty miles. Within minutes, he reached a level of inner concentration deeper than any he had experienced since back at Hokkaido. The three-dimensional world outside of his body faded, then disappeared. The noises of the sea and the gulls were still there but his ears did not pass on the sounds to his brain. Nor did the taste and smell of the salt register on his tongue or in his nose. Even his skin failed to register the fine sea spray that was around him. He had managed to completely eliminate any sensory perception or conscious thought and in his subconscious there was only a single unbelievably beautiful face.

Emiko.

Chapter 28

Sakai and Alicia walked slowly westward along Kalia Road toward Fort DeRussy, once the home of the nisei 442nd Regimental Combat Team of World War II fame. The army installation, now housing the Armed Forces Recreation Center, occupied a choice section of Waikiki Beach and featured a 420-room full-service hotel with a great expanse of green park on one side and a wide strip of beachfront that rivaled any of the other hotels. Hale Koa—the House of the Warrior—a modern high rise with rooms that had either a partial or full view of the ocean, had been constructed with armed forces recreational funds generated by BX sales all over the world. Exclusively for active duty and retired service personnel, the Hale Koa was the cause for green eyes among every hotel owner along Waikiki, and the city had tried time and time again to reclaim the property, which the Department of Defense defended with a fury usually reserved for exotic weapons systems. The hotel continued a tradition of rest and relaxation that Fort DeRussy had provided for the military back before World War II. Rates were well below those of comparable civilian establishments and graduated according to the rate or rank of the prime occupant. The top rooms were ninety dollars for the colonels and above but only thirty-five for the lowest enlisted. The Hale Koa was one of the few truly democratic assets accessible to the members of the military and reservations were mandatory, most rooms being booked months in advance.

The presidential dinner was scheduled for 8:00 P.M. in DeRussy Hall, the largest event room of the Hale Koa, and the attendees would be primarily active and retired members of the military stationed or living in Hawaii.

Kalia Road was alive with the early-evening pedestrian traffic of residents and tourists. A number had completed their day on the Waikiki sands and were wandering toward the few public parking areas to retrieve their vehicles. Others were handsomely clothed in evening wear, consisting primarily of cocktail dresses or the more traditional flowered muumuus for the ladies, slacks and colorful aloha shirts for the men. Most wore sweet-smelling leis and were on their way to the many spectacular hotel restaurants that featured Polynesian entertainment along with gourmet food. Another segment walked a bit awkwardly, their overindulged bodies straining the tight shorts and out-of-place mainland sport shirts or too-small halters, depending upon their sex. Middle-aged and overweight, they made up a large portion of the tourists who daily arrived and departed the islands, taking with them once-in-a-lifetime memories and leaving behind cash registers stuffed with megabucks.

The monied orientals from Japan were also there, primarily young married couples who chattered incessantly when the women were not suffering from a severe case of the giggles. All had cameras hanging around their necks despite the fading light and most wore tummy packs containing their personal items. There were a few older couples, mama-san shuffling a respectful half pace behind papa-san, and both looking a bit uncomfortable at being so near the beach of the island where, a half century before, some of them had aspired to storm with fixed bayonets. But only in the old folks' concerned imagination did any of the native Hawaiians pay any attention to them, and the other Americans were having too much of a good time to be bothered about the peaceful yen invasion of the nineties. A number of the luxury high rises towering above the evening street crowd were owned and managed by the overseas Japanese, and all were partially occupied by the superambitious natives of the dragon islands.

"It's a lovely night." Alicia slipped her arm over Sakai's and let it hang loosely.

"As nice as those in Australia?"

"You are developing a perchance to tease. Do you know that?"

"Don't mean to. I just wanted to remind you there are a lot of lovely places in the world."

"Well, I wouldn't want to *live* here."

"Oh?" Sakai would gladly welcome an assignment in the islands.

"Too commercial. Great for visits, too hectic for the overall goal of life."

"Which is?"

"Peace and contentment. A sense of being. Time to enjoy the ones you love—and yourself."

"I suppose I'd have to agree with that. Actually, I feel quite content tonight, don't you?" Sakai asked.

"Well—except for one thing."

"What's that?"

"I wish you were an inch taller."

Sakai laughed. "All Japanese are short. Besides, I'm as tall as you."

"Five-feet-five—big deal."

"You never complained before."

"And I'm not complaining now. Just a thought."

They had reached the curved driveway leading up to the entrance of the Hale Koa.

The open-air lobby was packed with people, a number of them residents setting out on their night's adventures. Others, obviously, were presidential dinner guests and were milling around enjoying last bits of conversation before proceeding up the stairs that led to the second-floor dining hall. Sakai stopped by the security desk and obtained his and Alicia's table assignment from the agent manning it. They were the last to arrive of the eight assigned to table ninety-nine, although it was still fifteen minutes before the scheduled dinner hour. They found their way-out-in-left-field round table elegantly draped in white linen and formally set.

"I guess I know how you rate," Alicia murmured aside to Sakai as he pulled out her chair.

Their dinner companions were retired Chief Quartermaster and Mrs. Bobby Chase, active duty USAF Colonel and Mrs. Lee Scottfield, and Mr. and Mrs. Willie Oko, fourth-generation Hawaiian residents and retired civil service workers at the Pearl Harbor Naval

Base. Chief Chase had been at the helm of the U.S.S. *Nevada* on that fateful 1941 Sunday when she had tried to make it out of Pearl Harbor. Unfortunately, rather than risk further damage, which would have sunk her and blocked the harbor entrance, the captain had decided to beach the warship at Waipio Point. Chief Chase would never forget his despair at hearing the sound and feeling the vibrations of the keel bottoming out on the sands aside the entrance channel.

Colonel Scottfield was the first to speak after the introductions, and he addressed Sakai. "State Department? I thought only military were invited to this dinner."

Mr. and Mrs. Oko exchanged tolerant glances at Scottfield's slightly insensitive statement.

"I'm a former marine." Sakai wondered why he felt he had to defend his presence.

"A gyrene! Pleased to be in your presence."

For an instant, Sakai thought Charlie Porter was present, then he realized it was Chief Chase who had spoken.

"Mrs. Oko, that's a beautiful muumuu," Alicia interjected, anxious to steer the conversation away from who was whom.

"Thank you."

Mrs. Colonel Scottfield waited for a similar compliment, her smile frozen. Mrs. Chase took a polite sip of her water.

"In fact, all of you ladies look ravishing this evening." As he spoke, Sakai nudged Alicia's leg with his. Looking across the table, he added, "Are you fully retired, Chief?"

"Yes. No worries. No obligations. No money."

"He is a volunteer at the naval hospital," his wife added.

"Good for you." The colonel made a conscious effort to put a ring of sincerity in his voice, realizing that his former statement could have been better worded. "How about you, Mr. Oko?"

"I have a small flower shop on the windward side."

Everyone smiled, and Mrs. Chase sipped her water again.

"How about you, Colonel? Hickam?" Sakai asked.

"Yes, base engineer. We've been here almost a year."

All looked toward the head table as one of the occupants leaned over and spoke into the microphone. "Ladies and gentlemen, our Commander-in-Chief." Automatically, everyone stood as the president and his wife entered, followed by Admiral and Mrs. DeHart. All took their places except the president, who stopped briefly in front of the microphone. "I can think of no place where I would rather be this evening. Please, take your seats and enjoy your dinner."

A burst of spontaneous applause rewarded the president's homey style.

"He's navy, you know," remarked Chief Chase with considerable pride. Colonel and Mrs. Scottfield were the only ones at the table who did not acknowledge Chase's remark with a nod or smile.

Over in the opposite corner of the dining room, a Marine Corps dance orchestra began a medley of Broadway show tunes.

Sakai was pleased that the conversation around the table softened during the dinner and by dessert everyone was on a first-name basis. The waiters were replenishing coffee and tea as Admiral DeHart stood and took his place behind the small podium on the head table.

"Ladies and gentlemen, permit me to speak for all of us when I extend our welcome to the president and our lovely first lady.

"This dinner is in response to the president's personal request that his first evening in the islands be spent with you who serve your country with such devotion and sacrifice—"

Hearty applause interrupted the admiral's remarks, and those at the table with Sakai and Alicia pushed back their chairs to join in the standing ovation. DeHart waited patiently until everyone resumed their seats. This was the way the commander-in-chief *should* be received, and he knew that the president would not forget such an enthusiastic welcome. It might even earn him a spot among the Joint Chiefs.

"This is not the night for lengthy introductions. We all know the military record of our commander-in chief, our comrade in arms. He is present in these islands to honor the supreme effort of those who have gone before us and to participate in a very historic occasion. His remarks will address that occasion.

"Ladies and gentlemen, it is my great honor to present the President of the United States of America!"

Once more everyone stood, and this time the applause was augmented by loud whistles. Obviously, the president could not have picked a more partisan audience for making his first public remarks concerning the Mutual Defense Treaty for the Western Pacific.

As he stood, his arms raised and his smile stretching the limits of his thin face, the bevy of press photographers crowded around the head table and flooded it with the bright strobe effect of their camera flashes. A deep baritone came over the dining room speakers. "The president has requested that no further still pictures be taken until the conclusion of his remarks."

A few of the members of the fourth estate fired off a few more just to show their displeasure at the restriction and then, at the urging of a colonel seated at one end of the head table, reluctantly joined their companions who stood aside along the walls of the dining room. As the president adjusted the microphone and began to prepare his notes for his remarks, several of his staff quietly moved over to the press corps and escorted the late shooters from the dining room. Sakai could only imagine the ire the press had at the network TV cameramen, who, on a small platform on the opposite side of the dining room, were permitted to continue their coverage. The president's press secretary would have to take a lot of flak over that decision.

"Admiral and Mrs. DeHart, members of the active and retired forces and your ladies, honored guests. Forty-seven years ago, when I was a young dive-bomber pilot in the Pacific, I gathered great comfort from the camaraderie of my shipmates. Those of us who serve or have served in the military know how special that relationship is. Therefore, I think it only fitting that I speak tonight, first to you who man the bulwarks of our Pacific defense, of a very significant new treaty between our country and the sovereign nation of Japan.

"Tomorrow morning, Prime Minister Hoikata will arrive and later tomorrow he and I will sit down and affix our signatures to a mighty piece of paper. That paper will welcome Japan as a full partner in the defense of the Pacific peoples and our mutual national interests. There are a number of provisions to this treaty. Many concern trade and cultural exchanges. But the most important provisions, ones that we have not announced publicly until now, concern the restoration of the armed forces of the nation of Japan and the assumption by that great modern nation of the security of a large segment of our Pacific responsibilities."

Sakai could see that the journalists were scribbling furiously and glancing anxiously at one another. Obviously, they had not been provided an advance copy of the president's remarks.

"We are entering a new era of American leadership of the free world. By recognizing the willingness, even the desire, of Japan to assume her share of world responsibilities, we set the precedent for all of our allies in assuming their fair share."

Oops! thought Sakai. *The NATO boys just went to emergency session!*

"With a decreased worldwide financial and force committment, we can turn more of our resources inward, toward the economic and social needs of our own country—*without*, I add, any reduction in our intent to work alongside our allies in the preservation and protection of our mutual way of life.

"On Saturday, December 7, 1991, Prime Minister Hoikata will accompany me aboard the *Arizona* Memorial, where we shall formally dedicate this treaty to all those, of all nationalities, who in their own way made the ultimate sacrifice—for much the same purpose—fifty years ago.

"Upon ratification of this treaty by the Congress of the United States and the Diet of Japan, Admiral DeHart will oversee the lease-transfer of two aircraft carriers, the U.S.S. *Midway* and the U.S.S. *Coral Sea*, to the Japanese navy, complete with all of the hardware of their aircraft wings, and the Commander-in-Chief, Pacific Fleet, will assume the responsibilities for training the men and women of the Japanese navy in the operation of those carriers and their air wings. Japan will commence immediate construction of its own carrier fleet and the *Midway* and the *Coral Sea* will be returned upon operational assignment of the Japanese carriers."

Sakai thought that Colonel Scottfield was going to have to reach up and use his hand to reposition his lower jaw. It had dropped abruptly at the president's last remarks. Instead, Scottfield turned angrily to his wife.

"The fucker's gone stark raving bonkers."

Mrs. Scottfield responded with a shocked "Lee!"

Scottfield quickly turned toward the other ladies at the table. "Excuse me."

The Okos and Chases were having a hard time disguising their amusement at the colonel's reaction. Alicia patted Sakai's crotch, her hand hidden under the table. Not sure how to interpret her reaction, Sakai kept his expression unchanged.

For the third time, the room was filled with applause, but not as spirited as before. The president continued.

"We will also share with the Japanese navy—and I remind you

that Japan is already one of the world's leading producers and users of nuclear energy with a demonstrated record of expertise in that field—our techniques and procedures of nuclear propulsion as used in our surface fleets. . . ."

The silence that greeted the president's latest remarks was complete. He immediately sensed the sudden discomfort of his audience, perhaps even hostility among some, and hastily continued. "In return for these dramatic provisions, we will have at our side a viable new armed force and a committment by the Japanese people to share in our goal of global peace and prosperity . . ."

Sakai heard little of the remainder of the president's remarks, most of which concerned the details of the trade and cultural aspects of the treaty. His attention was monopolized by his own thoughts and a number of questions surfaced. The reinstatement of the Japanese military would not be of great concern to the majority of Americans, but giving away technology was always a sensitive issue. Also, was the president hurting his international cause by announcing the details of the treaty this night? Was Hoikata making a simultaneous announcement in Japan? He better or the president was making the faux pax of the century. How much money was involved in the aircraft carrier lease arrangements? Was the treaty designed to make an appreciable difference in the balance of payments between the U.S. and Japan? Would there be a quid pro quo adjustment to the U.S. budget, each dollar saved by Defense winding up in social budgets, or had the president made that remark in a more general sense?

Generous applause awarded the president's final remarks, and after Admiral DeHart's mandatory "Thank you, Mr. President," the president and his wife danced the first dance on the tiny area set aside for that purpose. Under the watchful eye of his Secret Service staff, several preselected couples joined them. At the conclusion of the number, the president waved his hands and followed his escorts out of the dining room, Admiral and Mrs. DeHart in trail.

The band resumed and the tiny dance floor became shoulder-to-shoulder bodies, including Chief and Mrs. Chase, who determinedly edged their way into the pack.

Colonel and Mrs. Scottfield made their good-byes and walked away, the colonel still showing signs of impending military budget shock. The Okos rose and politely expressed their pleasure at having been at the table before starting toward the dance floor, then reversing themselves and giving one final wave before exiting the dining room.

"Want to stay a while?" Alicia asked.

"I'm too horny. Let's go."

"My, my, you're catching my disease."

The quiet walk back to the Royal Hawaiian in the cool night air was refreshing after the stuffiness of the crowded dining hall at the Hale Koa. As they entered the lobby of the pink landmark, Sakai let Alicia's hand drop from his.

"I want to stop by the command center for a moment. Meet me in the bar?"

"Sure—but don't take too long. I don't want the edge to wear off."

"Promise."

Murray Franklin was still out with the president and his party. There seemed to be nothing happening. Sakai sat down and picked up a copy of the detailed schedule of events for Friday and Saturday. He had not bothered to examine the one in his briefing packet. He looked for the time of the president's and the prime minister's visit to the *Arizona* Memorial since he had been asked to be part of that ceremony.

> *Saturday, December 7, 1991:*
> 0700 Presidential party departs for *Arizona* Memorial from park landing.
> 0730 Prime Minister Hoikata's remarks.
> 0735 President's remarks.
> 0740 Navy Hymn by Marine Corps band.
> 0745 Flyby by World War II SBD and Japanese Zero.
> 0755 President and Prime Minister place lei on water.
> 0800 Japanese national anthem followed by colors and the U.S. national anthem.
> 0815 Flyby by aircraft of U.S. military services and the JSDF.
> 0820 Nonsectarian benediction.
> 0825 President and Prime Minister depart *Arizona* Memorial.

A penciled line had been drawn through the words "Japanese Zero."

Alicia was seated in the open-air lounge halfway through a Mai Tai and quietly looking out at the moonlit waters off Waikiki. Sakai ordered a scotch.

"Big doin's this weekend," Alicia remarked.

"It's a momentous occasion."

"You seem let down. Don't you approve of the treaty?"

"It's not that. There was no news in the command center. Genda and Ohiro are still out there somewhere."

"Thousands of miles away, George."

"True. I just don't like to feel my job is not done yet. I keep trying to think of something I've overlooked."

"George . . ."

"Okay. I'm sorry." Sakai downed his scotch in one swallow. "I think I would like to jump your bones now."

Alicia drained her glass. "Only if I can jump yours."

"Lady, you got a deal."

As they walked out of the lounge hand in hand, Alicia looked aside at Sakai. "If only you were an inch taller."

Sakai licked his lips. "I'll grow a couple inches before we get to the room."

Alicia pinched his upper arm.

Chapter 29

Saburo Genda sat up, his body warm and sticky with sweat. His breathing slowed and he began to appreciate his return to reality. The nightmare had returned again and he had wakened screaming his wife's name. As he painfully pulled his legs under him and reached down to push himself up, he realized that sleeping on the hard Palmyra runway under the wing of the Zero had severely stiffened his body. His bones not only ached, they felt as if they were as brittle as dried wood.

He was pleasantly surprised, however. He had expected to be much weaker. After his collapse on Canton, he knew the end could not be far away. And during the flight to Palmyra he had experienced several periods of light-headedness, as if he were not really present but observing the flight of the Zero from another plane of reference. But his head was clear enough at the moment; all he asked was one more good day.

Breathing through his mouth in an effort to ease the pain, he stood and rubbed his lower back. It was not yet dawn, but his watch showed four-thirty-six. It would not be long. The ever-present sea breeze cooled him and as he walked aimlessly around the airplane, swinging his arms, his joints loosened and some of the aches faded.

There were lightning flashes to the east and puddles on the runway but Genda could not remember hearing or feeling any rain. At least for a while, he had slept soundly. Finally wide awake, it was a good time to walk the remaining stretch of runway and check its condition. There was enough night visibility for that and he did not feel the need for more sleep.

As he slowly proceeded down the runway, a naked stroller on a naked island in the vast Pacific, he considered a morning start-up and check of the airplane. The worst thing in the world for a flying machine was for it to just sit. All sorts of minor discrepancies seemed to materialize: oil leaks, hydraulic seepage, electrical glitches, any number of things. But to start the Zero and properly warm the engine would require several gallons of precious fuel. He could not afford that.

The best part of the runway seemed to be drifting to the center. He could probably start off on the left side and ease to the center as he accelerated. It took him sixteen minutes to examine the estimated three thousand feet of runway remaining. At the end, he looked back toward the airplane. In the darkness, the sides of the airstrip had a tendency to fade into the island foliage. An abundance of large-leafed pandanus trees were very close along the sides of the runway, some as tall as twelve feet. He planned a night takeoff, and if he drifted off to one side on his run he could catch a wing. He would have to figure some way of keeping himself aligned with the runway heading. His compass and heading indicator would provide a broad check, but precise tracking would be difficult on a runway only eighty or so feet wide, particularly if there was a crosswind. There were runway lights installed but obviously they were inoperative, and he doubted that the island generator would be usable, assuming there was one still present. He stooped and examined the terrain just off the end of the runway. There was some looseness to the crushed coral. Perhaps he could erect a pole on the runway centerline. He could wrap the top with gasoline-soaked rags and light them just before his takeoff. The flame would give him a point to keep dead ahead. The idea was worth further thought.

By the time he had walked back to the airplane, there was light to the east and he could see well enough to conduct a walkaround of the resting Zero. The tailwheel had taken a beating; the rough runway had scored and cut it in a number of places. The main tires had fared much better. There seemed to be no hydraulic or fuel leaks. There were some minor dents to the underside of the fuselage where bits of coral had been thrown up on his landing. Suddenly, his eyes narrowed. The left landing light was broken, the glass shattered, also most probably by flying coral from the old, neglected runway. Quickly, he took several side steps to examine the right light. It was shattered also. With no landing lights to illuminate the runway and no runway lights to guide him, there was a great danger that he could run off the side of the runway and into the pandanus trees!

The centerline pole was even more essential now. There might be something in the shacks that he could use to burn at its tip. He would check, but he had all day. For the time being, he would jump into one of the rain collectors and bathe. Then he would lay out the items he would take with him on the last leg of his journey. The realization that his task was nearing completion renewed his strength and determination. He almost wished there were someone present on the island with whom he could share his excitement and anticipation.

Still, the isolation of Palmyra suited him well. There was ample opportunity for complete relaxation and undisturbed thought. Why had the natives given up such a spot? It wasn't a garden of Eden and their living must have been spartan—but certainly feasible. Perhaps one drawback was the lack of soil for growing yams and other roots. Then again, they probably had been corrupted when the Americans came in and built the runway, the natives sharing in the packaged food and drinks provided the new occupants. Palmyra was a great distance from the nearest island, and he had known of some island colonies who had lost their fishing and even sailing skills when exposed to modern conveniences. Why work for something when it was handed to you? With grim humor, he recalled that such an aspect of human nature was not confined to the so-called primitive peoples.

There was a small diesel generator, but it was hopelessly rusted and short of a number of components. Still naked from the night before, Genda eased himself into the rainwater. The chill contracted every inch of his skin and he could actually feel his testicles retract, desperately seeking the warmth of his inner body; he would much have preferred the hot springs of Takaragawa, but after a few minutes his body adjusted to the cold water and the soak seemed to give him a bit more strength.

. . .

The giant Japan Air Lines 747 taxied slowly into the position that twenty-four hours before had been occupied by Air Force One. Prime Minister Hoikata descended the deplaning ladder to the same red carpet and was greeted first by the president. Mrs. Hoikata followed, strikingly dressed in a brilliantly colored silk kimono and coordinated obi. While her clothing was traditional, her makeup, hair, and easy smile were very modern. The first lady instinctively started to embrace her but abruptly held herself in check as Mrs. Hoikata greeted her with the traditional bow. However, as soon as the Japanese prime minister's wife stood erect she grinned even more broadly and held out her arms in a pleasant gesture that obviously pleased the first lady and the onlookers.

Within minutes, the prime minister and his party had been whisked away in limousines toward the naval station. There, along with the president and his wife, they would attend a welcoming breakfast hosted by CINCPAC. Afterwards, Admiral Togakagi, the designated head of the new Japanese Armed Forces, would have a private visit with Admiral DeHart and they would discuss the broad concept of the transfer of the American carriers to the Japanese navy and the requirements for training.

After an informal noon luncheon and a brief ceremony at the Punchbowl National Cemetery, the two national leaders would set their signatures to the mutual defense treaty.

Sakai checked into the Secret Service command post after his own breakfast. Murray Franklin would have a full day with the president and Sakai had to be content with the duty agent's briefing. There were no changes to the schedule of events and nothing else was of particular interest. Sakai had no obligations until the state dinner that evening.

Returning to his hotel, he stopped by the front desk to pick up his key, and the clerk handed him a folded message. He was to call Sammy Lee at the Punchbowl FAA Flight Service Office.

Lee had some startling information. "George, we have a report from an Argentine freighter that it has picked up aircraft wreckage in the southern Pacific. They have a piece carrying a portion of the aircraft registry number. It's incomplete but the numbers that are readable agree with those assigned to the hijacked MU-2."

"Where was the wreckage exactly?"

"About eight hundred miles due east of Canton Island and some two hundred south of the equator. I have the latitude and longitude."

"Has the wreckage definitely been identified as an MU-2?"

"No, that will have to wait for examination by the experts. The ship's first port of call is Nauru, and that's several days' steaming from their last position. We'll have someone accept the pieces and get them to Honolulu. Incidentally, we have no missing plane reports—other than the MU-2 and the Zero."

"We're looking at the better part of a week then."

"At least."

"No body?"

"Nothing but the wreckage. And damned little of that. They searched the area for about an hour."

"Thanks Sammy. Let me know."

"Sure."

Sakai rummaged around his room for the *National Geographic* map that Lee had given him. He laid it out on the side table. Why would Genda and Ohiro have taken off almost due east from Canton? There was hardly anything out there except several tiny islets. Maybe they were headed for Christmas Island. That was fairly large but it was several hundred miles north of the reported crash position. It had an airport. Other than that, there was just nothing. They couldn't have been trying for South America; the distance was far too great. He sat lost in thought until Alicia walked in from her room.

"What is it?"

Sakai pointed to his penciled X on the map. "Aircraft wreckage, picked up by an Argentine freighter. It could be the MU-2."

Alicia leaned over to examine the map. "Where were they going?"

Sakai sat back; obviously, Alicia's remark had triggered another thought. "Maybe *they* weren't going anywhere. Only parts of the MU-2 were found—although they haven't been positively identified. Maybe Genda and Ohiro weren't together. If they were, of course, it's doubtful they would have both crashed at the same spot."

"Can't they conduct a search of the area?"

"Hell, it's way out in nowhere. We might have a navy ship nearby. I don't know."

"Do you mind a layman's thought?"

Sakai looked up at Alicia, surprised. "No, of course not."

"Why are you so sure that Genda and Ohiro are the ones who hijacked the two aircraft?"

"Majuro, Funafuti, and Canton all reported the pilots were Japanese and the station chief at Canton said the descriptions fit."

Alicia just shrugged, exercising her female prerogative to remain unconvinced.

"What if it is the MU-2, but they weren't together?" Sakai mused. "If Ohiro went east, where would Genda have gone?" Sakai studied the map island by island, drawing a line through those with airports. The Zero wasn't at any of those; there would have been a report. The Zero *had* to be on one of the others—or in the drink. There was no other possibility. And if Genda was on one of the other islands, one without an airport, or he had crashed at sea, either on the route Ohiro had taken or on some other, he could no longer be a threat to anyone. There was the remote possibility that if he had picked the right island, he could live out his days there, but with his leukemia, which must be progressing rapidly now, he had very few days left. Maybe they would never know Genda's fate. He would die on some godforsaken Pacific outcropping and be buried by natives or just rot away—a fast process in the equatorial Pacific belt. That would be no great tragedy, but it would leave a mystery unsolved.

But why did he have such a strong, unexplainable feeling that he would meet Genda again? Perhaps, as the great Yogi Berra had once said, "It ain't over 'til it's over."

Genda waited until after the tropical sun was well on its drop toward the western horizon before gathering his materials. He had a two-by-two ripped from one of the shacks, some piano wire he found in another, and several odd rags. Also, he had a blob of soft tar that he had scraped from under the tin roof of one of the small buildings and a short length of electrical wiring.

At the takeoff end of the runway, exactly aligned with the centerline, he forced the two-by-two into the crushed coral until it would stand by itself. Then he ran four strands of the piano wire down from near the top of the piece of lumber to the ground and tied the ends around large chunks of broken coral. The blob of tar had been kneaded and pressed into the rags and the whole ensemble tied securely to the top of the pole. The device wasn't too steady, but it should last for the time he would need it. The only problem remaining was that he had no match to light the rags. He did have a possible solution to that dilemma, however, one that was somewhat ingenious but could blow his airplane sky high if he didn't conduct it properly, but he felt very strongly about the need for some kind of light at the end of the runway. Once he crawled into the cockpit enveloped by the night darkness, he would require all the help he could muster to assure a safe takeoff. Visibility across the nose of the Zero would be poor until he had sufficient speed to lift the tail. During those few seconds, he would just have to do the best he could on directional control. He wasn't overly concerned. He had made hundreds of night takeoffs. But they had all been on well-lighted, broad, long runways. This one would be different.

Returning to the shack area, he consumed his last meal. Ohiro had provided him with some packaged food, but there was some staleness present, brought on by the passing of the three hot, humid days since they had left Pohnpei. Filling his water bottle with fresh rainwater from one of the galvanized catchers, he walked back out to the Zero and lay under the wing. He would rest and try to get some sleep. To allow for last-minute preparations, he must wake himself two hours prior to midnight.

Sakai and Alicia found the state dinner in the Royal Hawaiian's oceanfront Monarch Room a highly upscaled replay of the one the night before at the Hale Koa. There were several differences, naturally. Formal wear was required, and Alicia used the occasion to purchase and wear an evening creation from Hawaii's top designer that reflected the spirit of Polynesia by providing only the barest minimum of body coverage.

The arrival of the president and the prime minister and their entourage was more ritually orchestrated, but the food was not nearly up to the standard of the meal they had consumed the evening before at the Armed Forces Recreation Center hotel.

The president's remarks were brief; details on the treaty had been revealed and most of the questions answered at his and the prime minister's joint press conference earlier in the afternoon. Hoikata's dinner speech was delivered in excellent English and stressed Japan's desire to assume her worldwide responsibilities as opposed to just western Pacific obligations. The very confident prime minister used the occasion to boldly project his country's intention to become the number-one financial, economic, and technological nation, but he discreetly steered away from mentioning a parallel objective for the emerging Japanese military forces. The press, particularly the Soviet editors and key journalists, would later editorialize on that at some length.

The Marine Corps band alternately played popular American and Japanese music, the latter with a such a genuine feel that the prime minister commented favorably on it at the end of his prepared remarks. In return, perhaps with tongue in cheek, the band played an unusually rousing version of the Marine Corps Hymn at the conclusion of their performance. Hoikata, to the surprise and delight of everyone present, clapped his hands enthusiastically in time with the spirited military march. The dinner ended on that note with a contagious feeling among the attendees that they had witnessed part of a truly extraordinary development of Japanese national purpose.

Sakai noted with mixed emotions that Hoikata was every bit the polished political performer that the Soviet Gorbachev had been on his earlier visits to the Western countries back in 1988 and '89. Perhaps more so.

Later that evening, after unwinding with Alicia over several scotches, Sakai went to bed unsure of just what he had witnessed at the state dinner.

One thousand miles southwest of Oahu a mature line of tropical thunderstorms steadily moved eastward, and the eight-mile-high, anvil-shaped cumulonimbus clouds began to release the tons of water they had absorbed during the long Pacific day. Torrential rains returned to their source and violent winds swirled around the dozens of intense low pressure areas under the cloud bases. The seas reacted by building and falling in a great secondary swell system topped by windswept waves and a fury of spray, and the few mariners in the area anxiously set their watertight conditions and prepared for the front's passage.

Encountering the resistance of a gigantic high pressure cell over the eastern Pacific, the mighty squall line turned slightly to the north, its center now destined to pass directly over the tiny island of Palmyra.

Chapter 30

The tremendous clap of thunder not only jarred Genda from his light sleep, it actually seemed to move him slightly across the surface of the runway. Startled, he stood and surveyed the dark skies around the island. They were pitch-black, but in every direction except the northeast bolts of lightning were shattering the darkness with streaks of silver so intense Genda's eyelids inadvertently slammed shut in response to each brilliant burst of electrical energy. Every few minutes, the entire sky would light up with what Genda's mother used to refer to as sheet lightning. In keeping with her Christian belief, she had jokingly claimed it was God briefly cycling the lights of Heaven to let the faithful know that He was still there and all was well.

There was a thin rain falling, but Genda knew that it was only the prelude. The storms would very soon drench the island. He also knew that the massive clouds were sufficiently widespread to take hours in passing. Using a flash of lightning for momentary illumination, he squinted at his watch. Ten-thirty P.M. He had overslept.

His intention had been to rise and methodically prepare himself for his last flight, much as he had on August 15, 1945. But there was not enough time now. It would be a race to get into the air before the full fury of the storm struck. An early departure could throw off his timing, but that was unavoidable. He must leave as soon as possible.

Ignoring his underwear, he jerked on his flying suit, socks, and shoes. Retrieving his cotton money belt, he zipped it open and pulled out the two *hachimakis* he had carried for the last forty-six years. Pulling on his helmet, he tied the headbands securely over it.

His *haiku*! He had to leave his last message to the mortal world where it would eventually be found. Fortunately, he had already written it. He could not run, the exertion would be too much, but he could trot over to the shacks. He read his last words one more time:

> There is no honor but service;
> There is no life but death.
> The majesty of Fuji-san
> can only impress the living.
> It is the next world that
> excites the spirit—and Michio Ohiro
> has made it possible for me to
> enter it with the blow of a
> warrior—for a samurai does not
> stay alive in dishonor.
>
> Saburo Genda
> Flight Petty Officer
> ·Imperial Japanese Navy

Genda fixed the folded paper under a piece of coral inside the sturdiest shack. Anyone entering would be sure to find it.

Back at planeside, he hastily drew a few ounces of fuel from one of the wing drain points, collecting the thin stream of aviation gasoline in a small can. He went forward and unsnapped the square cover over the electrical contacts used to receive an outside power cable. It took a minute to climb on the wing, reach inside the cockpit, and turn on the battery power. Back at the power receptacle, he poured a tiny bit of the gasoline on a tar-smudged rag. He twisted together the two wires of one end of the short length of electrical wiring he had obtained earlier. Holding the fuel-wetted rag close to the other end of the wiring, he held the end of one of the exposed wires tightly against one of the electrical contacts of the external power receptacle. Taking a deep breath, he touched the remaining wire to the other electrical contact. There was an instant spark and he jerked the flaming rag away from the airplane.

As fast as his weakened legs would allow, he carried the small fire to the end of the runway and ignited the combustible mass at the top of his alignment pole. By the time he returned to the waiting Zero, he was walking with considerable effort through a steady rain. It took a herculean effort to climb into the Zero. Feeling around in the side pouch, he found the last of his sake. To hell with the urgency of the situation. He would enjoy a last toast. Raising the hardened clay bottle to his lips, he lifted a clenched fist, shouted *"Banzai!"* and gulped down the rice wine. It warmed and strengthened him.

The rain forced him to close the canopy and he engaged the engine starter. To his joy, the Nakajima caught on the second revolution of the propeller and he adjusted the power for his warmup. To attempt a takeoff with a cold engine would be to risk misfires and plug fouling, possibly even engine failure.

While waiting, he ran over his pretakeoff checklist. He would have given several gallons of fuel—well, maybe one gallon—for landing lights. They would have made his night takeoff a snap.

He was ready, and the engine almost ready. Just a few more degrees of cylinder head temperature. He would check his magnetos on his takeoff run, but regardless of their condition he would be going as long as they supported combustion. One final task: He pulled back the propeller control lever and watched his RPMs decrease, then pushed it forward and watched them increase. The control was working properly.

Over the engine cowling, he could see the glow of the flame at the end of the runway but not the flame itself. He would have to get the tail up for that. The rain was heavy now and the wind gusts were rocking his wings with considerable force. His airspeed needle was jumping up as high as twenty-five knots. He couldn't wait any longer. He released his brakes. Easing on the power, he worked his rudders to keep his heading steady and as soon as he had sufficient airspeed, he pushed the stick forward to raise the tail. It came up just in time for him to see his runway alignment flame flicker and disappear. It had drowned—and he was committed.

But the intense lightning, coming so frequently that it provided almost constant illumination, lit up the runway as well as the noon-day sun. The rain, now a quick series of fierce waves, pounded his windshield and eliminated any forward visibility, but Genda lowered his goggles, slammed back the canopy, and leaned out the left side of the cockpit.

Thoroughly soaked, the rain stinging his face with the fury of a thousand hornets, he yelled with absolute glee as the Zero roared straight down the center of the runway and lifted into the air. With two quick motions, he pulled the canopy shut and retracted his landing gear, holding his heading steady to climb straight ahead. He dared not look outside the cockpit now; he must concentrate upon his instruments, and besides, he could not see the horizon or even the boiling surface of the Pacific. Genda turned his instrument lights up to their brightest position.

Following the indications of his INS and concentrating on his artificial horizon, he banked smoothly around to his enroute heading. At eight hundred feet, he entered the base of the clouds and a world of turbulent terror. The Zero jerked and rolled and Genda was thrown violently about the cockpit. Only his tight seat belt and shoulder harness kept him from banging the top of the canopy. Desperately, fearing that at any minute the Zero would be thrown out of control, he fought the stick and rudders. For a brief moment he was sure that the airplane was going to be thrown completely onto its back and his mouth dried with concern over the possibility of structural failure. The Zero was not the most structurally sound fighter of World War II, the designers having been more interested in saving weight in the interest of combat maneuverability. Unlike the sturdy Hellcat produced by the Grumman "Iron Works," the Zero disintegrated under the slightest burst of machine gun fire. Thunderstorm penetration had been strictly forbidden.

He passed two thousand feet—for the third time—and could only imagine how his struggle was affecting his fuel consumption. He was alternately ramming the throttle forward and jerking it back as his airspeed rose and dipped with no predictable pattern, the Zero's forward progress completely at the mercy of the storm winds.

Sweating such that the salty fluid began to enter and sting his eyes, Genda fought the gods of the air and managed to muscle the Zero up another two thousand feet. Going higher did not seem to make much sense. He doubted there would be any less turbulence, and besides, he needed maximum forward motion to get out of the storm as soon as possible. The ride was still much too violent to engage the autopilot, but after a few minutes he found to his relief that he could hold his altitude within five hundred feet of that desired and there was some noticeable decrease to the turbulence.

Unexpectedly, he momentarily broke out into clear air, but all around he could see the angry thunderstorms. There were several dead ahead but there were also gaps of lesser weather intensity and he steered for them. He plunged again into the darkness and there was another endless eighteen minutes of uncertainty and another sudden emergence into clear sky. Genda felt reborn. Ahead were only the stars.

Fine-tuning his altitude to four thousand feet, Genda engaged the autopilot and set his throttle and mixture controls for the most economical cruise. His fuel flow dropped to sixteen and a half gallons per hour. For the first time in forty minutes, he could relax. Of the utmost priority was a long drink from his water bottle.

Before turning down the cockpit lights, he checked the time, then the position indicators of the INS. He wasn't certain, but it appeared that he was less than a half hour ahead of his schedule. The INS gave a running latitude and longitude and he had no chart, but mental calculations could be made and he was confident he was not far off.

A momentary dizziness alarmed him. For just an instant he felt like he was going to pass out. He had not experienced that particular light-headedness before, even when he had fainted back on Canton. That time, the lights had simply gone out. It could be the result of the strain of the past hour. He put a hand on his chest and felt for his heartbeat. It wasn't hard to find but it wasn't racing. He estimated it to be close to ninety per minute. That should not be too unusual, considering his near-death experience within the thunderstorms.

There was moonlight and he could clearly see the water below. The Pacific glistened as the swells picked up the light of the moon and reflected the rays toward the Zero. Now, the air was almost calm, only an occasional jolt reminding Genda of his recent trip through the heavens of Hell.

For the next hour he monitored the northward flight of his precious flying machine. It had weathered the worst that nature could throw at it. Almost a half century old, it droned through the Pacific night with a confident smoothness that made Genda feel as if he could fly clear around the world. His eyelids became very heavy but he fought sleep for another half hour. Finally, he had to surrender. There just was no way he could resist. He retightened his harness in the event he encountered some unanticipated clear-air turbulence, took another long drink of his water, and dropped his seat a notch. Within moments, he knew he was asleep but he also knew in his pilot's heart that any change in the engine rhythm, any sudden jolt by the playful atmosphere, and he would be wide awake in an instant.

The change in engine rhythm came almost immediately. In fact, the strong Nakajima quit completely and Genda wakened cursing his stupidity. He had taken off on one of his full main fuel tanks but had switched to the belly tank when setting up his cruise condition. It had run dry. Lowering the nose to keep flying speed, he switched the fuel selector to the left wing tank. The engine sputtered, caught, and settled into a smooth rhythm once more. He had lost almost five hundred feet and elected to stay where he was. There was no need to reclaim the altitude. He pulled the release handle to his belly tank and felt a slight jolt as the tank fell away.

Once more he dozed, and when he next opened his eyes another hour had passed. But the nap had renewed his energy and he took stock of his situation.

Four hours out, he had covered six hundred and forty-eight miles! That was excellent considering his low power setting and an indicated airspeed of one hundred and twenty-three knots. Taking into consideration his altitude and outside air temperature, he had enjoyed an average tailwind component of better than thirty knots! At thirty-five hundred feet? In clear and nonturbulent air? There had to be a huge high pressure cell somewhere off to his right, or a very tight low to his left. Whatever, he had picked up enough speed that his fuel remaining should no longer be a critical factor. His gauges indicated ninety-eight gallons remaining. At his current fuel flow, he had almost six hours of endurance left—and he was only four hundred and two miles away from his first landfall! Three hours—six-thirty A.M. Perfect.

The Zero was cruising in clear air now and the myriad of stars overhead were blinking their friendly reassurance that all was stable in the heavens. There was no need for heat in the cockpit; the warm Pacific air cooled slightly as it passed through the fresh air inlets and Genda was quite comfortable. He felt alert and capable. There was some pain, mostly in his arms, but it was tolerable, and his hands were free of the pinpricky numbness that sometimes invaded them. He still had plenty of water and it remained fresh and cool. He was not hungry, and even if he were there were still several candy bars that would give him a quick injection of sugar. All in all, Saburo Genda had the situation well in hand.

An hour later, he was not so optimistic. His tailwind had disappeared. Ground speed: one hundred and twenty-eight knots. His ETA at first landfall had slipped to almost seven A.M. Not a worry yet, but certainly a concern.

Chapter 31

The president was having second thoughts about the schedule he had insisted on for the Pearl Harbor memorial service. Five in the morning was a bit too early to crawl out of bed after his evening with Prime Minister Hoikata. Their private tête-à-tête had evolved into a long session of war stories and reminiscences. The old Jap was several years senior to the president in age and had commanded a ragged company of militia on western Honshu when the war had ended. Prior to that, he had spent three years in constant retreat out of Manchuria and then the Pacific islands, including a successful participation in the then-secret withdrawal from Guadalcanal. He had a remarkable record of survival for a Japanese soldier, confiding to the president that there were several times when he should have opened his stomach and died a hero's death but he had never lost faith that he would escape to fight again, and he had been right.

During the occupation years, Hoikata had been part of the Japanese liaison staff assigned to MacArthur's headquarters in Tokyo and had soon made a name for himself as an innovative and cooperative minor official. That led to a political career that had spanned the last forty years, culminating in the top position of prime minister. Uno's demise as a result of the sex-and-payoff scandals in 1989 had indirectly opened the door for Hoikata, and he was a man of rigid morals and strict integrity. Unswervingly pro-American, he was to the president the ideal man to take Japan into her new role of equal partnership with the United States in the military defense of the western Pacific.

By 5:45 A.M., the president and his wife had gulped down their papaya juice and coffee and were dressed for the morning's crowded schedule.

At 6:15 A.M., they prayed briefly in the base chapel at Hickam and at 6:45 A.M. arrived at the Pearl Harbor Memorial Park. Leaving their limousine, they greeted Prime Minister Hoikata and his wife, who also had just arrived after their return from the leeward side of the island, where they had prayed at the Byodo-in temple in the Valley of the Temples Park. An exact replica of the nine-hundred-year-old Buddhist temple at Uji in the Kyoto area of Japan, the magnificent structure had been selected by Hoikata for his special-day morning prayers even though it meant he and Mrs. Hoikata had risen an hour earlier than the president and first lady.

At the same moment when the two leaders were walking toward the boat landing at the *Arizona* Memorial Park, Saburo Genda was grinning with an almost ecstatic flush of satisfaction as his eyes roamed the southwest coast of the big island of Hawaii.

He decided to stay at thirty-five hundred feet for the time being. In all probability, the air traffic radar on the big island had picked him up, but since he was well below the positive control zone and not squawking any IFF codes, his blip would be of little concern to the controllers manning the scopes. In fact, they would figure he was a local flight operating under visual flight rules and scrub his return from their screen. What irony that would be—fifty years back almost to the minute, six soldiers manning the crude radar at Kahuku Point on the northern tip of Oahu had also detected unknown aircraft. They had been mistakenly identified as a flight of B-17s arriving from the mainland when in fact the returns had been the Japanese attack force.

Genda pointed the Zero toward the channel between Hawaii and Maui and increased his speed. He had sufficient fuel remaining to carry out his intentions and now the important factor was timing. Certainly, the Americans would have some sort of special ceremonies scheduled for this historic day, and he was quite sure that they would have something precisely at 7:55 A.M., perhaps a moment of silence or a rifle salute out on the memorial. Maybe they would elect noise, and the ship's whistles would all sound in unison and bells throughout the city ring. Whatever the event, Genda intended that at exactly that time he would swoop down from the Pali pass and pick his target.

In 1941, there had been ninety-six U.S. Navy ships in the harbor, including the battleships *Nevada*, *Arizona*, *Tennessee*, *West Virginia*, *Maryland*, *Oklahoma*, *Utah*, *California*, and *Pennsylvania*, all but the latter tidily tied up to the great round quays off Ford Island: Battleship Row. But there had been no carriers present.

Genda knew that there would be carriers there on this day!

First, he would treat the early risers to a display of the Zero's magnificent maneuverability and orbit low around the waters of Pearl Harbor long enough for the news media to film and photograph the resurrection of the Imperial Navy and record the historic attack of the last *kamikaze*. He reasoned that there would be no armed aircraft on alert and that the ships in the harbor would figure his presence as part of the day's activities. The Americans were very gullible. They would have no idea that the Zero had flown halfway across the Pacific and in its cockpit there would be a pilot of the *Tokkotai* Special Attack Corps of the Imperial Navy. Too bad he would never read or see the accounts of his feat, although, perhaps, in his spirit life he would be aware of such things. He would like that.

According to the newspaper article he had read on his flight out of Osaka, there was even a chance that the American president and Prime Minister Hoikata would be on the memorial. Genda had no desire to threaten the peaceful sleep of the American sailors entombed on the *Arizona*, but once his intentions were known, there would be an attempt to remove the president and Japanese prime minister from the memorial. That could give him an opportunity to strike them. If not, there would surely be some suitable target present at Pearl Harbor.

Sakai and Alicia sat in the navy-manned fifty-foot shuttle boat as it approached the inspirational, sway-backed, permanent memorial structure that spanned the beam of the sunken U.S.S. *Arizona*. Along with the other members of the official party, they were preceding the president and the prime minister and everyone would be in their assigned positions by the time the dignitaries arrived in style. The president and his wife, along with Prime Minister and Mrs. Hoikata as well as Admiral and Mrs. Togakagi would be escorted by Admiral DeHart and they would ride across the waters of Pearl Harbor to the memorial in CINCPAC's personal white-and-chrome U.S. Navy barge, although Sakai had always wondered why such a sleek cabin cruiser became a barge when assigned to an admiral. How did the old song go?

> The officers, they ride in a motorboat,
> The captain, he rides in his gig.
> But the admiral arrives on his great barge
> For it makes the old bastard feel big.
> Oooooooh, too-ra-lie, too-ra-lie . . .

"What are you humming?" Alicia asked.

Sakai had not realized he was being vocal with his thought. "Sorry, just something. I wish I could remember the exact words."

The sky of the Saturday morning was tourist blue and the waters of the harbor were waking up with gentle movements, the low waves slapping against the boat's wooden hull as the bow of the fifty-footer cut through them. The air was crystal clear, but to the north the purple peaks of the mountains had still to wipe their wakeup haze away and the dip in their ragged profile that was the Pali pass was partially shrouded by the gray veil of a morning shower.

The coxswain rang his bell and the engineman downshifted the speed of the engine as the boat made a wide sweeping turn to come alongside the steel-plated landing platform attached to the memorial.

A respectful silence marked the demeanor of those in the boat as it glided port-side-to the landing, and when someone did speak it was in an intuitive whisper. Sakai knew that everyone around him was experiencing the same slight chill as he stepped onto the memorial and offered his assistance to Alicia. He had visited the *Arizona* several times before and as on each of those prior visits the moment his foot had stepped onto the platform his eyes moistened.

The long white structure ran amidships just aft of the number-two main gun turret, and just below the surface of the water was the clear outline of the sunken battleship, the national ghost of the surprise attack on Pearl Harbor, the 1,177 souls still entombed within her shattered hull sacred in the national conscience of all Americans. Just as it had for the past fifty years, a small trickle of oil was rising from the depths and threading its way from the ship.

The exterior of the sway-backed memorial structure featured an irregular cutout symbolizing the Tree of Life and twenty-one six-sided openings, seven in the middle of each long side and a corresponding seven in the roof, all together symbolizing a perpetually silent twenty-one-gun salute. From the stub of the mainmast of the *Arizona*, only a few feet in front of the exact center of the memorial, rose a gleaming stainless steel pole and at its top flew the colors of the United States.

The interior of the memorial was divided into three sections. The first, directly off the landing, contained the ship's bell, removed from the sunken corpse and proudly displayed as testimony that in a very spiritual way, the U.S.S. *Arizona* was still a U.S. Navy ship of the line. The Secret Service had used one corner of the room to set up the ever-present array of presidential communications equipment.

The main section was the largest, and the large openings not only provided an excellent view toward the bow and stern of the ship but let in the majestic sunshine of the Hawaiian heavens and enabled the ever-present harbor breezes to flow through the structure. The last compartment featured a glistening white marble wall upon which were inscribed the names of the men entombed below, a memorial not unlike the Vietnam wall in Washington. At the moment, a segment of the Marine Corps Headquarters Band was already in place in front of the wall.

Sakai and Alicia and the other invited guests were escorted to their positions in the rear of the center section. All stood, conversing quietly, as they waited for the official party to arrive.

Rounding the eastern tip of Maui, Genda dropped to just a hundred feet above the water and stayed close aboard the rugged coastline. While he was still confident that the Honolulu air traffic center would treat him as a local flight, it would be better to use the hills of Maui and Molokai to mask his approach. He did not intend for any detection to take place before he began his dive from over the Pali.

·   ·   ·

Long-time *paniolo* (Hawaiian cowboy) David Makaka and his seven-year-old granddaughter, Lani, rode easily in their saddles, Makaka having been the head wrangler on Maui's Hana Ranch for the last fifteen years and Lani having sat a cow pony before she walked. They were leisurely driving three strays toward the main herd and anticipating a big breakfast back at the main ranch house where Makaka's wife was head cook.

"Grandfather, look! There's an airplane!" Lani stood in her stirrups with excitement. The airplane would come very close to them.

Makaka reined his spirited mount to a stop beside his granddaughter and searched in the direction of her excited waving. There was an airplane flying very fast just below the tops of the high bluffs. It passed within fifty yards of him and Lani, the pilot even returning the child's enthusiastic wave. At first, Makaka thought it to be one of the usual sight-seers out for a morning flight around the island, but the bright red meatball on the afterside of the fuselage instantly jarred his memory back fifty years. Suddenly, he was a ten-year-old paperboy for the *Honolulu Star-Bulletin*, sleepily untying his bundles of heavy Sunday papers at his assigned corner in Pearl City. Then, a whole sky full of identical airplanes had swooped low overhead and banked sharply toward Ford Island.

My God . . . , he first thought. The Zero was not one of the modified U.S. trainers that had been used in several filmed re-creations of that attack; instead, the speeding green-and-black airplane was authentic, complete to the oriental pilot with a white-and-red headband tied around his helmet. Makaka would never forget that vision. Obviously, however, the flight of the Zero had to have something to do with the ceremonies taking place over on Oahu.

"Look at it, Grandfather!"

Makaka nodded. Strange, how its sudden appearance had brought back the bad memories, complete in every frightening detail. A mind growing old, thought Makaka, may forget some things, but it never loses an image of diving planes and burning ships and a sky full of orange fireballs and black smoke and a young boy's innocent realization that death had come on a peaceful Sunday morning. Even stranger was the feeling that before him and Lani, the racing ghost of the past had no idea that its mission had been completed a half century ago. Makaka found his mouth opening and his voice erupting. "No, stop! Wait!"

Lani stared at her grandfather, confused. "He can't hear you, Grandfather."

"What? Oh . . . no, of course not." Makaka turned up the collar of his Levis jacket as the Zero disappeared in the direction of Oahu. There seemed to be a slight chill to the air. "Come on," he said, "let's go get some of Grandma's breakfast."

Admiral DeHart's barge slid quietly up to the landing, where two four-man ranks of white-uniformed sideboys stood waiting at rigid attention. It eased to a stop and the president stepped onto the landing to stand for a moment as the great brass bell of the *Arizona* tolled a series of double clangs and a navy boatswain announced, "United States of America—arriving." The sideboys snapped the inside edges of their hands against their foreheads as the boatswain rendered ship's honors by the shrill call of his silver pipe.

Next came, "Prime Minister, Japan—arriving," then "Commander-in-Chief Pacific—arriving," and finally a most unusual announcement, "Commander, Japanese Armed Forces—arriving." In a slight break of tradition but in consideration of the prominence of the top four dignitaries attending the ceremonies, lesser officials were received with silent hand salutes by the officer-of-the-deck and the eight sailors manning the landing. The four ladies in the official party, the two Japanese wives diplomatically in Western dress, were escorted to their position in front of the assembled guests while the president, Hoikata, DeHart, and Togakagi took their places at the center front of the memorial. Ahead of them, beyond the flagpole, the quiet waters of Pearl Harbor lapped against the rusted round base of the *Arizona*'s number-two main battery, the hollow steel casement all that remained of the mighty three-gun, sixteen-inch turret that along with all the main guns had been powerless to defend the ship.

The red, white, and blue colors at the top of the flagpole had hung limp in the morning calm, but now a fresh breeze stimulated the cloth and it snapped into a new position, fully streamed aft—as if the *Arizona* had suddenly gotten under way.

Genda let the Zero drift out to seaward as he approached Molokai. He would still be below any radar beams. His watch read 7:25 A.M. He should be right on time.

Without warning, the lightness in his head that he had felt before returned and his vision blurred. He shook himself and wiggled in his seat to clear the feeling and it did disappear as suddenly as it had come. There was water left in his bottle and he drained it. Somewhere in one of the leg pockets was a bottle with the last pills the doctor back in Sapporo had given him. He fumbled around until he found it and popped two of the oblong pellets into his mouth. He had no idea whether they would help, strongly suspecting they were for prolonged effect, not for quick remedy to whatever was happening to him. In any event, he did not like the way his mind was drifting out of and back into reality.

Prime Minister Hoikata read in English from a small white card. "On this sacred anniversary, I carry a message from the people of Japan to the brave warriors who sleep here. In the inexplicable way of international relations, we once found ourselves on the opposite sides of a great conflict. Now, recognizing the passing of that time, and the realization that within the deepest recesses of our souls we all share the same goals of peace and tranquillity, we ask you to accept our hand and national honor in a partnership that will prevent another happening such as that to ever occur again. History records many tragedies. Let history now be the only chronicle of the tragedy that in its ultimate end has brought our two peoples together; let the minds and thoughts of the new generations think only of brotherhood among nations."

Sakai listened very closely to the words. Hoikata had selected them with great care, staying clear of an outright apology for the sneak attack—after all, the men of the Imperial Navy had been under the impression that war had already been declared—but clearly implying that there was a sense of national regret. The crafty old politician had probably succeeded in drafting words that would placate both Japanese and Americans.

The president accepted Hoikata's bow with an awkward one of his own, then spoke without reference to any notes. "The peace that was won in 1945 has even up to this moment never been a confident one, and those who would deny the United States of its pursuit of national interests are still present. To the men of the U.S.S. *Arizona*, and the people of the United States, I pledge that this new relationship between our country and the nation of Japan will insure that the days of uncertainty are behind us. It may very well be that our new treaty of mutual trade, cultural exchange, and defense will complete the task that the heroic crew of the *Arizona* began with their ultimate sacrifice, and make any further thought of global conflict unacceptable to any nation or groups of nations. On behalf of the people of the United States, I welcome the people of Japan into this new relationship and pray that our association has the blessings of the men of the *Arizona*, who will forever witness this event from their position of eternal rest."

With the president's last word, the Marine Band softly began the inspirational music of the Navy Hymn.

Genda banked sharply south toward the northern coast of Oahu. Reaching down on the right console, he set his radio to the UHF emergency frequency. There would be a number of units in Pearl Harbor guarding it and when it came time to announce his identity, he would do so on the emergency channel.

He was now on the original course of the 1941 attack. Ahead, he could see the cut of Kaneohe Bay and the wide runways of the modern-day Marine Corps air station that bordered it. Fifty years ago, it had been a seaplane base and the ramps had been lined with the great-winged PBY patrol planes. The forbidding cliffs of the leeward side of the mountain range that cut across Oahu rose before him and he adjusted his heading to approach the Pali pass. Two hundred and thirty miles behind him, he could sense the ghost of the Special Attack Force flagship, the Imperial Navy's fast attack carrier, *Akagi*. On it, the ethereal presence of Vice Admiral Nagumo, the commander of the strike force, waited anxiously for the first reports of the attack. Around him steamed his five companion carriers, the *Kaga*, the newer and considerably larger *Zuikaku*, the big *Shokaku*, and the light carriers *Hiryu* and *Soryu*. All of the floating airfields were defended by the spirits of a formidable surface fleet, including the battleships *Hiei* and *Kirishima*, and the deadly new cruisers *Tome* and *Chikuma*. An array of fast destroyers circled the big ships and the light cruiser *Abukuma*, three screening submarines, and eight support tankers.

The ships were not the only ghosts present.

The sky around Genda and his Zero was also full. Up and to his right flew Commander Mitsuo Fuchida, the aggressive and skilled leader of the air group in his especially marked Nakajima B5N Kate with the distinctive red-and-yellow stripes around its tail. Instead of a torpedo, Fuchida carried a modified sixteen-inch battleship shell destined for the U.S.S. *Maryland.* All around the brilliant Fuchida were Lieutenant Commander Shigeru Itaya's forty-three Zero fighters, Lieutenant Commander Kakwichi Takahashi's fifty-one Val dive bombers, and Lieutenant Commander Shigaharu's forty Kate torpedo bombers of the first wave of the gigantic air assault. Behind Fuchida were another forty-eight Kates rigged for horizontal bombing.

The giant formation approached the northern coast of Oahu and began its dispersal for the coordinated attack, the dive bombers heading for Hickam and Ford Island, the torpedo bombers anxiously positioning themselves for their attack on the big ships. The horizontal bombers would follow.

Genda kept his eyes glued on Fuchida's aircraft, anxiously waiting for the flare signal that would signify the attack had begun.

It came almost immediately, the single bright flare erupting from Fuchida's bomber and arcing high over the formation, the signal that they had achieved surprise.

"Tora! Tora! Tora!" yelled Genda as he started a maximum-performance dive toward the mountain gap of the Pali.

Chapter 32

"Mister Sakai, would you join us please?"

The president's request was totally unexpected. Sakai had been watching the beautifully restored Douglas SBD dive bomber make several passes across the bow of the *Arizona* and it took a moment for the reality of the request to sink in. "Yes, Mr. President."

The guests parted to let him through and the president indicated that he should stand between him and the prime minister.

"Prime Minister Hoikata, I would like to present George Kohji Sakai."

Sakai returned Hoikata's bow, being sure to hold his a moment after the prime minister stood erect. Hoikata offered his hand as the president completed the introduction.

"George is a second-generation Japanese-American, Mr. Prime Minister. His parents immigrated from Kyushu in 1939 and became American citizens in 1946. They ran a very popular bakery in San Jose, California, and I am told they produced the best pastries in the western United States."

After spending almost four years in a detainment camp, thought Sakai, but he was pleased that his thought was without malice. It probably would have been improper for the president to have mentioned the incident.

"I thought it would be only fitting that George join us in laying this wreath upon the waters of Pearl Harbor since in his blood flows both the heritage of the United States and Japan."

"I would agree most heartily with such a thoughtful act, Mr. President. Mr. Sakai, I am honored to have you join us."

"*Domo arigato,*" Sakai replied, bowing several times in the way of sincere appreciation.

The blue-and-gray dive bomber made one last pass and then pulled up in a wide arc to circle the harbor. Two enlisted marines came forward with a giant flower lei and held it while the president, Hoikata, and Sakai placed their hands on it. The marines released their grip and stepped smartly back. Following the president's lead, Hoikata and Sakai leaned forward over the front of the memorial and together the three men let the fragrant necklace drop gently onto the water. It floated back against the memorial, bobbing gently, held there by the wind.

Sakai was uncertain as to what he should do next. The president seemed to detect his confusion and said under his breath, "Please, remain with us."

The Marine Corps band began the national anthem of Japan, the lilting melody a bit strange to the Western ear but filling everyone with appreciation for the significance of the moment. Sakai said a silent prayer that the men of the *Arizona* would understand the intent of the ceremony and take some comfort from it.

Listening, he idly gazed out over the water at the clutter of buildings and houses along the northern reaches of Pearl Harbor and the green fields and purple mountains beyond. He let his eyes enjoy the panorama of beauty, slowly shifting them eastward across the Aloha Stadium area and up to the Pali. He could almost envision how it had been on that fateful day so many years past, a swarm of black dots approaching the fleet resting in the harbor, another swarm diving onto Hickam and Ford Island. It must have been chaos. By contrast, on this equally peaceful and sunlit morning, there was only one dot in the sky. *One dot?* There shouldn't be *any* dots on this day. Sakai strained to identify the tiny form that was rapidly growing wings. Certainly, there was a restricted airspace warning over the entire harbor. Yet the form, now easily identifiable as a fast-moving aircraft, was starting a steep descent.

The last notes of the Japanese anthem died and there was a brief drumroll before the first stirring notes of the Star-Spangled Banner began.

Oh-ooo, say can you see . . .

Sakai joined the president in placing his right hand over his heart but his eyes were riveted on the winged intruder. It was coming very fast, swooping down from the Pali across the Fort Shafter Military Reservation then banking toward Pearl Harbor.

. . . what so proudly we hailed at the twilight's last gleaming . . .

It was a low-winged aircraft with a large round engine and definitely hauling ass straight for the memorial! Sakai took only a moment to run the head-on view through his mind. He was not an aviator and certainly not of the World War II generation but he knew enough about the conflict to recognize that the airplane was a radial-engined fighter.

. . . the bombs bursting in air . . .

Sakai's heart went into overdrive—it was a Zero! With one motion, he grabbed the president and threw him to the deck while shouting, "Murray! It's Genda!" Everyone on the memorial could see the aircraft now. A horde of Secret Service agents rushed forward and covered Sakai, the president, and Hoikata with their bodies. Sakai knew it was a futile effort. If Genda smashed into the memorial, they would all die in the flaming impact. Instead, the Zero leveled off only a few feet above the water and less than fifty yards away pulled up and over the structure, rotating gracefully in a victory roll.

Genda howled with glee dispite the dizziness caused by his rapid roll. Whatever was taking place on the *Arizona* had been thoroughly interrupted. The people down there had been frantically throwing themselves onto the deck of the memorial structure as he swept over them. They had nothing to fear; there was no way he would harm the memorial or the *Arizona*. He had nothing but the greatest respect for those men still on board the sunken battleship. But as he pulled up in a climbing turn he saw his target. Three huge nuclear carriers were tied up at the naval base piers.

Sakai squirmed his way free of the mass of bodies on top of him. "Murray! It's Genda! I have to talk to him!"

"How in the hell do you propose to do that? We have to get the president off here!"

"No! No! If he intended to crash into the memorial he would have done so. Right now, this is the safest place in the whole harbor. I know him, believe me. He would not dishonor the men of the *Arizona*. I'm sure of it."

"We'll be taking one hell of a chance."

"No, god-damn it! If he sees a boat speeding away from here, he will figure it is high brass and just might decide to make them his target. I need to talk to him. Can we come up on the international aircraft distress frequency?"

"We can come up on any god-damned frequency you need, but this better be quick."

Already, Sakai could hear the agent manning the communications array sending out an alert to security forces around the harbor and also to CINCPACFLT. There would be at the least a duty destroyer somewhere in the harbor, perhaps a cruiser, and they would already be going to general quarters, even if pierside. The order would undoubtedly be to shoot the Zero down if it came within range. Another agent handed Sakai a headset with a lip mike attached. "Simultaneous on 121.5 and 243," shouted the agent, informing Sakai that both the VHF and UHF distress frequencies were simultaneously available.

"Captain Genda, this is George Sakai. Captain Genda, do you hear me?" Any reply was overshadowed by the roar of one of the president's USMC helicopters arriving over the memorial.

"Get that damned thing away!" Sakai shouted. "We have to be able to hear!" One of the agents spoke into his microphone and the chopper tipped forward and sped away.

"Captain Genda! This is George Sakai. Do you hear me?"

Genda watched the special green marine helicopter turn away from the memorial and hover over Ford Island. The president of the United States *was* on the *Arizona* Memorial! And in all probability, so was Hoikata. What phenomenal timing! Now if only some boat or the helicopter would take him off! Then he heard the incredible "Captain Genda, this is George Sakai. Do you hear me?" It was the nisei who had visited him on Hokkaido and arrested him on Guam!

"Nisei, I do not believe this. Why is it that everywhere I go, you are?"

. . .

Sakai could not contain the sigh of relief that rose from his lungs. He could talk to Genda. Now, if only he could say the right things. "Captain Genda, do not do this. Land and you will have a fair trial. Do not disgrace yourself—" He had started to say "again" but thought better of it. Nothing would be served by openly condemning Genda.

"I did not order the attack on the aircraft at Osaka," Genda replied, repeating the statement he had made on Guam.

"We know that, Captain. We understand your bitterness. Let us talk about it."

"The president of the United States, he is on the memorial," Genda stated.

Sakai took a deep breath. The old warrior was no dummy. He must have seen the distinctly marked presidential helicopter. "Yes, Captain. Also Prime Minister Hoikata. A great new treaty has been signed. Are you aware of that?"

"No, nor do I wish to be."

Sakai took a quick glance outside. The Zero was in a tight circle about a thousand feet directly over the memorial. "Do not dishonor the men of the *Arizona*, Captain."

"I would not do that. You know that, nisei."

You bet your sweet ass I do, you crafty old bastard.

"Captain Genda, land at the airport. We have people waiting for you."

"No, nisei, I cannot do that."

Genda studied the three massive carriers. He carried no bombs. But a vertical dive onto one of the flight decks would send parts of the Zero down several decks and certainly set off jet fuel fires. But he also noticed a pair of gray navy Hornets approaching from the direction of the Barbers Point Naval Air Station. He could see the deadly heatseeking Sidewinder missiles on their wingtips. That was one miscalculation he had made: not figuring on any alert aircraft. It was peacetime. He dropped down to five hundred feet and tightened his turn. They would not release a missile if there was any chance it would crash into the memorial. Not with the president on it. As he expected, the Hornets broke off and began a wider circle outside his own.

"Nisei, if the navy planes fire at me, I come down on the memorial. I do not want to do that—but I will."

"They have been instructed to hold their fire, Captain."

"What the shit is going on?" Admiral DeHart questioned. "Why haven't the Hornets bagged the son of a bitch?"

"He's too close, Admiral," Franklin responded. "He just threatened to crash the memorial if they try. He's only up five hundred feet and in a constant bank. They release a missile and we're charcoal."

The president stuck his head out the entrance to the memorial. Hell, he could see the red characters on Genda's headband. "Who *is* that?"

"Captain Saburo Genda, Japanese Maritime Self Defense—"

"The terrorist?" the president interrupted. "I read the reports on the car-bombing and the United shootdown at Osaka. How in God's holy name did the son of a bitch get here with a Zero? I thought he died on Guam."

Genda kept his turn as tight as safety would allow, thanking the designers of the Zero for providing him with an airplane that could hold a sixty-to-ninety-degree bank at only one hundred and fifty knots. His turn radius was a very tight six hundred and fifty feet.

With some amusement, he noticed the SBD also circling, well outside the orbit of the Hornets. What did that idiot feel he could do? It would take one hell of an aviator to bag a Zero with a fighter. An unarmed dive bomber wouldn't even be able to get within ramming position.

"Captain Genda, both the president and Prime Minister Hoikata urge you to land. They promise a complete and fair hearing of your grievances."

"Will they agree to resurrect my mother and father? Will they call back from the dead my Emiko? If they can do these things, I will rejoice and land at once!"

"You know they cannot do that, Captain."

"And stop referring to me as Captain. I am Flight Petty Officer Saburo Genda of the Special Attack Corps of the Imperial Japanese Navy."

. . .

"Oh, sweet Jesus," Franklin exclaimed. "He thinks he's back in the war years!"

Genda studied the memorial below, then once more the carriers. They were probably a quarter mile away. It would take only a few seconds to fly over into position for his attack. But that would be all the time the Hornets needed. Just the hint of his nose swinging away from overhead the *Arizona* and the feisty Navy fighters would be all over him. It was an impasse—unless he wanted to take out the memorial. No, a samurai would not dishonor the grave of an opponent who had fought an honorable battle. And the men on the *Arizona* had fought just such a fight. The more he studied the outline of the *Arizona* just below the surface of the water, the more conscious he became of the mass sacrifice her crew had made. The president of the United States had also fought honorably. Sakai knew that. And even stupid Hoikata had overcome several defeats to fight again against the island-hopping enemy during the awful last days. Perhaps they were not the ones to die with him this day. He checked his fuel gauges. Fifteen minutes left, twenty at the outside. The high-speed approach to Oahu and maneuvering power had sucked his fuel like a hungry child at a mother's breast. He would have to make a decision soon.

"You're the antiterrorist specialist here, George. What do you suggest?" The president asked his question in a gentle manner. He knew that what was going to happen was probably not up to anyone on the memorial. But they had to keep trying.

Sakai said the only thing that came to his head. "It isn't over until the fat lady sings, Mr. President." *God! What a stupid thing to say.*

Prime Minister Hoikata tilted his head. He didn't understand at all. What fat lady? Why was she going to sing?

Genda felt very tired. He adjusted the elevator trim tab until the Zero was practically flying itself and he needed only light control pressures to keep it in its bank. But even that was an effort. His arms and legs were very heavy and his chest had a fullness he had not experienced before. Once more that strange light-headed calmness came over him. He cracked the canopy a bit wider to let in the cool air and swept his gaze over the harbor.

The damage was devastating, with great corkscrew columns of black smoke rising from the burning battleships tied alongside Ford Island. A great orange ball erupted from one of the naval station dry docks where the destroyers *Cassin* and *Downs*, along with the battleship *Pennsylvania*, were berthed for overhaul and repair. Shigaharu's torpedo bombers were just pulling up from their deadly runs and their steel fish were burying themselves in the helpless hulls of the *West Virginia*, the *California*, the *Utah*, and the *Arizona*. The *Nevada* was under way, reaching desperately for the Pearl Harbor channel and the relative safety of the open sea. Itaya's fighters were still strafing the Ford Island airfield and the American PBYs and Kingfishers were burning furiously, their fabric gone and aluminum skin and frames twisting and breaking apart in the intense heat. The *Maryland* reeled under the force of the modified sixteen-inch shell that Fuchida had planted firmly on her superstructure. Takahashi's dive bombers were striking almost every ship in the harbor, their whistling bombs dropping unerringly onto their helpless targets. Small craft were everywhere, trying valiantly to pick up the wounded and dead that swam and floated amid the burning oil slicks. Genda was awed at the scope of the destruction, the Americans having been caught completely by surprise. For the first time in his life, Genda saw the war as a terrible two-edged sword, striking both sides with equal ferocity. Thousands below were dying—most of them as innocent and unsuspecting as his own mother and father had been at Nagasaki.

". . . Genda, Captain Genda, this is George Sakai. Do you hear me?"

Sakai's call jerked Genda back into the land of reality, and he was startled to see that he was in a spiral and passing three hundred feet. He added power and pulled up. Still shaken from his hallucination, he anxiously searched the still blue waters of Pearl Harbor. The American fleet was quietly at anchor or tied alongside the great piers, the white memorial still below him.

"Captain Genda! Do you hear me?"

"Yes, nisei. . . . I am very tired."

"Captain, we know you are ill. You need medical treatment. Please land. Let us help you. Don't bring disgrace upon yourself and your people. It is time, Captain, time to forgive."

Genda made his decision. He had demonstrated that a Thunder God could achieve the impossible. Alone, he had flown over a vast segment of the Pacific; and undetected, he had penetrated the airspace of the most powerful nation on earth. He was even holding off a pair of the most deadly naval fighters flying. Most significant of all, he was in effect holding the president of the United States as a hostage.

"I have made my decision, nisei."

"What is it, Genda-san?"

Genda fixed his eyes on the three nuclear carriers. "I want safe passage around the perimeter of the harbor. I want all to see the magnificent Zero of Imperial Japan and wonder at the skill of the Thunder Gods."

"And then?"

"I will land."

"Whadda you think?" Franklin asked.

Sakai could only shake his head. He did not know what to think. Was Genda maneuvering for an opening to attack one of the ships in the harbor? The man certainly knew he could not fly away.

"You will not carry out any attack?" Sakai asked over the radio.

"You have my word, nisei."

"I say we let him do it," Sakai decided.

"I agree. Get him away from the president," Franklin urged.

The president held up a hand. "I think this should be my decision. George, how honorable a man do you think Genda is—really is?"

"If nothing else, despite all that he has done and caused to be done, I think he is a man who has his own sense of honor."

"Will he stand by his word?"

"Yes, Mr. President."

"Then I say we give him his moment in the sun. Then, after he lands, we hang the son of a bitch."

Sakai relayed the decision. "You have safe passage, Genda-san. Afterwards, the Hornets will escort you to the airport."

It was Genda's turn to ponder the integrity of a man's word. Once he left his orbit, the Hornets could destroy him at will. They had split up and taken position one hundred and eighty degrees from one another in their orbit. The instant Genda broke his own circle, one could be immediately upon him. Under the circumstances, however, Genda knew that his decision was preordained.

"I am leaving my orbit."

. . .

The pair of Hornets closed and took station, one on each wing of the Zero. Genda remained at five hundred feet throughout his entire circuit of Pearl Harbor, leaving his canopy open so that those on the ground could see the contrast of the white-and-red *hachimaki* with his helmet. Then he gave a hand signal that he intended to climb. The Hornet pilots gave him a thumbs-up reply but one backed off to take a station a half mile behind him.

"Follow me," said the other and pulled out ahead.

Genda knew his moment had arrived. The carriers were less than a mile away.

"He's going to do it," the president said, obviously relieved.

Yes, Mr. President, thought Sakai, but God forbid, not what I think.

Genda called his lead escort. "I have the field in sight." Directly below him was the open water of Pearl Harbor. Off to his left were the three carriers. He lowered his landing gear. The two Hornets quickly resumed their wing positions. Genda turned to each and rendered a hand salute. Both returned it, but neither knew why the pilot of the Zero had made such a gesture. It seemed right out of a movie.

Now! Genda jerked his control stick into his stomach and kicked hard right rudder. The Zero snap-rolled over on its back before the Hornet pilots could react, and as his aircraft reached its inverted position, Genda kicked opposite rudder and thrust the stick forward to break the stall. The Zero paused inverted, still between the Hornets.

"Holy shit!" exclaimed one of the Hornet pilots. "What's he trying to do?"

Genda grinned at his success in catching the Hornets by surprise and pulled his nose through to dive away from the escorting fighters.

"Jesus! Let's take him, Shooter!" yelled the Hornet pilot.

Too late, thought Genda. They had absolutely no chance of getting into firing position before he would complete his maneuver.

Sakai had watched the Zero flip over and start down. The two Hornets were making an incredible attempt to get into firing position but Sakai knew they would never make it. "Genda! Don't do it!"

"*Sayonara, nisei*. Never forget the blood that flows in your veins."

Sakai watched the Zero plunge straight down. It was already past a safe pullout altitude. *But Genda wasn't aiming for the carriers!* Incredibly, the scene seemed to shift into slow motion. For an instant, the bright morning sun bounced off the diving Zero and spread a flash of silver spokes across the blue Hawaiian sky. Using borrowed Secret Service binoculars, Sakai could actually see Genda turn his face toward the memorial and bow with his upper body before facing forward again. Only one more word came just an instant before the airplane hit the water. "Emiko. . . ."

The Zero disintegrated upon contact, the heavy Nakajima engine plummeting to the bottom of the harbor and sending a geyser of frothy water a hundred feet into the air. The droplets caught the rays of the morning sun and split them into the colors of the visible light spectrum. A faint multicolored rainbow appeared and then quickly faded as the water fell back.

For a long moment, no one on the memorial spoke or moved. Then everyone silently followed the president's lead and walked back to their ceremonial positions.

"What has happened here today, Mr. President?" Hoikata asked. "I don't understand."

The president kept his gaze on the swirl of water where the Zero had entered the harbor. The ancient SBD was passing over it, dipping its wings in salute. The president quietly answered Hoikata. "The end of the war, Mr. Prime Minister, the end of the war. Gentlemen, I believe we were in the middle of our national anthem." The president placed his right hand over his heart. The lei had floated out a bit and was halfway between the memorial and the skeleton of the number-two main turret mount. The band took up the anthem at the precise note upon which they had stopped.

. . . gave proof through the night . . .

Sakai raised his own right hand and placed it over his heart. It was about to pound through his chest. As he listened to the music and sang the words, he was filled with pride and the love of his land and his flag and his part in Genda's decision to die in an honorable fashion. And he was very proud of his Japanese heritage that placed such a high priority on the honor and dignity of life—and death. Then he felt the warmth of Alicia's body pressing against him and his other hand found one of hers. She pulled it tightly against her hip.

"I love you, George."

Sakai kept his eyes on the flag, but his former wife's presence caused his thoughts to stray.

Perhaps the life of a nisei sheep farmer in the Aussie outback wouldn't be the most awful thing in the world after all.

ABOUT THE AUTHOR

M. E. MORRIS lives and writes in Colorado Springs, Colorado, in the shadow of Pikes Peak. A former career naval aviator, he injects his novels with generous doses of military flavor and he enjoys a loyal readership in Great Britain and Japan, as well as in the United States. While his works fall within the thriller genre, each has its own subgenre, from techno-thriller to action-adventure. And each reflects his professional background, formal education, and experience in the fields of the military, aviation, and international affairs.